A HELLION IN HER BED

"A perfectly matched pair of protagonists who engage in a spirited battle of wits and wiles, and a lively plot blending equal measures of steamy passion and sharp wit come together brilliantly in the second addition to Jeffries's tempting new Hellions of Halstead Hall series."

—*Booklist* (starred review)

"Wonderfully original. . . . It's more than the original plotline that captures readers; it's Jeffries's sense of humor, her engaging characters, and delightfully delicious sensuality that spice things up!"

—*RT Book Reviews* (4½ stars)

"Rich with family interaction and overflowing with scintillating wit and heart-stopping sensuality, this addition to Jeffries's addictive series satisfies while cleverly doling out tidbits that will keep readers eager for the next installment. "

—*Library Journal*

"Engaging . . . fun and moving."

—*Romance Reviews Today*

"A winning hand of hearts and spades!"

—Fresh Fiction

"Another enjoyable romance that will entertain readers from cover to cover."

—Reader to Reader

"*A Hellion in Her Bed* enchants with its likable characters. . . . Amusing and poignant."

—Single Titles

"Yet another delicious love story from Sabrina Jeffries."

—Romance Junkies

"A lively, energetic romance with two smart, strong-willed protagonists that are sure to capture your heart."

—*Joyfully Reviewed*

THE TRUTH ABOUT LORD STONEVILLE

"Jeffries pulls out all the stops with a story combining her hallmark humor, poignancy, and sensuality to perfection."

—*RT Book Reviews*

"The first in a captivating new Regency-set series by the always entertaining Jeffries, this tale has all of the author's signature elements: delectably witty dialogue, subtly named characters, and scorching sexual chemistry between two perfectly matched protagonists."

—*Booklist*

"Lively repartee, fast action, luscious sensuality, and an abundance of humor."

—*Library Journal*

"*The Truth About Lord Stoneville* has the special brand of wit and passion for which Sabrina Jeffries is recognized, where each enthralling scene will thoroughly capture your imagination."

—Single Titles

"Sabrina Jeffries . . . starts another excellent series that will alternatively have you laughing, crying, and running the gamut of emotions."

—*Romance Reviews Today*

Sabrina Jeffries

A Lady Never Surrenders

POCKET BOOKS

New York   London   Toronto   Sydney   New Delhi

Pocket Books
A Division of Simon & Schuster, Inc.
1230 Avenue of the Americas
New York, NY 10020

Manufactured in the United States of America

ISBN-13: 978-1-61793-647-0

To my dear sister, Jamie McCalebb, who was part of the inspiration for Celia—you're the best sister a woman could have!

To my mom, Gladys Martin, who fled a hurricane and ended up putting in line edits on my book! Thanks, Mom, you're the best.

And to Becky Timblin, for all the things you do. Thanks for everything!

Acknowledgment

Much thanks goes to Wagner Dias da Silva, for his invaluable input concerning the Italian and Portuguese phrases in the book. It was greatly appreciated!

Dear Readers,

Thank heavens Celia has taken seriously my demand that she marry. She has gathered several gentlemen here for a house party so she can make her choice.

Only one thing worries me—Jackson Pinter. The Bow Street Runner is showing a most inappropriate interest in her. I do not like it. He is apparently the bastard son of some nobleman who never claimed him, so he needs to marry well in order to further his ambition to be Chief Magistrate. That means he might consider her a very good choice for a wife.

It would not bother me if I did not suspect that she, too, harbors a secret interest in the man. I have caught them alone together on more than one occasion, and sometimes she gazes on him with such alarming evidence of a budding infatuation. . . .

My other grandchildren think I should not interfere. Even my dear Isaac (yes, I have become quite friendly with that audacious cavalry general) says I meddle in matters beyond my ken. But she is so young and naïve! I cannot stand by and do nothing if his interest is merely in her rank and fortune. I did that once with her mother; I will not do it again.

Isaac, the old fool, insists that Mr. Pinter's fascination for her is decidedly *not* mercenary. He claims that the man follows her with his eyes every time they are near each other. While I concede that Mr. Pinter does seem rather . . . intrigued by her, that does not necessarily mean that he is in love with her. He can desire her money *and* her body without caring a whit about *her*.

Meanwhile, she has a duke, an earl, and a viscount sniffing at her heels, none of whom needs her money. She could be a duchess, my Celia! Why should she settle for a mere Runner, even if he *is* working hard to solve the murders of her parents? Can you blame me for wanting something more for her?

Sincerely,
Hetty Plumtree

Prologue

Halstead Hall
1806

Celia roused to the sound of grown-ups whispering in the nursery. The tickle in her throat made her want to cough. But if she did, the grown-ups would tell Nurse to put more nasty stuff on her chest, and Celia hated that. Nurse called it a mustard plaster. It was greasy and yellow, and it smelled bad.

The whispers got louder until they were right behind her. She lay still. Was it Mama and Nurse? Either one would put the mustard plaster on her chest. She kept her eyes shut so they would leave her be.

"We can meet at the hunting lodge," whispered one voice.

"Shh, she might hear you," whispered the other.

"Don't be absurd. She's asleep. And anyway, she's only four. She won't understand."

Celia frowned. She was *almost* five. And she did too understand. Lots and lots. Like how she had two grandmamas—Nonna Lucia in heaven and Gran in

"I know, dearie. But you want the cough to go away, don't you?"

Celia frowned. "I guess."

Nurse clucked at her, then got a glass and poured something from a bottle into it. "Here, this will help."

She gave it to Celia to drink. It tasted odd, but she was thirsty, so she drank it as Nurse set about preparing the mustard plaster.

By the time Nurse started patting it on, Celia felt *so* sleepy. Her eyelids were so heavy she forgot about the bad-smelling stuff on her chest.

She slept a long time. When she woke again Nurse gave her gruel but said the mustard plaster could wait until night. Then she gave Celia more of that odd drink, and Celia got sleepy again. The next time she awoke, it was dark.

Lying there confused, she listened to her older sister Minerva and her older brother Gabe fight over who got the last pear tart. She wouldn't mind a pear tart; she was hungry.

Nurse came in again, with two men: Gabe's tutor, Mr. Virgil, and Tom, Celia's favorite footman. "Minerva," Nurse ordered, "you and Gabe go down to the study with Tom. Your grandmother wants to speak to you."

After they left, Celia lay there, not sure what to do. If Minerva and Gabe were getting treats from Gran, she wanted some, but if Nurse meant to give her another mustard plaster . . .

She'd better keep quiet.

"You're not going to wake the girl?" Mr. Virgil asked Nurse.

"It's better if she sleeps. She has to hear it eventually, and the little dear won't understand. How can I tell her that her parents are gone? It's too awful."

Gone? Like when they went off to London and left her and Minerva and Gabe at Halstead Hall?

"And for her ladyship to shoot his lordship?" Nurse went on. "It ain't right."

Papa went out shooting birds with guests sometimes. Her older brother Jarret told them all about it. The birds fell to the ground, and the dogs picked them up. And they never flew again. But Mama wouldn't shoot Papa. Must be another "ladyship." There were lots of them here for the house party.

"It is upsetting," Mr. Virgil said.

"And we both know her ladyship didn't mistake him for an intruder. She probably shot him because she was angry with him over his soiled doves."

"Mrs. Plumtree said it was an accident." Mr. Virgil sounded stern. "If you know what's good for you, madam, you'll speak nothing to gainsay that."

"I know my duty. But what her ladyship did after she shot him . . . How could she leave the poor children without a father *or* a mother? That's an abomination."

'Bomination sounded bad. And she began to fear it *was* Mama they were talking about.

"As Dr. Sewell wrote in 'The Suicide,'" Mr. Virgil said in his loftiest voice, "'The coward sneaks to death, the brave live on.' It's sheer cowardice, is what it is. And I'm disappointed that her ladyship has proved a coward."

Celia began to cry. It couldn't be Mama. Mama was *not* a coward! *Coward* was bad. Papa had explained it to her. It meant someone wasn't brave. And Mama was always brave.

"Now look what you've done," Nurse said. "You've woke the lass."

"Mama isn't a coward!" Celia sat up in bed. "She's brave! I w-want to see her. I want to s-see M-Mama!"

Nurse picked her up and smoothed back her hair. "Shh, now, dearie, calm down. It's all right. Do you want something to eat?"

"No! I want Mama!" she wailed.

"I can take you down to see your grandmama. She'll explain everything."

Panic seized her chest. Why wouldn't they let her see Mama? Whenever Celia had one of her coughs, Mama always came if she asked. "I don't *want* Gran! I want Mama!" She was crying hard. "I-want-Mama-I-want-Mama-I-want-Mama—"

"She'll make herself sick again with sobbing," Nurse said. "Hand me that paregoric elixir, Mr. Virgil."

Mr. Virgil had a funny look on his face, like someone had struck him. "The girl will have to learn the truth eventually."

"She's in no state to hear it right now." Nurse pressed a cup to Celia's lips, and the drink that made her sleepy poured into her mouth. She nearly choked on it before she got it down. It did stop her wailing.

Nurse gave her more. Celia didn't mind. She was thirsty. She drank it, then whispered, "I want Mama."

"Yes, dearie," Nurse said soothingly. "But first, let your old nurse sing you a song, all right?"

Her eyelids felt heavy again. "Don't want any songs," she complained, laying her head on Nurse's shoulder. She glared at Mr. Virgil. "Mama isn't a coward," she spat.

"Of course not," Nurse said soothingly. She picked up something and laid it in Celia's arms. "Here's the pretty new doll your mama gave you."

"Lady Bell!" Celia clutched it to her.

Nurse carried her over to the rocking chair and sat to rock her, back and forth, back and forth. "Is there a song you want me to sing to you and Lady Bell, my sweet?"

"Sing me about William Taylor." The lady in "William Taylor" wasn't a coward, and *she* had shot someone.

Nurse shivered. "Do you hear what the lass wants, Mr. Virgil? It's downright spooky."

"Clearly she understands more than you realize."

"How do you know that song, dearie?" Nurse asked her.

"Minerva sings it."

"I'm not going to sing you that," Nurse said. "I'll sing another. 'Golden slumbers kiss your eyes / Smiles awake you when you rise / Sleep, pretty wantons, do not cry . . .'"

Celia pushed fitfully against Nurse's chest. She usually liked hearing about the golden slumbers, but not tonight. She wanted to hear about the lady who got a pistol and "shot her true love William with the bride on his right arm." The captain in the song made the lady a commander for shooting William. That meant the lady was brave, right? And since Mama had shot someone, Mama was brave, too.

But she shot Papa.

That couldn't be right. Mama wouldn't shoot Papa.

Her eyelids got heavy. She didn't want to sleep. She had to explain how Mama couldn't be the "ladyship." Mama was brave. Celia would tell them so.

Because Celia was brave, too. Not a coward . . . never a coward . . .

Chapter One

Ealing
November 1825

When Bow Street Runner Jackson Pinter entered Halstead Hall's library, he wasn't surprised to find only one person there. He was early, and no one in the Sharpe family was ever early.

"Good morning, Masters," Jackson said, inclining his head toward the barrister who sat poring over some papers. Giles Masters was husband to the eldest Sharpe sister, Lady Minerva. Or Mrs. Masters, as she'd chosen to be called.

Masters looked up. "Pinter! Good to see you, old fellow. How are things at Bow Street?"

"Well enough for me to take the time to hold this meeting."

"I daresay the Sharpes have run you ragged investigating their parents' deaths."

"Murders," Jackson corrected him. "We've determined that for certain now."

"Right. I forgot that Minerva said the pistol found at

the scene had never been fired. A pity no one noticed it nineteen years ago, or an investigation might have been mounted then and a great deal of heartache prevented."

"Mrs. Plumtree paid off anyone who might have explored further."

Masters sighed. "You can't blame her. She thought she was preventing scandal."

Jackson frowned. Instead she'd prevented the discovery of the truth. And that was why she'd ended up with five grandchildren stuck in the past, unable to go on with their lives. That's why she'd laid down her ultimatum— all of them had to marry by the end of the year or none would inherit. So far, they'd obliged her. All but one.

In his mind arose an image of Lady Celia that he swiftly squelched.

"Where is everyone?"

"Still at breakfast. They'll be trooping across the courtyard soon, I'm sure. Have a seat."

"I'll stand." He strode over to the window that overlooked the Crimson Courtyard, named for its red tile.

Being at Halstead Hall always made Jackson uneasy. The sprawling mansion shrieked "aristocracy." Having spent his early childhood in a Liverpool slum before moving to a terrace house in Cheapside at age ten, he found Halstead Hall too large, too sumptuous—and too full of Sharpes.

After nearly a year with them as his clients, he still wasn't sure how he felt about them. Even now, as he saw them walking across the courtyard beneath a cloud-darkened November sky, he tensed up.

They didn't *look* as if they planned to spring anything on him. They looked happy and content.

First came the great lord himself—Oliver Sharpe, the ninth Marquess of Stoneville, said to be a near copy of his olive-skinned, black-haired, and black-eyed father. Initially Jackson had despised the man, having made the mistake of believing the gossip about him. He still thought Stoneville had chosen the wrong path after his parents' deaths, but since the marquess seemed to be making up for it now, perhaps there was good in him after all.

Beside him walked Lord Jarret, whose blue-green eyes and black hair were said to make him look more a blend of his half-Italian father and blond mother. He was Jackson's favorite of the brothers. No-nonsense and even-tempered, Jarret was the easiest to talk to. And once his scheming maternal grandmother, Mrs. Hester Plumtree, had allowed him to take over the family business, the man had flourished. Jarret worked hard at Plumtree Brewery; Jackson could admire that.

After him came Lord Gabriel with his new wife, Lady Gabriel, on one arm. No doubt the other two men's wives were in their confinement—Lady Stoneville was expected to deliver within the month, and Lady Jarret wasn't far behind. But Jackson wouldn't be surprised to hear of an impending child soon from the youngest Sharpe brother. The couple seemed very much in love, which was rather astonishing, considering that their marriage had initially been contracted just to fulfill Mrs. Plumtree's ridiculous ultimatum.

That august woman clung to Gabe's other arm. Jackson admired Mrs. Plumtree's determination and pluck—it reminded him of his beloved aunt Ada, who'd raised him and now lived with him. But what the elderly woman was demanding of her grandchildren reeked of hubris. No one should have such power over their descendants, not even a legend like Hetty Plumtree, who'd singlehandedly built the family brewery into a major concern after the death of her husband.

Behind her, the two Sharpe sisters came out to cross the courtyard. He dragged in a heavy breath as the younger one caught his eye.

Masters approached to look out the window, too. "And there she comes, the most beautiful woman in the world."

"And the most maddening," Jackson muttered.

"Watch it, Pinter," Masters said in a voice tinged with amusement. "That's my wife you're talking about."

Jackson started. He hadn't been staring at Mrs. Masters. "I beg your pardon," he murmured, figuring he'd best not explain.

Masters would never accept that Lady Celia was to her sister as a gazelle was to a brood mare. The newly wedded barrister was blinded by love.

Jackson wasn't. Any fool could see that Lady Celia was the more arresting of the two. While Mrs. Masters had the lush charms of a dockside tart, Lady Celia was a Greek goddess—willowy and tall, small-breasted and long-limbed, with a fine lady's elegant brow, a doe's soft eyes. . . .

And a vixen's temper. The damned female could flay the flesh from a man's bones with her sharp tongue.

She could also heat his blood with one unguarded smile.

God save him, it was a good thing her smile had never been bestowed on *him*. Otherwise, he might act on the fantasy that had plagued him from the day he'd met her—to shove her into some private closet where he could plunder her mouth with impunity. Where she would wrap those slender arms about his neck and let him have his way with her.

Confound her, until she had come along, he'd never allowed himself to desire a woman he couldn't have. He'd rarely allowed himself to desire *anyone*, only the occasional whore when he felt desperate for female companionship. Now he couldn't seem to *stop* doing so.

It was because he'd seen too little of her lately. What he needed was a surfeit of Lady Celia to make him sick of her. Then he might purge this endless craving for the impossible.

With a scowl, he turned from the window, but it was too late. The sight of Lady Celia crossing the courtyard dressed in some rich fabric had already stirred his blood. She never wore such fetching clothes; generally her lithe figure was shrouded in smocks to protect her workaday gowns from powder smudges while she practiced her target shooting.

But this morning, in that lemon-colored gown, with her hair finely arranged and a jeweled bracelet on her delicate wrist, she was summer on a dreary winter day, sunshine in the bleak of night, music in the still silence of a deserted concert hall.

And he was a fool.

"I can see how you might find her maddening," Masters said in a low voice.

Jackson stiffened. "Your wife?" he said, deliberately being obtuse.

"Lady Celia."

Hell and blazes. He'd obviously let his feelings show. He'd spent his childhood learning to keep them hidden so the other children wouldn't see how their epithets wounded him, and he'd refined that talent as an investigator who knew the value of an unemotional demeanor.

He drew on that talent as he faced the barrister. "Anyone would find her maddening. She's reckless and spoiled and liable to give her future husband grief at every turn." When she wasn't tempting him to madness.

Masters raised an eyebrow. "Yet you often watch her. Have you any interest there?"

Jackson forced a shrug. "Certainly not. You'll have to find another way to inherit your new bride's fortune."

He'd hoped to prick Masters's pride and thus change the subject, but Masters laughed. "You, marry my sister-in-law? That, I'd like to see. Aside from the fact that her grandmother would never approve, Lady Celia hates you."

She did indeed. The chit had taken an instant dislike to him when he'd interfered in an impromptu shooting match she'd been participating in with her brother and his friends at a public park. That should have set him on his guard right then.

A pity it hadn't. Because even if she *didn't* despise him and weren't miles above him in rank, she'd never make him a good wife. She was young and indulged, not the sort of female to make do on a Bow Street Runner's salary.

But she'll be an heiress once she marries.

He gritted his teeth. That only made matters worse. She would assume he was marrying her for her inheritance. So would everyone else. And his pride chafed at that.

Dirty bastard. Son of shame. Whoreson. Love-brat. He'd been called them all as a boy. Later, as he'd moved up at Bow Street, those who resented his rapid advancement had called him a *baseborn upstart.* He wasn't about to add *money-grubbing fortune hunter* to the list.

"Besides," Masters went on, "you may not realize this, since you haven't been around much these past few weeks, but Minerva claims that Celia has her eye on three very eligible potential suitors."

Jackson's startled gaze shot to him. Suitors? The word *who* was on his lips when the door opened and Stoneville entered. The rest of the family followed, leaving Jackson to force a smile and exchange pleasantries as they settled into seats about the table, but his mind kept running over Masters's words.

Lady Celia had suitors. Eligible ones. Good—that was good. He needn't worry about himself around her anymore. She was now out of his reach, thank God. Not that she was ever *in* his reach, but—

"Have you got news?" Stoneville asked.

Jackson started. "Yes." He took a steadying breath and forced his mind to the matter at hand. "As you know, your father's valet insists that your father wasn't having an affair with Mrs. Rawdon nineteen years ago."

"Which I still don't believe," Stoneville put in. "She certainly led me to think otherwise when she . . . er . . . was found in my room."

In his lordship's bed, to be precise. Although the entire family now knew of Mrs. Rawdon's seduction of the six-teen-year-old heir on the day of his parents' deaths, it wasn't something they liked to dwell on, least of all Stoneville.

"I'm aware of that," Jackson said. "Which is why I've been trying to confirm it through another source."

"What source?" Mrs. Masters asked.

"Mrs. Rawdon's former lady's maid, Elsie. The valet wouldn't have been the only servant with private infor-mation. If your father and Mrs. Rawdon were involved, her lady's maid probably knew of it, too." He sucked in a breath. "Unfortunately, I haven't yet located Elsie."

"Then why are we here?" Jarret asked, always right to the point.

"Because while searching for her, I discovered a curious circumstance. It seems that her last place of employ was with a rich gentleman in Manchester."

Although the others took a moment to catch the signif-icance of that, Jarret and Gabe realized it at once. They'd been with Jackson at the inquest of Halstead Hall's for-mer head groom, Benny May, whose body had been found after he'd traveled to visit a "friend" in Manchester.

"Surely you don't think that Elsie might have had

something to do with Benny's death," Mrs. Plumtree exclaimed, horror showing in her aging features.

"I have no idea," Jackson said. "But it seems quite the coincidence that Benny would travel to where Elsie had been, only to end up dead shortly after he left that city."

"*Had* been?" Gabe asked. "Elsie left Manchester?"

"She did. I find that suspicious. According to her family, she sent them a quick note saying she was leaving her post and heading to London to look for a new one. Apparently, she'd always refused to tell them the identity of her employer. They suspected she was involved with the man romantically. Whatever the case, I'm having trouble finding her. No one in Manchester seems to know anything. But she told her family she would send them word as soon as she settled in London."

"Is it possible we're barking up the wrong tree with Elsie and Benny?" Stoneville asked. "The authorities were never sure he was murdered. He might have been the victim of a hunting accident. Elsie might have moved on because she didn't like her employer. Their both being in Manchester at the same time could be coincidence."

"True." But in Jackson's business, genuine coincidences were rare. "I did learn she was younger than your mother."

"Quite pretty, too, as I recall," Stoneville said.

"How strange that Mrs. Rawdon would have a fetching young lady's maid," Mrs. Plumtree said. "That's asking for trouble, men being what they are."

"Not all men, Gran," Mrs. Masters said stoutly.

Mrs. Plumtree cast a glance about the table, then smiled. "No, not all men."

Jackson fought to shield his thoughts. Masters did seem an excellent husband, but he'd already reformed by the time he'd begun courting his wife. And the Sharpe men seemed devoted to their wives, but would it last?

His mother had been seduced by a nobleman, a brash young lord in Liverpool with a penchant for sweet maidens. Instead of marrying her, the arse had married a wealthy woman and set up Jackson's mother as his mistress, abandoning her when Jackson was two. So Jackson had no illusions about what marriage meant to the aristocracy.

Don't blame your father, Mother had said as she lay dying in his aunt and uncle's home. *If not for him, I wouldn't have you. And that made it all worth it.*

He couldn't see how. The memory of her emaciated body lying on that bed …

With an effort, he tamped down his anger and forced himself to pay attention to the matter at hand. "I'm waiting to hear from Elsie's family about her location in London. I heard from Major Rawdon's regiment in India that he'd taken a three-year post in Gibraltar, so I've sent a letter there asking him questions concerning the house party. Until I get responses, I should stay close to town rather than returning to Manchester on a probable wild-goose chase." He glanced to the marquess. "With your lordship's approval."

"Whatever you think is best," Stoneville murmured. "Just keep us apprised."

"Of course."

Taking that for a dismissal, Jackson headed out the door. He had another appointment this afternoon, and he had to stop at home to pick up the report his aunt was transcribing. Only she could transform his scribbles into legible, intelligible prose. If he left now, he might have time to eat before—

"Mr. Pinter!"

He turned to find Lady Celia approaching. "Yes, my lady?"

To his surprise, she glanced nervously at the open door to the library and lowered her voice. "I must speak to you privately. Do you have a moment?"

He ruthlessly suppressed the leap in his pulse. Lady Celia had never asked to talk to him alone. The singularity of that made him nod curtly and gesture to a nearby parlor.

She preceded him, then stood looking about her with uncharacteristic anxiousness as he entered and left the door open, wanting no one to accuse him of impropriety.

"What is it?" he asked, trying not to sound impatient. Or intrigued. He'd never seen Lady Celia looking unsure of herself. It tugged annoyingly at his sympathies.

"I had a dream last night. That is, I'm not sure if it actually was a dream. I mean, of course it was a dream, but . . ."

"What's your point, madam?"

Her chin came up, and a familiar martial light entered her gaze. "There's no need to be rude, Mr. Pinter."

He couldn't help it; being this close to her was doing uncomfortable things to him. He could smell her perfume, a tempting mix of . . . whatever flowery things noblewomen wore to enhance their charms.

Her charms needed no enhancement.

"Forgive me," he bit out. "I'm in a hurry to return to town."

She nodded, taking his excuse at face value. "Last night I had a dream that I often had as a child. I don't know if it was because we'd been working in the nursery, or Annabel and Maria were discussing . . ." When he raised his eyebrow, she steadied her shoulders. "Anyway, when I used to have it, it seemed unreal, so I assumed it was only a dream, but now . . ." She swallowed. "I think it might also be a memory of the day my parents died."

That caught his attention. "But you were only four."

"A few weeks shy of five, actually."

Right. She was twenty-four now, and the murders had happened nineteen years ago last April. "What makes you think it's a memory?"

"Because I heard Papa making an assignation with a woman to meet her at the hunting lodge."

A chill coursed down his spine.

"In the dream, I assume it's Mama, but even there she doesn't behave right."

"In what way?"

"Papa used to call Mama '*mia dolce bellezza*,' and she would blush and tell him he was blind. Well, in the dream the man called the woman '*mia dolce bellezza*,' and she got angry. She told him she hated it when he did that. Don't you see? She probably resented being called the same thing he called his wife."

"I don't suppose you could tell who she was from the voice."

She sighed. "Unfortunately, they were both whisper-ing. I only know it was Papa because of the '*mia dolce bellezza.*'"

"I see."

"If it really happened, it means Mama somehow found out about Papa's assignation. That's why she asked Benny not to tell Papa where she was going. Because she wanted to catch him and his mistress in the act. And whoever Papa was going there to meet arrived first and shot Mama."

"Then when your father showed up, she shot him, too?" he said skeptically. "Now that she'd ensured that her lover was free to marry her?"

Lady Celia's expression turned uncertain. "Perhaps Papa was angry that she'd killed Mama. Perhaps they struggled for the gun and it went off."

"So she reloaded the gun after shooting your mother. She lay in wait for your father—her lover—with a loaded gun."

"I-I don't know. All I know is what I heard."

"Which might have been a dream."

She sighed. "It might. That's why I came to you with it rather than mentioning it during our family meeting. I didn't want to get everyone excited about it until we were sure."

"We?"

"Yes. I want you to investigate and find out if it might have been real."

The plea in her lovely hazel eyes tugged at him, but she was asking the impossible. "I don't see how I can—"

"Other things happened in the dream," she said hastily. "Gabe's tutor, Mr. Virgil, came in later, and my nurse-maid sang to me. I overheard things." She drew a folded sheaf of paper from her pocket and held it out to him.

Reluctantly, he took it.

"I wrote down everything I could recall," she went on. "I figured you could talk to Mr. Virgil and Nurse and find out if I'm remembering that part correctly. If not, then the rest doesn't matter. But if I am . . ."

"I understand." She might have stored something important in her memory. But which parts? How could he sort the wheat from the chaff?

He skimmed the neatly penned words, and something leapt out at him. "Your nurse gave you medicine?"

Lady Celia nodded. "She calls it paregoric elixir. I suspect that Annabel and Maria's discussion about it yesterday was what prompted my dream."

"You do know that paregoric contains opium."

"Does it?" A troubled frown crossed her brow. "My sisters-in-law did say they would never use it on their own children."

"I'm told that doctors disagree on its usefulness." He weighed his words. "You may not realize this, but opium can sometimes provoke—"

"I know," she said tersely. "Dreams and phantasms and things that aren't real." She met his gaze. "But I feel in my bones that it *was* real. I can't explain it, and I know I might be wrong, but I think it at least deserves attention, don't you? If we discover it really is a memory, we might piece together who was missing early that morning and figure out Papa's mistress by a process of elimination." Her chin came up. "Besides, Nurse gave me the paregoric *after* I overheard the conversation."

"Unless she gave you some to sleep the night before," he said gently.

Her face fell, and he felt her disappointment like a punch to the gut.

He cleared his throat. "I agree it's worth pursuing. Your nurse is on my list of people to track down anyway, and Mr. Virgil is certainly of interest. I'll speak to them both and we'll continue from there." He shoved the paper in his coat pocket. "You were right to come to me with this."

She smiled at him then, the first smile she'd ever given him. It brought life to her face and a softness to her features that blazed a path through to his very soul.

"Thank you," she said.

God save him, he must keep his wits about him. "You're welcome." He turned for the door. He had to get out of here. If she ever guessed what she did to him, she'd mock him mercilessly for daring to raise his gaze so high. "If that's all—"

"Actually," she said, "I need something else from you, too."

Confound it all, he'd nearly escaped. Slowly he faced her once more. "Yes?"

She took in a breath, then lifted her chin. "I need you to investigate my suitors."

Chapter Two

Celia realized she'd shocked Mr. Pinter when his thick black brows drew together in a frown. His lean form seemed even more rigid than usual, and his angular features—the arrow of a nose and bladed jaw— even more stark. In his severe morning attire of black serge and white linen, he radiated male disapproval.

But why? He knew she was the only "hellion" left unmarried. Did he think she would let her brothers and sisters lose their inheritance out of some rebellious desire to thwart Gran's ultimatum?

Of course he did. He'd been so kind and considerate during her recitation of the dream that she'd almost forgotten he hated her. Why else were his eyes, gray as slate after a storm, now so cold and remote? The blasted fellow was always so condescending and sure of himself, so . . . so . . .

Male.

"Forgive me, my lady," he said in his oddly raspy voice, "but I was unaware you had any suitors."

Curse him for being right. "Well, I don't . . . exactly.

There are men who might be interested but haven't gone so far as to offer marriage." Or even to show a partiality to her.

"And you're hoping I'll twist their arms so they will?" he drawled.

She colored under his piercing gaze. "Don't be ridiculous."

This was the Mr. Pinter she knew, the one who'd called her "a reckless society miss" and a "troublemaker."

Not that she cared what he thought. He was like her brothers' friends, who saw her as a tomboy because she could demonstrate a rifle's fine qualities. And like Cousin Ned. *Scrawny bitch with no tits—you don't have an ounce of anything female in you.*

Curse Ned to hell. Surely she'd filled out a bit in the ten years since their . . . private encounter. Surely her sharp features had softened into more womanly ones.

But she still had Papa's unfashionable olive skin and ungainly height, and Mama's boyish frame. She still had deplorably straight brown hair, not to mention the most boring hazel eyes.

Celia would give anything to look like her sister. To fill out gowns in all the right places. To have wavy tresses with streaks of gold in them, eyes of brilliant jade, and features as classically perfect as a porcelain doll's. Celia was sometimes described as pretty, but next to Minerva . . .

She swallowed her envy. She might not have her sister's looks, but she did have other appealing qualities. For one thing, men were comfortable around her because of her interest in guns and shooting.

"You may find this hard to believe, Mr. Pinter," she went on defensively, "but some men *enjoy* my company. They consider me easy to talk to."

A ghost of a smile touched his handsome face. "You're right. I do find that hard to believe."

Arrogant wretch. "All the same, there are three men who might consider marrying me, and I could use your help in securing them."

She hated having to ask him for that, but he was necessary to her plan. She just needed one good offer of marriage, one *impressive* offer that would show Gran she was capable of gaining a decent husband.

Gran didn't believe she could, or she wouldn't be holding to that blasted ultimatum. If Celia could prove her wrong, Gran might allow her to choose a husband in her own good time.

And if that plan didn't work, Celia would at least have a man she could marry to fulfill Gran's terms.

"So you've finally decided to meet Mrs. Plumtree's demands," he said, his expression unreadable.

She wasn't about to let him in on her secret plan. Oliver might have employed him, but she was sure Mr. Pinter also spied for Gran. He would run right off and tell her. "It's not as if I have a choice." Bitterness crept into her tone. "In less than two months, if I remain unmarried, my siblings will be cut off. I can't do that to them, no matter how much I resent Gran's meddling."

Something that looked oddly like sympathy flickered in his gaze. "Don't you want to marry?"

"Of course I want to marry. Doesn't every woman?"

"You've shown little interest in it before," he said skeptically.

That's because men had shown little interest in *her.* Oh, Gabe's friends loved to stand about with her at balls and discuss the latest developments in cartridges, but they rarely asked her to dance, and if they did, it was only to consult her on rifles. She'd tried flirting, but she was terrible at it. It seemed so . . . false. So did men's compliments, the few that there were. It was easier to laugh them off than to figure out which ones were genuine, easier to pretend to be one of the lads.

She secretly wished she could find a man she could love, who would ignore the scandals attached to her family's name and indulge her hobby of target shooting. One who could shoot as well as she, since she could never respect a man who couldn't hit what he aimed at.

I'll bet Mr. Pinter knows his way around a rifle.

She scowled. He probably *thought* he was a grand shot, anyway. For a man whose lineage was reputedly unsavory, Mr. Pinter was so high in the instep that she privately called him Proud Pinter or Proper Pinter. He'd told Gabe last week that most lords were good for only two things—redistributing funds from their estates into the gaming hells and brothels in London, and ignoring their duty to God and country.

She knew he was working for Oliver only because he wanted the money and prestige. Secretly, he held them all in contempt. Which was probably why he was being so snide about her marrying.

"Be that as it may," she said, "I'm interested in marriage

now." She strode over to the fireplace to warm her hands. "That's why I want you to investigate my potential suitors."

"Why me?"

She shot him a sideways glance. "Have you forgotten that Oliver hired you initially for that very purpose?"

His stiffening posture told her that he had. With a frown, he drew out the notebook and pencil he always seemed to keep in his pocket. "Very well. Exactly what do you want me to find out?"

Breathing easier, she left the fire. "The same things you found out for my siblings—the truth about my potential suitors' finances, their eligibility for marriage, and . . . well . . ."

He paused in scratching his notes to arch an eyebrow at her. "Yes?"

She fiddled nervously with the gold bracelet she wore. This part, he might balk at. "And their secrets. Things I can use in my . . . er . . . campaign. Their likes, their weaknesses, whatever isn't obvious to the world."

His expression chilled her even with the fire at her back. "I'm not sure I understand."

"Suppose you learn that one of them prefers women in red. That could be useful to me. I would wear red as much as possible."

Amusement flashed in his eyes. "And what will you do if they all prefer different colors?"

"It's just an example," she said irritably. "In truth, I'm hoping you can provide me with more substantive information. You might discover that one of my suitors supports a by-blow. I could use that to—"

"Your brother pays me to make sure your suitors are acceptable and eligible," he ground out, "not to help you blackmail men into marriage."

Too late, she remembered that *he* was a by-blow. "I didn't mean it like that! If I knew a suitor had an illegitimate child that he cared enough about to support, then I'd know he liked children. So I could ramble on about how much *I* like children. That's all."

That seemed to mollify him only slightly. "In other words, you'll pretend to be someone else in order to snag a husband."

"Oh, for heaven's sake," she said defensively, "it's no different than what half the women in society do to catch a man. I don't want to waste my time in pointless flirtation when a little inside knowledge will improve my aim on the targets."

He flashed her a condescending smile.

"What is it?" she snapped.

"Only *you* would approach courtship as a marksman approaches a shooting match." He licked the tip of his pencil. "So who *are* these hapless targets?"

"The Earl of Devonmont, the Duke of Lyons, and Fernandez Valdez, the Visconde de Basto."

His jaw dropped. "Are you insane?"

"I know they're rather beyond my reach, but they seem to like my company—"

"I daresay they do!" He strode up to her, strangely angry. "The earl is a rakehell with a notorious reputation for trying to get beneath the skirts of every woman he meets. The duke's father was mad, and it's said to run in his family, which is why most women steer clear of him. And Basto is a Portuguese idiot who's too old for you and clearly trawling for some sweet young thing to nurse him in his declining years."

"How can you say such things? The only one you know personally is Lord Devonmont, and you barely know even him."

"I don't have to. Their reputations tell me they're utterly unacceptable."

Unacceptable? Three of the most eligible bachelors in London? Mr. Pinter was mad, not her. "Lord Devonmont is Gabe's wife's cousin. The duke is Gabe's best friend, whom I've known since childhood, and the viscount . . . well . . ."

"Is an oily sort, from what I hear," he snapped.

"No, he isn't. He's very pleasant to talk to." Really, this was the most ridiculous conversation. "Who the devil do *you* think I should marry, anyway?"

That seemed to take him aback. He glanced away. "I don't know," he muttered. "But not . . . That is, you shouldn't . . ." He tugged at his cravat. "They're wrong for you, that's all."

She'd flustered Mr. Pinter. How astonishing! He was *never* flustered. It made him look vulnerable and much less . . . stiff. She rather liked that.

But she'd like it even better if she understood what had provoked it. "Why do you care whom I choose, as long as you're paid? I'm willing to pay extra to ensure that you find out everything I want to know."

Once more he turned into Proud Pinter. "It isn't a matter of payment, madam. I choose my own assignments, and this one isn't to my taste. Good day." Turning on his heel, he headed for the door.

Oh, dear, she hadn't meant to run him off entirely. "So you're reneging on your agreement with Oliver?" she called out.

He halted.

She pressed her point hastily. "At the very least, you owe me an investigation of my suitors' backgrounds. If you don't give me *that*, I'll tell my brother you've refused to do what he hired you for."

When he clenched his hands into fists, a twinge of guilt assailed her. He'd been so nice about her dream earlier that she felt bad forcing his hand. But blast it—it *was* his job. Mr. Pinter had done it for Minerva and Gabe; he sure as the devil could do it for *her*.

He faced her once more, his expression now carefully bland. "I daresay when I tell him whom you're considering, he'll side with me. He was *not* happy when your sister chose Mr. Masters."

"But that worked out well, which I'll remind him of if he protests. He won't, though—he knows how important it is that I marry."

Mr. Pinter searched her face so intently that it made her uncomfortable. "And what of love?" he asked in a hoarse rasp. "Do you love any of these men?"

He had the audacity to speak of that when he *knew* her situation? "Gran isn't giving me a chance to fall in love."

"So tell her you want more time. As long as she knows that you're open to the idea, I'm sure she'll—"

"Give me a reprieve? You know better than that. She'll say that I've had nearly a year already, and I frittered it away."

She'd be right, too. But Celia had hoped that her siblings' devious plans would work and put an end to Gran's diabolical ultimatum. Instead, her brothers and sister had all given in and married.

Or rather, they'd fallen in love. It wasn't fair. It had been easy for her beautiful sister to find a husband—she'd simply gone after the man she'd always wanted. Gabe had married his best friend's sister, Jarret had found a wife who loved brewing as much as he, and Oliver had practically fallen into the perfect woman.

But Celia had no old beaus waiting in the wings, no best friends with eligible brothers, and no fellow sharpshooters who fancied her. She had three men who *might* consider marrying her. She had to make do with that.

"It's too late for love, Mr. Pinter," she said wearily. "Gran is breathing down my neck, and this is hardly the season for matrimony. There are a few country balls and little else before the end of the year. The likelihood of my stumbling upon any other eligible gentlemen at this late date is quite small."

"There must be someone else, someone more—"

"No one whom I know, whom I'm comfortable with. At least I like these gentlemen. I can see myself married to one of them." *Possibly. If worse came to worst.* "And since they're all titled and wealthy, Gran would find them irreproachable." Which was the point, though she couldn't tell *him* that.

His expression turned cynical. "So that's what you're looking for in a husband," he said coldly. "A rich man of rank."

"No!" How like him to assume she was mercenary. "That's what *Gran* is looking for. I merely want a man I can tolerate. But if my suitors are wealthy, at least they won't marry me simply to gain my fortune." *As Papa had done with Mama.* "I prefer not to marry a fortune hunter."

"I see." A muscle ticked in his jaw. "Still, wealthy lords and fortune hunters aren't your only choices. Surely there are other respectable gentlemen."

"Why are you being so stubborn about this?" Suddenly it dawned on her. "Wait, is it because my suitors are noblemen? I know that you consider titled gentlemen to be beneath contempt, but—"

"That's not true," he grumbled. "I count Lord Kirkwood and his brother among my friends, and even, if I venture to be presumptuous, your brothers. It's not *all* men of rank I find beneath contempt—just the ones who prey on women. Like Devonmont. And probably the other two, as well."

"To my knowledge, none of them has ever taken advantage of a respectable female. Even my brothers had their . . . dalliances as bachelors."

"So did your father."

He *would* point that out. "That's different. Papa broke his marriage vows. That doesn't mean my suitors would do so." She swallowed. "Unless you think it impossible for a woman like me to keep men like them satisfied and happy?"

He started. "No! I wasn't trying to say . . . That is—"

"It's all right, Mr. Pinter," she said, fighting to keep the hurt out of her voice. "I know what you think of me."

His gaze locked with hers, confusing her with its sudden fierceness. "You have no idea what I think of you."

She twisted her bracelet nervously, and the motion drew his eyes down to her hands. But as his gaze came back up, it slowed, lingering on her bosom.

Could Mr. Pinter . . . Was it possible that he . . .

Certainly not! Proper Pinter would never be interested in a reckless female of her stamp. Why, he didn't even *like* her.

She'd dressed carefully today, hoping to sway him into doing her bidding by showing that she could look and act like a lady, hoping to gain a measure of his respect.

But the intimate way his gaze continued up past her bosom to her throat, and then paused again at her mouth, was more how her brothers looked at their wives. It wasn't so much disrespectful as it was . . . interested.

No, she must be imagining that. He was merely trying to make her uncomfortable; she was misinterpreting the seeming heat in his glance. She refused to let herself be taken in by imagining what wasn't there. Not after the nasty things Ned had said to her when she was fourteen.

I only kissed you to win a bet, you know.

She'd learned her lesson then. Men had an annoying habit of pretending interest in a woman just to gain something they wanted. Just look at Mama, dreaming of fairy tales when Papa had been dreaming only of finance.

Well, *she* would marry a man who didn't need or want her fortune. Mr. Pinter didn't fall into that category.

And given how blank his expression became as his gaze met hers, she'd been right to be skeptical. He would never be interested in her in *that* way.

He confirmed it by saying, with his usual formality, "I doubt any man would consider your ladyship unacceptable as a wife."

Oh, when he turned all hoity-toity, she could just *murder* him. "Then we agree that the gentlemen in question would find me satisfactory," she said, matching his cold tone. "So I don't see why you assume they'd be unfaithful."

"Some men are unfaithful no matter how beautiful their wives are," Mr. Pinter growled.

He thought her beautiful?

There she went again, reading too much into his words. He was only making a point. "But you have no reason to believe that these gentlemen would be. Unless there's some dark secret you already know about them that I do not?"

Glancing away, he muttered a curse under his breath. "No."

"Then here's your chance to find out the truth about their characters. Because I prefer facts to opinions. And I was under the impression that you do, too."

Take that, Mr. Pinter! Hoist by your own petard. The man always insisted on sticking to the facts.

And he was well aware that she'd caught him out, for he scowled, then crossed his arms over his chest. His rather impressive chest, from what she could tell beneath his black coat and plain buff waistcoat.

"I can't believe I'm the only person who would object to these gentlemen," he said. "What about your grandmother? Have you consulted *her*?"

She lifted her eyes heavenward. He was being surprisingly resistant to her plans. "I don't need to. Every time one of them asks to dance with me, she beams. She's forever urging me to smile at them or attempt some flirtation. And if they so much as press my hand or take me for a stroll, she quizzes me with great glee on what was said and done."

"She's been letting you go out on *private strolls* with these scoundrels?" Mr. Pinter said in sheer outrage.

"They aren't scoundrels."

"I swear to God, you're a lamb among the wolves," he muttered.

That image of her, so unlike how she saw herself, made her laugh. "I've spent half my life in the company of my brothers. Every time Gabe went to shoot, I went with him. At every house party that involved his friends, I was urged to show off my abilities with a rifle. I think I know how to handle a man, Mr. Pinter."

His glittering gaze bored into her. "There's a vast difference between gamboling about in your brother's company with a group of his friends and letting a rakehell like Devonmont or a devilish foreigner like Basto stroll alone with you down some dark garden path."

A blush heated her cheeks. "I didn't mean strolls of *that* sort, sir. I meant daytime walks about our gardens and such, with servants in plain view. All perfectly innocent."

He snorted. "I doubt it will stay that way."

"Oh, for heaven's sake, why are you being so stubborn? You know I must marry. Why do you even care whom I choose?"

"I *don't* care," he protested. "I'm merely thinking of how much of my time will be wasted investigating suitors I already know are unacceptable."

She let out an exasperated breath. Of course. With him, it was always about money. Heaven forbid he should waste his time helping her.

"Your family has also hired me to investigate your parents' deaths," he went on. "Would you rather have this scheme of yours draw my attention away from that matter?"

Leave it to him to try and make her feel guilty about that. "Of course not, but you said that you're waiting to hear from Major Rawdon and Elsie's family. Aside from questioning my nurse and Mr. Virgil, you aren't terribly busy right now, are you?"

Hah! He certainly didn't like *that* observation. Eyes like ice bored into her. "I do have to *find* your nurse and Mr. Virgil. And I have other clients. But if you could present me with more acceptable choices, I'm sure I could find time to examine *their* backgrounds and give you a thorough report."

"If I had other choices, I would have presented them," she snapped. "But if you know of some eligible gentlemen you can strong-arm into courting me, then by all means, tell me. I'm open to suggestions."

He blinked. "There has to be some fellow—"

"Right." Lifting her skirts, she headed for the door. "Thank you for your time, Mr. Pinter. I can see I'll have to pursue this on my own."

"What's that supposed to mean?"

She glared at him. "That should be obvious. Since you refuse to investigate the gentlemen I've chosen, I shall have to do it myself."

Chapter Three

Jackson gaped at her, wondering how this had all turned so terribly wrong. But he knew how. The woman was clearly daft. Bedlam-witted.

And trying to drive him in the same direction. "You can't be serious. Since when do you know anything about investigating people?"

She planted her hands on her hips. "You won't do it, so I must."

God save him, she was the most infuriating, maddening— "How do you propose to manage that?"

She shrugged. "Ask them questions, I suppose. The house party for Oliver's birthday is next week. Lord Devonmont is already coming, and it will be easy to convince Gran to invite my other two. Once they're here, I could try sneaking into their rooms and listening in on their conversations or perhaps bribing their servants—"

"You've lost your bloody mind," he hissed.

Only after she lifted an eyebrow did he realize he'd cursed so foully in front of her. But the woman would turn a sane man into a blithering idiot! The thought of her wandering in and out of men's bedchambers, risking her virtue and her reputation, made his blood run cold.

"You don't seem to understand," she said in a clipped tone, as if speaking to a child. "I have to catch a husband *somehow*. I need help, and I've nowhere else to turn. Minerva is rarely here, and Gran's matchmaking efforts are as subtle as a sledgehammer. And even if my brothers and their wives could do that sort of work, they're preoccupied with their own affairs. That leaves *you*, who seem to think that suitors drop from the skies at my whim. If I can't even entice *you* to help me for money, then I'll have to manage on my own."

Turning on her heel, she headed for the door.

Hell and blazes, she was liable to attempt such an idiotic thing, too. She had some fool notion she was invincible. That's why she spent her time shooting at targets with her brother's friends, blithely unconcerned that her rifle might misfire or a stray bullet hit her by mistake.

The wench did as she pleased, and the men in her family let her. Someone had to curb her insanity, and it looked as if it would have to be *him*.

"All right!" he called out. "I'll do it."

She halted but didn't turn around. "You'll find out what I need in order to snag one of my choices as a husband?"

"Yes."

"Even if it means being a trifle underhanded?"

He gritted his teeth. This would be pure torture. The underhandedness didn't bother him; he'd be as underhanded as necessary to get rid of those damned suitors. But he'd have to be around the too-tempting wench a great deal, if only to make sure the bastards didn't compromise her.

Well, he'd just have to find something to send her running the other way. She wanted facts? By thunder, he'd give her enough damning facts to blacken her suitors thoroughly.

Then what?

If you know of some eligible gentlemen you can strong-arm into courting me, then by all means, tell me. I'm open to suggestions.

All right, so he had no one to suggest. But he couldn't let her marry any of *her* ridiculous choices. They would make her miserable—he was sure of it. He must make her see that she was courting disaster.

Then he'd find someone more eligible for her. Somehow.

She faced him. "Well?"

"Yes," he said, suppressing a curse. "I'll do whatever you want."

A disbelieving laugh escaped her. "*That* I'd like to see." When he scowled, she added hastily, "But thank you. Truly. And I'm happy to pay you extra for your efforts, as I said."

He stiffened. "No need."

"Nonsense," she said firmly. "It will be worth it to have your discretion."

His scowl deepened. "My clients always have my discretion."

"But the only client in my family actually paying you at the moment is Oliver. I want to be your client on my own terms, especially since you must keep my plans secret from him and Gran."

That roused his suspicions. "And why is that?"

Her expression grew guarded. "In case this doesn't turn out how I want."

Under his pointed stare, she flushed. Damn if it didn't make her look even prettier.

She dropped her gaze to the jewel-encrusted bracelet she kept twisting about her slender wrist. "They think me incapable of gaining a husband, and I mean to prove them wrong. But I don't want them knowing I've stooped to such devious tactics to accomplish it. It's embarrassing." She glanced up at him. "Do you understand?"

He nodded. Pride was a powerful motivator. Sometimes the urge to prove people wrong was the only thing that kept a man—or a woman—moving forward.

"This conversation will stay between us," he said tightly. "You may depend upon that."

Relief shone in her lovely face. "All the same, I wish to pay you for whatever work isn't covered by your arrangement with Oliver."

He was *not* taking money from her for this. "I tell you what. Assuming that all goes well and you gain one of these gentlemen as a husband, you may cover my fee from the money you inherit from your grandmother."

"But what if it *doesn't* go well? You still deserve compensation for your efforts. Gran gives me an allowance. Just tell me what you want."

What he wanted was *her*, naked in his bed, gazing up at him with a smile as she opened her arms and drew him down to kiss that thoroughly enchanting mouth.

But that was impossible for more reasons than he could count.

"My clients only pay me if they get results," he lied. "So until you achieve your goal, there's no fee."

She eyed him skeptically. "Surely you require at least a pledge of some kind." She unclasped her bracelet and held it out to him. "Take this. It's worth a few pounds, I'll warrant."

More like a few *hundred* pounds. Leave it to a fine lady like her to act as if it were some bauble.

When he merely stared at it, she added softly, "I insist. I don't want to be obligated to you in case this doesn't work out. You could always sell it or give it to your sweetheart. Or perhaps your mother."

He tensed. "I don't have a sweetheart, and my mother is dead."

Her face fell. "I'm sorry, I forgot that your mother . . . That is . . ." She drew back the bracelet. "How awful of me to remind you of it."

The gentle regret in her voice clutched at his gut. He'd never seen this side of her. "It's fine. She died a long time ago."

Her eyes searched his face. "Some wounds even time doesn't heal, no matter what people say."

They shared a glance borne of their mutual loss, both their mothers vilified in death as they'd been wronged in life.

"You live with your aunt," she said hesitantly. "Is that right?"

He cleared his throat. "Actually, she lives with *me*. My uncle willed their house in Cheapside to me when he died last year, with the condition that she be allowed to live there until her death. I'd planned to remain in my regular lodgings, but she's been so lonely of late . . ." Realizing he was revealing more than he wanted, he said, "Anyway, I moved in last week."

She held out the bracelet again. "Then keep this as a surety and give it to her if our agreement doesn't prove fruitful."

"She could never wear that," he countered. It was too expensive for even the widow of a lauded magistrate to sport at church or in the shops.

A flush filled her cheeks. "Oh, of course. I see."

He hadn't expected her to take his meaning, but her mortification showed that she had. He'd never thought Lady Celia was so perceptive. Or sensitive.

"My aunt's wrists aren't as delicate as yours," he added hastily. "It wouldn't fit her." When relief showed in her eyes, he was glad he'd lied. "Still, I'll accept it as a gesture of good faith on your part, though I fully expect to return it in a few weeks." He took the bracelet from her.

"Of course." Her bright smile warmed him. "So, what do you think of the idea of inviting the gentlemen to the house party? It will give me more chances to get to know them, and Halstead Hall is certainly large enough to accommodate a few more guests."

What an understatement. The marquess's seat was called a "calendar house" because it had three hundred and sixty-five rooms, seven courtyards, fifty-two staircases, and twelve towers. Henry VIII had given it to the first marquess.

"And if you attend, too," she went on, "you can investigate the gentlemen more easily."

Damn. Attending a house party would mean vails to pay the servants and fine clothes for him, a definite strain on his funds. Especially now that he was trying to do improvements on the house he'd inherited.

But if her idiot suitors were staying at Halstead Hall with her, then by thunder, he'd be here, too. They wouldn't take advantage of her on *his* watch. "We're agreed that you won't do any of that foolish nonsense you mentioned, like spying on them, right?"

"Of course not. That's what I have you for."

Her private lackey to jump at her commands. He was already regretting this.

"Surely the gentlemen will accept the invitation," she went on, blithely ignoring his disgruntlement. "It's hunting season, and the estate has some excellent coveys."

"I wouldn't know."

She cast him an easy smile. "Because you generally hunt men, not grouse. And apparently you do it very well."

A compliment? From *her*? "No need to flatter me, my lady," he said dryly. "I've already agreed to your scheme."

Her smile vanished. "Really, Mr. Pinter, sometimes you can be so . . ."

"Honest?" he prodded.

"Irritating." She tipped up her chin. "It will be easier to work together if you're not always so prickly."

He felt more than prickly, and for the most foolish reasons imaginable. Because he didn't like her trawling for suitors. Or using him to do it. And because he hated her "lady of the manor" role. It reminded him too forcibly of the difference in their stations.

"I am who I am, madam," he bit out, as much a reminder for himself as for her. "You knew what you were purchasing when you set out to do this."

She frowned. "Must you make it sound so sordid?"

He stepped as close as he dared. "You want me to gather information you can use in playing a false role to catch a husband. *I* am not the one making it sordid."

"Tell me, sir, will I have to endure your moralizing at every turn?" she said in a voice dripping with sugar. "Because I'd happily pay extra to have you keep your opinions to yourself."

"There isn't enough money in all the world for that."

Her eyes blazed up at him. Good. He much preferred her in a temper. At least then she was herself, not putting on some show.

She seemed to catch herself, pasting an utterly false smile to her lips. "I see. Well then, can you manage to be civil for the house party? It does me no good to bring suitors here if you'll be skulking about, making them uncomfortable."

He tamped down the urge to provoke her further. If he did, she'd strike off on her own, and that would be disastrous. "I shall try to keep my 'skulking' to a minimum."

"Thank you." She thrust out her hand. "Shall we shake on it?"

The minute his fingers closed about hers, he wished he'd refused. Because having her soft hand in his roused everything he'd been trying to suppress during this interview.

He couldn't seem to let go. For such a small-boned female, she had a surprisingly firm grip. Her hand was like her—fragility and strength all wrapped in beauty. He had a mad impulse to lift it to his lips and press a kiss to her creamy skin.

But he was no Lancelot to her Guinevere. Only in legend did lowly knights dare to court queens.

Releasing her hand before he could do something stupid, he sketched a bow. "Good day, my lady. I'll begin my investigation at once and report to you as soon as I learn something."

He left her standing there, a goddess surrounded by the aging glories of an aristocrat's mansion. God save him—this had to be the worst mission he'd ever undertaken, one he was sure to regret.

I prefer not to marry a fortune hunter.

With a scowl, he tucked her bracelet into his coat pocket. No, she only preferred fools and lechers and sons of madmen. As long as they were rich and titled, she was content, because then she knew they weren't after her money.

Yet he couldn't even despise her for that. Traveling between two worlds made him all the more aware of how hard it would be to live in the one he hadn't been born to.

Still . . .

I know what you think of me.

If he wasn't careful, one day he'd show her exactly what he thought of her. But if that day came, he'd better be prepared for the consequences.

Chapter Four

*H*etty was finishing up a conversation with Gabe's wife, Virginia, when she saw Mr. Pinter leave the blue parlor, looking agitated.

Had he been in there with Celia all this time? Alone?

That could not be good. The others thought he and Celia hated each other, but Hetty was not so sure, at least on his part. The man watched the girl when he thought no one was looking.

What Hetty wanted to know was *why*. Did Celia actually interest him? Or was the Runner hoping to further his ambitions by marrying a rich wife? It would not be the first time a man of low degree had levered his position as an employee of a great family into a more direct connection.

Either way, he should not be having private conversations with Celia.

Virginia walked off, leaving Hetty to block Mr. Pinter's path as he approached. "I take it that my granddaughter has been giving you the rough side of her tongue again."

He halted, an inscrutable expression on his face. "Not at all," he said smoothly. "We had a perfectly cordial conversation."

"And may I ask what it concerned?"

"No, you may not."

She frowned. "How very unaccommodating of you, Mr. Pinter. Have you forgotten that you are in my grandson's employ?"

"I have obligations to others in your family also, which means I owe them my discretion. So if that's all—"

"What obligations could you possibly have to my granddaughter?" Hetty demanded as she saw Celia leave the parlor and catch sight of them.

Celia hurried up. "Leave him be, Gran. He's doing what Oliver hired him to do—investigating my suitors. We were consulting on that."

"Oh." Hetty glanced at Mr. Pinter. The man could be so damned hard to read sometimes. "Why didn't you say so, Mr. Pinter?"

"Because I'm in something of a hurry, madam. So if you'll both excuse me, I'll bid you good day."

With a cursory bow, he strode off. Hetty noticed that Celia watched him go with the same sort of veiled interest that he sometimes had in watching her.

Her eyes narrowed. There had to be more to this than they were saying. They had been in that parlor an awfully long time. And Mr. Pinter's responses had bordered on rudeness. The man was direct and frank, but never rude.

Her granddaughter, on the other hand . . . "He seemed in an awful rush to get away. What did you say to him in there, anyway?"

Two spots of color appeared on Celia's cheeks, another alarming sign that something was afoot. "I merely laid out everything he needed to know to gain the full background on my suitors."

"And which suitors are these? The last time I asked, you said you had none."

"Things are progressing well with Lord Devonmont, the Duke of Lyons, and the Visconde de Basto. That's why I need more information."

Ah. Well, that wasn't so bad. Devonmont and Lyons were eminently eligible. Devonmont was a bit wild, but that never worried her. Her late husband had been wild until he married. Her grandsons, too. Marriage had settled them right down.

It did not settle your son-in-law.

Hetty grimaced. All right, so that had been her one failure. She should never have encouraged Lewis Sharpe to marry her daughter—although then she would not have five delightful grandchildren, with two great-grandchildren on the way.

With any luck, Celia would bring her more. "Basto," Hetty mused aloud. "I do not recall that one."

"Oh, we met at the ball where Gabe and Virginia first danced together a few months ago. Since then we've seen each other often enough, but rarely at the affairs you attend. He hates leaving his ailing sister alone in the evening. But he's very nice and seems to dote on me when I do see him. He's Portuguese, I believe."

"Foreign, eh?" Hetty frowned. "Then I am glad Mr. Pinter is looking into his background. You have to be careful with foreigners."

"Right. I wouldn't want to rush into marriage with a stranger," Celia said tartly. "Oh, wait, yes, I would. My grandmother has dictated that I must."

Hetty stifled a smile. "Sarcasm does not become you, dear girl."

"Draconian ultimatums don't become *you*, Gran."

"Complain if you must, but I still mean to see you married by year's end."

Firm treatment was the only way to handle her grandchildren. Celia in particular had been too much indulged; it was time to nudge her out of the nest.

Celia glared at her. "Fine. Then I'll need your help."

That put Hetty instantly on her guard. Celia never asked for anyone's help. She had some fool notion she was an independent woman. "What do you wish from me?"

"I'd like you to add the duke and the viscount to the guest list for the upcoming house party. Having them visit here will make it easier for me to determine their intentions."

"And bring them up to snuff?" Hetty prodded.

Her granddaughter bristled. "I've no doubt they'll all make offers if given the chance," she said hotly. "They are half in love with me already."

"And what about you? Are you half in love with *them*?"

Celia's eyes glittered. "I didn't think love was part of this equation, Gran."

"It most certainly is. Do not mistake that. I want you to marry for love."

Seizing Hetty's hand, Celia turned earnest. "Then don't give me a deadline. Let me do it in my own way."

"As you have been until now, keeping every man at arm's length, scaring them away with your target shooting?" Gran shook her head. "You cannot fall in love if you do not let a man close. And you will not let a man close unless you have a reason. I know you. If I rescind that ultimatum, you will bury yourself on this estate and never come out."

A sad smile crossed Celia's face. "I told him you'd say that."

"Who?"

"It doesn't matter." Celia drew a heavy breath. "So will you add them? Two more guests can hardly make much difference."

Hetty stared at her. "Maria wanted it to be a more private affair, only Oliver's closest friends and family, since she is so far along in her confinement and can't see to the guests the way she would like."

"I thought that was why you and Minerva and Virginia were doing most of the work," Celia retorted.

"Well, yes, but—"

"And the duke *is* a friend of the family. He may be more a friend of Gabe's than Oliver's, but I don't think Oliver or Maria would mind."

"They might mind having that foreigner Basto wandering the house."

"Do you want me to marry or not?"

Hetty clutched her cane. "I tell you what. I shall include them if you will reveal what you discussed with Mr. Pinter in the drawing room."

"I already told you—"

"Nonsense. He said something about having an obligation to you."

"Yes. An obligation to research my suitors."

"Nothing more?"

Guilty color rose in her granddaughter's cheeks. "Why would you think there was anything more between me and Mr. Pinter?"

Because you blush when his name is mentioned. Because he follows you with his eyes. Because I do not know what to make of him, and that worries me.

It was always better to play dumb until one had all the facts. "Is he to be invited to this house party?"

"Of course," Celia said with false-sounding lightness in her voice. "It's the best way for him to discover information about my suitors."

"Then I hope the man has appropriate clothing for the affair. I doubt that Bow Street Runners wear the sort of evening attire suitable for dining with dukes and marquesses."

A frown knit Celia's brow. "I hadn't thought of that."

Good. It was time she considered such things if she had any romantic interest in the man. "Well, no matter." She waved a hand dismissively. "Considering the large fee he charges, I am sure he can afford to buy what he needs."

"I-I didn't mean for him to suffer any financial burden

over this." Celia's face showed a worrisome amount of concern for the strain on Mr. Pinter's pocketbook.

Hetty levied a searching glance on her. "Should I invite his aunt as well?"

Celia looked genuinely confused. "I don't see why. This is no social visit. He'll be here to work."

"Of course." Hetty let out a breath. Perhaps everything *was* just as it appeared. Though the girl seemed to be up to something suspicious, it didn't seem to involve any deep feelings for Mr. Pinter.

Now if only she could be as sure about Mr. Pinter's feelings for Celia . . .

STILL BROODING OVER his unsettling bargain with Lady Celia, Jackson hurried into his uncle's house in Cheapside and headed for his study. He had less than an hour to be at his office to meet with his client, and he had to pick up the report he'd promised the man.

"Jackson!" Aunt Ada called to him from the parlor.

"Not now, Aunt," he barked. "I'm late."

Ada Pinter Norris came out into the hall, a wiry little bundle of sheer will. It sometimes amazed him that she and his mother had been sisters. Mother had been tall and dark like him, while the top of Aunt Ada's graying blond head barely reached his shoulder. "Have you eaten? Don't answer that—I know you haven't."

He entered his study and scanned his desk but didn't see the papers. "I have to be at the office by—"

"Is this what you're looking for?" she asked.

He turned to find her waving a sheaf of paper. "Yes, thanks."

But when he reached for it, she shoved it behind her back. "Not until you eat."

"Oh, for God's sake, Aunt Ada—"

"None of that swearing, now. If you mean to be chosen as Chief Magistrate, you can't talk like a dockworker."

With a lift of his eyebrow, he held out his hand. "I won't be chosen as anything if I don't satisfy those who require my help."

"Humph. They can wait a few minutes." Her eyes glittered a warning. "I mean it. Don't make me throw these in the fire."

He flashed her his darkest scowl. "You wouldn't dare."

She set her shoulders. "Try me. And while those black looks of yours might intimidate criminals, they won't work on me. They didn't when you were ten, so they certainly won't now."

"Then I'll have to resort to force." He fought a smile as he stalked toward her. "I outweigh you by a good five stone. I could snatch those papers before you got anywhere near a fire."

"I could bash you over the head with a skillet, too."

The idea of his sweet-natured aunt bashing him over the head with anything made him laugh. He held up his hands. "Fine, I'll eat. But I must make it quick."

Clucking her tongue at him, she headed for the kitchen. He followed, shaking his head. It had been so long since he'd lived in the same house with her that he sometimes forgot how stubborn she could be.

"I don't know what to do with you," she groused as he sat down at the kitchen table. She filled a plate with stew and set it before him. "Always in a rush. Never taking time to eat properly. That will end now that you're living here. I won't see you work yourself into an early grave like Wil—"

She broke off with a little moan that cut him to the heart.

"I'm sorry, Aunt," he said. "I didn't mean to upset you."

"Don't mind me," she whispered, wiping tears from her eyes. "It's just . . . I miss him so. It comes up at the oddest times."

"I know," he said softly. "I miss him, too."

Uncle William, the magistrate, had taught him everything. God only knew what would have happened if Jackson and his mother had continued to live their hand-to-mouth existence in Liverpool. The day his uncle had responded to Mother's letter by coming to snatch them from the jaws of poverty had been the day Jackson had finally started to breathe again.

"Eat." His aunt pressed a fork into his hand. "I don't want to make you late."

He snorted but started right in on the stew. He hadn't realized how hungry he was.

With open curiosity on her face, she sat down beside him. "So how did the meeting with the Sharpes go?"

"Well enough," he said between bites. "I've been invited to their house party."

Her face lit up. "That's wonderful. I knew that your association with them would do you good. Is it very exclusive? Will there be many important people there?"

"A duke and an earl, for one." He swallowed some ale. "Do I have any clothes suitable enough for the evenings there?"

"Lord, no."

"I was afraid of that." He sighed. "There's no time to get anything made up at the tailor's, either. The house party is next week."

"Next week!" She pursed her lips. "Your uncle's clothes ought to be fine enough. He dined with lords of Parliament occasionally. You're the same height as he is— *was*—and I could probably take in the waist . . ."

"I hate to ask you to do all that work."

"Nonsense. You can't pass up a chance to make important connections simply for lack of a decent coat."

"It's not what you think. I'm working."

Her face fell. "Working?"

"I'm investigating Lady Celia's potential suitors."

"Oh," she said in a small voice.

He glanced at her, surprised to find her looking stricken. "What's wrong?"

"I didn't know she *had* suitors."

"Of course she has suitors." Not any he could approve of, but he wasn't about to mention that to his aunt. "I'm sure you read about her grandmother's ultimatum in those reports you transcribed. She has to marry, and soon, too."

"I know. But I was rather hoping . . . I mean, with you there so often and her being an unconventional sort . . ." When he cast her a quizzical look, she went on more forcefully, "There's no reason *you* couldn't offer for her."

He nearly choked on his bread. "Are you out of your mind?"

"She needs a husband. You need a wife. Why not her?"

"Because marquess's daughters don't marry bastards, for one thing."

The coarse word made her flinch. "You're still from a perfectly respectable family, no matter the circumstances of your birth." She eyed him with a sudden gleam in her eye. "And I notice you didn't say you weren't interested."

Hell. He sopped up some gravy with his bread. "I'm not interested."

"I'm not saying you have to be in love with her. That would perhaps be asking too much at this point, but if you courted her, in time—"

"I would fall in love? With Lady Celia? That isn't possible."

"Why not?"

Because what he felt for Celia Sharpe was lust, pure and simple. He didn't even know if he *wanted* to fall in love. It was all fine and well for the Sharpes, who could love where they pleased, but for people like him and his mother, love was an impossible luxury . . . or a tragedy in the making.

That's why he couldn't let his desire for Lady Celia overcome his reason. His hunger for her might be more powerful than he cared to admit, but he'd controlled it until now, and he would get the best of it in time. He had to. She was determined to marry someone else.

His aunt was watching him with a hooded gaze. "I hear she's somewhat pretty."

Hell and blazes, she wouldn't let this go. "You *hear*? From whom?"

"Your clerk. He saw her when the family came in to the office one time. He's told me about all the Sharpes, how they depend on you and admire you."

He snorted. "I see my clerk has been doing it up brown."

"So she's *not* pretty?"

"She's the most beautiful woman I've ever—" At her raised eyebrow, he scowled. "Too beautiful for the likes of me. And of far too high a consequence."

"Her grandmother is a brewer. Her family has been covered in scandal for years. And they're grateful to you for all you've done so far. They might be grateful enough to countenance your suit."

"You don't know the Sharpes."

"Oh, so they're too high and mighty? Treat you like a servant?"

"No," he bit out. "But . . ."

"By my calculations, there's two months left before she has to marry. If she's had no offers, she might be getting desperate enough to—"

"Settle for a bastard?"

"Ignore the difference in your stations." She seized his arm. "Don't you see, my boy? Here's your chance. You're on the verge of becoming Chief Magistrate. That would hold some weight with her."

Setting his fork down, he leaned back in his chair. "First of all, I'm not on the verge of anything. Just because Sir Richard Birnie is retiring doesn't mean they'll choose me to replace him."

That was his hope, of course, and everything he'd done had been to further that aim, as his aunt well knew. He'd served as an assistant magistrate for the past couple of years, ever since he'd been instrumental in solving the murder of the first Lady Kirkwood. But even at thirty-two, he was still quite young to become Chief Magistrate.

"Secondly," he went on, "a Chief Magistrate is about as far beneath a marquess's daughter as a tree is beneath the moon."

A mutinous look crossed his aunt's face. "Sir Richard started out as a saddler's apprentice. He got himself a knighthood partly because he married a wife with good connections."

"A wealthy baker's daughter. That's a far cry from a lady of rank."

"That doesn't mean it can't happen. You're a fine man, a handsome man, if I do say so myself. You're young and strong, with a good education and gentlemanly manners—better manners than Sir Richard, anyway. And now that you own this house—"

"She lives in a mansion!" Snatching his arm free, he rose. "Do you really think she'd be happy here in Cheapside, with the butchers and merchants and tradesmen?"

Her aunt looked wounded. "I thought you liked this neighborhood."

Damn. "I do, but . . ." There was nothing for it but to tell her the truth. "She can't stand me, all right? I'd be the last person on earth she'd want to marry." Snatching up the report, he headed for the door. "I have to go."

"Jackson?"

"What?" he barked.

"If that's true, she's a fool."

Lady Celia was no fool. She simply knew better than to take up with a man who didn't know the identity of his own father. He managed a curt nod. "I'll see you tonight, Aunt."

As he left the house, an age-old anger weighed him down. He wouldn't hurt Aunt Ada for the world, but she didn't understand. Ever since he'd started working for the Sharpes, she'd hoped that his association with them would raise him up in the world, and nothing he said dampened that hope.

No doubt she believed that his father's supposedly noble blood made him somehow superior to every other bastard. But one day she would learn. An unclaimed bastard was an unclaimed bastard, no matter who his father was.

Chapter Five

A week later, on the first night of the house party, the guests gaily mingled about the great hall and a bit of impromptu dancing was in progress, but Celia felt rather blue.

Put her with a group of men bragging about their exploits and trying to outdo each other, and she was perfectly at home. But at more formal affairs, she ran into trouble. Men turned into such silly creatures when faced with ladies in fine dresses. They spouted ridiculous compliments or talked only of the weather, as if females were too stupid for anything else. Or they retreated en masse to the card room.

She wasn't adept at flirting, like Minerva, and she didn't read widely, like her sister-in-law Maria. All she could talk about was shooting, and that rarely enticed a man to view a woman as a romantic prospect.

But that wasn't the only reason for her depressed spirits. Her suitors were *not* acting according to plan.

Although Lord Devonmont was here, the Visconde de Basto had said he could come to Halstead Hall only during the day. He was reluctant to leave his sister alone at night with just servants to watch after her. And the duke *still* hadn't arrived. He'd accepted the invitation to the house party but apparently hadn't thought it necessary to show up in a timely fashion. He hadn't sent word about the reason for his lateness either. Like a typical duke, he was doing everything at his leisure and assuming that the world would go along. That didn't bode well for his manageability as a husband.

The worst part was that Mr. Pinter had shown up too late for her to get him alone and ask what he'd discovered about her suitors. How was she to go on without some inside information? He *knew* he was supposed to provide her with that. Instead, he prowled among the guests like a panther stalking prey.

As he came near where she stood, she noted that at least Gran's fears about his clothing had been for naught. Though out of date, his tailcoat of cobalt blue superfine with gilt buttons and his waistcoat of sky blue silk were perfectly respectable. The color turned his gray eyes into a mesmerizing azure, and his chest and shoulders filled out both coat and waistcoat rather impressively.

Not that she cared. Nor did she care how his white trousers clung to calves that were surprisingly muscular or how his thighs strained against the fabric. So what if he cut a fine figure in evening attire? His stern manner ruined it all.

Although right now his manner was anything but stern. He was speaking amiably to Lady Kirkwood, who said something that made him laugh. Astonishing! The man could laugh! It quite transformed his face, softening the sharp edges and sweetening his expression.

A lump caught in Celia's throat. Why had *she* never seen him laugh?

And why was he making merry with the Kirkwoods, anyway? Shouldn't he be off questioning her suitors' servants and sneaking into their rooms? Getting information? Lord Kirkwood wasn't good friends with any of her choices.

Mr. Pinter caught her gaze on him, and his laughter died. Then he offered her a nod as cool as any she'd ever seen.

That sparked her temper. She nodded with equal coolness and deliberately turned her back on him, only to find Lord Devonmont approaching.

"May I have this dance, madam?" he asked with a genuine smile.

If Lord Devonmont could smile at her, why couldn't that blasted Bow Street Runner?

"I would be delighted," she said in an effusive voice that she hoped carried to the officious Mr. Pinter. "How good of you to ask."

His eyes twinkled as he offered her his arm. "How good of you to accept."

As he led her to the floor, she cast a furtive glance back to where Mr. Pinter was watching her and Lord Devonmont with his usual impenetrable gaze. It made a shiver skitter down her spine.

Then the waltz began. Lord Devonmont was an excellent dancer, thank heaven. She enjoyed dancing almost as much as she enjoyed shooting. It was physical and energetic, and she was rather good at it.

They took a few turns in a comfortable silence. Then she couldn't resist peeking in the direction of the Kirkwoods to see if Mr. Pinter had noticed her skill at waltzing. But he wasn't with them anymore. Had he finally gone off to do his job? Was he even now slipping into Lord Devonmont's room?

"Looking for someone?" Lord Devonmont asked.

Oh, dear, she'd been too obvious. "Certainly not," she said lightly.

He raised an eyebrow. "So you weren't watching for Lyons?"

That startled her. "Why on earth would you think that?"

"You're in the market for a husband, and Lyons is unattached." His voice deepened. "As am I."

Blast, she couldn't have him catching on to her plans so quickly. He might bolt. "Really, Lord Devonmont, it's not what you—"

"Call me Pierce. We're practically family." He said it in that husky, roguish voice her brothers used to use on women they wanted to bed. Her brothers hadn't always been discreet in their flirtations.

Coming from Lord Devonmont, however, it took her completely by surprise. Surely he wasn't trying to . . . seduce her. "You're a second cousin to my brother's wife—that's hardly a family connection."

"Then call me Pierce because we're friends." He bent in close in the turn, eyes gleaming as they dropped to her lips. "*Intimate* friends, if I get my wish."

This time there was no mistaking his meaning. But

he was so practiced and smooth that she couldn't help herself—she laughed. When that made him frown, she tried to suppress her amusement, but that only made her laugh harder.

"What's so funny?" he muttered.

"I'm sorry," she said, swallowing her amusement. "It's just that I've heard my brothers make such insinuations to women in that tone of voice for years, but I've never been on the receiving end."

Pierce's sensual smile would rival that of Casanova. "I don't know why not," he said in a lazy drawl. His gaze raked her appreciatively as they swirled about the room. "Tonight, in that purple gown, you look particularly fetching. The color suits you."

"Thank you." Minerva had been trying to get her to stop wearing browns and oranges for years, but Celia had always pooh-poohed her sister's opinions. It was only after Virginia had said exactly the same thing last month that she'd begun to think she should listen. And to order new gowns accordingly.

"You're a lovely woman with the figure of a Venus and a mouth that could make a man—"

"You can stop now." Her amusement vanished. She'd be flattered if he meant a single word, but clearly this was just a game to him. "I don't need the full rogue treatment, I assure you."

Interest sparked in his eyes. "Hasn't it occurred to you that I might be sincere?"

"Only if you're sincerely trying to seduce me."

He cast her a blatantly carnal glance as he held her

tighter. "Well, of course I'm trying to seduce you. What else would I be doing?"

She pitched her voice over the music. "I'm a respectable woman, you know."

"What has that got to do with anything?"

She arched an eyebrow at him as they moved in consort.

"Even a respectable woman might be tempted into, say, slipping out with a gentleman for a walk in the moonlit courtyard. And if said gentleman should happen to steal a kiss or two—"

"Lord Devonmont!"

"Fine." He smiled ruefully. "But you can't blame me for trying. You do look ravishing this evening."

"There you go again," she said, exasperated. "Can you never talk to a woman as if she's a normal person?"

"How dull that would be." When she frowned, he shook his head. "Very well. What scintillating topics of conversation did you have in mind?"

That was easy. She'd been wondering something ever since his cousin had married her brother. "When you offered to marry Virginia a few months ago, was it just to save her from my brother's attentions or were you really hoping she would accept?" In other words, was he looking for a wife or not?

The sudden glint in his eyes told her he might have guessed her goal. "That's far too serious a conversation for a party. Can't we just keep flirting?"

Though his voice held a certain hardness now, she refused to let him change the subject. "I merely wondered if Virginia left you brokenhearted. If you were still holding a tendre for her."

A shuttered look crossed his face. "No one leaves me brokenhearted, my dear lady. Not even my cousin."

The uncomfortable silence that descended made her regret being too direct. But what else was she supposed to do? She didn't have time to be coy. She had to know if he was amenable to marrying. Because if he weren't, she wouldn't waste her efforts on him.

Unfortunately, the waltz was ending. And since he'd already stood up with her for a previous set, they couldn't dance again without the other guests speculating that there was something more serious between them.

Would he ask her to dance anyway? That would certainly make his intentions clear.

But he did not. After leading her from the floor, he bowed most politely and headed off toward the card room.

She sighed. That had gone badly. How was she supposed to snag a husband if she didn't have a knack for flirting?

When she headed over to pick up her reticule, a hand grabbed her arm. "Come with me to the retiring room," Virginia murmured and dragged her off.

What the devil?

As soon as they entered the small parlor designated for the ladies, Celia pulled free of her sister-in-law. "What's this all about?"

Virginia planted her hands on her hips. "I do hope you haven't set your sights on Pierce."

Celia blinked. "Was I that obvious?"

"Not you. *Him.* The rascal enjoys entertaining himself by flirting shamelessly with respectable young females. But he never means anything by it. I have warned him often—"

"I'd thank you *not* to warn him," Celia said a little stiffly. "You never know, he might be ready to settle down. He proposed marriage to *you*, didn't he?"

"Because he was testing Gabriel's resolve, that's all. He had no intention of marrying me, I assure you." Virginia searched her face. "You're not in love with Pierce, are you?"

Celia considered lying, but there seemed little point. "No. He's a bit too much like my brothers to suit me. Though they did manage to settle down into wedded bliss, so perhaps your cousin—"

"Did he suggest taking you for a walk in the moonlight?"

"How did you know?"

Virginia sighed. "That's what he does. I think it's a kind of challenge for him—to see if he can get young women to let him steal a kiss. If he succeeds . . ." She trailed off with a frown.

"If he succeeds, then what?" Celia prodded.

"Frankly, I'm not sure. That's as far as the girls ever get in complaining to me about him. First, they tell me he kissed them and it was like communing on some 'ethereal plane.'" She snorted. "Then they protest that they were *sure* he loved them. And then they start crying. It all goes downhill from there."

"You don't think he actually—"

"No!" She chewed on her lip. "That is, I don't think so. It's hard to know with Pierce. He's so unpredictable." Her gaze met Celia's. "But I'd hate to think of him getting you off alone and attempting—"

"You needn't worry about that," Celia said. "That's what I have Betty for."

"Betty?"

Celia reached into her reticule and pulled out her ladies' pocket pistol.

Virginia leapt back. "Oh, my word! Does your family know you carry that around?"

"I doubt it. I don't think they'd approve."

"I should say not!" Virginia surveyed it curiously. "Is it loaded?"

"Only with powder. There's no ball."

"Thank heaven for that. Still, aren't you worried it will go off by itself?"

"No. It has two protections to keep it from firing accidentally. I made sure of that when I purchased it." She hefted the pistol. "I've been told that ladies of the evening use this sort of gun to frighten customers who try to hurt them."

"Told by whom?"

"My gunsmith, of course."

"How on earth did you find a gunsmith?"

Celia shrugged. "Gabe introduced me to his."

Virginia rolled her eyes. "You and my husband are mad, I swear."

"I suppose we are." With a faint smile, she stroked the pearl handle. "I learned how to shoot from him."

After Celia had been forced to crown Ned with a brick to get him off her in the garden shed that awful day, she'd gone right to Gabe and asked him to teach her. Thank heaven, he'd taken her seriously. Because from then on she'd felt safe in the knowledge that no man could ever get her at a disadvantage again.

Virginia peered uncertainly at the pistol. "Only powder in it, right?"

"Enough to make a very loud bang. But I daresay it would quite frighten a fellow if fired."

"I daresay." Virginia began to grin.

"What?" Celia asked.

"Perhaps it wouldn't be such a bad idea for you to go for a moonlight walk with Pierce. He could use a little shaking up."

Celia laughed. Then they both started laughing.

By the time they left the retiring room, she was almost hoping that Lord Devonmont would indeed take her out somewhere and try to ravish her. Though she'd already fired her pistol in a controlled situation, she'd been wanting to test it under more typical conditions.

But it wasn't Lord Devonmont whom she practically ran into as she and Virginia entered the ballroom. It was the Duke of Lyons.

"Well, if it isn't Lady Celia," he said with his usual dukely reserve. "And Lady Gabriel, too. What a pleasure."

Both women dropped into curtsies.

"Come now, let's not stand on ceremony. I've known you both since you were in leading strings."

"True," Celia remarked. Gabe and Virginia's late brother Roger had been close friends to the duke when he was still a marquess. "And you and I have also been in shooting matches together a time or two."

His manner cooled a fraction. "We have indeed."

Oh, dear, since she always beat him, she probably shouldn't have mentioned that. No man liked to be reminded of such failures.

He glanced about the great hall, which was devoid of music at the moment. "Have I arrived too late for the dancing?"

"I believe the ladies taking turns at the pianoforte are pausing to indulge in some refreshment," Celia said. "I'm sure they'll start again soon."

"I should apologize for my lateness," he said smoothly. "I had a bit of trouble with my curricle. It lost a wheel."

"How awful!" Virginia exclaimed. "It's such a fine curricle, too."

"I think so."

They fell silent. Celia was wondering how to move the conversation along when Virginia said, "Since there's no dancing just now, Your Grace, you ought to tour the orangery. We decorated it for his lordship's birthday tomorrow. I'm sure Lady Celia would be willing to show it to you."

A strange look crossed his face before he smiled and offered Celia his arm. "I'd be delighted to see it."

He sounded as if he meant that. As Celia took his arm, she caught him casting her a rather calculated glance. What was *that* about? She didn't really know him all that

well. He'd been abroad off and on throughout her come-
out.

As they skirted the room, he said, "You look different
tonight, Lady Celia."

How was she to respond? Make some coy remark? She
opted for directness. "In what way?"

"More like a lady than usual. Most of the time when I
see you, you're dressed in smocks for shooting."

"Oh. That's probably true."

They walked a moment in silence. Then he said, "Perhaps we should lay our cards on the table." His glittering
green gaze met hers. "You need a husband to gain your
inheritance. I need a wife to bear my heir. There's no reason we couldn't come to some agreement on the matter."

She gaped at him. The duke was making it easy for her,
and with practically no effort on her part.

So where was the exultation she'd expected? Where was
the triumph that she'd beaten Gran at her game?

"You are very direct, Your Grace," she said, scrambling
to find her purchase in this odd conversation.

"I gather that your situation requires haste."

"Yes, but . . . well . . . this is hasty even for me. What
did you do? Wake up this morning and decide to acquire
a wife?"

A thin smile cracked his reserve. "Not quite. I've given
the matter some thought for the past few months, ever
since Gabe suggested it."

"My brother suggested that you marry me?" she said irritably. Gabe truly doubted she could gain a husband on
her own, didn't he?

"He planted the seed." They walked out the ballroom door and headed across the courtyard toward the orangery. "May I be frank?"

"You seem to be going that direction already," she muttered. "I don't think you need my permission to continue."

He chuckled. It was a surprisingly warm sound for a man she'd always thought rather cold. "As I'm sure you know, my father had a . . . problem."

"You mean, his madness?" As long as they were being frank . . .

"Yes," he said after a moment's hesitation. "Any woman who takes me on risks watching me go mad and perhaps passing it on to her children. So marriage to me might not be an advantage. I've known that for some time. It's why I haven't made any offers before. I am willing to risk marrying, for obvious reasons, but many women may not wish to take the same risk. I thought that perhaps in your case—"

"Given my limited choices and the urgency of my situation," she said cynically, "I might be willing to risk it, too."

"Exactly."

She struggled not to show her hurt feelings. She wasn't sure which was worse, having a man desire her only because it was "a kind of challenge" or having a man want her only for the convenience of it. Was she really so very unmarriageable?

Tears stung her eyes as they entered the orangery. The Buzaglo stove that had been newly installed kept it surprisingly warm for winter, and the gas lanterns cast a soft light over the tile walkway.

Ten potted orange trees were ranged in a line along the windows. On the opposite wall was a row of benches so people could sit and enjoy the scent and sight of orange trees in bloom or in full fruit. But even the bright ribbons jauntily festooning the pots couldn't cheer her.

Because something else had occurred to her. How could she let Lyons make an offer if she meant to refuse him? He would think she was refusing because of the madness in his family. And if word got around that he'd offered and been rejected, it would worsen his situation. She couldn't do that to him.

But her only other choice was to marry him. She wasn't sure how she felt about that, either. It was hard to imagine spending her life with such a lofty personage. "So this would be strictly a marriage of convenience."

"Not exactly. I would hope we could have a normal, amiable marriage."

Amiable. Like friends.

He stopped to search her face. "I shall give you time to think about it, my dear. I know I've sprung this on you rather precipitously. But may I assume that you are at least interested in my proposition?"

She might be. If . . . "Tell me something, Your Grace. Do you find me at all . . . appealing as a woman?"

He appeared startled. "Forgive me. I suppose my offer sounds rather cold-blooded."

"A bit, yes."

That brought a glint to his eye. "Then perhaps this will set your mind at ease." He reached up to catch her by the chin, then lowered his mouth to hers.

She held her breath. A kiss would certainly soothe her misgivings.

But as his lips touched hers, soft, coaxing . . . cool, she felt a stab of disappointment. It wasn't that there was anything wrong with his kiss. It was just too . . .

Careful. Reserved. As if he were testing the waters. She didn't want a man to test the waters with her. She wanted him to seize her in an impassioned embrace and show her in no uncertain terms that he found her desirable. That he wanted—

"I suggest you release the lady, sir," growled a familiar voice, jerking her up short. "Or you won't like the consequences."

THE SIGHT OF the duke taking liberties had made something boil up inside Jackson that he couldn't suppress. He'd uncharacteristically acted on impulse, and already regretted it.

Because the duke now pulled back with the languid motion of all such men of high rank to fix him with a contemptuous stare. "I don't believe we've met, sir."

Jackson fought to rein in the wild emotions careening through him. Lady Celia was glaring at him, and the duke was clearly irritated. But now that Jackson had stuck his nose in this, he would see it out.

"I'm Jackson Pinter of the Bow Street Office. This lady's brother has hired me to . . . to . . ." If he said he'd been hired to investigate suitors, Lady Celia would probably murder him on the spot.

"Mr. Pinter is investigating our parents' deaths," she explained in a silky voice that didn't fool Jackson. She was furious. "And apparently he thinks that such a position allows him the right to interfere in more personal matters."

When Jackson met her hot gaze, he couldn't resist baiting her. "Your brother also hired me to protect you from fortune hunters. I'm doing my job."

Outrage filled the duke's face. "Do you know who I am?"

An eminently eligible suitor for her ladyship, damn your eyes. "A man kissing a young, innocent lady without the knowledge or permission of her family."

Lady Celia looked fit to be tied. "Mr. Pinter, this is His Grace, the Duke of Lyons. He is no fortune hunter. And this is none of your concern. I'll thank you to keep your opinions to yourself."

Jackson stared her down. "As I said the other day, madam, there isn't enough money in all the world for that."

The duke cast him a considering glance. "So what do you plan to do about what you saw, sir?"

Jackson tore his gaze from Lady Celia. "That depends upon you, Your Grace. if you both return to the ballroom right now, I don't plan to do anything."

Was that relief or chagrin he saw on the duke's face? It was hard to tell in this bad light.

"As long as you behave yourself with propriety around Lady Celia in the future," Jackson went on, "I see no reason for any of this to pass beyond this room."

"That's good of you." The duke offered Lady Celia his arm. "Shall we, my lady?"

"You go on," she said coolly. "I need to speak to Mr. Pinter alone."

Glancing from her to Jackson, the duke nodded. "I'll expect a dance from you later, my dear," he said with a smile that rubbed Jackson raw.

"Of course." Her gaze locked with Jackson's. "I'd be delighted."

The minute the duke was gone, however, any "delight" she was feeling apparently vanished. "How *dare* you interfere! You should be upstairs searching my suitors' rooms or speaking to their servants or something useful instead of—"

"Do you realize what could have happened if I hadn't come along?" he snapped. "This room is private and secluded, with a nice hot stove keeping it cozy. All he would have had to do was lay you down on one of those damned benches that are everywhere and—"

He caught himself. But not quickly enough.

"And what?" she prodded. "I would have let him ravish me like the wanton I am?"

Confound it all. "I wasn't saying that."

"That's what it sounded like. Apparently you have some notion that I have no restraint, no ability to resist the attentions of a man I've known since childhood."

"You have no idea what a man can do to a woman!" Jackson shouted.

She paled. "It was just a kiss."

He strode up to her, driven by a madness he couldn't control. "That's how it begins. A man like him coaxes you into a kiss, then a caress, then . . ."

"I would never let it go beyond a kiss," she said in outrage. "What sort of woman do you think I am?"

He backed her toward the wall. "The sort who is too trusting to realize what some men are really after. You can't control every situation, my lady. Some men take what they want, and there isn't a damned thing you can do about it."

"I know more about the true nature of men than you think." She stopped short as she came up against the wall. "I can take care of myself."

"Can you?" He thrust his hands against the wall on either side of her, trapping her.

He thought of his mother and the heartbreak she'd endured because some nobleman had taken a fancy to her. A roiling sickness swamped him at the idea of Lady Celia ever suffering such a thing because she was too reckless and naïve to recognize that she was *not* invincible.

Bending in close, he lowered his voice. "You really believe you can stop any man who wants to hurt you, no matter how strong and determined he is?"

Challenge shone in her eyes. "Absolutely."

It was time someone made her realize her vulnerability. "Prove it," he growled. Then he brought his mouth down on hers.

Chapter Six

elia froze. She couldn't believe it—Proper Pinter was *kissing* her. Hard, boldly, with more feeling than the duke.

Good heavens.

Stung by the challenge he'd laid down, she fumbled for the pistol in her reticule, but she'd just got it in her hand when he whispered hoarsely against her lips, "Sweet God, Celia . . ."

He'd never called her by only her Christian name. He'd certainly never said it so . . . desperately. It made her hesitate with the pistol in her hand.

He took her mouth once more, and her world shifted on its axis as his kiss became wilder, more consuming. This wasn't about a challenge anymore—not when he kissed her as if her mouth held the secret to eternity. Such lovely, drugging kisses made her blood dance through her veins.

His mouth slanted over hers, and his tongue swept the seam of her lips with an urgency that made her throat ache. Remembering how Ned had kissed her, she parted her lips for him.

He went still for the briefest instant. Then with a groan, he slipped his tongue into her mouth. Ohhh, that was *amazing*. When Ned had done it she'd found it messy and disgusting, but Mr. Pinter's kiss was as opposite to Ned's as sun was to rain.

Slow and sensual, he dove inside with hot strokes that had her eager for more. How could this be happening to her? With *him*? Who could ever have guessed that the passionless Mr. Pinter could kiss so very passionately?

Scarcely aware of what she did, she slipped her free hand up to clutch his neck. He pressed into her, flattening her against the wall as he ravished her mouth with no remorse. His whiskers abraded her chin, his mouth tasted of champagne, and the smell of orange trees sweetened the air around them.

It was delicious . . . intoxicating. *Paradise*.

She forgot the pistol in her other hand, forgot that they were in full view of anyone who might be outside the orangery windows, forgot that he'd just been lecturing her as if she were some ninnyhammer. Because he was kissing her now as if she were an angel. *His* angel. And Lord help her, but she wanted him to keep kissing her like that forever.

But a noise from the nearby stove—the crackle of a log as it settled—seemed to jerk him to his senses. He tore his lips from hers and stared down at her a moment, his eyes wild, his breathing heavy.

A change came over his face, turning his expression to cold stone. "You see, Lady Celia?" he said in his harsh rasp. "A man can do anything he wants if he has a woman alone."

Her pleasure died instantly. Had this just been about teaching her a lesson?

Anger roared up in her. How *dare* he? Remembering the pistol, she shoved it up under his chin and cocked the hammer. "And if he does, the woman has a right to defend herself. Don't you agree?"

The surprise on his face was immensely gratifying, but it didn't last long. Eyes narrowing, he leaned closer to hiss, "Go ahead then. Fire."

She swallowed. Though there was no ball, the powder alone would do serious damage. She could never . . .

While she hesitated, he removed the pistol from her numb fingers. His glittering gaze bore into her. "Never brandish a gun unless you're prepared to use it."

She crossed her arms over her chest, feeling suddenly exposed. "Most men would be cowed by the very sight of a pistol," she muttered.

"*I* wasn't."

"You're not most men," she said tightly.

He acknowledged that with a curt nod. Then he walked over to one of the pots, aimed down at the dirt, and fired. When the smoke cleared from the muzzle flash, he noted the lack of a hole in the dirt and faced her.

"Powder." He glared at her. "Did it occur to you that unless you fired at point-blank range, you might merely anger the man you're aiming for?"

"I only need it for men who get close to me," she bit out.

"All the same, the next time you need to protect yourself, forget the pistol and bring your knee up between the man's legs as hard as you can. It'll make your point just as effectively and give you plenty of time to escape."

Color flooded her cheeks. Since she had brothers, she knew what he meant, but it wasn't something she would ever have thought to do. A pity, for it would have served her well with Ned. "Why are you telling me this?"

"I want you to know how to defend yourself if someone's taking liberties."

"Even if the someone is you?"

A strange light glinted in his eyes as he pocketed her pistol. "*Especially* if it's me."

What did he mean by that? "Mr. Pinter, about our kiss . . ."

"I was making a point," he said tersely. "Nothing more. Complain to your brothers about it and get me dismissed if you must, but don't worry—regardless of what you do, it won't happen again."

She caught her breath. How could he be so nonchalant? He'd kissed her so convincingly, so sweetly . . .

It started that way with Ned, too, and it meant nothing to him either. He did it only to impress his friends.

Mr. Pinter headed for the door.

Choking down her hurt, she called out, "Where are you going?"

He paused to cast her an icy glance. "I have suitors' rooms to search and servants to interrogate, remember?"

"I want my pistol back," she snapped.

"You'll get it tomorrow. Given your foolish belief that carrying it will protect you in any circumstance, it's better that you don't have it to hide behind. Perhaps then you won't be tempted into private encounters with randy gentlemen."

A hot blush seared her cheeks. "The only randy gentleman I need protection from is *you*. Next time I have you in my sights, I *will* shoot you."

"Then you'd better not miss," he drawled. "Because if you ever aim a gun at me again, I'll have you arrested for assaulting an officer of the law."

While she was still gasping, he strode from the orangery. She picked up her reticule and flung it at the door just as it closed. He was a beast! A monster! And he'd even made her forget to ask him if he'd learned anything about her suitors!

Tears started in her eyes. It was so . . . so *typical* of him to rattle her by saying such an awful thing. She would swear he did it on purpose. He was always riding roughshod over her. Kissing her passionately one minute and threatening to have her arrested the next—the unnatural devil!

She collapsed onto a bench, struggling to hold back her tears. She would not cry over him. She would *not*! Men were dreadful creatures. And Gran wanted her to *marry* one of them?

Oh, heavens, what was she to do? Lord Devonmont was obviously not interested in marriage. The viscount would arrive in the morning, and if he offered for her,

Gran might abandon her ultimatum just to keep a foreigner out of the family.

Then there was the duke. His kiss might not have thrilled her, but at least he sought a respectable connection, and Gran would be mightily impressed by an offer from him. Celia just wasn't sure if she could take advantage of that.

But she would see her way through this somehow. Then Mr. Pinter would regret being so awful to her.

JACKSON STRODE THROUGH a door and into a hallway to avoid the servants running across the courtyard toward the orangery, no doubt drawn by the pistol shot. Let Celia deal with them. He couldn't stand to speak to anyone right now.

What an idiot he was! Had he really thought he could get away with kissing a marquess's daughter?

And not just any marquess's daughter, either. Celia, looking oh so tempting in her sumptuous purple gown. Lovely, angry Celia.

Lady Celia, he reminded himself. But he'd never be able to think of her like that again, not when the taste and smell of her still filled his senses.

Hearing voices behind him, he slipped into an empty room to wrangle his emotions into some semblance of control. But it was no use. He could still feel her body yielding to his, still hear her rapid breathing as he'd taken every advantage.

Damn her and her soft mouth and her delicate sighs

and her fingers curling into the nape of his neck so that all he wanted to do was press her down onto a bench . . .

"Hell and blazes!" He thrust his hands through his hair. What in thunder was he supposed to do about her?

And why had she let him kiss her, anyway? Why had she waited until he'd made a complete fool of himself before she'd drawn that damned pistol?

Oh. Right. That was why. To make a fool of him *herself.* To lull him into a false sense of security so she could prove she could control any situation.

Well, he'd stymied that, but it was little consolation. He'd behaved like a damned mooncalf, devouring her mouth as if he were a wolf and she were supper. If he'd allowed her to speak of their kiss, she probably would have pointed out exactly how insolent he'd been. Would have warned him never to do anything so impudent again.

She didn't need to tell him. He'd learned his lesson.

Yes. He had.

The memory of her mouth opening beneath his surged up inside him, and he balled his hands into fists.

No. He hadn't. All he'd learned was that he wanted her more intensely now than ever. He wanted to kiss her again, and not just her mouth but her elegant throat and her delicate shoulder and the soft, tender mounds of her breasts. . . .

A curse exploded out of him. This was insanity! He had to stop making himself mad by thinking about her as if—

"There you are, sir," said a voice behind him. "I thought that might have been you who came in here."

"What the hell is it?" he growled as he rounded on whoever had been fool enough to run him to ground.

It was John, Stoneville's longest-serving footman and the one the marquess trusted most. The man paled. "I-I beg your pardon, but I thought you'd like to know what I found out about Nurse and Mr. Virgil. You did ask me to look into it."

"Yes, I remember. Thank you." Jackson had turned to John because although the footman hadn't been with the family at the time of the deaths, he knew nearly everyone who had. Jackson forced himself to smile, to relax, to behave as if he were *not* standing here thinking of how much he wanted to ravish the youngest lady of the house. "Forgive me, I have quite a few things on my mind right now, and that's made me irritable."

Unbidden, Celia's—*Lady* Celia's—words leapt into his mind: *It will be easier to work together if you're not always so prickly.*

He suppressed a snort. It would never be easy to work with *her*.

Warily, John approached to hand him a piece of paper. "I'm afraid I haven't located all the servants you've asked about yet. But here's a list of the ones I have. I'm nearly certain that Nurse—Mrs. Duffett, that is—lives in High Wycombe. I've written down the last address anyone had for her, but if you'll give me a day to talk with a pensioned servant in Ealing, I'll confirm it and any others on the list."

Jackson took the paper. "I would appreciate that, thank you."

Normally he'd go over to High Wycombe and check out the address himself, but it was nearly two hours' ride away and he'd need at least half a day. He dared not be away from Halstead Hall that long with Lady Celia's damned suitors trying to get her off alone. So it could wait until the end of the house party.

As John turned to go, something occurred to Jackson. "By the way, did you happen to find out if the nurse ever used paregoric elixir with the children?"

"Oh! Yes, I forgot. The steward said he seems to remember that it appeared in the estate bills from time to time. But he would have to check to be sure. He wanted to know if you wished him to do that." John frowned. "And he was a bit curious as to why you wanted to know."

Curious wasn't good—not if Jackson was to keep this particular line of inquiry secret for Lady Celia's sake. "Something one of the Sharpes said made me wonder about it. But tell him not to bother."

He'd just ask the nurse when he met her, though he wasn't sure it was even worth mentioning.

I feel in my bones that it was real.

He sighed, remembering how fervently Lady Celia had spoken those words. No matter how much trouble she gave him, and how much he wanted to steer clear of her, he couldn't just dismiss her dream without following it up. She might be the most aggravating female ever to come into his sphere, but she deserved better than that.

Chapter Seven

Celia wasn't surprised to find herself alone at the breakfast table. It was still early for people to be up, considering that the dancing and card playing had gone on until well past one in the morning. Normally she would still be abed, too, but she hadn't been able to sleep.

It wasn't because of her suitors, either. Lord Devonmont's flirting later in the evening had demonstrated that her mention of marriage hadn't sent him fleeing. And the duke had danced with her twice. The second time he'd made himself quite amiable, forcing her to seriously consider the possibility of accepting his offer.

Only one thing had her balking: his cool kiss. Especially when compared to Mr. Pinter's hot ones.

Curse that man. No matter how much she told herself his kisses hadn't meant anything, her wounded pride wanted to believe otherwise. Her wounded pride insisted they'd been too passionate to be meant only as a lesson.

Her wounded pride was a blasted nuisance.

"The Visconde de Basto, my lady," said a voice from the door.

With a start, she turned to find a footman ushering the viscount into the breakfast room. "Good morning, sir," she rose to say cheerily, glad to be distracted from her thoughts. "You've arrived early, I see."

Smiling broadly, he strode over to take her hand and lift it to his lips, brushing a kiss against it in the Continental fashion. "I did not want to miss one moment of my time with such a lovely lady."

Sometimes she had to strain to make out his words through his thick accent, but she'd caught that perfectly well. "I'm glad you did." She gestured to the sideboard. "Do have some breakfast."

"Thank you, I believe I shall. I left town without eating." He winked at her. "I was in a great hurry to see you."

She bit back a laugh. Sometimes he was the Portuguese version of Lord Devonmont.

As he strolled to the sideboard, she took her seat and tried to ignore what he wore, but his outrageous attire was one of his few flaws. She understood that fashions were different in Portugal, but really, she'd never seen such a peacock!

Still, she could tell that a fine form lay beneath his red velvet waistcoat and green satin breeches. Fortunately his coat was brown, which helped to mitigate the vividness of the other colors, though he did wear his cravat in an elaborate and rather old-fashioned knot.

Unbidden, Mr. Pinter's remark about him flitted into her head: *Basto is a Portuguese idiot who's too old for you and clearly trawling for some sweet young thing to nurse him in his declining years.*

She scowled. Why on earth would Mr. Pinter think the man so old? Lord Basto's hair was black as night, where even Oliver's was starting to show threads of gray. She would guess him to be Oliver's age—late thirties at most. That was only fifteen years older than she, certainly not out of the realm of possibility for a husband.

She did wish he wasn't quite so hairy, though. He kept his full beard and mustache neatly trimmed, and she understood that it was quite common abroad, but no man in England wore full whiskers. The first thing she'd do if they married was persuade him to shave.

He sat down next to her at the table with a plate full of eggs and sausage and cast her a serious glance. "I must apologize, my lady. I wish that I could join you here in the evenings as well, but it is very hard on the . . . how do you say it . . . company . . . for my ailing sister."

"Company? Oh, you mean a companion?"

He smiled gratefully. "Yes, that is the word. The companion must speak Portuguese, and that is not so easy to find. I could only hire the one lady, and she can only come in the day."

"Yes, I suspect there are few Englishwomen who speak Portuguese. You're lucky you found one who did."

"I am sure that is true." He slanted a glance at her. "I do not dare to hope that you speak it."

"I'm afraid not." When he looked disappointed, she

added, "But your English is very good, so there's no need."

His eyes twinkled. "You are too kind, my lady. Indeed, you are the most amiable Englishwoman I have ever met."

She laughed. The viscount was rapidly rising on her list. "Some people don't find me amiable." *Like a certain unfeeling Bow Street Runner.*

He struck a hand to his chest. "I cannot believe that! You are such an *alma brilhante* . . . a bright soul. How can anyone not see it?"

She grinned at him. "They must all be blind."

"And deaf." He tapped his temple. "And not very right in the head."

"Excellent, my lord," she said. "You grasped that idiom quite well."

He looked surprised by that, then smiled. "I have to learn if I am to impress the *senhora.*"

She cast him a coy glance. "And why would you want to impress me, sir?"

Picking up her hand, he pressed a kiss to it again and this time didn't release it. "Why would I not?" His wistful expression tugged at her sympathies.

"You'd better eat your eggs before they get cold," she said, gently withdrawing her hand.

He sighed and did as she bade. After a moment, he said, "I understand that your father's family is foreign, like me. Is that true?"

"Yes, Papa's mother was from Tuscany."

"So he was half-Italian. Is that why your mother married him? Because she liked foreigners?"

He said it so hopefully that Celia snorted. "I think she liked that he was a marquess but didn't realize what that meant."

He frowned. "I do not understand."

"My father was used to living how he pleased, to being fawned over as a marquess. He didn't change his behavior once he was married."

"What do you mean?"

"He wasn't faithful to my mother. But she'd married him because she thought they were in love. So his infidelities broke her heart."

"I see. And you know for certain that he was not faithful?"

We can meet at the hunting lodge.

No, that was *too* personal to speak of. "I only know because my siblings speak of it. I don't remember anything of those years. I was too young."

"That is good," he said.

She glanced at him, eyebrow raised.

He cast her a searching glance. "No child should have to witness their parent's—how did you say it?—infidelities."

"I quite agree." She gave him a sad smile. "Though I'm surprised you feel that way. I assumed that being from the Continent and of a privileged class—"

"I would approve of such behavior?" He sounded insulted.

But she persisted. "Perhaps. Many noblemen marry for money, to make sure that their estates are taken care of. Mama fancied herself in love with Papa, when all he wanted was her fortune."

"And you fear that a man will marry *you* for *your* fortune," he said, surprising her with his insight.

"Can you blame me? I want a man to like me for myself, not for what I can provide him."

"That is very wise of you. And you have a right to expect it, too." He turned pensive. "But sometimes people want many things, not just one. Money, an amiable wife . . . peace."

Peace? What a strange choice. "And what do *you* want, sir?"

As if realizing he'd revealed too much about himself, he cast her a bland smile. "I want everything, of course. Who does not?" He patted her hand. "But I will settle for an amiable wife." It was as close to making a declaration of his intentions as he'd come.

So of course Mr. Pinter chose that inopportune moment to enter the breakfast room. "And whose amiable wife are you settling for, sir?" he said in a snide tone.

His gaze dropped to the viscount's hand resting on hers, then darkened. She resisted the urge to snatch her hand free.

The viscount bristled, tightening his hand almost possessively on hers. "Do I know you, sir?"

"Not yet. The name is Jackson Pinter." He came to stand directly across the table and bent forward over it to offer his hand to Lord Basto, forcing the viscount to release her hand to take it. "Some would call me Mrs. Plumtree's 'lackey,'" he added with a side glance at Celia. "Though I work for Lord Stoneville."

She colored, remembering the conversation they'd had

a few months ago, when she'd called him that. He was clearly spoiling for a fight. No doubt he was still smarting over her pulling a pistol on him last night. "Mr. Pinter does investigations of all kinds," she explained. "For money."

Mr. Pinter's slate-gray eyes bore into her. "Some of us cannot live on our family's fortune, my lady."

"While some of us are very fond of biting the hand that feeds them." If he could throw her past words at her, then she could throw back what he'd said to *her* months ago.

She was surprised when a reluctant smile tugged at his lips. "A hit direct, madam. Perhaps I should get out of the line of fire while I still have my head."

"Perhaps you should refrain from putting yourself *in* the line of fire in the first place," she quipped. "An officer of the law ought to know better."

"Know better than what?" Oliver asked as he entered with the duke at his side.

Generally, she liked being in a room full of men. But when it was her brother, two suitors, and the only man whose kisses had ever affected her, there was a bit too much manliness in the air for her taste.

"Your sister and I were just having one of our usual discussions," Mr. Pinter said.

"You mean she was raking you over the coals again," Oliver said.

"I believe the coal raking was mutual this time," she said lightly.

Oliver snorted. She could feel the viscount's gaze on her, and the duke seemed to be watching both her *and* Mr. Pinter. It was very unsettling.

"So you're investigating the deaths of the Sharpes' parents, are you?" the duke asked Mr. Pinter in a conversational tone.

As Celia groaned, Oliver swung his gaze to her. "You *told* him about that?"

Last night, she'd been so worried that Mr. Pinter might tell the duke his role in investigating her suitors that she'd blurted out something the family had been keeping fairly quiet until now.

"I'm afraid I'm the one who told him, your lordship," Mr. Pinter said. "I assumed that he knew, given his friendship with your brother."

She was shocked that Mr. Pinter would lie to Oliver to spare her embarrassment. Especially since he depended on Oliver for part of his livelihood.

Mr. Pinter's eyes met hers, and a faint smile curved his lips.

"Sorry, old chap," the duke said, his curious gaze on her and Mr. Pinter. "No one said it was a secret." He cast a veiled glance at the viscount. "I shouldn't have brought it up."

Looking confused, Lord Basto leaned over to whisper, "I had heard that your mother shot your father as an accident and then shot herself. Is that not so?"

"It's . . . complicated," she murmured, aware of Oliver's dour gaze on them.

"I see the cat is out of the bag," Oliver grumbled. "Just so you know, Mr. Pinter is here to explore the possibility that our parents were murdered. If you gentlemen wouldn't mind, we'd rather that information not be spread too widely."

"What information?" said a fresh voice from the doorway. Lord Devonmont. And he had Gabe with him.

"Good heavens," Celia said, "what are all you men doing up so early?"

Gabe laughed. "We're going shooting, of course. Well, except for Jarret. He has to be at the brewery." He glanced at the viscount. "You'll come with us, Basto, won't you?"

"I would be delighted."

"Speaking of shooting, my lady," Mr. Pinter said as he came around the table, "I looked over your pistol as you requested. Everything seems to be in order."

Removing it from his coat pocket, he handed it to her, a hint of humor in his gaze. As several pairs of male eyes fixed on her, she colored. To hide her embarrassment, she made a great show of examining her gun. He'd cleaned it thoroughly, which she grudgingly admitted was rather nice of him.

"What a cunning little weapon," the viscount said and reached for it. "May I?"

She handed him the pistol.

"How tiny it is," he exclaimed.

"It's a lady's pocket pistol," she told him as he examined it.

Oliver frowned at her. "When did you acquire a pocket pistol, Celia?"

"A little while ago," she said blithely.

Gabe grinned. "You may not know this, Basto, but my sister is something of a sharpshooter. I daresay she has a bigger collection of guns than Oliver."

"Not bigger," she said. "Finer perhaps, but I'm choosy about my firearms."

"She has beaten us all at some time or another at target shooting," the duke said dryly. "The lady could probably hit a fly at fifty paces."

"Don't be silly," she said with a grin. "A beetle perhaps, but not a fly." The minute the words were out of her mouth, she could have kicked herself. Females did not boast of their shooting—not if they wanted to snag husbands.

"You should come shooting with us," Oliver said. "Why not?"

The last thing she needed was to beat her suitors at shooting. The viscount in particular would take it very ill. She suspected that Portuguese men preferred their women to be wilting flowers.

"No thank you," she said. "Target shooting is one thing, but I don't like hunting birds."

"Suit yourself," Gabe said, clearly happy to make it a gentlemen-only outing, though he knew perfectly well that hunting birds didn't bother her.

"Come now, Lady Celia," Lord Devonmont said. "You were eating partridges at supper last night. How can you quibble about shooting birds?"

"If she doesn't want to go, let her stay," Gabe put in.

"It's not shooting birds she has an objection to," Mr.

Pinter said in a taunting voice. "Her ladyship just can't hit a moving target."

She bit back a hot retort. *Don't scare off the suitors.*

"That's ridiculous, Pinter," Gabe said. "I've seen Celia—ow! What the devil, Oliver? You stepped on my foot!"

"Sorry, old chap, you were in the way," Oliver said as he went to the table. "I think Pinter's right, though. Celia can't hit a moving target."

"Oh, for heaven's sake," she protested, "I most certainly *can* hit a moving target! Just because I choose not to for the sake of the poor, helpless birds—"

"Convenient, isn't it, her sudden dislike of shooting 'poor, helpless birds'?" Mr. Pinter said with a smug glance at Lord Devonmont.

"Convenient, indeed," Lord Devonmont agreed. "But not surprising. Women don't have the same ability to follow a bird in flight that a man—"

"That's nonsense, and you know it!" Celia jumped to her feet. "I can shoot a pigeon or a grouse on the wing as well as any man here."

"Sounds like a challenge to me," Oliver said. "What do you think, Pinter?"

"A definite challenge, sir." Mr. Pinter was staring at her with what looked like satisfaction.

Blast it all, had that been his purpose—to goad her into it?

Oh, what did it matter? She couldn't let a claim like his or Lord Devonmont's stand. "Fine. I'll join you gentlemen for the shooting."

"Then I propose that whoever bags the most birds gets to kiss the lady," Lord Devonmont said with a gleam in his eye.

"That's not much of a prize for *me*," Gabe grumbled.

She planted her hands on her hips. "And what if *I* bag the most birds?"

"Then you get to shoot whomever you wish," Mr. Pinter drawled.

As the others laughed, Celia glared at him. He was certainly enjoying himself, the wretch. "I'd be careful if I were you, Mr. Pinter. That person would most likely be *you.*"

"Oho, man, you've really got her dander up this time," Gabe exclaimed. "What on earth did you do?"

Mr. Pinter's gaze met hers, glinting with an unholy amusement. "I confiscated her pistol."

As Gabe gasped, Oliver shook his head. "You'll learn soon enough—never take away one of Celia's guns. Not if you want to live."

"I'm not that bad," Celia grumbled as the duke and the viscount eyed her with a twinge of alarm, though Lord Devonmont's grin broadened. "I've never shot a person in my life."

"There's always a first time," Gabe teased.

"Oh, for pity's sake." She regarded them all stoutly. "I promise not to shoot any of you. How about this? If I win, you gentlemen owe me a rifle. Between the five of you, I'm sure you can afford a decent one."

"Five?" Mr. Pinter said. "Don't I get a part in this little game?"

She stared him down. "I thought you had *certain duties* to attend to." He should be investigating her suitors.

"Whatever duties he has for me will keep, Celia," Oliver said. "Do come with us, Pinter. I want to see how well you handle a fowling piece."

Mr. Pinter smiled at her. "I'd be honored, my lord. As long as her ladyship doesn't mind."

Of course she minded. But if she tried to cut him out, they'd say she was afraid he would beat her.

"Not in the least," she said. "Just be prepared to contribute your part for my rifle."

But as she headed for the door, it wasn't the rifle she was worried about. It was that blasted kiss. Because if *he* won . . .

Well, she'd just have to make sure he didn't.

Chapter Eight

*T*aking aim as the grouse rose, Jackson fired, bringing down another one. He moved forward with
the others as the dogs raced off to pick up the birds. The
six men and Celia were spread out in a line across the
field so that each of their kills would be clearly delin-
eated, but it made it hard to keep track of how many the
others had shot.

The dogs loped back to lay the birds at Stoneville's feet.
Since Jackson had no dogs of his own, his lordship had
gamely relinquished the use of them to him. Apparently, Stoneville meant to gain his amusement solely from
watching Jackson bait Celia.

Jackson wasn't entirely sure why, but neither did he
care. He cared only about making sure he shot well
enough to beat Celia's three suitors, to prevent them
from gaining the kiss.

So you can gain it yourself.

He scowled as they halted in their new spot to reload.
Nonsense. But if he did happen to win it, he would treat
her like the lady she was. Devonmont was just the kind

of joking fellow to be impudent with her in front of everyone. Lyons had already had a taste of her lips, so he might very well think to make his second taste more intimate. And Basto, who already had a fondness for holding her hand, confound the insolent devil—

Jackson swore under his breath. He was acting like some jealous idiot. All right, so he *was* jealous, but this wasn't about that. He merely wanted to keep Celia from making an enormous mistake.

When she'd tried to get out of shooting, Jackson had realized she was serious about choosing one of these idiots as a husband. Clearly, she thought if she pretended to be some milk-and-water miss, it would help her chances.

So he'd made sure she didn't do any such thing. If they were worthy of her, they had to be worthy of the *real* her, not the pretend one she presented. Personally, he thought them all fools for not seeing she was putting on an act.

And couldn't *she* see that a marriage built on such deceptions would fail?

No, she was too blinded by her determination to prove her grandmother wrong about her. Well, he couldn't let her stumble into some idiotic engagement with gentlemen who didn't deserve her. Especially not after what he'd learned about them.

"I see you're no stranger to grouse shooting, Mr. Pinter," Lyons called over as he, too, reloaded.

"My uncle took me a few times," Jackson answered.

The beaters flushed the grouse. As the birds rose, he and the others fired. He hit another grouse.

They were piling up. For the competition, Stoneville

had designated a time limit of two hours. Jackson wasn't sure how much time had passed, but he would guess from the position of the sun that the end of the first hour was nearing.

Assuming he got to keep his kills, his aunt would be ecstatic over the abundance of game birds for their table. "Would that uncle be William Norris, the magistrate?" Stoneville asked Jackson as they all trudged forward again.

"Yes. His friends liked to hunt. Sometimes I went along."

"And here I thought you only fired at people," Celia called over from the other side of him.

"I rarely need to shoot in the course of performing my duties. But I do have to use my pistol occasionally." He slanted a glance at her. "Unlike you, my lady, I don't carry mine for show."

Her cheeks pinkened, but she merely sniffed and halted to reload again. So did he.

He probably should stop tormenting her about her damned pocket pistol, but it still shook him. Powder or no powder, such a weapon could easily provoke a man to attack her.

Still, Jackson admitted that it probably wouldn't have that effect on this lot. They didn't seem the bullying sort, just the coax-a-woman-into-their-bed sort. As for their shooting abilities, Lyons was a good shot, but Devonmont didn't seem to take the sport seriously. Basto was the big surprise. Clearly he'd had some experience with guns. He was deft in his loading and a decent shot, too. But he wasn't particularly fast. He kept stealing glances at Celia that were filled with longing and perhaps desire.

Jackson didn't like that one bit. When he gave her his report, he would emphasize the viscount's utter unsuitability as a suitor. Devonmont's, too.

Lyons's unsuitability was more murky. But Jackson could still make a case against the man, and he fully intended to do so as soon as he could get her alone. Preferably in a public area where what happened between them last night couldn't occur again.

Liar. You want to kiss her so badly you can taste it.

It was a wonder he could shoot straight with her standing so near. She'd dressed to entice again today, this time in a heavy redingote the color of the forest. It turned her hazel eyes just green enough to remind him she was a Sharpe, with the same eyes as most of them. The expensive tailoring of her wool attire, a cross between a gown and a coat, reminded him she was a lady and an heiress, especially since she'd refrained from wearing her usual smock.

He'd never seen her shoot and had assumed that her prowess must be exaggerated. It was not. He hadn't been able to keep track of her kills while focusing on his own, but he was fairly certain the number came close to his. He noted her concentration, the care she took in aiming, the way she compensated for wind and other variables. He'd never met another woman like her. She was magnificent.

"Listen, lads," Devonmont called out. "I'm freezing over here. Might we take a few moments to warm our blood with a bit of drink?"

"Go right ahead," Celia said archly. "I'll just keep shooting."

"That's no way to treat our guests, sis," Stoneville chided. "We should probably move to the east field anyway—this one's just about played out. Gentlemen—and lady—put down your guns and come have some refreshment. We've got wine and ale, and Cook sent out some fine things in case we got hungry, too."

The gentlemen seemed happy to rest, but Celia looked disgruntled. Jackson hid a smile. One would think she'd leap at the opportunity to flirt with her suitors, but she was bent only on winning. He liked that about her.

The footmen quickly set up a table with plates of bread, butter, cheese, and cake. But it was the pewter mugs of ale that Jackson welcomed, needing something to heat his blood. The weather was brisk, and he noticed Celia shivering, even in her wool redingote, though she didn't seem to notice it herself. She was preoccupied by the servants who were counting the birds in the bags to give them a report of who was ahead in the shooting.

Jackson poured her a mug of ale and walked over to hand it to her. "Drink this, my lady. It will warm you."

"Thank you," she murmured as she took the mug.

His fingers brushed hers, and her gaze shot up to meet his. For a long moment they stared at each other, and he was reminded of how soft her mouth had been last night, how sweet her scent as he'd backed her against that wall and—

"Lady Celia, will you have some lemon cake?" Basto asked in a hard voice that was far too possessive.

She jumped as if caught in a naughty act. Pasting a smile to her face, she strolled over to the viscount. "I would adore some, thank you," she said without a backward glance at Jackson.

Meanwhile, he couldn't keep his eyes off her. How could she even tolerate that arse, let alone welcome his attentions? Every word out of the fellow's mouth was prompted by a desire to gain her fortune.

But she didn't know that yet.

"So, Gabe," the duke said as he poured himself some wine, "after this is over, you should try out my new Manton detonator gun with the percussion caps."

"Thanks, old chap, but Celia got one a couple of months ago. We've been giving it a regular try-out—I believe she's using it today. It's a fine gun, isn't it, sis?"

The duke frowned. "Manton told me I was one of the first to have it."

"*One* of the first," Jackson emphasized. "It appears Lady Celia was the first."

She shot him a warning look. He ignored it.

"What Mr. Pinter meant to say," she said smoothly, "was that Mr. Manton probably tells all his customers that."

"That is *not* what I meant to say, my lady," Jackson retorted, unreasonably annoyed. "I said what I meant, and I'd thank you not to put words in my mouth."

"I'd thank you not to provoke m—" She caught herself, casting a furtive glance at her listening suitors. "Forgive me, sir. I wasn't trying to 'put words in your mouth.'"

"Of course you were." He was more than willing to draw her fire if it drove her into showing her real self. "That's why you spoke as if you could read my thoughts. Which we both know you can't." If she could, she'd know that right now he wanted nothing more than to drag her away from these curst gentlemen and kiss every inch of her.

"I say, Pinter," Gabe put in, "you're awfully argumentative today."

"The word you're looking for is 'prickly,'" Celia said, a militant glint in her eye. "Mr. Pinter doesn't like having a mere woman speaking for him."

That sparked his temper. "I don't like having *anyone*, man or woman, speaking for me. I daresay you feel much the same."

She colored but didn't turn away, her eyes flashing at him.

"Meanwhile," Devonmont put in, "I've never even heard of a percussion cap. Anyone care to enlighten me?"

Celia tore her gaze from Jackson. "How can you not have heard of it? That's all anyone has been talking about!"

"Really?" Devonmont looked amused. "I need to go out into society more."

"Indeed, you do," Celia said stoutly. "Only last week at the Knightons' affair, Lord Templemore told me that Manton now refuses to make flintlocks unless by special request. It's astonishing!"

"Astonishing indeed," Devonmont said with a glint of humor in his eye. "So what is a percussion cap, again?"

"Oh, you are hopeless." She let out an exasperated breath. "I can't believe you know so little about firearms."

"I can't believe you know so much," Devonmont countered. "Never seen a woman as keen on guns as you. It's rather chilling."

"Isn't it, though?" Jackson put in. "Better watch it, Devonmont. Her ladyship is liable to shoot first and ask questions later if she finds you doing anything she doesn't approve of."

"I may just take your caution to heart, Pinter." Devonmont winked at Celia. "Then again, some things are worth risking life and limb for."

Celia looked startled, then cast Jackson a smug smile. With a snort, he drank more ale. Devonmont was really starting to irk him. They all were.

"So, Lord Devonmont," Celia said, turning her back on Jackson, "would you like me to show you the difference between a percussion gun and a flintlock?"

"By all means," Devonmont replied. "Though I can't promise to remember any of it later, explain away."

That was all the invitation she required. Carrying her new gun over, she launched into an animated description that would do a gunsmith proud.

Where the blazes had she learned so much about the subject? And why would a woman who'd been raised believing that her mother had shot and killed her father, not only learn to shoot, but *embrace* shooting? Had she ever seen anyone killed with a gun? Or was the process of aiming and firing merely a mechanical problem to her?

He didn't understand that side of her at all. And somehow he felt that if he could puzzle it out, he'd find the key to who she was.

Then he happened to glance at the viscount, and his blood stilled. The viscount's eyes followed Celia's every move, and his finger kept stroking his goblet as if he wanted to stroke some part of her.

Jackson gritted his teeth. No way in hell was he letting that bloody foreigner—or Devonmont, or even the duke—stroke anything of hers. "Are we going to stand around all day discussing which guns are more effective at killing," he snapped, "or are we actually going to kill something?"

Gabe exchanged a glance with his sister. "You're right. 'Prickly' is the word."

"Mr. Pinter is probably just eager to earn his kiss," Stoneville put in. "And given how the numbers stand right now, he may very well do so."

They all pivoted to look at his lordship.

Stoneville chuckled. "Devonmont has killed a pathetic eight brace of birds, Gabe a respectable fifteen, Basto an impressive seventeen and a half, Lyons an even more impressive nineteen, and Pinter an astonishing twenty brace. My sister is tied with him at twenty brace."

"Good show, Pinter!" Gabe said amiably. "You must beat her so none of us have to pay for a blasted rifle."

"Here now, Gabe," the duke cut in irritably, "I have as much chance of beating her as Pinter does. I'm only behind by one brace."

"I don't care who beats her," Gabe said. "Just make sure one of you does, in case I can't catch up. She'll pick the most expensive gun in Manton's shop."

"You're such a pinchpenny, Gabe," Celia teased as they tramped back over the field, headed toward the east end of the estate.

"That's because I need every guinea I have, in case you don't marry."

The lord might have meant the comment as a joke, but clearly Celia didn't take it that way. When the blood drained from her face, Jackson felt a stab of sympathy. He could understand why she wanted to show her family that she could find a decent husband. But *decent* was the operative word.

"Oh, I daresay Lady Celia will be married sooner than you think," the duke remarked. When he slid a knowing glance at Celia and she smiled faintly, Jackson felt his heart drop.

The duke seriously had his eye on her. And apparently she knew it.

Confound it all.

As they stopped, Jackson began loading his gun with quick, efficient movements. That blasted duke could look all he wanted, but he was *not* marrying Celia.

Nor even getting another chance to kiss her. Not if Jackson had anything to say about it.

* * *

CELIA SHOT ANOTHER bird. She wasn't fond of hunting, but the challenge of a moving target appealed to her. Unfortunately, she shouldn't be rising to the challenge. She should let one of the gentlemen win their little wager and steal a kiss. That would help her cause far more than beating them.

But what if Mr. Pinter won? What if he kissed her as he had last night? It would be just the sort of thing he'd do, to put off her suitors by making it appear she had an interest elsewhere. That perhaps he had an interest in her, too.

Perhaps he does.

She snorted. The only interest he had was in ruining her life. He *still* hadn't reported to her about her suitors. He would much rather be here, trying to upset all her plans, than doing his job.

He shot well, though. She'd give him that. The man knew his way around a firearm.

"So, my dear," the duke said from the position he'd taken beside her after they'd had their refreshments, "you seem to have mastered the percussion gun fairly well."

She debated how to answer as they tramped forward. Being careful of a man's pride was more difficult than she'd expected. "Not as well as I'd like. There's less delay in firing, so you have to aim differently, and sometimes I forget. What about you?"

"The same, though I could never have managed as well if I'd used it today. I'll have to stop going back and forth between it and the flintlock. But I need more time to practice before I start using the percussion gun exclusively."

"I need more practice myself," she said.

"Perhaps we could practice together at Marsbury House sometime," he said.

"I would enjoy that." She ignored the niggle that said encouraging the duke's suit was wrong when she wasn't sure she wanted to marry him.

"Yes, Lady Celia always enjoys showing a man how to use his gun," Mr. Pinter put in. "You couldn't ask for a better tutor, Your Grace."

When the duke stiffened understandably, she glared at Mr. Pinter. "His Grace needs no tutoring. He shoots quite well. And manages to remain civil at the same time, which is more than I can say for you, sir."

Why was Mr. Pinter being so difficult? Bad enough that he'd goaded her into this competition—must he also make her suitors resent her? So far they'd taken her participation in this competition in stride, but if he kept provoking them . . .

Mr. Pinter scowled as they all halted to reload. "Civility is for you aristocrats." His voice was sullen. "We mere mortals have no sense of it."

"Then it's a miracle anyone ever hires you to do anything," she retorted. "Civility is the bedrock of a polite society, no matter what a man's station."

"I thought money was the bedrock," he countered. "Why else does your grandmother's ultimatum have all of you dashing about trying to find spouses?"

It was a nasty thing to say and he knew it, for he cast her a belligerent look as soon as the words left his mouth.

"I don't know why you should complain about that," she said archly. "Our predicament has afforded you quite a good chance to plump your own pockets."

"Celia," Oliver said in a low voice, "sheathe your claws."

"Why? He's being rude."

The beaters flushed the grouse. Mr. Pinter brought down another bird, a muscle ticking in his jaw as they all fired. "I beg your pardon, my lady. Sometimes my tongue runs away with my good sense."

"I've noticed." She caught the gentlemen watching them with interest and forced a smile. "But since you were good enough to apologize, let us forget the matter, shall we?"

With a taut nod, he acknowledged her request for a truce.

After that, they both concentrated on shooting. She was determined to beat him, and he seemed equally determined to beat the other gentlemen. She tried not to dwell on why, but the possibility of another kiss from him made her nervous and excited.

As the end of the second hour of shooting approached, her hands grew clammy. While she and the others kept shooting, Oliver asked for a count from the gamekeeper. She and Mr. Pinter were still neck and neck, and the duke had dropped behind them by one more.

She heard a curse from Mr. Pinter and glanced his way. "What's wrong?"

"Just a misfire, my lady," he said tersely. "I believe I need a new gun."

Should she go on? The others were, so she must, too, yet it seemed somehow unfair to take advantage of something that had nothing to do with his shooting ability. The servants hurried to provide him with a new flintlock, but he'd already lost ground.

When Oliver called time a few moments later, she'd beaten them all. But she'd beaten Mr. Pinter by only one bird.

"It appears, Lady Celia, that you've won a new rifle," the duke said graciously.

"No," she answered. They all stared at her. "It doesn't seem sporting to win a challenge only because one of my opponents had a faulty firearm. Which *we* provided to him, by the way."

"Don't worry," Mr. Pinter drawled. "I won't hold the faulty firearm against you and your brothers."

"That's not the point. This should be fair, and it isn't."

"Then we'll move forward," Oliver said, "and let the servants flush the grouse again. Pinter can take one more shot. That's probably all that the misfire delayed him by. If he misses, then you've won squarely. If he hits his target then it's a tie, and we'll decide on a tie breaker."

"That seems fair." She glanced over at Mr. Pinter. "What do you say, sir?"

"Whatever my lady wishes." His eyes met hers in a heated glance.

She had the unsettling feeling that he referred to more

than just the shooting. "Well, then," she said lightly. "Let's get on with it."

The beaters headed forward to flush the grouse, but either because of where the grouse had last settled or because of the beaters' position, the birds rose farther away than was practical.

"Damn it all," Gabe muttered. "He won't make a shot from here."

"You can ignore this one, and we'll have them flushed again," Celia said.

But Mr. Pinter raised his gun to follow their flight. With a flash and the pungent smell of black powder igniting, the gun fired and white smoke filled the air. She saw a bird fall.

No, not one bird. He'd hit *two* birds with an impossible shot.

Her breath lodged in her throat. She'd hit two with one shot a few times, due to how they clustered and how well the birdshot scattered, but to do it at such a distance . . .

She glanced at him, astonished. No one had ever beaten her—and certainly not with such an amazing shot.

Mr. Pinter gazed at her steadily as he handed off the gun to a servant. "It appears that I've won, my lady."

Her mouth went dry. "It does indeed."

Gabe hooted, pleased at having escaped buying her a rifle. The duke and the viscount scowled, while Devonmont just looked amused as usual.

All of that fell away as Mr. Pinter's gaze dropped to her mouth.

"Well done, Pinter," Oliver said, clapping him on the shoulder. "You obviously more than earned a kiss."

For a moment, raw hunger flickered in his eyes. Then it was as if a veil descended over his face, for his features turned blank. He walked up to her, bent his head . . .

And kissed her on the forehead.

Hot color flooded her cheeks. How dared he kiss her last night as if she were a woman, and then treat her like a child in front of her suitors! Or worse, a woman beneath his notice!

"Thank heavens *that's* done," she said loftily, trying to retain some dignity.

The men all laughed—except Mr. Pinter, who watched her with a shuttered expression.

As the other gentlemen crowded round to congratulate him on his fine shot, she plotted. She would make him answer for every remark, every embarrassment of this day, as soon as she had the chance to get him alone.

Because no man made a fool of *her* and got away with it.

Chapter Nine

*T*he rest of the afternoon seemed endless to Jackson, though it was probably only an hour or so. They ate more, drank more, and the gentlemen joked more. Celia was subdued, which seemed to rouse her suitors to flirt outrageously with her. Couldn't they see she was angry? It didn't take a crack investigator to notice the signs.

The problem was he didn't know the reason for her anger, which seemed directed at *him*. It must be because he'd beaten her. She was definitely the sort to be a sore loser.

If he made a remark, she answered coldly, while she responded to the other gentlemen with a smile. He'd assumed that after last night, she would treat him a bit more warmly, but no such luck. It was starting to eat at him. After all, she was the one who'd insisted that he shoot again—it was her fault that he'd won.

Was it the kiss that had sparked her temper? No, how could that be? He'd kissed her with infinite politeness.

By the time the group trudged back across the estate toward the manor, he was in a foul mood. He didn't care that he'd won, or that Gabe kept clapping him on the shoulder and praising his shooting, or that Stoneville asked his advice about estate matters. His entire attention was centered on the damned suitors who trailed after Celia like hungry wolves.

And on the damned female who bedeviled him with every smile she bestowed on the others. They didn't deserve her smiles, and he meant to make sure she knew it.

The opportunity came more quickly than expected. They had just entered the east wing from the garden. The duke and the viscount were ahead of them, discussing Portuguese politics, while Gabe and Devonmont walked a bit behind them to talk about horse racing. Celia dragged her feet, prompting Jackson and Stoneville to do the same. When the others were well ahead, she stopped with a look of horror on her face.

"Oh dear, I believe I left my gun loaded. I was so distracted by Mr. Pinter's success that I forgot. I must tell the servants at once."

Stoneville's eyes narrowed on her. "Are you sure? I can't imagine your making such a mistake."

"It's that new percussion gun. I forgot about the cartridges; it's truly awful of me. The servants won't know how to handle it." Her gaze shifted to Jackson. "Would you help me with it, Mr. Pinter? You're probably best acquainted with how to unload these new guns."

The veiled reference to his behavior the night before gave him pause, as did her look of challenge. "Certainly, my lady. I'm happy to help in any way."

Stoneville glanced from her to Jackson. "Are you sure you need the help?"

"Of course. And Mr. Pinter deals with this sort of mishap daily, given the raw recruits he trains at Bow Street, so let him do what he does best."

It wasn't Jackson's job to train anyone at Bow Street—there were underlings who did that—but since it rapidly became apparent that her ladyship's "mishap" was just a ruse to enable them to speak privately, he played along. "Yes, a common occurrence." He offered her his arm. "I can handle it well enough."

"Thank you, Mr. Pinter," she said as she curved her hand into the crook of his elbow.

He could feel his lordship's eyes watching them as they headed down a different hall that led toward the servants' quarters in another wing, but at least the man didn't protest her purpose any further.

As soon as they were out of sight, she tugged him down an unlit passage. "This way. There's a place where we can speak privately. No one ever comes here."

He soon found himself in a secluded part of the manor. The musty scent and closed doors told him that the chambers hadn't been opened in some time. Then she unlocked a door with a key that she kept on a chain around her neck and went inside.

The room was clearly an unused parlor, since all the furniture, save one settee and a writing table stacked with books, was protected from dust with white canvas covers. But the settee and table had been drawn up to the fireplace, and it was clear from the ashes in the hearth that a fire had been laid there not long ago. A short-handled broom nearby and a wool blanket completed the image of someone's private retreat.

Hers.

"Don't they give you a large enough sitting room, my lady?" he asked as she bent to ladle some coals into the hearth, then used a flint and some kindling to get a fire going.

She eyed him from beneath lowered lashes. "You have no idea what it's like to be surrounded by a family like mine. We have enough space for a hundred guests, yet everyone seems determined to stay in the same ten rooms. My family doesn't know the meaning of privacy."

Straightening, she turned to face him. "Sometimes I just want to get away from them all. Especially lately, with Gran breathing down my neck about marrying. Sometimes I go shooting, and sometimes . . ." She shrugged.

"You come here to hide."

Her eyes glittered at him. "Escape. It's not the same."

He went over to the table and picked up a book, then smiled at the title: *Ammunition: A Descriptive Treatise.* He went through the others—*Instructions to Young Sportsmen in All that Relates to Guns and Shooting, The Shooter's Companion* . . . and oddly enough, a book called *Emma.*

When that one made him raise his gaze to her in question, she colored. "Don't tell Minerva about that. She won't be happy to hear I'm reading a novel by a woman she considers her competitor, even though the authoress is dead."

"I wouldn't dream of mentioning it. Though I'm surprised that you read novels."

"I do have other interests than shooting, you know."

"I never said otherwise."

"But you think me a complete tomboy. Admit it."

He measured his words. "I think you a woman with a few unusual interests that happen to be similar to those of some men. Those interests don't, however, make you a tomboy."

No tomboy would fire his blood the way she did right now in her elegant redingote, despite the black smudges of powder along its sleeves and the mud caked along its hem. And no tomboy would have kept him up last night imagining what it would be like to raise her skirts so he could run his hands along the pale swaths of thigh that lay above her garters.

"And yet," she said hoarsely, "you kissed me as if I were some mannish chit beneath your notice. God forbid you should treat me as a desirable woman in front of my suitors. It might give them ideas."

He stared at her, thunderstruck. She was angry because he'd accorded her the respect she deserved? "Forgive me, my lady," he said acidly. "I didn't think you'd want me to toss you down in the grass and ravish you. I see I was mistaken."

Two spots of color appeared on her cheeks. "There is a vast space between ravishing me and treating me like a child. The gentlemen expected you to kiss me on the lips, as they would have. You won such a kiss, after all. When you didn't take it, I'm sure they thought it was because

I was somehow . . . unattractive to you. And that only hurts my cause."

Her *cause*, which was to be affianced to one of those arses. Anger boiled up in him. "Let me see if I understand you correctly. You wanted me to kiss you with some degree of passion so your suitors would be convinced of your desirability as a woman. Is that right?"

She cast him a resentful look, then nodded.

He strode up close, unable to contain his temper. "Isn't it enough for you that they're already barking at your heels like randy hounds? That they're seizing your hand at the breakfast table and inviting you for tête-à-tête practice sessions at their estates?"

"What good does that do me when you seek to turn their affections away at every turn? You provoked me to accept that shooting challenge because you wanted me to frighten them off with my enthusiasm for guns. Admit it."

All right, so that was true. But he had good reasons for it. "I *wanted* them to see you for who you really are and not for the woman you keep pretending to be."

"*Pretending* to be?" she said in a choked voice. "And who is that? A lady worthy of marriage? You wanted to expose me as some . . . adventuress or man in woman's attire or . . . oh, I don't know what."

"No!" he protested, suddenly all at sea in their argument.

"You know what, Mr. Pinter? Ever since we made our agreement, you've only made matters worse, for some nefarious reason of your own." She planted her hands on her hips and gave him a look of pure defiance. "So you're dismissed from my employ. I no longer require your services." With her head held high, she strode for the door.

Hell and blazes, he wouldn't let her do this! Not when he knew what was at stake.

"You don't want to hear my report?" he called out after her.

She paused near the door. "I don't believe you even *have* a report."

"I certainly do, a very thorough one. I've only been waiting for my aunt to transcribe my scrawl into something decipherable. Give me a day, and I can offer you names and addresses and dates, whatever you require."

"A day? Just another excuse to put me off so you can wreak more havoc." She stepped into the doorway, and he hurried to catch her by the arm and drag her around to face him.

He ignored the withering glance she cast him. "The viscount is twenty-two years your senior," he said baldly.

Her eyes went wide. "You're making that up."

"He's aged very well, I'll grant you, but he's still almost twice your age. Like many vain Continental gentlemen, he dyes his hair and beard—which is why he appears younger than you think."

That seemed to shake her momentarily. Then she stiffened. "All right, so he's an older man. That doesn't mean he wouldn't make a good husband."

"He's an aging roué, with an invalid sister. The advantages in a match are all his. You'd surely end up taking care of them both. That's probably why he wants to marry you."

"You can't be sure of that."

"No? He's already choosing not to stay here for the house party at night because of his sister. That tells me that he needs help he can't get from servants."

Her eyes met his, hot with resentment. "Because it's hard to find ones who speak Portuguese."

He snorted. "I found out this information *from* his Portuguese servants. They also told me that his lavish spending is a façade. He's running low on funds. Why do you think his servants gossip about him? They haven't been paid recently. So he's definitely got his eye on your fortune."

"Perhaps he does," she conceded sullenly. "But not the others. Don't try to claim that of them."

"I wouldn't. They're in good financial shape. But Devonmont is estranged from his mother, and no one knows why. I need more time to determine it, though perhaps your sister-in-law could tell you, if you bothered to ask."

"Plenty of people don't get along with their families," she said stoutly.

"He has a long-established mistress, too."

A troubled expression crossed her face. "Unmarried men often have mistresses. It doesn't mean he wouldn't give her up when he marries."

He cast her a hard stare. "Are you saying you have no problem with a man paying court to you while he keeps a mistress?"

The sigh that escaped her was all the answer he needed. "I don't think he's interested in marriage anyway." She tipped up her chin. "That still leaves the duke."

"With his mad family."

"He's already told me about his father, whom I knew about anyway."

"Ah, but did you know about his great-uncle? He ended his life in an asylum in Belgium, while there to receive some special treatment for his delirium."

Her lower lip trembled. "The duke didn't mention that, no. But then our conversation was brief. I'm sure he'll tell me if I ask. He was very forthright on the subject of his family's madness when he offered—"

As she stopped short, Jackson's heart dropped into his stomach. "Offered what?"

She hesitated, then squared her shoulders. "Marriage, if you must know."

Damn it all. Jackson had no right to resent it, but the thought of her in Lyons's arms made him want to smash something. "And of course, you accepted his offer," he said bitterly. "You couldn't resist the appeal of being a great duchess."

Her eyes glittered at him. "You're the only person who doesn't see the advantage in such a match."

"That's because I don't believe in marriages of convenience. Given your family's history, I'd think that you wouldn't either."

She colored. "And why do you assume it would be such a thing? Is it so hard to believe that a man might genuinely care for me? That he might actually want to marry me for myself?"

The hurt in her words set him back on his heels.

"Why would anyone wish to marry the reckless Lady

Celia, after all," she went on in a choked voice, "if not for her fortune or to shore up his reputation?"

"I didn't mean any such thing," he said sharply.

But she'd worked herself up into a fine temper. "Of course you did. You kissed me last night only to make a point, and you couldn't even bear to kiss me properly again today—"

"Now see here," he said, grabbing her shoulders. "I didn't kiss you 'properly' today because I was afraid if I did I might not stop."

That seemed to draw her up short. "Wh-What?"

Sweet God, he shouldn't have said that, but he couldn't let her go on thinking she was some sort of pariah around men. "I knew that if I got this close, and I put my mouth on yours . . ."

But now he *was* this close. And she was staring up at him with that mix of bewilderment and hurt pride, and he couldn't help himself. Not anymore.

He kissed her, to show her what she seemed blind to. That he wanted her. That even knowing it was wrong and could never work, he wanted to have her.

She tore her lips from his. "Mr. Pinter—" she began in a whisper.

"Jackson," he growled. "Let me hear you say my name."

Backing away from him, she cast him a wounded expression. "Y-you don't have to pretend—"

"I'm not pretending anything, damn it!"

Grabbing her by the sleeves, he dragged her close and kissed her again, with even more heat. How could she not see that he ached to take her? How could she not know what a temptation she was? Her lips intoxicated him, made him light-headed. Made him reckless enough to kiss her so impudently that any other woman of her rank would be insulted.

When she pulled away a second time, he expected her to slap him. But all she did was utter a feeble protest. "Please, Mr. Pinter—"

"Jackson," he ordered in a low, unsteady voice, emboldened by the melting look in her eyes. "Say my Christian name."

Her lush dark lashes lowered as a blush stained her cheeks. "Jackson . . ."

His breath caught in his throat at the intimacy of it, and fire exploded in his brain. She wasn't pushing him away, so to hell with trying to be a gentleman.

He took her mouth savagely this time, plundering every part of its silky warmth as his blood pulsed high in his veins. She tasted of red wine and lemon cake, both tart and sweet at once. He wanted to eat her up. He wanted to take her, right here in this room.

So when she pulled out of his arms to back away, he stalked after her.

She didn't stop backing away, but neither did she turn tail and run. "Last night you claimed this wouldn't happen again."

"I know. And yet it has." Like someone in an opium den, he'd been craving her for months. And now that he'd suddenly had a taste of the very thing he craved, he had to have more.

When she came up against the writing table, he caught

her about the waist. She turned her head away before he could kiss her, so he settled for burying his face in her neck to nuzzle the tender throat he'd been coveting.

With a shiver, she slid her hands up his chest. "Why are you doing this?"

"Because I want you," he admitted, damning himself. "Because I've always wanted you."

Then he covered her mouth with his once more.

Chapter Ten

elia's head was reeling. He wanted her? Mr. Pinter *wanted* her?

Not Mr. Pinter. Jackson. *Jackson.*

She released a shuddering breath as he trailed kisses from her mouth to her ear, his breathing heavy and his heart racing beneath the hands she pressed against his chest.

He *did* want her. He was devouring her, dragging open-mouthed kisses along her neck and throat like a man starved. He still smelled of saltpeter and smoke—as masculine and earthy as the rasp of his faint whiskers against her skin. Desire welled up in her when he tongued the hollow of her throat.

She'd never experienced kisses and caresses like these before, tender and searing all at the same time. She was drowning in every one.

"Jackson . . ." she whispered.

"I love to hear my name on your lips," he rasped against her ear. "Say it again."

"Jackson . . . this isn't another lesson . . . is it?" She had to know. She had to be sure.

"It ought to be," he growled. "God knows you didn't learn the first one very well, or we wouldn't be here together, alone."

When he lifted her onto the table, knocking off some of the books, she gasped. "I've never been good with lessons."

He brushed a kiss over her lips. "Perhaps you haven't had the right teacher. Or the right lessons, my lady."

"Celia," she countered, burying her hands in his thick, raven hair. He had the most beautiful hair, soft to the touch, with lovely waves that spilled wantonly over her fingers. "If I'm to call you Jackson, you must call me Celia."

His eyes turned molten gray as they locked with hers. "Celia," he breathed. Then he brought his hands up to flick open the buttons of her redingote and pull out her lace tucker so he could toss it aside.

She caught her breath. "Wha-What are you doing?"

"Continuing your lessons." He spread open her redingote gown to expose her undergarments. "I want to taste you. Will you let me, sweeting?"

Sweeting? That alone would have softened her resolve, for no man had ever called her such a lovely thing. But the fact that he was asking for what Ned had tried to force from her melted her resistance even further.

"I'm willing to repeat a lesson as often as it takes to learn it," she said, shocked by her own boldness.

His response was to untie the top of her corset and pull the cups down to expose her chemise. She dragged in a long breath as the chill of the room made her nipples harden beneath the linen. The fire that leapt in his face was so hot it sparked flames low in her belly.

"What lesson is this?" she choked out.

His wild gaze met hers. "That even a low bastard can be tempted above his station when a lady is as lovely as you."

"A lady? Not a tomboy?"

"I wish you *were* a tomboy, sweeting," he said bitterly. "Then you wouldn't have viscounts and earls and dukes vying for your favors."

Was he jealous? Oh, how wonderful if he was! "And Bow Street Runners?" she prodded.

He shot her a dark glance that was apparently supposed to serve as her answer, for he then bent to close his mouth over one linen-draped breast.

Good. Heavens. What deliciousness was this? She shouldn't allow it. But the man she'd been fascinated with for months was treating her as if he truly found her desirable, and she didn't want it to stop.

Clutching his head to her, she exulted in the hungry way he sucked her breast through her chemise, turning her knees to water and her blood to steam.

He pleasured her breast with teeth and tongue as his hand found her other breast and teased the nipple to arousal. Her pulse leapt so high she feared she might faint. "Jackson . . . ohhh, *Jackson* . . . I thought you . . . despised me."

"Does this feel like I despise you?" he murmured against her breast, then tongued it silkily for good measure.

A sensual tremor swept through her. "No." But then, she'd been a fool before with men. She wasn't good at understanding them when it came to *this*. "If you desired me all along, why didn't you . . . say anything before?"

"Like what? 'My lady, I keep imagining you naked in my bed?'" He slid one hand down to her hip. "I'm not fool enough to risk being shot for impertinence."

Should she be thrilled or disappointed to hear that he imagined her in his bed? It was more than she'd expected, yet not enough.

She dug her fingers into his shoulder. "How do you know I won't try shooting you now?"

He nuzzled her breast. "You left your pistol on the breakfast table."

A strange excitement coursed through her. It made no sense, considering what had happened the last time a man had got her alone and helpless. "Perhaps I have another hidden in this room."

He lifted his head to gaze steadily into her eyes. "Then I'd best keep you too busy to use it."

Suddenly he was kissing her again, hard, hungry kisses . . . each more intoxicating than the last. He filled his hands with her breasts and fondled them shamelessly, distracting her from anything but the taste and feel of him.

A moan escaped her, and he tore his mouth from hers. "You shouldn't let me touch you this way."

"Yet I am," she gasped against his cheek. "And you aren't stopping, either."

"Say the word, and I will." Yet he dragged her skirts up and pressed forward between her legs. "This is mad. We're both mad."

"Are we?" she asked, hardly conscious anymore of what she was saying.

Because it felt utterly right to be in his arms, as if she'd waited ages to be there. Her heart had never clamored so for anyone else.

"I don't generally take advantage of my clients' sisters," he rasped as his hands slid to grip her thighs. "It's unwise."

"I'm your client, too. Do I look as if I'm complaining?" she whispered and drew his head down to hers.

With a groan, he covered her mouth with his once more. They kissed a long while, their breaths entwining, their hearts pounding in tandem. His thumbs swept up the insides of her thighs just above her garters, and a delicious anticipation made her lean into him, wanting him to touch her, to caress her—

"Celia! Where are you, girl?"

The sound came from not far away, outside the room. They both froze. It was Gran!

She tore her mouth from his in a panic. "You have to go." She shoved at his shoulders. "She can't find you here. She mustn't!" Gran would have him dismissed before Celia could even discover how he felt about her. How *she* felt about *him*.

He hesitated, his eyes hungry, his lips parted. Then an odd disappointment flickered in his face before he pulled away and that infernal detachment of his hardened his features again. "No, indeed. Your grandmother mustn't find you being mauled by the likes of me."

"Jackson—" she began.

"I'm going," he said sharply and strode for the window.

Before she could call him back or protest his words, he'd opened it and passed through into the courtyard, closing the window behind him.

"Celia, I know you are back here somewhere!" Gran cried, much closer now.

Frantically, Celia leapt off the table and buttoned up her gown. At the last minute, she spotted her tucker on the floor and stepped on top of it, just as Gran hobbled in.

Gran halted, then searched the room with eyes that were sharp and keen as always. "Why did you not answer me?"

Celia forced a smile. "I did," she lied. "You must not have heard." What on earth was Gran doing here, anyway?

"Oliver said that you were with Mr. Pinter in the servants' quarters, but they said they had not seen either of you. And that all the guns were already in order and placed in their racks."

She clapped her hand to her chest dramatically. "Oh, thank heaven! We headed there, but then I remembered I had a book that explained how to unload the new percussion guns, so I sent him back to the house. I came here, figuring I could handle unloading the gun alone if I found the book passage I was remembering."

The explanation sounded inane, but it was the only excuse she could think of that was remotely convincing.

Gran didn't look convinced. Her gaze dipped down. "Do you generally look through your books on the floor?"

"Of course not. You startled me, that's all. I knocked them off." Crossing her arms over her chest, she went on the offensive. "And how did you know where to find me, anyway?"

"One of the servants told me to check this part of the north wing—she said she had discovered that someone had been burning coal in one of the fireplaces." Gran's gaze narrowed. "Eventually I find out everything that goes on in this house, girl. Do not think to hide anything from me."

Celia fought not to swallow and give herself away. Gran was like a shark when she scented blood in the water. "And what would I hide from you?"

"That you and Mr. Pinter are up to something."

"He's investigating my suitors—nothing more."

Gran swept her gaze around the room again. "I hope that is true. He cannot afford even the appearance of impropriety."

"Impropriety? I can't imagine what you mean."

Her grandmother arched one eyebrow. "Do not play the fool with me. This is not the first time you have been off alone with him. You must consider how that looks."

"To whom?"

"To everyone. He cannot afford to have people gossiping about you and him—"

"No, of course not," she said bitterly. "Because then you'd have to dismiss him, even after all he's done for our family."

Gran's gaze turned steely. "Actually, he cannot afford it because he is very near to being appointed Chief Magistrate. Any appearance of impropriety toward a client's sister might scuttle that appointment." Gran searched her face. "Unless, of course, he married the woman. A rich wife of rank would enhance his chances."

It took all of Celia's control to appear unconcerned, though her heart clamored in her chest. Jackson was in line for an important appointment? Why had he never mentioned it?

Because he knew what you'd think of his overtures. Because he knew it would put you on your guard while he was pretending to desire you madly.

No, she couldn't believe that his sweet kisses and caresses had been calculated. They'd been too reckless, too impassioned. Could such a thing really be feigned? He'd always been forthright with her—it wasn't in him to misrepresent himself.

Was it?

She forced a smile to her lips, determined not to let Gran's words affect her until she could learn the truth. Gran was known for her devious strategies. This might merely be one more of those.

But to what purpose?

"I don't know why you think Mr. Pinter would be caught in an impropriety with *me,* of all people. He can't stand to be in the same room with me."

"Yet he beat your suitors this afternoon so he could gain a kiss from you."

Celia gave a brittle laugh. "Rather, so he could avoid having to pay his portion of the rifle they would have owed me if I'd won. Mr. Pinter is nothing if not careful with his money. Didn't you hear the whole tale? He gave me a peck on the forehead. Hardly the action of a man seeking my favors."

With an attempt at nonchalance, she bent to pick up a book. "In any case, even if he was trying to court me, it's not as if I would fall for his tricks. I have three perfectly eligible suitors here this week—why should I care if a Bow Street Runner dangles after me?"

Gran watched her carefully. "So you have no feelings for the man."

"I have a duke practically in my pocket," she managed. "What would I want with Mr. Pinter?"

Who made her blood race and her heart soar. Who made her hope, for the first time, that she might still find a man to love her. A man she could love.

Love? He'd said nothing of love or even affection. He'd spoken only of desire. For that matter, he'd said nothing of marriage.

Then again, if what he wanted was a rich and influential wife, he'd be a fool to make that too obvious too soon.

Blast it all! Gran was muddling her mind, playing with her heart. And for what? To make sure she didn't marry too low? It was hardly fair, under the circumstances.

"I do find it odd," she went on, "that you should care how Mr. Pinter feels about me. I thought all you wanted was to have some man marry me. He would be as good as any."

Gran winced. "Not if he is after your fortune. That is what happened to your mother, and I regret to this day that I did not see beneath your father's winning smiles and title to his mercenary motive."

Celia swallowed past the lump in her throat. "Well, since Mr. Pinter has no title and barely knows *how* to smile, you needn't worry. If he has a mercenary motive, he's hiding it well." She surreptitiously kicked her tucker under the table as she stepped forward. "Now, let's go have some tea, shall we?"

After another hard look about the room, Gran took the arm Celia offered and let her granddaughter accompany her out the door. But while they walked down the corridor, Celia's mind kept stumbling over Gran's revelation.

A rich wife of rank would enhance his chances.

It wouldn't be the first time a man had pretended to find her fetching for his own reasons. But if Gran's suspicions about Jackson's motives proved true, it would definitely be the last. Because Celia would rather enter a loveless marriage with the Duke of Lyons than be used by Jackson Pinter.

Chapter Eleven

That night, Jackson stood in the corner of Halstead Hall's spacious ballroom, downing one glass of punch after another and wishing he could be anywhere else. But of all the events of the house party, he couldn't miss his lordship's birthday ball. Even Lord Basto had chosen to stay this evening instead of going home to his sister, though he'd said he would return to London later.

Jackson surveyed the room, trying not to fix on the one person who interested him. Celia was merrily dancing with that damned Lyons, letting the duke put his hands all over her while Jackson could only stand and watch.

He'd made a muck of things today. He'd let his feelings show, and now he was paying for it. All evening, Celia had vacillated between ignoring him entirely and giving him veiled glances that he didn't know how to interpret.

Meanwhile, he couldn't tear his gaze from her. She danced like a creature from another realm—a sparkling fairy of the forest. He must have been under some enchantment to think he could ever have such a sprite for his own, yet the illusion persisted, no matter how he fought it. After tasting her this afternoon, he ached to claim her before them all.

Sheer madness. She belonged here among her kind, not in Cheapside with a bastard. Perhaps one day, if he became Chief Magistrate . . .

But she would never let her brothers and sisters lose their fortune. She would choose a suitor long before then.

That suitor could be you.

He stifled a bitter laugh. What a ridiculous pipe dream. So far she'd given no indication that their encounter this afternoon had meant anything to her but a moment's enjoyment. If she'd wanted to be caught with him, wanted to force the issue, she could have. It certainly would have solved her problem of how to gain a husband, because he would have offered for her right then.

But she'd panicked at the idea of her grandmother catching them together. No doubt their interlude had just been a case of a gently bred female indulging her curiosity about men.

It wouldn't be the first time a lady dallied with a man beneath her rank merely because he gave her pleasure. He'd seen plenty enough young ladies with infatuations for their footmen that came to nothing, plenty enough gently bred females who swooned over tutors they had no intention of marrying. There was no reason to believe that Celia felt more for him than just an unwise desire.

And even if she *did* have some vague notion that they could marry, even if he could set her mind at ease about his not being interested in her fortune, it wouldn't make a difference. She couldn't possibly be happy married to him, given his station and hers. How could she?

The butler appeared at the entrance to the ballroom and announced in a voice that could barely be heard over the music, "Mr. and Mrs. Desmond Plumtree and Mr. Edward Plumtree."

Jackson's jaw dropped. "What the devil are they doing here?" he muttered as Desmond strolled in with his wife and son.

"Desmond is still my nephew, after all," said a voice very near him.

Mrs. Plumtree, of all people. That put Jackson instantly on his guard. He still had no idea why she'd shown up in the north wing this afternoon, or if she realized he'd been in there alone with her granddaughter.

"I beg your pardon, madam," he said stiffly as he tossed back the remainder of his punch and girded himself for doing battle with Mrs. Machiavellian Plumtree. "I meant no disrespect."

"Believe me, I understand your surprise." She stared over to where her nephew and great-nephew stood talking to Stoneville and looking awkwardly about them. "It was Minerva's idea to invite them."

"Even after the two of them threatened her life?"

"Minerva doesn't see it that way. She considers it a misunderstanding borne of Desmond's idiotic resentment of our family. But Jarret has been working with Desmond and Ned to make their mill more successful, and he and Minerva thought it might be a good idea to mend fences.

I confess I was eager for that, too. They are still my family, after all."

The dance ended, and the duke led Celia over to a chair on the wall opposite from the Plumtrees. She didn't seem to have noticed their entrance—no doubt she'd been too busy dancing to hear them being announced. The duke said something to her, then headed off to the room that held the punch table.

The minute the man was gone, Ned broke away from his parents and sauntered over to where Celia sat. She caught sight of him, and the blood drained from her face.

Jackson's eyes narrowed.

"I don't think all your grandchildren agree with your assessment," he said, nodding to where Celia had risen stiffly to greet Ned.

Mrs. Plumtree followed his gaze. "Celia has never liked the fact that Desmond hires children in his mills. Even though Jarret has put an end to that practice, she still dislikes her cousin for it."

"It's not Desmond she's reacting to."

Ned stepped nearer and she took a quick step back, raising the hackles on the back of Jackson's neck. He moved forward, but Mrs. Plumtree laid a hand on his arm. "It is none of your concern, Mr. Pinter."

"Even if you trust the fellow, madam, I don't," he snapped. "Look at how your granddaughter stands, as if poised for flight. Look at her *face*. It's not dislike of his father that plagues her. She looks almost frightened. Or rather, she looks as if she's pretending *not* to be frightened. And that's not a look I've seen on her before."

"If that is true, the duke will take care of matters," Mrs. Plumtree said smoothly. "He's approaching her now."

Jackson held his breath as Lyons came to Celia's side and Celia visibly relaxed. She said something to the duke, who took her arm and led her away. Only then did Jackson let out his breath. But Ned continued to watch her with palpable tension, and that worried him.

Then Celia glanced over at Jackson, catching sight of him and her grandmother standing together, and the mix of emotions on her face made a new concern take hold of him. What exactly had Mrs. Plumtree told Celia after he'd left the room this afternoon? Whatever it was seemed to have made her cautious around him. God save him, between that and her odd reaction to Ned, he didn't know what to think.

"You see?" Mrs. Plumtree remarked. "The duke has matters well in hand."

"It appears so," he clipped out. That was all he could manage. He couldn't stand that the duke had been the one to protect her and not him.

"A tactful response," she said, gazing out over the dancing couples. "You will make a very good Chief Magistrate, I think."

Shock swept over him that he fought mightily to disguise. So she knew of that, did she? "I'm only one of several possible candidates, madam. You do me great honor to assume I'll be chosen."

"Masters tells me that the appointment is all but settled."

"Then Masters knows more than I on the subject."

"And more than my granddaughter as well," she said.

His stomach knotted. Damn Mrs. Plumtree and her machinations. "But I'm sure you took great pains to inform her of it."

The woman hesitated, then gripped the head of her cane with both hands. "I thought she should have all the facts before she threw herself into a misalliance."

Hell and blazes. And Mrs. Plumtree had probably implied that a rich wife would advance his career. He could easily guess how Celia would respond to hearing that, especially after he'd fallen on her with all the subtlety of an ox in rut.

His temper swelled. Although he'd suspected that Mrs. Plumtree wouldn't approve of him for her granddaughter, some part of him had thought that his service to the family—and the woman's own humble beginnings— might keep her from behaving predictably. He should have known better.

"No doubt she was grateful for the information." After all, it gave Celia just the excuse she needed to continue in her march to marry a great lord.

"She claimed that there was nothing between you and her."

"She's right." There never had been. He'd been a fool to think there could be.

"I am glad to hear it." Her sidelong glance was filled with calculation. "Because if you play your cards right, you have an even better prospect before you than that of Chief Magistrate."

He froze. "What do you mean?"

"You may not be aware of this, but one of my friends is the Home Secretary, Robert Peel. Your superior."

"I'm well aware who my superior is."

"It seems he wishes to establish a police force," she went on. "He is fairly certain that it will come to pass eventually. When it does, he will appoint a commissioner to oversee the entire force in London." She cast him a hard stare. "You could be that man."

Jackson fought to hide his surprise. He'd heard rumors of Peel's plans, of course, but hadn't realized that they'd progressed so far. Or that she was privy to them.

Then it dawned on him why she was telling him this. "You mean, I could be that man if I leave your granddaughter alone."

A faint smile touched her lips. "I see that I was right to consider you a very perceptive fellow, Mr. Pinter."

It took all his will to tamp down his anger. He did *not* like being ordered about by anyone, but especially by a woman who'd let her long acquaintance with the aristocracy convince her that she had the right to run roughshod over whomever she pleased.

"And if I choose to ignore your 'bribe,' madam?" he snapped.

She stiffened, then shifted her gaze to where Celia was dancing again with that bloody duke. "I might decide to disinherit my granddaughter."

He gaped at her. "You would cut her off even though she has met your ultimatum?"

"I might. If she chooses badly." Color rose in her cheeks. "I never said I would give my money to them if they married. I only said I would *not* give it to them if they did not."

"And here I thought you were an honorable woman. I guess I'm not so perceptive after all."

She flinched. "The rest of them would get their money. Just not her." She searched his face. "*If* I thought it best, that is."

A futile anger choked him that he barely understood; he'd known all along that nothing could come of his foolish attraction to Celia.

Still, if she had her inheritance, she might stoop to marry him. At least he wouldn't be forcing her to give up all her creature comforts along with her place in society. Then she might not mind that the high sticklers wouldn't accept her.

But without the money?

He could easily afford a wife, but not one used to living like *this*. Glancing around at the liveried footmen and the glittering ballroom with its crystal chandeliers filled with beeswax candles, he choked down the bile rising in his throat. He remembered how casually she'd spoken of offering him an expensive bracelet as payment, probably because she knew there was plenty more where that came from.

How could he think for even one moment that she would consider giving all this up for him? If wealth and position didn't matter to her, she wouldn't be seeking a lofty lord for a husband at this very moment.

He forced himself to meet Mrs. Plumtree's questioning glance. "As I said before, there's nothing between me and your granddaughter. She has no interest in being married to a nobody's bastard." And certainly not one whose modest income was nothing to that of a lady of her means. "I'm sure she'll choose a suitor more to your liking in due time."

"You misunderstand me, sir," she said irritably. "I am only trying to protect her."

"By driving her into the arms of the first man of rank who offers for her? Whether or not she loves him or he loves her? Do you think so little of her worth?"

Mrs. Plumtree glowered at him. "You are impertinent, sir."

"I'll be even more impertinent if that's what it takes to keep Lady Celia from making a mistake she may regret the rest of her life." He glanced over to where Basto was now holding her far too close in the waltz. "The viscount there isn't as young as he appears, nor are his finances as healthy as *they* appear. And the earl has a longtime mistress. Did you know that?"

"How can I trust you to tell the truth about these men?"

"Do you really think you can trust *them*? Lady Celia's future is tied inextricably to a fortune. That muddies the water with any man."

"Even the duke? I should think he has no need to marry for money or anything else."

Jackson tensed. "That's true. Except for the rumors of madness in his family, he is eminently eligible." And that irritated Jackson beyond all endurance. "But she doesn't love him."

Mrs. Plumtree cast him a searching glance. "How do you know?"

Because she spent the afternoon in my arms, letting me kiss and caress her, eagerly responding to my desire for her. Even hinting that she might feel the same. Until she tossed me from the room in a panic when she realized what I've known all along—that mere mortals like us can never cross the divide.

Still, that didn't mean he had to stand by and watch her suffer in a marriage to the wrong man. "Because Lady Celia told me."

He cursed himself even as he said the words. It was a betrayal—he'd promised to keep their conversations private—but he refused to watch her marry a man she clearly didn't love. That would be as bad as marrying a man like him and losing her fortune.

"She's trying to gain a husband so precipitously only because you're forcing her to," he went on. "If you'd just give her a chance—"

"She has had plenty of chances already."

"Give her another." Remembering Celia's insecurity over being thought a tomboy, he added, "This little experiment is sure to have increased her confidence with men. If you allow her more time, I'm sure she could find a gentleman she could love, who would love her in turn."

"Like you?" Mrs. Plumtree asked.

He gave a caustic laugh. "Your granddaughter isn't fool enough to fall in love with a man of my rank. So you're wasting your bribes and threats on me, madam."

"And what about you? How do you feel about *her*?"

He'd had enough of this. "I suspect that whatever I say, you'll believe what you wish." He knew better than to reveal how he felt about Celia, especially when he wasn't even sure himself. "Now, if you'll excuse me, I see a servant with whom I need to speak about the investigation into your daughter's and son-in-law's murders."

"Have you heard something?" she asked, a sudden catch in her voice.

"I'm following new leads, that's all."

"Will they require your leaving the house party?"

Though he detected nothing in her voice beyond curiosity, she must be itching to have him out of the way. He hated to fall in with her wishes, but . . .

He glanced over to where Celia stood with the duke and her brothers, telling some story that had Lyons laughing uproariously, and the ache in his chest grew almost unbearable.

"Yes," he heard himself say. "If John has the information I've been waiting for, I'd like to go tomorrow morning. I should be back by evening."

She looked from him to Celia, and a thoughtful expression crossed her face. "I shall make sure that Oliver is informed of the reason for your absence."

"Thank you." With a curt bow, he headed for John.

He'd done everything he could to dissuade Celia from making a bad match. Perhaps his words would bear fruit if he wasn't here to provoke her. Or perhaps Mrs. Plumtree would come to her senses.

Whatever the case, he couldn't endure watching how matters played out. Better that he get away where he could think. Where he could breathe. Where he wouldn't make a fool of himself over a woman he had no business desiring.

Before *she* made a fool out of *him*.

HETTY WATCHED Mr. Pinter walk off and wondered if perhaps she had gone too far. The way he had looked at Celia . . .

"There you are," said a voice close by.

She turned to see General Isaac Waverly approaching.

The faint flutter in her chest at the sight of him, looking so dashing in evening attire, made her smile ruefully. Who would ever have guessed that after all these years a man would come along who could make her heart race and her blood run quick? She had thought herself too old for such things.

Apparently she was wrong.

Isaac cast her a knowing grin as he approached. "I've been charged with telling you that it's nearly time to bring out the cake." He offered her his arm. "Maria wants to have the family all together for it."

Shifting her cane to her other hand, she took his arm with a smile. "Lead on, kind sir."

As they skirted the room, he nodded to where Mr. Pinter was now deep in conversation with John. "What's that all about?"

"I am not sure," she said, "but I believe that Mr. Pinter is going off tomorrow for a bit. He told me it had to do with a lead he has in Lewis's and Pru's murders, but he would not say exactly what."

Some sound nearby made her turn her head. But there was no one near them, no one standing in the open door to the card room, which they were passing. So why did she feel as if she were being watched?

She shook off the thought. All this talk of murder had her jumpy.

"Pinter is leaving for the day?" Isaac commented. "That's a pity."

"Why?"

"Haven't you noticed how he looks at Celia sometimes? I think he might have set his sights on her."

"I thought so, too. Until just now."

"Just now?"

"He did not react exactly as I expected when I—" Oh, dear, perhaps she should not mention that. Isaac might not approve.

"Hetty?" Isaac prodded. "What mischief have you been up to now? You weren't warning him off, were you?"

The disapproval in his tone made her bristle. "And what if I was? The man is the love child of a light-heeled wench and God knows whom."

Isaac's jaw tautened. "I didn't know you were such a snob."

"I am *not*," she protested. "But given his circumstances, I want to be sure he is interested in Celia for something other than her fortune. I watched my daughter marry a man whom she thought loved her, only to discover that he was merely a more skillful fortune hunter than most. I do not want to make that mistake again."

He sighed. "All right. I suppose I understand your caution. But Pinter? I've never seen a less likely fortune hunter. He talks about people of rank with nothing but contempt."

"And does that not worry you? She is one of those people, after all."

"What it tells me is that he doesn't think much of marrying for rank or fortune."

She gripped his arm. "I suppose. And I must admit that when I hinted I could disinherit her if she married too low—"

"Hetty!"

"I would not do it, mind you. But *he* does not know that. It is a good way to be sure how he feels about her."

"You're playing with fire," he gritted out. "And what did he say to it?"

"He told me she would never marry anyone as low as him, then tried to convince me to rescind my ultimatum for her so she could marry a man she loved. And that was after I made it clear that it could not be him. He was very eloquent on the subject of what she deserved. Accused me of not knowing her worth, the impertinent devil."

"Good man, our Pinter," he muttered.

"I beg your pardon?" she said, bristling.

"A man in love will fight to see that the woman he cares for is given what she deserves, even if he can't have her." Isaac eyed her askance. "Even if some meddler has dictated that marrying her would ruin her future forever."

A chill ran down Hetty's spine. She had not considered her tactic in quite that light.

"Be careful, my dear," Isaac said in a low voice. "You've been dabbling in your grandchildren's lives to such good effect you've forgotten that the heart is beyond your purview."

Was he right?

No. He was ignoring one very important thing. "Suppose he really is in love. What about her? She never has anything good to say about him."

"Yet she blushes whenever he enters a room. And she stares at him a good deal. Or hadn't you noticed that, either?"

"As a matter of fact, I have." Gazing up at him, she softened her tone. "But I do not want her hurt, Isaac. I must be sure she is desired for herself and not her fortune. Her siblings had a chance of not gaining their inheritance unless the others married, so I always knew that their mates loved them, but she . . ." She shook her head. "I had to find a way to remove her fortune from the equation."

"I still say you're taking a big risk." He glanced beyond her to where Celia was talking to the duke. "Do you really think she'd be better off with Lyons?"

But she doesn't love him . . . If you'd just give her a chance—

"I do not know," Hetty said with a sigh. "I do not know anything anymore."

"Then you shouldn't meddle. Because there's another outcome you haven't considered. If you try to manipulate matters to your satisfaction, she may balk entirely.

Then you'll find yourself in the sticky position of having to choose between disinheriting them all or backing down on your ultimatum. Personally, I think you should have given up that nonsense long ago, but I know only too well how stubborn you can be when you've got the bit between your teeth."

"Oh?" she said archly. "Have I been stubborn with you?"

He gazed down at her. "You haven't agreed to marry me yet."

Her heart flipped over in her chest. It was not the first time he had mentioned marriage, but she had refused to take him seriously.

Until now. It was clear he would not be put off any longer. He looked solemnly in earnest. "Isaac . . ."

"Are you worried that *I* am a fortune hunter?"

"Do not be absurd."

"Because I've already told you that I'll sign any marriage settlement you have your solicitor draw up. I don't want your brewery or your vast fortune. I know it's going to your grandchildren. I only want *you*."

The tender words made her sigh like a foolish girl. "I realize that. But why not merely continue as we have been?"

His voice lowered. "Because I want to make you mine in every way."

A sweet shiver swept along her spine. "We do not need to marry for that."

"So all you want from me is an affair?"

"No! But—"

"I want more than that. I want to go to sleep with you in my arms and wake with you in my bed. I want the right to be with you whenever I please, night or day." His tone deepened. "I love you, Hetty. And when a man loves a woman, he wants to spend his life with her."

"But at our age, people will say—"

"Our age is an argument *for* marriage. We might not have much time left. Why not live it to the fullest, together, while we're still in good health? Who cares what people say? Life is too short to let other people dictate one's choices."

She leaned heavily on his arm as they reached the steps leading up to the dais at the front of the ballroom. He did have a point. She had been balking at marrying him because she was sure people would think her a silly old fool.

But then, she had always been out of step with everyone else. Why should this be any different? "I shall think about it," she murmured as they headed to the center of the dais, where the family was gathering.

"I suppose I'll have to settle for that. For now." He cast her a heated glance. "But later this evening, once we have the chance to be alone, I shall try more effective methods to persuade you. Because I'm not giving up on this. I can be as stubborn as you, my dear."

She bit back a smile. Thank God for that.

Chapter Twelve

ear midnight, Celia came out of the retiring room, then stopped short. She had the strangest sensation someone was watching her. But a quick glance around showed that no one was there. How odd. A servant must have passed by and glanced her way.

Though it was early, the ball was ending, so the staff was already scurrying about, putting things in order as the musicians packed up their instruments. Maria and Annabel had gone to bed at eleven. Virginia and Gran appeared to be headed there now, as Gabe and the general joined the other gentlemen, who seemed to be gravitating toward the card room, even her suitors.

The Plumtrees were here somewhere, but Jarret said they planned on staying at the inn in Ealing. Thank heaven. At least she didn't have to worry about running into Ned in the hall tonight.

She hadn't seen him in years until this summer, when he'd been caught trying to hurt Giles and Minerva. Even then, she hadn't been alone with him, which was why when he'd approached her at the ball, she'd had quite a start.

Fortunately, he hadn't had time to do more than ask her to dance. She'd refused. Then the duke had come along, and she'd told her suitor she needed to speak to Maria about the cake. That had extricated her from Ned. She'd managed to avoid him the rest of the evening, too.

Him and Jackson.

She sighed. She hadn't tried to avoid Jackson, curse him, but he'd clearly tried to avoid *her.* Indeed, he'd disappeared from the ball after his conversation with John, the one that had followed his worrisome conversation with Gran.

"You look rather anxious," said a voice beside her.

She glanced over to see her sister standing there. Relief coursed through her. It had been a long time since she'd had a good chat with Minerva, and if ever she needed such a thing, it was now. "Are you staying the night?"

With a laugh, Minerva glanced over to where her husband was headed into the card room with Jarret. "It appears so. Why?"

Making a split-second decision, Celia grabbed her sister's arm. "Because I need some sisterly advice."

Minerva smiled broadly. "*That* I can give. I'll meet you in your room in half an hour. Just let me get out of this gown and into something more comfortable."

A short while later they were snug in Celia's room with a roaring fire, some chocolate to drink, and plenty of blankets to wrap about them as they sat on Celia's bed in the candlelight.

"So tell me, dearest," Minerva said as she lifted the cup of chocolate to her lips. "What is it you need advice about?"

Celia sighed. "My suitors."

"Ah." Minerva sipped some chocolate. "You did seem rather beleaguered by gentlemen this evening. The duke danced with you three times. That's practically a proposal of marriage."

Celia stared into her cup. Should she tell Minerva? Perhaps she should. Her sister had a way of cutting through all the nonsense to get right to the bone of things. "Actually, he's already proposed marriage."

Minerva looked startled. "Why, that's wonderful!" She eyed Celia closely. "Isn't it?"

"I'm not sure."

Her sister's gaze sharpened. "Do you love him?"

"I wish people would stop asking me that," Celia muttered under her breath.

"What people?"

"Gran." She swallowed. "Mr. Pinter."

"Mr. Pinter?" Minerva echoed with decided interest.

"It's not what you think," Celia protested. "I hired him to find out the truth about my suitors, so he wanted to know if I was in love with any of them."

Minerva arched one eyebrow. "And why should he care?"

"That's what *I* said. And ever since, he's been baiting me in front of them and telling me awful things about them to blacken them in my mind."

"Even Lyons?" Minerva said.

"Well, no. I mean, I'm sure you've heard about the madness in the duke's family, but beyond that, Jackson hasn't found a single thing—"

"Jackson?"

Celia colored. "Mr. Pinter." When Minerva kept staring, she added sullenly, "We've been in each other's pockets because of the investigation. That's all."

"Ah." Minerva sipped more chocolate. "Get back to the part about the duke offering marriage."

"It wouldn't be a love match. His Grace just figures that since I need a husband and he might have trouble finding a wife, what with the madness in his family and all, we could simply . . . agree to marry."

"I see. And you approve of that?"

Celia stared sightlessly at the printed bed hangings, with their faded blue and yellow flowers against a light green field. "I don't know. I mean, I like him well enough, I suppose. We've known his family forever. He doesn't seem to care about the scandal in ours, and he's an excellent shot—"

"That would certainly be at the top of *my* list of requirements for a husband," Minerva broke in, eyes twinkling. "'Must be able to hit a bull's-eye at fifty paces.'"

"Fifty paces! Are you mad? It would have to be a hundred at least."

Her sister burst into laughter. "Forgive me for not knowing what constitutes sufficient marksmanship for your prospective mate." Her gaze grew calculating. "I hear that *Jackson* is a very good shot. Gabe said he beat everyone today, even you."

"Don't remind me," Celia grumbled.

"Gabe also said he won a kiss from you."

"Yes, and he gave me a peck on the forehead," Celia said, still annoyed by that. "As if I were some . . . some little girl."

"Perhaps he was just trying to be polite."

Celia sighed. "Probably."

I didn't kiss you "properly" today because I was afraid if I did I might not stop.

"The thing is . . ." Celia bit her lower lip and wondered just how much she should reveal to her sister. But she had to discuss this with *someone*, and she knew she could trust Minerva. Her sister had never betrayed a confidence. "That wasn't the first time Jackson kissed me. Nor the last."

Minerva nearly choked on her chocolate. "Good Lord, Celia, don't say such things when I'm drinking something hot!" Carefully she set her cup on the bedside table. "He *kissed* you?" She seized Celia's free hand. "More than once?"

Celia nodded.

Her sister cast her eyes heavenward. "And yet you're debating whether to enter into a marriage of convenience with Lyons." Then she looked alarmed. "You did *want* the man to kiss you, right?"

"Of course I wanted—" She caught herself. "He didn't force me, if that's what you're asking. But neither has Jackson . . . I mean, Mr. Pinter . . . offered me anything important."

"He hasn't mentioned marriage?"

"No."

Concern crossed Minerva's face. "And love? What of that?"

"That neither." She set her own cup on the table, then dragged a blanket up to her chin. "He's just kissed me. A lot."

Minerva left the bed to pace in front of the fireplace. "With men, that's how it starts sometimes. They desire a woman first. Love comes later."

Unless they were drumming up desire for a woman for some other reason, the way Ned had. "Sometimes all they feel for a woman is desire," Celia pointed out. "Sometimes love never enters into it. Like Papa with his females."

"Mr. Pinter doesn't strike me as that sort."

"Well, he didn't strike *me* as having an ounce of passion until he started kissing me."

Minerva shot her a sly glance. "How is his kissing?"

Heat rose in her cheeks. "It's very . . . er . . . inspiring." Much better than Ned's, to be sure.

"That's rather important in a husband," Minerva said dryly. "And what of the duke? Has he kissed you?"

"Once. It was . . . not so inspiring." She leaned forward. "But he's offering marriage, and Jackson hasn't even hinted at it."

"You shouldn't settle for a marriage of convenience. Especially if you prefer *Jackson.*"

I don't believe in marriages of convenience. Given your family's history, I would think that you wouldn't, either.

Celia balled the blanket into a knot. That was easy for

Jackson to say—he didn't have a scheming grandmother breathing down his neck. For that matter, neither did Minerva.

"Gran won't relent," Celia said. "I'd hoped that perhaps if I . . . Oh, it doesn't matter. That probably wouldn't have worked anyway."

"What wouldn't have worked?"

Celia explained her plan to garner an impressive offer of marriage so she could throw it back in Gran's face. Then she told Minerva of her qualms about exposing Lyons to public humiliation.

"I see your dilemma," Minerva said. "Why don't you go to Gran and tell her of the duke's offer, then say you don't love him? Perhaps she'll give in then."

"Or perhaps she'll call the duke in, welcome him as her future grandson-in-law, and start planning the wedding. Remember how she announced Oliver's engagement at that party before he even had a chance to stop it? If she does that to me, I won't be able to cry off without embarrassing myself *and* the duke. I don't want to risk that. He's a nice man, no matter how he kisses."

Minerva sighed. "You've got a point. Gran is so unpredictable. And she would probably *love* to see you married to a duke."

"I know."

"Perhaps you should take the bull by the horns. Ask Jackson to marry you."

Celia glared at her sister. "And what if he agrees for the wrong reason?"

"What do you mean?"

"Gran says he's up for some important appointment. What if he just wants a rich wife because it would help him become Chief Magistrate? What if that's the only reason he's been kissing me?" And complaining about her suitors. And trying to blacken their reputations to her.

Minerva arched an eyebrow. "If that were the case, you would think he'd have offered marriage the minute you started talking about suitors."

"If he had deeper feelings for me," Celia countered, "you would think he'd have offered marriage then, too. He hasn't."

Like this afternoon—if he'd wanted to marry her, he could have just stayed to let Gran catch them together. He must have known Gran would make them marry, yet he'd left when Celia had asked him to.

Then again, he might have feared that Gran would simply have him dismissed. For a man of Jackson's ambitions, that would have been enough to send him fleeing.

"Oh, blast, this is all so confusing!" she complained. "How is a woman supposed to figure out what a man really wants?"

"If you learn the answer to that question, do be a dear and tell the rest of us," Minerva quipped. "Though as far as I can tell, men are simple creatures, for all their posturing. They want food, drink, and a wench to bed, not necessarily in that order."

"And love?" Celia asked.

Minerva smiled. "That, too. Some men do, anyway. You'll just have to spend some time with Mr. Pinter and find out if that's what he wants from you."

"And how on earth am I supposed to spend time with him when he's been avoiding me ever since the last time we kissed?"

"Perhaps he's worried about the difference in your stations."

"That didn't keep him from kissing me." She scowled. "Besides, you've heard what he says about our sort. If anything, he thinks himself above us, not below us. He didn't even ask me to dance tonight! He could have. No one would have thought anything of that. Instead, he spent the entire ball standing about, looking disapproving, and talking to servants."

"Perhaps because *you* spent the entire ball in the company of your suitors."

Celia released an exasperated breath. "What else was I supposed to do? I'm not allowed to ask a man to dance. And at least I know what my suitors want. Lord Devonmont wants to seduce me, the viscount wants peace in his old age, and the duke wants to marry me. I don't have any idea what Jackson wants, other than to drive me mad."

And to make her want him. She'd spent half the evening remembering his sweet kisses that afternoon and his fierce words about desiring her.

Had any of it been feigned? It was hard to know. Still, even tonight she'd caught him gazing at her with such hunger . . .

A rush of heat through her body made her bite back an oath.

"There's still a couple of days left until the house party is over," Minerva pointed out. "Why don't you just see how matters progress? Tell the duke you need time to consider his offer, and use that time to try to figure out what's going on with Mr. Pinter."

"In other words, 'let his behavior be the guide of your sensations.'"

Minerva scowled. "Have you been reading Jane Austen?"

Oops. She'd forgotten that she'd read the line in *Emma*.

"Don't get me wrong—she's a good choice," Minerva said tartly. "And I *suppose* that is good advice. Though I'd also advise you to decide what it is you want from him. Marriage?"

"I don't know. That's the trouble."

But an hour later, after Minerva had left and Celia was lying alone in her bed, she realized that she did know *one* thing she wanted from him. More time alone together. More chances to see how she felt, and if it was real or just borne of some madness of the moment.

Only now did she realize how much she'd been protecting herself from feeling anything for a man. But whenever she was with him, she didn't want to protect herself. He made her *want* to feel.

She fell asleep, dreaming of Jackson's mouth on hers, his hands on her body. And she awoke only a few hours later, touching herself.

Even as she came fully awake, she continued the shameful behavior. She laid her hand on her breast, remembering how he'd sucked and fondled it. Her fingers seemed to move of their own accord, stroking the nipple through her nightdress. It made her blood run hot . . . but it still wasn't as good as when *he'd* done it.

Just thinking of how he'd pressed between her legs and dragged his thumbs up her naked thighs . . .

Oh, heavens, what would it be like to have him touch her down *there*, between her legs? Ned had been trying to do that very thing when she'd hit him with the brick. At the time, she'd been appalled that he would even attempt it.

But now, after coming so close to having Jackson caress her there, it didn't seem quite so appalling. In fact . . .

With her cheeks flaming, she pressed her hand against the part of her that seemed to ache for his touch. Trying not to think of how wicked she was being, she rubbed herself there. Heavens, but it felt so good! Closing her eyes, she imagined it was Jackson's hand rubbing her, and making her grow more and more damp, more and more achy. . . .

A creak inside the wall was all the warning she got before the servants' door opened and Gillie, her maid, crept in.

She froze, grateful that the covers were over her. As Gillie built the fire, Celia lay there, pretending to be asleep, utterly mortified. Look what that curst man had done to her! He had her *touching* herself like some wanton.

After Gillie left, Celia tried to go back to sleep, but it was impossible. Her mind and body both were too agitated. When an hour had passed with sleep eluding her, she leapt from the bed and began to pace. This was madness. She couldn't believe she was letting the man do this to her! She had to get out of the house. Sitting around and brooding over Jackson would only make her insane.

She rang for Gillie. It was near dawn—the other guests would all be in bed. So she could do the one thing that always helped calm her agitation.

Go target shooting.

Chapter Thirteen

Shortly after dawn, around half past seven, Jackson headed out on horseback to interview Mrs. Duffett, with Mrs. Plumtree's words still ringing in his ears. He wished the ride to High Wycombe wasn't so long. He was in no mood to be alone with his thoughts.

To gain time, he cut across the estate instead of riding up the drive to the road. Thank God, it was too early for snow—bad enough that the wind was sharper than usual today.

He hadn't ridden far when he heard a pistol shot near-by. He'd seen Halstead Hall's gamekeeper having break-fast in the kitchen when he left, so it couldn't be him. The house party guests had stayed up late dancing and playing cards, so he doubted they'd be hunting this early. Besides, he didn't hear dogs.

That left only one possibility—poachers.

He could just mention it to the gamekeeper when he got back . . . but the idea of someone shooting anything willy-nilly on the estate unsettled him. A second shot decided him. Spurring his horse into a gallop, he rode toward the sound.

But when he crested the hill, the sight that greeted him made him pause. At the bottom of the hill stood Celia in a riding habit, her gun pointed in his direction. He halted just as she spotted him.

After emptying the gun by firing it in the opposite direction, she set it on the ground facing away from them, picked up her skirts, and came up the hill with fire in her eyes. "Are you *trying* to get yourself killed?" she cried.

Only then did he notice the target that was set into the hill below him. So *this* was where she did her shooting practice. He should have known she'd have a secret spot for it.

"Pardon me for interrupting," he said dryly as she approached. "When I heard shots, I thought it was poachers."

"And you were going to confront them alone?" She planted her hands on her hips. "What if there were several, armed and ready to shoot?"

The very idea made him roll his eyes. "In my experience, poachers run when they see someone coming. They don't brandish guns." He couldn't resist taunting her. "You're the only person who does *that*, my lady."

At his use of her title, she stiffened. "Well, you could have been hurt all the same. You really mustn't sneak up on people like that. And what are you doing up so early, anyway?" Her eyes narrowed. "You can't be going to London—you're heading in the wrong direction."

"I'm off to High Wycombe. Apparently your old nurse lives there, so I'm going to question her about the events on the morning of your parents' deaths. That way I can confirm if your dream is just a dream or something more."

Her face lit up. "Let me go with you."

Hell and blazes. This is what he got for sticking his nose where it didn't belong.

"No," he said harshly. "That would decidedly *not* be a good idea."

Turning his horse around swiftly, he spurred it into a gallop and rode back the way he'd come. The last thing he needed was her trying to join him.

Unfortunately, that wasn't enough to dissuade her. In no time, she had run down the hill, fetched her gun and her horse, and galloped after him. Within minutes she was riding up beside him. With a curse, he slowed his horse to a trot.

"Why wouldn't it be a good idea?" she asked.

Because the sight of you so delicately perched on your sidesaddle makes my blood heat and my hands itch to touch you.

"If you go missing, everyone will worry."

She snorted. "First of all, it's barely an hour after dawn. 'Everyone' will be asleep for another several hours. Secondly, my maid Gillie knows to say that I'm sleeping off a headache, as she always does when I'm target shooting." She flashed him a sheepish smile. "Gran doesn't approve of the shooting, you know. So I get a *lot* of headaches."

He gritted his teeth. Of course Celia did what she must to get her own way.

"No one ever questions it," she went on. "So we can be to High Wycombe and back before anyone realizes I'm gone."

"There are other reasons for you not to join me. For one thing, the minute I introduce you, Mrs. Duffett will temper her answers. I'll be asking about your father's philandering, among other things, and she'll balk at telling the truth if you're there."

"So introduce me as your sister, who has come along to take notes. I doubt she'll recognize me. She hasn't seen me since I was nine, when I was short and scrawny and my hair was much lighter."

"That isn't the point," he bit out. "Why the bloody hell do you want to be there, anyway?"

She blinked at his sharp tone, then stared off at the fields ahead. "I have to know, don't you see? I have to hear for myself whether it was a dream or something that really happened." She cast him a pleading glance. "You never know what might come up in your interrogation. Nurse might say something that triggers another memory in me."

Damn it, she was right. If it were any of the other Sharpes, he wouldn't balk. But the idea of spending several hours in her company was both intoxicating and terrifying.

"If you don't let me go along," she continued, "I'll just follow you."

He scowled at her. She probably would; the woman was as stubborn as she was beautiful.

"And don't think you can outride me, either," she adde

"Halstead Hall has a very good stable, and Lady Bell is one of our swiftest mounts."

"Lady Bell?" he said sarcastically. "Not Crack Shot or Pistol?"

She glared over at him. "Lady Bell was my favorite doll when I was a girl, the last one Mama gave me before she died. I used to play with it whenever I wanted to remember her. The doll got so ragged that I threw her away when I outgrew her." Her voice lowered. "I regretted that later, but by then it was too late."

The idea of her playing with a doll to remember her late mother made his throat tighten and his heart falter. "Fine," he bit out. "You can go with me to High Wycombe."

Surprise turned her cheeks rosy. "Oh, thank you, Jackson! You won't regret it, I promise you!"

"I already regret it," he grumbled. "And you must do as I say. None of your going off half-cocked, do you hear?"

"I *never* go off half-cocked!"

"No, you just walk around with a pistol packed full of powder, thinking you can hold men at bay with it."

She tossed her head. "You'll never let me forget that, will you?"

"Not as long as we both shall live."

The minute the words left his lips, he could have kicked himself. They sounded too much like a vow, one he'd give anything for the right to make.

Fortunately, she didn't seem to have noticed. Instead, she was squirming and shimmying about on her saddle.

"Are you all right?" he asked.

"I've got a burr caught in my stocking that keeps rubbing against my leg. I'm just trying to work it out. Don't mind me."

His mouth went dry at her mention of stockings. It brought yesterday's encounter vividly into his mind, how he'd lifted her skirts to reach the smooth expanse of calf encased in silk. How he'd run his hands up her thighs as his mouth had tasted—

God save him. He couldn't be thinking about such things while riding. He shifted uncomfortably in the saddle as they reached the road and settled into a comfortable pace.

The road was busy at this early hour. The local farmers were driving their carts to market or town, and laborers were headed for the fields. To Jackson's relief, that made it easy not to talk. Conversing with her was bound to be difficult, especially if she started consulting him about her suitors.

After they'd traveled a few miles, she asked in a conversational tone, "Does your aunt mind that you're away this week?"

At least she'd picked a safe topic. "No. She understands I'm working."

"I suppose she's very proud of you."

"Do you find that surprising?" he drawled.

"No!" She cast him a considering glance. "Why shouldn't she? You're a very skilled investigator, I'm told."

"But not skilled enough to suit your ladyship," he said, feeling a perverse urge to bait her.

"I didn't say that. From what I've seen, you're ver

thorough." She turned her gaze to the road ahead. "It's no wonder that you're being considered for the position of Chief Magistrate."

His stomach knotted. He should have known that every conversation with Celia had the potential to be a bog-ridden moor. "I suppose your grandmother told you about that."

A troubled expression crossed her face. "She says you must be careful not to be accused of any impropriety. That it would hurt your prospects for advancement. She says I should take care not to let you be caught in that position."

"Oh, she does, does she?" Mrs. Plumtree was even more Machiavellian than he'd given her credit for. "And I see you listen to her very well, for here we are, alone together again. At your instigation."

A blush suffused her cheeks that so enhanced her beauty, he had to look away. "Don't worry," she said, "no one will ever know about this. I'll make sure of that."

"Like no one knew about our being alone together yesterday?"

"No one did!" she protested.

"Right. And your grandmother didn't guess that we'd been together, either. The last time anyone saw us, we were walking off arm in arm, remember?"

"Oh, but I told her some nonsense about how we parted before I came into the north wing."

"And she believed you," he said skeptically.

"Yes." She chewed on her lower lip. "Well, I think she did."

"Doesn't sound like it."

Her brow knit with worry as she glanced over at him. "What did she say to you last night at the ball?"

That she'll disinherit you if I'm fool enough to offer for you.

No, he couldn't reveal that. Celia liked being told what to do about as much as he did. She might attach herself to him just to annoy her grandmother. He didn't want her that way. Especially when she had no idea what it was like to live without money.

"She asked about my intentions toward you." He steadied his nerve to speak words that might hurt her. "I told her there was nothing between us."

"Did you?" Her expression was impenetrable as she shifted her gaze to the road ahead. "Fortunately, I told her the same thing."

He gripped the reins. So much for hurting her.

"But you know Gran," Celia went on lightly. "She'll think what she wants, no matter what either of us say."

"Well," he managed, "her mind will surely be put to rest about you and me when you announce that you're marrying the duke."

"*When* I announce it?" she echoed, then fell silent for a long moment. "There's something I . . . ought to have mentioned before."

He gritted his teeth. Damn, damn, damn. She must have already announced it, last night after he'd left the ball. It was set in stone now. She was planning to let that bloody duke into her bed and her life, even though she didn't—

"I never had any intention of marrying the duke."

Stunned, he turned to gape at her, a jolt of relief shooting straight to his soul. Then he caught himself. He could be reading her words entirely wrong. "Oh? Have you fixed on one of the others instead?"

She took a deep breath. "Actually I'd planned for another outcome entirely."

His blood clamored in his chest. "What do you mean?"

"I was hoping that if I gained an offer from a man of high rank, I could throw it back in Gran's face to prove I am just as marriageable as any woman. Then she would realize that her ultimatum was foolish, and she would rescind it."

Sweet God. *That,* he hadn't expected. "I see," he muttered, rendered practically speechless by her revelation. All this time he'd assumed that she *wanted* to marry one of those arses. If she hadn't really . . .

No, he couldn't allow himself to hope. Nothing had really changed.

"I know, I know," she went on, "you don't have to say it—it was a stupid plan. I didn't think it through."

He weighed his words. "If it was a stupid plan—and I'm not saying it was—it's only because you misconstrue your grandmother's feelings about your eligibility to marry."

She snorted. "She thinks no one would ever marry 'a reckless society miss' and a 'troublemaker.'"

He winced to hear his own words thrown back at him. Celia was all that . . . and so much more. Not that he dared tell her. Bad enough that he'd revealed too much of how he felt yesterday. For now, she could chalk it up to mere desire. If he started paying her compliments, she might guess how far his feelings went, and that wouldn't do.

So he tempered his remarks. "Your grandmother is merely worried that you will waste yourself on some man who doesn't deserve you." *Like a bastard Bow Street Runner.* "I suspect that if you tell her you're going to marry the duke, she won't be a bit surprised. And she certainly won't agree to rescind the ultimatum, now that she's finally achieved what she wanted."

"Yes, I've come to that conclusion myself. And besides . . . well . . . it wouldn't be fair to involve him in such a plot behind his back when he's a genuinely nice man offering marriage. If word got out that he had offered and I'd accepted, only to turn him down, people would assume I'd done it because of the madness in his family. That would just be cruel."

Now that Jackson knew she wasn't actually going to marry the duke, he could be open-minded. "It certainly wouldn't be kind," he agreed. "But I'd be more worried that if word got out, you'd be painted as the worst sort of jilt."

She shrugged that off. "I wouldn't care, as long as it freed me from Gran's ultimatum."

It took him a moment to digest that. "So you lied when you said at our first discussion of your suitors that you had an interest in marriage?"

"Of course I didn't lie." Her cheeks pinkened again. "But I want to marry for love, and not because Gran has decided I'm taking too long at it. I want my husband to genuinely care for me." Her voice shook a little. "And not just my fortune." She cut him a sidelong glance. "Or my connections."

He stiffened in the saddle. "I understand." Oh yes, he understood all right. Any overtures he made would be construed as mercenary. Her grandmother had made sure of that by telling her of his aspirations.

Not that it mattered. If he married her, he risked watching her lose everything. A Chief Magistrate made quite a lofty sum for someone of Jackson's station, but for someone of hers?

It was nothing. Less than nothing.

"So what do you plan to do?" he asked. "About your grandmother's ultimatum, I mean."

She shook her head. "If presenting her with an offer and begging her forbearance didn't work, my original plan was just to marry whichever of the three gentlemen had offered."

"And now?"

"I can't bring myself to do it."

He stopped clenching the reins. "Well, that's something then."

"So I find myself back where I started. I suppose I shall have to drum up some more suitors." She slanted a glance at him. "Any ideas?"

Chapter Fourteen

Celia didn't know how to make it any plainer. If Jackson was interested in marriage, now was the time to speak up. She'd made it clear how she felt about being married for her fortune and connections. All he had to do was step in and declare that he didn't care about any of that, that he was madly in love with her, and all would be well.

Instead, he said stiffly, "I can't imagine how I could help you in that regard, my lady."

The "my lady" particularly hurt. She'd thought that they'd moved past his acting like Proud Pinter, and her hurt made her peevish. "Well, you kept insisting when I hired you that there must be some suitable gentlemen out there who would marry me. So go find some, blast you. So far, all you've done is criticize the ones I found for myself."

He flashed her a small smile. "Excellent point."

"I know," she shot back.

Though now it occurred to her that his vehement protests over her choice of suitors were odd. Given his heated caresses yesterday, his behavior smacked of jealousy. So if he cared enough to be jealous of the other men, why didn't he care enough to court her himself?

I told her that there was nothing between us.

Was that just his way of soothing Gran's fears and protecting his pride? Or had their encounter yesterday truly been only a dalliance?

"For a man whose task is to solve problems," she grumbled, "you create more than you solve."

"In my defense, I'm not used to matchmaking work," he pointed out.

"Clearly."

They rode a few minutes in silence. Slowly it dawned on her that she really wasn't sure what his job entailed, aside from his work for Oliver. Indeed, she didn't know much about him at all. Perhaps if she could learn more, she could figure out why he liked to kiss her passionately one minute and ignore her the next.

"So," she said, "do you have a good chance of becoming Chief Magistrate?"

For some reason, that made him stiffen. "Reasonably good, I suppose."

"What exactly does the Chief Magistrate do?"

He eyed her askance. "Why do you want to know?"

"I'm curious, that's all. And we do have another hour and a half of riding ahead of us. Indulge me."

"Very well." He tugged his beaver hat more firmly down on his forehead. "Do you know anything about the magistracy?"

"They're judges, right?"

"At Bow Street, it encompasses a great deal more. There's some work running the office, some work supervising the junior officers, and some work serving as a judge."

"If you're acting as a judge, why don't you have to be a barrister?"

"That's how the system is run. Magistrates are appointed. The present Chief Magistrate started out as a saddler's apprentice. Magistrates are given some training in the law, but the position is more supervisory than anything. In London, being Chief Magistrate puts you in charge of all seven magistrate's offices."

Oh my. "That sounds terribly important."

"Terribly," he echoed in a dry tone.

As the wind kicked up, she drew her cloak more tightly about her. "How does your aunt feel about your becoming Chief Magistrate?"

He gave a rueful smile. "She's chomping at the bit to see me in such a lofty post. She preened like a peacock when they made me assistant magistrate."

"Oh! I didn't realize you were already a magistrate."

"Assistant," he emphasized. "I serve as that in addition to my duties as a Runner. I was given the appointment two years ago."

"After you solved the first Lady Kirkwood's murder?"

He shot her a surprised look. "You knew about that?"

"Of course. That's why Oliver hired you—because his friend Lord Kirkwood praised your abilities to the skies."

A mysterious smile played over his lips.

"What's so funny?" she asked.

"I was just thinking it must have annoyed you tremendously to have me, of all people, be hired by your brother after I kicked you and your other brother's friends out of Green Park."

She chuckled. "I suppose it did at the time. But . . ."

"But . . ."

Her hands tightened on the reins. "Shall I make another confession?"

"Please do," he drawled. "I'm taking note of every one in case I ever have to blackmail you."

"Very funny. But the truth is . . . that shooting match in Green Park really was ill-advised. I knew it at the time, but I let myself be carried away by the moment—and the insistence of several young gentlemen. You were right to put a stop to it."

"Of course I was right."

"Jackson!"

He laughed. "Well, I was, and you know it." Sobering, he leveled her with a steady glance. "You have good sense when you choose. I noticed just now that your practice target was set into a hill to prevent injury to anyone who might stray into the area. The only way you would have hit me when I rode up was if you chose to. You're not generally stupid with guns, by any means. Nor reckless."

She sniffed. "That's not what you said the other night when you lectured me about my pistol."

"Only because you weren't prepared to follow through." His gaze narrowed on her. "Don't pull a gun on a man unless you mean to shoot it."

"I've already had the lecture, remember?"

He broke into a smile. "Sorry. My uncle used to say I was born trying to tell people what to do." He grew pensive. "And that *he* was born trying to tell them where to go."

The sudden grief that washed over his face made her heart twist for him. "He was a magistrate, too, wasn't he?"

"One of the best."

She eyed him closely. "I suppose you miss him awfully."

After a moment, he nodded. "He was the closest thing I ever had to a father."

"Was he your mother's brother?"

"No. My aunt is my mother's sister."

That surprised her. "Then it was very kind of him to take the two of you in after . . . I mean . . ." Oh, Lord, she probably shouldn't have brought that up.

He shot her a veiled glance. "After my mother so spectacularly ruined her life?"

"Well . . . yes. It couldn't have been easy for a magistrate to take in his . . . unwedded sister-in-law and her—"

"Bastard," he clipped out.

"I was going to say 'child,'" she murmured.

His rigid demeanor made her wonder how many times he'd been called that word in his youth. Children could be cruel. She knew that better than anyone, thanks to the unrelenting gossip about her parents' scandalous deaths.

"You forget," she went on, "I now have a nephew who was born out of wedlock. George is a dear. It's not his fault that his mother bore him on the wrong side of the blanket. It's hardly even *her* fault, given the circumstances. She truly expected to marry her fiancé once he returned from the war. If he hadn't died—"

"Well, if my mother suffered from such a delusion, she didn't suffer for long." He fixed his gaze on the road ahead. "My father was apparently quite the dashing young fellow, but he was a spoiled lord, and after he convinced her to run away with him and took her innocence, he refused to marry her. He said he needed a rich wife. He loved her, but not enough to lower his expectations for the future."

"Oh, Jackson," she whispered, her heart in her throat.

But he didn't seem to hear. "Instead he found his rich wife somewhere near Liverpool and established Mother as his mistress there, then abandoned her when I began to consume too much of her attention. Apparently he didn't like competing with a child's affections."

"You keep saying 'apparently.' Didn't you know him at all?"

He shook his head no. "I was two when he left us to fend for ourselves. And Mother would never reveal his name or even his title."

No wonder he hated the nobility. She couldn't imagine what it would be like not to know who her father was, to go from day to day wondering if some man she worked for or met in society was the man who'd sired her.

It must have been very hard for him. "How did you live after he left?"

"Not badly at first. Mother did piecework for a seamstress, but when the machines came along, there was less of that. We moved to a poorer part of town, and she began working in the mill. Then she grew ill." His voice tightened. "I was ten. She'd already begun talking about seeking out her family when something happened to press her into doing so."

When he didn't go on, she said, "Oh?"

"I spent my days at a local charity school, and got into an altercation with a boy who called her a whore. I . . . um . . . called him a few choice words myself, and he grabbed me by the throat and started to choke me. He crushed my larynx. He would have killed me if the head-mistress hadn't ripped him off of me." He shot her a side-long glance. "That's why my voice sounds so rough. And that was when she went to her sister for help."

"Why didn't she go before then?

He gave her a hard stare. "For the very reason you mentioned—she feared that her presence in their house would ruin her brother-in-law's prospects. I later learned that they'd had no idea she was living so meanly. She'd lived with them after her parents died, but once she ran off to be with her lover she didn't keep in touch with them, out of shame or resentment. My aunt has always said that they would have taken her in at once if they'd known she was raising me alone."

A lump caught in Celia's throat. "Your aunt must be a very good person. And your uncle, too, of course."

His expression softened. "They're the finest I've ever known. They tried to save Mother, but she was too ill by then to be saved. After she died . . ." He broke off, his eyes misty. When he could go on, he said, "After that, Uncle William took me under his wing as an apprentice. I went with him every day to Bow Street." A faraway smile lifted his lips. "I learned the business from top to bottom. I'll always be grateful to him for that."

She was silent a long moment, taking it all in. What an incredible man Jackson was, to have suffered so much and still have come so far. "It must have been difficult for you, starting so young in a place like Bow Street. You must have worked very hard to have risen so high in such a short time."

"In my world, working hard is a requirement for everyone who wants to eat, my lady."

His taut tone, combined with his formal speech and his clear condescension, made her testy. "You forget, Jackson, that my family has always had one foot in your world. I know only too well that everything I eat and drink and wear comes to me because of the sweat and toil of my grandparents at their brewery. It certainly doesn't come from my father's people, who spent all their funds on wild living and left the estate practically bankrupt."

She twisted the reins in her hand, her voice turning acid. "Indeed, that's why Gran feels she has the right to lay down rules for our future. Because she's been paying for our past for a long time." Shooting him a resentful look, she added, "And that's why you think she has the right, too. Admit it."

His manner softened as he gazed over at her, a sudden spark of sympathy in his eyes. "Not anymore. I'll admit I agreed with her aims at the beginning, but . . .." He shook his head. "I can't approve of her methods, sweeting."

Sweeting?

Her eyes met his, and he flushed, then jerked his gaze away. "We'll reach High Wycombe before we know it," he said, his voice noticeably harder, "so we should probably discuss what I'm going to ask Mrs. Duffett."

She sighed. Every time she thought she was on the verge of figuring him out, he said something to confuse her.

One thing she *did* know—he was an even finer man than she'd realized. The kind of man she would be happy to marry. But only if he truly wanted to marry her.

She might have been willing to accept a marriage of convenience to the duke, since she cared for His Grace only as a friend. With Jackson, however, she needed more, because she *cared* far more. She could never endure living with him day after day, pining for him, enjoying his kisses, if his desire for her was all just part of his ambition.

So before she let her heart be fully engaged, she had to make sure that he wanted her for herself. Nothing less would do.

HIGH WYCOMBE WAS a quaint little market town northwest of London. They had no trouble finding a livery to feed and water their horses while they were in town, but they had a bit more trouble finding Mrs. Duffett. The directions John had given Jackson weren't easy to follow, so it was well past ten before they found the country road on the outskirts of the village.

As they walked toward the farmhouse, he risked a glance at Celia. He was worried about her. She'd grown

more subdued the closer they'd come to finding their
quarry. She would be very disappointed if she discovered
that her dream really was just a dream. And he hated that
she might doubt herself and her memories.

He still couldn't believe all she'd said to him on the
road. Or the many things he'd confessed to *her*, about
his mother and his childhood. He'd thought she would
be appalled to hear the sordid details. The fact that she
wasn't . . .

Damn it, there he went again, hoping for more.
But how could he not? Whenever he looked at her, he
wanted—

"Well? Shall we knock?" she asked.

He blinked. He hadn't even noticed that they'd reached
the doorway. "Of course." He rapped twice on the door.
When that brought no one, he rapped again.

"Coming, coming!" cried a muffled voice from inside.

The woman who opened the door was far too young to
be Celia's former nursemaid. Plump and harried-looking,
she tucked a lock of greasy blond hair up into her mob
cap. "Yes?"

"My name is Jackson Pinter, and this is my sister, Miss
Cordelia Pinter." Cordelia had been his mother's name.
"I work for Lord Stoneville. We were hoping to speak to
Mrs. Duffett on his behalf. We understood from those
who used to be in service with her at Halstead Hall that
she now lives here."

The woman blinked. "Oh. Yes. Come in." She stood
aside, casting surreptitious glances at his well-brushed
beaver hat and Celia's fine cloak. "I'm Anne Wyler, her

granddaughter. I live with me mum and dad up the road, but I look in on Granny once or twice a day to be sure she don't need anything. She don't see all that well, you know."

She lowered her voice with a glance back down the hall. "She and me dad don't really get along, so she prefers to stay here alone. But I'm sure she'd be happy to talk with you. She speaks fondly of her days working at Halstead Hall and at Mrs. Plumtree's town house in London. She tells stories about the family all the time. I'll go get her right away."

Guiding them to a small parlor, she bid them sit, then hurried off down the hall. "Granny!" she cried as she went. "You've got visitors, you do! They come all the way from Halstead Hall!"

"Jackson," Celia murmured as they took seats next to each other on the settee. "Look at that!"

He followed her gaze to the mantel, which held a motley assortment of baby shoes, notes with childish illustrations, tiny dresses, and lace caps—all proudly displayed beneath a framed print of Halstead Hall.

Celia's eyes filled with tears. "I remember that cap, the sweet one with the scalloped edges. It was my favorite when I was eight. Gran must have given it to her when I outgrew it."

She started to rise from the settee, but he placed a hand on her arm. "You're not Celia right now, remember? You don't know this woman."

A shuddering breath escaped her. "Of course."

Her gaze dropped to his hand, and he jerked it away.

"Perhaps you should give me your notebook and a pencil," she went on. "Since I'm supposed to be taking notes."

"Right."

He'd just passed it over when Anne appeared in the doorway to usher in a portly lady of about seventy, dressed all in gray, except for her snowy mob cap, her net tucker, and her white lace cuffs. He bit back a smile. His aunt, though quite a bit younger than this woman, kept just such a pair of fancy cuffs that attached under her sleeves for "company."

As he and Celia rose and Anne made introductions, Mrs. Duffett peered at them with a smile. "How delightful to make your acquaintance, sir! And you, too, Miss Pinter, of course. How is his lordship? I heard that he has finally married, along with two of his brothers and one of his sisters. I was so glad to hear of it. He was always a good boy."

"And he has become a fine man, too," Jackson said, conscious of Celia's gaze on him.

As they all sat down, he slid a glance at Celia, wondering if she could contain her reactions to a woman who must have been like a mother to her. Though Celia wore a carefully bland expression that gave nothing away, he noticed that her hands trembled in her lap.

Best get right to it, before she betrayed herself. "Mrs. Duffett," Jackson said, "his lordship has asked me to gather information for the family about the day of their parents' deaths. New evidence has come to light that what we believed happened that day might not be entirely correct."

"My, my," she said, touching one gray-gloved hand to her throat. "Do you think it wasn't suicide after all?"

His eyes narrowed. "Why do you ask?"

"It just seemed so odd. Her ladyship wasn't the sort to shoot herself. Drown herself, perhaps, but never shoot herself." She smoothed out her skirts. "She was always elegant, very aware of her appearance. Shooting is just so . . . messy, don't you think?"

"Quite," he said dryly. "Let's start with the events of that day in the nursery. I'd like a clearer picture of where his lordship and ladyship—and the children—were at every moment of the day."

"The children?"

"Yes. It would help with my mapping out the scene, you see."

"Oh." That seemed to confuse her momentarily, but then she said, "Well, I can tell you where the children were, but I'm not sure I remember the whereabouts of his lordship and ladyship at every moment."

"Anything you remember would be a help."

She pursed her lips, then glanced at her granddaughter. "Annie, dear, would you mind putting the kettle on for tea? I'm fair near to being parched, and I'm sure my guests are, too." As Anne rose, she added, "And when it's ready, bring some of that good quince pie, too."

"Yes, Granny." Anne left the room.

Mrs. Duffett smiled at Jackson. "A young man like you needs to keep up his strength. My Annie makes delicious quince pie." She leaned forward. "She's unattached, you know."

"You don't say," he muttered with a glance at Celia, who was clearly struggling not to laugh. "Now, about that day at Halstead Hall . . ."

"Of course. Let me see . . ." With a faraway look in her eye, she settled back against her chair. "Miss Minerva and Master Gabriel rose early as usual, the little rascals, but Miss Celia slept quite a while. She had a cough, you see, and whenever it plagued her, I gave her something for it that made her sleep."

"Paregoric elixir, you mean."

"Exactly." Then she caught herself and stiffened. "In my day there was none of this nonsense about its being bad for children. Sleep is important when a child is sick."

"Of course."

Her papery cheeks got pink. "She slept right through breakfast, she did. She was still fast asleep when her lady-ship came in to check on her—"

"Her ladyship?" he broke in, a sudden chill running down his spine. "You mean, Lady Stoneville?"

"Of course. She always came in to check on the chil-dren when they were ill."

When Celia caught her breath beside him, he shot her a warning glance. "And what of his lordship? Did he do the same?"

Mrs. Duffett gave a tinkling laugh. "Don't be silly. He never rose that early. Sometimes he would come in at night right before dinner and give them a little fun, but I daresay he was still abed that morning."

Perhaps it had been a dream, after all. "So you and her ladyship were alone with the children."

"Well, of course. I suppose someone might have come in later after I left with Master Gabriel and Miss Minerva—"

"You left the nursery?" Celia asked from beside him.

Mrs. Duffett looked startled at Celia's speaking up. "I took the children for a walk at her ladyship's insistence. She said she'd look after Miss Celia."

The ramifications of that hit him all at once. Celia had insisted that it was her father in the nursery that morning. But what if it hadn't been? What if it had been her *mother*?

What if her mother had arranged the assignation at the hunting lodge? It would explain why she'd ridden off before his lordship.

"Was her ladyship alone when you returned to the nursery?" Jackson prodded.

"Yes, but she only stayed a moment longer. She mumbled something about having to see to her guests and hurried off."

He thought back over what Celia had described. It was possible that while trying not to alert Nurse to her cough, Celia hadn't noticed her mother still there. Memory could be inexact in a young child.

Or the whole thing really had been just a dream.

Confound it all. He had to know more, but if he led Mrs. Duffett through the whole day, it would take forever, and they didn't have that long before people back at Halstead Hall would notice Celia's absence.

Perhaps it was time for another tack. "Let me ask you something. You seemed skeptical about Lady Stoneville taking her own life. If you were to hazard a guess as to what happened in the hunting lodge, what would it be?"

She lifted a hand to her throat. "I could never presume . . ."

"Humor me. It might lead the investigation in a new direction. And if, by some chance, the Sharpes were murdered, wouldn't you want to see their killer brought to justice?"

"Murdered!" she exclaimed.

He shrugged. "If her ladyship didn't kill herself . . ."

"Oh! I take your meaning, sir." She stared up at the print over the fireplace. "My word. Murdered?"

"It's quite possible. So tell me about the gossip at the time. What did you hear of the Sharpes and their affairs that might have led to murder?" When she looked uneasy, he prodded her. "I understand that his lordship was . . . indiscriminate with his affections?"

She colored. "Well, I don't like to speak ill of the dead, but . . ." She leaned forward. "He did have a lady friend or two."

He forced himself not to look at Celia for her reaction. After all, she knew of her father's indiscretions. "That must have upset her ladyship terribly."

"It did." She lowered her voice meaningfully. "Though there *was* talk that he wasn't alone in his entertainments. Some said that her ladyship had decided that what was sauce for the gander was sauce for the goose, if you take my meaning."

His blood pounded in his ears as everything Celia had told him flashed through his mind. The *"mia dolce bellezza*" could just as easily have been spoken by Lady Stoneville's lover, to tease her with words her husband might have used. *That* could have been why the woman got angry over it. And it would explain why her ladyship had been in the nursery when Mrs. Duffett came in. If his lordship had been there, he would have felt no need to leave. He would just have shooed his mistress out.

The way her ladyship must have done with her lover.

It would also explain why his lordship's valet had insisted that the man hadn't been involved with Mrs. Rawdon. Because he hadn't.

Apparently Celia had come to the same conclusions, for she jumped to her feet and said hoarsely, "No, Mama would never have . . . she could never . . . it's a lie! I don't believe it!" She cast him a frantic look. "Jackson, tell her it's not possible!"

Damn, damn, damn.

"'Mama?'" Mrs. Duffett squeaked. "Wait, I thought you were Mr. Pinter's . . . oh, dear, you can't be . . . I didn't realize—"

"Forgive me for the subterfuge," he said hastily. "But as you've probably guessed, this isn't my sister. This, I'm afraid, is Lady Celia Sharpe."

And she'd just sent his interrogation all to hell.

Chapter Fifteen

elia could tell from Jackson's stony expression that she'd ruined his plans for how this discussion should go, but she didn't care. She couldn't let such an idea stand! Mama would never have taken a lover. Never! Not when she hated Papa's infidelities so.

"Miss Celia?" Nurse squinted as she too rose from her seat. "Little Elf?"

"Papa was the one to call me Elf," Celia said absently, thumbing through her memories, trying to make sense of them in light of what Nurse was claiming about Mama.

"Aye. That's why we started doing it. It fit you then— you were such a tiny thing."

But she hadn't been a tiny thing in a long while. Even her siblings didn't call her Elf anymore, so it felt strange to have Nurse do so.

Nurse shocked her by seizing her in a great hug. "Oh, my dear girl, I can't believe it's you!" She peered at her with a misty gaze. "Look at you, all grown up. Why, you're so tall! And so elegant-looking, too. What a fine lady you've turned out to be."

"I . . . I . . . thank you." Celia was torn between wanting to embrace her old nurse and wanting to shake her for what she'd said. She stood there awkwardly, not sure what to do.

"Oh! I've got something to show you. Come!" Grabbing Celia by the hand, Nurse drew her to a trunk and opened it to reveal a trove of baby dresses and shoes and the like. "Your grandmother was always so kind about letting me keep a thing or two after you children outgrew it."

She began to rummage through the trunk. "Now where is it . . ." She picked up a worn primer. "Oh, look, this was your brother's. Master Gabe carried it everywhere after your parents . . . Well, anyway, he liked the pictures."

Shoving it into Celia's hand, she searched some more. "And here is Miss Minerva's red handkerchief." She shot Celia a knowing glance. "Your sister always did like the colorful ones. *You* liked the dainty ones—lots of lace. You loved them to be pretty and feminine."

"Did she?" Jackson sounded surprised as he came to stand beside them.

She felt his steady gaze on her, but couldn't return it, her mind still too full of turmoil.

"Oh yes," Nurse said. "It was strange really. She liked girlish clothes, but she wasn't squeamish like most girls. She was curious about everything, even bugs and spiders. Minerva would scream at the sight of a snake, but Miss Celia wanted to pick it up and examine it. She wanted to know how things worked." She cast Celia a sly smile.

"That is, until Master Ned caught her attention when she was nine. Then she turned all simpering and silly."

Jackson went rigid. "Ned Plumtree?"

Heavens, Celia had forgotten that her infatuation for Ned had started so early. Or that she'd often confided in Nurse about it.

"Yes, indeed." Mrs. Duffett patted Celia's hand. "How *is* your cousin? He made all the girls swoon in his day, and you were the worst, as I recall."

"Ned is fine," she said tightly, unable to meet Jackson's gaze. Swiftly she changed the subject. "What is it you were looking for in the trunk?"

"Oh!" Nurse rummaged a moment more, then pulled out a bedraggled fashion doll with one glass eye missing and half its hair worn off. "Do you remember this, dearie?"

"Lady Bell!" Tears stung Celia's eyes. "But I threw it away!"

"I know. I fished it out and kept it in case you missed it. You loved that doll so."

Celia held it close, her heart full as she stared at the ragged leather arms and the wax cheeks with the pink worn from them. "I remember the day Mama gave it to me. She'd returned from a shopping trip to London with gifts for us all."

But that was the Mama of her fondest memories. Not the frustrated woman who might have stood in the nursery making an assignation with a man other than Papa. She blinked back her tears.

Could it be true? Mama and another man, together?

Nurse touched her arm. "Forgive me, dearie, for gossiping about your mama. I am so very sorry."

"No," she said hastily, seizing Nurse's hand. "Don't be sorry. It's important that I hear it, even if it means . . ."

It was time to grow up, time to look at her parents with a hard eye. That's what it might take to find their killer.

Celia swallowed hard. "I'm not a little girl anymore. I need—" She glanced at Jackson. "*We* need to hear the truth. Please tell us whatever you remember. Any piece of information might be crucial."

Nurse stared into her face with worry in her eyes, then nodded. "Well then, come sit down. I'll see what I can recall."

When they were seated, Celia asked, "Was there ever any *evidence* that Mama had a . . . lover? Or was it just gossip?"

The old woman sighed. "Cook claimed she saw her ladyship kissing a man in the pantry late at night, but couldn't see who the man was. She knew it wasn't your papa because he had already gone to bed."

And sadly, their previous cook had been dead for some years.

"When did she see this?" Jackson asked. "During the house party? Or some other time?"

"She never said. Or if she did, I don't remember."

"Did she have any idea who it might have been?" Jackson prodded.

Nurse shook her head no. "We joked that it was Mr. Virgil. He always spoke glowingly of her ladyship."

"Not always," Celia put in, remembering her dream.

Her memory?

"Nurse, on the day my parents died, did you and Mr. Virgil discuss it while you rocked me to sleep?"

"You remember that?" Nurse said, looking startled.

A chill coursed down Celia's spine. "I think so. Mr. Virgil called Mama a coward, and it made me cry. And then I asked you to sing 'William Taylor.'"

Nurse grew very agitated. "Oh, dearie, that fairly gave me goose bumps."

"Why?" Jackson asked.

Both Nurse and Celia eyed him askance.

"I'm not familiar with the song," Jackson said defensively. "I asked my aunt about it after you mentioned it, Lady Celia, but she didn't know it either."

"It's an old English ballad that used to be one of our favorites," Celia explained. "William Taylor is on his way to be married when he's impressed. His bride-to-be dresses as a sailor and goes hunting for him in the navy. She serves aboard a ship, and in battle it's discovered that she's a woman."

Nurse took up the tale. "The captain asks why she's there, and she says she's looking for her true love. He tells her that her true love has married another, and she can find him walking the beach nearby. So she lies in wait for William, finds him with his new bride, and shoots him." She cast Celia a long glance. "It was downright spooky that you asked for that, dearie, given what had just happened."

"Not at all," Celia said. "You and Mr. Virgil were talking about people being shot. That was the only song I knew about such things. Besides, I always liked it because of what happened to the woman who shoots William." Celia gave Jackson a rueful smile. "The captain makes her the commander of a ship."

Jackson arched an eyebrow. "That *would* appeal to you."

"The important thing," she said, "is that it means my dream probably isn't just a dream."

"Probably," Jackson agreed.

"Dream?" Nurse asked.

Quickly Celia described the entirety of it, starting with what had happened that morning.

Nurse looked troubled. "To the best of my knowledge, that's a fair account of what happened that day. I didn't realize anybody was in the nursery with her ladyship that morning, but I suppose it's possible."

"Even if it is," Celia said, "we still don't know who it was. And we can't be sure he had anything to do with the murders. Why would he shoot Mama if he was in love with her?"

"I have some theories about that," Jackson said enigmatically. "But I'll need more information." He rose. "And we should be getting back anyway."

Anne came in just then, with an amply loaded tray. "You're leaving?" she said, disappointment on her face.

"Not yet, they aren't!" Nurse exclaimed. "You just put that tray down over here on the table," she told her granddaughter with a stubborn set to her chin. "We're going to have tea, we are."

"Mrs. Duffett, I do regret this, but—" Jackson began.

"Come now, you can't leave yet. I've barely had the chance to talk to my little girl here." She seized Celia's hand as she faced him down. "I want to hear all about the family—what they've been doing, how everyone is faring . . . what the people they married are like . . ." She brightened. "Did they come with you to town, Mr. Pinter? I mean, what with Lady Celia being unmarried, I know you didn't come here alone with her."

Celia shot Jackson a warning glance. "The family is back at Halstead Hall, I'm afraid, but we brought my maid. Unfortunately, she was famished, so we left her at the coaching inn down the road, since we weren't sure how long our visit to you would take."

Nurse seemed to swallow that tale whole, thank heaven. "Well then, no need to run off, eh? And you must be pretty famished yourself by now. Stay for tea at least."

Celia appealed to Jackson. "Can we? Perhaps Nurse will remember more details as we talk. And I have so many questions still unanswered, so many possibilities to—"

"It's past noon already," he warned.

"If we stay an hour, we'll still get home around three. People will barely have been up."

He glanced from her to the expectant faces of the other two ladies and sighed. "All right. An hour. But *only* an hour, do you hear?"

Celia nodded. It wasn't much time to unravel the secrets of a lifetime, but it would have to do.

* * *

TWO HOURS LATER, Jackson was torn between wanting to strangle Celia and wanting to comfort her as she said her tearful good-byes to Mrs. Duffett. He understood why Celia had dallied. She was clearly still reeling from the news that her mother might have had a lover, and she was trying to find any crack in that tale.

But if they didn't return to Halstead Hall before their absence was discovered, she'd be ruined. A young unmarried female couldn't just go off on a trip, no matter how short, with an unmarried gentleman. They'd have to marry.

Yes—they *would*, wouldn't they?

A powerful longing swept him as he watched her hug Mrs. Duffett. For one fleeting moment, he indulged the fantasy of being Celia's husband.

He would return to Cheapside every day after work at Bow Street to find her, his wife, waiting in his home to greet him with a kiss. They'd have a pleasant dinner, then walk down to Blackfriars Bridge and stroll across the Thames to watch the sun set in summer or the moon rise on a chilly night in winter.

Once they returned home, he'd write up his reports as she darned his socks—

A harsh laugh clogged his throat. As if a lady like her would ever darn socks. Or be satisfied with a simple walk across a bridge in the moonlight instead of a night at the theater.

You could afford a night at the theater from time to time, and new socks anytime your old ones get holes.

But only if he became Chief Magistrate. And once the children came along . . .

Children? That was quite the leap forward, considering that a marriage between them was impossible. Damn Mrs. Plumtree to hell.

"Lady Celia," he said, more sharply than he'd intended, "we have to go."

She broke away from Mrs. Duffett with a parting smile. "Yes, of course, Mr. Pinter."

At last they were walking back to the livery where their horses were stabled. He waited for her to speak, but she remained quiet while they fetched their horses and headed out of town.

After a few furlongs, he could no longer wait to broach the subject. Unlike this morning, when the road had been busy, it was practically deserted now, midafternoon. "I've been considering what Mrs. Duffett said in light of your memory of that morning."

She sighed. "So have I."

"And what conclusions have you drawn?"

"I simply can't believe Mama would have been unfaithful to Papa after how she railed at him for his own infidelities. It makes no sense."

"Celia . . ." he began in a low tone.

"I know." Her voice grew choked. "It makes no sense— but it has to be what happened. I can't make it work any other way. Mama wouldn't have come in to check on me only to leave me alone, then come back ten minutes later to check on me again . . . And Nurse is right—Papa rarely came into the nursery. He wouldn't have been there at all so early."

She took a heavy breath. "I keep thinking about everything I remember. The voices are just whispers—there's no reason to believe that Papa was there if not for the words, '*mia dolce bellezza*,' and that could just have been Mama's lover mocking Papa. I can easily understand how that would have annoyed Mama."

"That's my conclusion as well." He wished he could wipe out her pain, could go back and erase everything she'd heard. Aside from the betrayal she must feel, it must also be humiliating to know that her mother had been so indiscreet that even the servants had noticed. "So none of you ever suspected that your mother—"

"No. I daresay even Gran was oblivious." She stared blindly at the road ahead. "Though perhaps if you ask Oliver and Jarret, they might remember something pertinent. They were old enough to pick up on such clues. I was too young." Her face crumbled. "Oh, Lord, you have to tell them, don't you? It's going to destroy Oliver. He's always blamed Papa for everything that went wrong in their marriage."

Never had Jackson wished more that he had the right to hold her and soothe her hurt. He struggled for words that might make it better. "For all we know, this was her only indiscretion. No one could blame her, given your father's behavior."

"You don't believe it's Mr. Virgil, do you?" Celia asked.

"No. It had to have been Rawdon. Think of what your mother said that morning at your bedside: 'I loathe how she looks at me whenever you speak to me. I think she knows.' Mr. Virgil had no woman for her to compete with, that we know of."

"Unless that part really *was* a dream. I can't be sure."

"It doesn't seem like something a child would invent, does it?"

"I suppose not." She sighed. "I just don't understand how she could rail at Oliver for his behavior with Mrs. Rawdon. He told us months ago that she compared him to Papa, claiming that Oliver was becoming 'the same wicked, selfish creature as he is, sacrificing anyone to his pleasures.' Those are hard words coming from a woman who is doing the same thing."

"I find that people often use the hardest words for sins in others that they themselves commit. She was feeling guilty over what she'd been doing, so she lashed out at Oliver to cover her own guilt."

"That makes sense," she said in a sad voice. "And it shows how astute you can be when it comes to understanding people. I don't understand people at all. I thought I understood Mama's and Papa's marriage, but now . . ." She let out a long breath. "Do you think Mama was in love with . . . with the captain?"

"I don't know. Her words to Oliver that day imply that she might have been. She said that Mrs. Rawdon 'already had *him*.' That's what you tell a woman you envy."

"So you think Mrs. Rawdon killed Mama?"

"I'm not sure of that either," Jackson admitted. "How did she know about the assignation? We've already established that your father was the one to notice your mother riding off when he went to the picnic and apparently followed her."

The wind kicked up, and Celia drew her cloak more tightly about her. "Mrs. Rawdon could have followed her, too."

"Perhaps, but surely your mother would have taken measures to prevent that. And your father would have noticed, in any case. Besides, we've also established that it was midafternoon when they headed out for the hunting lodge. But Desmond heard the shots at dusk, hours later. If she'd followed them, she would have killed them right away."

"And Captain Rawdon was probably the man who showed up after they died, so his wife couldn't have followed *him* there," she said.

"It baffles me. I would suspect that it really was a murder-suicide, that your parents argued and your mother shot your father, except for the gun not being the one that was used to commit the murders."

"Perhaps Captain Rawdon tidied up the scene," she said.

"Why would he do that unless he was tidying it up for his wife?"

"And assuming that Mrs. Rawdon somehow learned of the assignation and killed them, why didn't Desmond see her leave?" Celia pointed out. "Where was she? Desmond never said exactly what he saw that day."

"We need to question him again," Jackson said. "I want more details about what he saw when he entered the lodge."

She was silent for a brief pace. "There's another possibility," she said softly. "Desmond could have some of the details wrong. Or perhaps the captain *had* been riding away, and he's covering up for him."

"Perhaps Desmond is lying for other reasons," Jackson said grimly. "We still can't be sure *he* had no part in it. And then there's Benny's death—the Rawdons are in Gibraltar. So who killed Benny? And why?"

"Could Mrs. Rawdon's lady's maid, Elsie, have been involved somehow, and Benny suspected it? Could *she* have killed Benny?"

"Then why wouldn't he have told me his suspicions when I first talked to him?" Jackson pointed out.

Neither of them had an answer.

They rode a few moments without speaking. The beech woods were thick and shadowed at this point in the road, lending a hush to their surroundings. This was the time to broach the subject of Ned. After what Mrs. Duffett had said concerning Celia and her young cousin, Jackson had to wonder how she'd gone from fancying him to being afraid of him. "Celia—"

A crack sounded somewhere nearby. He didn't register what the sound was until Celia's horse reared and another crack sounded. When he saw the blood seeping from her horse's shoulder and heard her cry, "What the devil?" he realized what was happening.

Someone was shooting at them.

Chapter Sixteen

$\mathcal{E}$verything happened quickly after that. Celia had barely registered the two pistol shots and was just feeling Lady Bell stagger beneath her when Jackson rode up next to her and hauled her off her horse and onto his.

As she grabbed his waist, he spurred his horse into a gallop. She glanced back to see Lady Bell stumble, but at least the mare was still moving. Celia strained to see who was shooting at them, but the smoke obscured her view and the person was firing from just inside the woods.

More shots followed, and Celia could hear hooves thundering behind her. Oh, Lord, someone really was trying to kill them! And in this heavily wooded, deserted stretch of road, the person might actually succeed.

"We have to leave the road," Jackson called back to her. "We're sitting ducks out here, and we can't outride anybody with two of us on one horse."

That was all the warning he gave her before he veered off into the forest. Beech branches ripped at them, forcing the horse to slow.

Jackson leapt from the saddle, then pulled her down beside him. "Come on! We're safer on foot." He paused only long enough to jerk the saddle bags from the horse, throw them over his shoulder, and then slap his horse on the rear to send it heading back to the road. "That ought to throw them off for a few minutes."

Then he grabbed her hand and dragged her along with him as he took off at a run deeper into the woods. Underbrush tore at her skirts as they rushed past bared branches and crashed through piles of leaves. He stopped abruptly, held a finger to his lips and dug through the saddle bag until he found his pistol and kit.

He swiftly loaded the gun, keeping an eye on the woods between them and the road. Back around that vicinity they could hear someone cursing as their assailant discovered that the horse emerging onto the road was riderless.

Jackson grabbed the pistol with one hand while he tried to tug her away again with the other.

She held firm. "Why can't we just stand and fight?" she whispered.

With a scowl, he pressed his mouth to her ear. "Those shots were too close together to be from one firearm, so I'm outgunned and possibly outmanned. I'm not risking you in a fight that I might not win."

Eyes darkening, he pulled her forward. "Now come on. We've got to find a hiding place, or at least somewhere less exposed."

They started moving again, this time more slowly as he cautioned her to make as little noise as possible. Fortunately, their pursuer wasn't taking such care, which made it easier for them to head away from him. So she and Jackson scrambled over logs, darted across long stretches of beech, skirted the edge of a pond. She had no idea where they were going—she could see the sky through the barren branches overhead, but the sun was already too low for her to fix its location. Did Jackson have a plan, or was he just leading her blindly through the woods?

It seemed as if they'd been running forever when they began climbing a rise. Suddenly, Celia tripped and fell over something protruding up from the ground. As Jackson helped her up, his gaze narrowed on what had made her fall.

He kicked away some debris to reveal what looked like . . .

"A chimney?" she asked, perplexed.

He arranged the pile of debris back over the chimney, then said, "This way." Looping an arm about her waist, he tugged her to the edge of the hill, which fell abruptly before them. He glanced over it, then followed the curve of the hill down and pulled her around to the front of the cliff they'd just been standing on.

He pushed some dead vines aside. "It's a poacher's cottage," he murmured. "Sometimes they build them into the sides of hills to make them harder for the authorities to find."

As the sounds of someone crashing through the brush above them came nearer, he shoved aside the vines to find a rotting door. He opened it, dragged her inside, then pulled the vines back over the opening before closing the door.

Touching his finger to his lips, he pulled her deep into the bowels of the long-abandoned cottage. At the back lay a hearth filled with debris, an open cupboard with a few cheap pans and various bits of crockery, a battered tin pail, and a bedstead with a moth-eaten blanket stretched halfway across a thin mattress. Pieces of straw stuck out from the mattress's worn cover.

"Stay here," he whispered, then went to the single window at the front of the cottage. So much growth lay over it that she doubted he could see much, though he tried, rubbing the panes with his elbow in a vain attempt to clear the grime.

Overhead came the sounds of hoofbeats, or perhaps even a couple of people tramping about. She couldn't be sure which. To her alarm, the activity shook some debris down the chimney into the hearth.

Oh, Lord, please don't let them see the chimney.

A sudden gunshot made her jump and clamp her hand over her mouth. Was their pursuer trying to get them to betray their hiding place? Or simply firing at shadows?

Casting her a warning look, Jackson returned his gaze to the window. He held his pistol at the ready, and she could tell from his grim expression that he was prepared to fight for her life.

The sounds of someone searching continued for what seemed like a long time. He and she stood frozen in their positions, until her back started to ache from being held stiff so long. She glided over to the mattress and sat down gingerly. He barely spared her a glance as he stood guard near the window.

It grew darker. This time of year the sun set at four, and since they'd left High Wycombe around two and had already been traveling for an hour when they were shot at, it would probably turn completely dark soon.

After a while, the sounds of searching moved away until all they could hear were the noises of the forest—birdsong, the rustle of small animals, wind whining through the trees.

She rose to approach Jackson. "Do you think they're gone?" she whispered.

"Probably. But we should stay put a while longer to be sure."

"Then what?"

It was barely light enough to see his face, but she could hear his breathing. "We'll stay here tonight. I fear we have no choice. By the time it's safe to leave it'll be too close to sunset, and there's no moon. We could never find our way back to the road through the woods in the dark, and even if we could, I'm not risking the possibility of your assailant lying in wait for us up ahead somewhere. We're lucky as it is that he—or she or them—didn't find us."

She digested that. "Are you sure it wasn't just an attempt at robbery?"

"In broad daylight? Hardly likely. Besides, there hasn't been a highwayman along this road in years. And why pursue us into the woods? A thief wouldn't go to that trouble if they hadn't been seen."

"So . . . so they really were after us."

"You," he said harshly, his eyes dark with anger. "They were after *you.* It was you they fired at, your horse that was hit."

"Lady Bell," she said in sudden anguish. "They shot Lady Bell."

"Only in the shoulder. She may still survive. With any luck, someone will find her on the road and care for her."

"I do hope so. Because I owe her a great debt. If she hadn't reared at the first shot, the one that missed, I might be lying in that road instead." A shudder wracked her. "And if you hadn't pulled me from the horse—"

"I lost half a lifetime when I realized—" He choked off whatever else he was about to say. "Best not to think about it." He squeezed her shoulder. "You survived, and that's all that matters."

"You saved my life."

He smiled faintly. "If you can't trust a Bow Street Runner to protect you, who *can* you trust?" His tone turned fierce. "I won't let anything happen to you, I swear."

"I know." She gazed up at him, her heart full.

He flushed, then jerked his gaze back to the window. "Can you hear anything?"

"Not anymore." She peered out the window, but all she could see were vines. "I don't understand how they found us. How could anybody have known I'd be traveling this way today, when even I didn't know?"

"Someone must have followed you when you left the house this morning."

"Why didn't they shoot me then?"

"You were carrying a rifle, remember? Perhaps they didn't want to risk it."

"Or perhaps it was *you* they followed."

"Though I told some people I was going off to pursue a lead, I deliberately didn't tell them where. And I can't see how anyone could have followed me without my realizing it."

"They wouldn't have had to follow closely," she said. "There's a hill where you can see the whole estate and the road. If they were watching for you from the hill, they would have seen us head off for High Wycombe together."

He nodded. "And they might have decided it was a good time to take their chance at eliminating you."

"Why?"

"I don't know. Because you heard something important the morning that your parents were killed? Because you know who the killer is without realizing it?"

"Then why not attack me on the road *to* High Wycombe? Weren't they worried about what I might learn from Nurse?"

"The road was too busy then, remember? They waited until it was deserted, when they were more likely to get away with murder."

"As they did with Benny."

"Exactly."

Her blood chilled. Someone had killed to silence Benny, had been willing to kill to silence *her*, probably the same someone in the nursery that day. It had to be Mama's lover, Captain Rawdon, because his wife wouldn't have known about Celia hearing that conversation.

But his being the killer made no sense in light of the facts. Besides, the Rawdons were in Gibraltar, as far as anyone knew.

"And there's another possibility," Jackson went on, his tone hard.

She swallowed, still having trouble comprehending that someone wanted her dead. "Oh?"

"Desmond might have decided to eliminate his competition for your grandmother's fortune. If you marry, he loses all chance at it, so he may think that killing you would give him a shot since that would defeat your grandmother's demand."

"Surely he's not stupid enough to believe that Gran would hold to her ultimatum if something happened to one of us."

A low laugh escaped him. "Desmond doesn't strike me as particularly bright."

"True." She gazed out the window at the dying light, and a shiver wracked her.

"You're cold," he murmured.

"No," she said, then realized that she was indeed cold, not only from the merciless truths hitting her, but from the plain fact that it was winter and night was falling.

Jackson removed his surtout and laid it over her cloak. "I should start a fire before it gets too dark to see."

"Don't you need supplies for that?"

He smiled. "I've got gunpowder and a spare flint for

the pistol. That, and some straw from that mattress over there, should be all I need." He glanced back at the hearth. "There's still logs by the fireplace."

"Aren't you worried our pursuers will see the smoke come out of the chimney?"

"We'll just have to pray that they're far enough away not to notice. Which reminds me . . ." He removed his coat and handed it to her. "After I get the fire started, hang this over the window. We don't want any light showing through."

When he walked to the fireplace, she realized she'd never seen him in shirtsleeves. He was always much too formal for that.

But he didn't look the least bit formal as he knelt to start the fire. He looked rough and disheveled and thoroughly capable of eluding murderers and taking care of her while hiding deep in the woods.

A thrill coursed through her. Being forced to survive in such primitive conditions was far beyond her experience, but she suspected that he felt perfectly comfortable with it. If she had to be in danger, she couldn't think of any man she trusted more to keep her safe.

She watched until he got the fire going. Then she covered the window before going to join him at the hearth, where he fed logs into the blaze. "Aren't you glad now that we had something to eat at Mrs. Duffett's?" she said, trying to lighten the mood.

He arched an eyebrow at her. "If we'd left earlier—"

"I know. We might have avoided this." She tipped up her chin. "Or we might not."

A chuckle escaped him, relieving her tension. "Have it your way." He rose and walked to the saddlebags to fish out a wrapped package. "Though I'm even gladder that your cook is fond of me." He tossed the package to her, then pulled out another. "She wouldn't let me leave this morning without loading me down with food for the day."

She tore open the paper to find a ham and cheese sandwich. "Oh, I do love Cook," she breathed as she fell on it with gusto. The tea and cake hadn't held her for long. "At least we won't starve," she said between bites.

He eyed her askance as he devoured his own sandwich. "I believe we can survive for one night without a sumptuous dinner at Halstead Hall, don't you?"

Noting his condescension, she asked, "Does it bother you that we eat so well?"

He blinked, then frowned. "Of course not," he clipped out. "Why shouldn't you, if you can afford it?" Finishing off his sandwich, he picked up the pail. "I'm going to make sure the chimney is clear and see if I can't find some water while there's still light. The former residents must have had some source of it."

"You're leaving me alone?" she squeaked.

"You'll be fine." He handed her the pistol. "Shoot if you have to." His eyes gleamed at her. "I know you know how."

He headed for the door, and she cried, "Wait!"

When he paused to look at her questioningly, she hurried up to hand him his surtout. "You'll need this. It's freezing out there." As she helped him into it, she whispered, "Be careful."

He tipped his hat. "Always, my lady," he said in that husky rasp that never failed to make her heart turn over. Then he walked out.

After he was gone, she took off her bonnet and gloves and surveyed her surroundings. The fire wouldn't last long with so little wood. It would be difficult to keep warm all night when the wind blew through the cracks in the walls as if through an open window.

But perhaps she could do something about that. She searched the room and found a broken-down chair in one corner. She dragged it over to the fireplace, then examined the cupboard to see if she could break it up and use it for firewood, too. It was made of flimsy deal—it wouldn't burn long, but it was something.

Now if only there were some stones or bricks to heat in the fire and use to warm their feet . . .

After a quick search, she found bricks under the bed that must have been used for that very purpose, and she put them in the fire to heat. In rummaging through the saddlebags, she discovered a flask of something pungent. She took a swig and nearly choked on the strong liquor. My, my, wasn't Jackson full of surprises?

After another gulp that burned all the way down, she began to feel quite a bit warmer. Removing her wool cloak, she hung it on a hook by the fire to heat so they could use it as a cover. She tossed the moth-eaten blanket aside and thumped the mattress to make sure there weren't any nasty creatures nesting inside it, then put the blanket back on. But she was *not* going to sleep with that next to her skin.

Her petticoats! She removed one, ripped it in half and spread it over the moth-eaten blanket. That was better. Not that anybody could sleep well on a straw mattress anyway, but—

That's when it hit her that there was only one bed. She caught her breath. It was only logical that they would share it. It was also only logical that sharing a bed could lead to sharing other things . . .

Her cheeks heated. If that happened, there would be no going back. She'd be irrevocably ruined.

Oh, what was she thinking? She'd be ruined either way, even if they spent the entire night here as chaste as nuns.

Of course, it was possible that Jackson wouldn't *want* to share her bed or anything else. They'd been together all day, and he hadn't once tried to kiss her. And even if he did desire her, he might balk at seducing her, with him being so honorable and all.

On the other hand, if he were interested in her fortune, he might take this chance to secure her.

But she couldn't believe that. He didn't seem the sort. And even if he were, it hardly mattered anymore. Once they returned home after a night spent in the woods together, Gran would almost certainly *insist* that they marry. And if Gran didn't, Oliver would.

So if she had to marry him anyway, they might as well . . .

She blushed again. Oh, she truly was brazen. But why not? If for some reason he refused to marry her tomorrow, she'd be ruined all the same, so why not take this chance to see what it was like to experience lovemaking with a man she cared for? Mama had taken a lover, blast it—why shouldn't she?

A little fluttering started in her belly that wouldn't be quelled, even after she took another swig of Jackson's liquor.

At that moment the door opened, making her start. She glanced about her for the pistol, which she must have laid somewhere, but it was only Jackson.

"Looks like you've been busy," he said as he set down the pail to survey the room.

"You found water!"

"There was a stream close by." His gaze fixed on what she held in her hand. "I see you found my brandy."

Refusing to be embarrassed, she walked over to hand the flask to him. "I did indeed." She shot him a mischievous glance as he drank some. "Who would guess that the estimable Mr. Pinter, so high in the instep, drinks strong spirits?"

He scowled at her. "A little brandy on a cold day never hurt anyone. And I'm not high in the instep."

"Oh? Didn't you tell Gabe only last week that most lords were only good for redistributing funds from their estates into all the gaming hells and brothels in London, and ignoring their duty to God and country?"

When he flushed, she felt a twinge of conscience, but only a twinge. He looked so charming when he was flustered.

"I wasn't implying that your family . . ."

"It's all right," she said, taking pity on him. He *had* saved her life, after all. "You have good reason to be high

in the instep. And you're not far wrong, in any case—
there are many lords who are a blight upon society."

He was quiet a long moment. "I hope you realize that
I don't think that of your brothers. Or your brother-in-
law. They're fine men."

"Thank you."

Removing his surtout, he walked over to hang it on top
of her cloak, then stood there warming his hands at the
fire. "I wish I could say the same about your cousins."

Oh dear. That was the last thing in the world she wanted to talk about, especially after what Nurse had told him
today.

She busied herself with hunting through his saddlebags
for more food. "Desmond and Ned have always been . . .
difficult."

"Yet you were infatuated with Ned when you were a
girl." He continued to sip the brandy, his gaze steady on
her.

Seizing a pear, she took a couple of bites as she wondered how to answer. "It didn't last long."

"I figured that." When she shot him a startled glance,
he added, "I saw your reaction to him at the ball last
night."

Had she been that obvious?

"What did he do to you?" Jackson prodded as he
capped the flask and tucked it into a pocket of his surtout.

She ate the rest of the pear. How much should she tell
him? What would Proper Pinter think of her if she revealed everything?

Oh, she could easily guess, and she couldn't bear it.

"Did he hurt you?" Jackson asked in a harsher voice. "I swear, if he laid a hand on you—"

"It wasn't like that," she murmured.

With a darkening expression, Jackson approached her. "Then tell me what it was like."

"It was a long time ago, really. Nothing to speak of."

"I saw your face last night," he said softly. "For one moment, you were afraid of him, and I want to know why."

"I wasn't afraid—"

"Damn it, Celia, tell me what he did!"

She swallowed hard, then turned her back to him. "I-I think he tried to deflower me."

Chapter Seventeen

*R*ed-hot rage seized Jackson. "*Deflower* you!" he choked out. "You mean he tried to *rape* you?"

"No!" She whirled on him with a look of alarm. "I-I told you, it wasn't like that! I mean, it wasn't . . ." She dropped her gaze to her hands. "Oh, I should never have said anything."

He struggled to restrain his anger. He was an investigator, for God's sake—he ought to know by now that you didn't get the truth out of someone by overreacting. Taking her gently by the arm, he led her over to the bed.

"Start at the beginning." He urged her to sit, then took a seat next to her, though not too close. She needed some distance just now. "Tell me what happened. I promise, I'll just sit here and listen." Even if it killed him, and it very well might.

With a nod, she stared off across the room. "It was all my fault, really."

"It was *not* your fault," he snapped.

She eyed him askance. "I thought you were going to sit and listen."

He sucked in a steadying breath. "Right. Go on."

"I'd fancied Ned for years, you see. The summer after I turned fourteen, he was seventeen and on holiday from school, so his family came to visit us at Gran's town house. They stayed a couple of weeks." She pleated her skirt nervously. "He was quite the dashing fellow back then. He rode well—he and Gabe used to race down Rotten Row all the time—and he was a very good dancer. So when he noticed me . . ."

Her voice grew choked. "You have to understand—boys never noticed me, not next to Minerva. She'd just had her come-out, and there were men after her everywhere. She said they were all fortune hunters, but it didn't seem that way to me. Of course, I wasn't out yet so I didn't get to witness much of her success firsthand. But at the few events I attended, she was always the belle of the ball, and I was just the scrawny sister."

It took some doing for him to keep his mouth shut at that, but somehow he managed it.

"Then Ned started flirting with me," she went on, "and I was terribly flattered. All of us children would go to Hyde Park, and he would escort me as if I were already grown. He . . . he paid me compliments and picked me flowers—" Her voice hardened. "His attentions were all a lie, but I didn't find that out until later."

All a lie? Did she mean because the arse was trying to get under her skirts?

"Anyway, Gran held a large party one summer day, and after everyone else went inside for supper, Ned convinced me to go into the garden shed with him."

The troubled expression that crossed her face made Jackson want to find Ned Plumtree and beat him to a bloody pulp. He curled his hands into fists so hard that his fingernails dug into his palms.

"At first it was everything I wanted," she said. "He . . . He kissed me. It wasn't awful, but it wasn't as nice as I'd expected. He was so, well, clumsy at it." She sighed. "I didn't like it much. But I figured it was what happened when a boy kissed a girl, you know?"

No, he didn't know, though he could well imagine a sweet young Celia eager for her first kiss. As his mother had probably been.

But his mother had been old enough to realize what she was doing. Celia had only been fourteen.

He choked back his anger. "You didn't have anything to compare it to."

"Exactly." Her voice lowered. "But when he . . . put his hands on my bosom . . . I knew that wasn't right."

The urge to kill ripped through him again.

"I told him he shouldn't do that," she went on, "and he just kept . . . squeezing, so hard that it hurt." The words tumbled out of her now, one after another, in rapid succession. "And then he started dragging up my skirts with his other hand, and I told him to stop it, and he shoved me down on the floor and got on top of me and his hands were all over me, so—" She scowled. "So I hit him with a brick."

The abrupt cessation of her tale made him blink. "You . . . you what?"

She cast him a furtive glance from beneath her lowered lashes. "Hit him on the head with a brick. I hit him pretty hard. He started cursing and rolled off of me, and I jumped up and ran out the shed door."

"Sweet God," he muttered, his heart leaping into his throat as he realized how close she'd come to being violated.

"He caught up to me in the garden and said some vile things, but I still had the brick, so I threw it at him and ran into the house."

He gaped at her. "Where was your family while all this was going on?" he asked hoarsely. "Your brothers, your sister?"

"They were at supper. Being the youngest, I and my younger cousins were relegated to the children's table, so no one was paying much attention to us at that point. Besides, it all happened so fast . . . I managed to slip in and sit down before anyone even noticed I wasn't there."

A ghost of a smile crossed her lips. "They did notice later that Ned was missing, however. When they asked me if I'd seen him, I told them he'd been complaining of a headache ever since he'd fallen off his horse earlier in the day and hit his head."

She looked smug. "He *hated* that. He was so proud of being known for his riding skills, and after that everyone called him Clumsy Plumtree for a while. And he didn't dare correct me for fear that I would tell them what really happened."

"Why didn't you, damn it?" Jackson gritted out.

She eyed him askance. "Oliver would have shot him on the spot."

"Good. I've a mind to do that myself the next time I see him."

"I'm not going to let you shoot Ned," she said stoutly. "That wouldn't help your chances at being chosen Chief Magistrate." He was about to protest that he didn't give a bloody damn about being chosen Chief Magistrate right now, when she added, "And I wasn't going to let Oliver do it either, not with all the rumors that he'd shot Mama. We had enough scandal in our family as it was."

She crossed her arms over her chest. "Besides, if anyone ever shoots Ned, it's going to be me."

And just like that, everything fell into place. "Ah, so *that's* when you convinced Gabe to teach you how to shoot. That's why you carry a ladies' pocket pistol in your reticule."

She gave him a terse nod. "I wasn't about to let anything like that happen to me ever again."

A sudden chill swept him. How could she think herself so alone? "Leaving the possibility of scandal aside, you should have told your family. They could have dealt with Ned privately."

"And then they would have found out how reckless I was," she whispered. "How pathetic and stupid, too stupid to . . . see that Ned didn't care about me . . . to realize he was just poking fun . . ."

With a little moan, she rose from the bed, but he grabbed her hand and tugged her back to face him. "It wasn't *your* fault that Ned took advantage of your youth and your attraction to him to attempt a seduction, for God's sake."

"You don't understand—it *was* my fault." She ducked her head, refusing to look at him. "I should h-have known better. Boys had never looked at me in that way . . . but I thought h-he really liked m-me. All the while, he was just . . ."

Tears welled in her eyes that tore at his soul. "When I wouldn't l-let him . . . you know . . . he told me he h-hadn't really wanted to, anyway," she stammered, her hand squeezing his painfully, "since I was a . . . a scrawny b-bitch with no tits and not an ounce of anything f-female in me."

"Oh, sweeting," he whispered, drawing her down onto his lap so he could hold her close. She was breaking his heart.

All their conversations came back to haunt him.

Unless you think it impossible for a woman like me to keep men like them satisfied and happy?

You wanted to expose me as some . . . adventuress or man in woman's attire or . . . oh, I don't know what.

You kissed me last night only to make a point, and you couldn't even bear to kiss me properly again today—

Hell and blazes. The clues had been there all along, and he'd ignored them. *This* was the reason for her leaping to such strange conclusions about her attractiveness when he spent every waking hour resisting the urge to take her to bed. And this was why she was determined to prove her grandmother wrong about her ability to marry.

He held her close as she gulped air, clearly fighting back sobs. "He told me he only d-did it to w-win a bet. H-his friends said he could never get a m-marquess's daughter to g-give him a k-kiss, so he bet them that he could."

"That's a lot of bloody nonsense," he hissed, then regretted the sharpness of his tone when her face darkened in confusion. "I'd bet good blunt he only said those things because he was smarting over your rejection. A spoiled brat like Plumtree would hate having his pride pricked. When he found he couldn't cow you into letting him do as he pleased, he attempted to bring you down to his level by speaking vile untruths."

Brushing a kiss to her damp cheeks, he wished he had the bastard in front of him now so he could thrash him within an inch of his life for making her doubt herself. "It's what arses like him do if they don't get their way. So don't believe a word of it. No boy in his right mind would find you unattractive."

She gazed into his face, still looking uncertain. "I *was* rather thin then, and I've never had . . . had much in the way of a bosom."

"Your bosom is fine," he whispered, thinking of how luscious her breasts had tasted, how firm and beautiful they'd looked through the damp linen of her shift when he'd dared to open her gown for a peek. "And even if Plumtree meant what he said, that only shows what a fool he is. To have a goddess like you in his arms and not appreciate it . . ."

He kissed her, unable to resist the lush, succulent

mouth so close to his. He put everything he felt into it, so he could wipe out any hurt the Neds of the world had given her.

When he broke away, realizing he was treading dangerous ground, she said hoarsely, "You weren't always so . . . appreciative. When I said that men enjoyed my company, you said you found that hard to believe."

"*What?*" he retorted with a scowl. "I never said any such thing."

"Yes, you did, the day that I asked you to investigate my suitors. I remember it clearly."

"There's no way in hell I ever . . ." The conversation came back to him suddenly, and he shook his head. "You're remembering only part, sweeting. You said that men enjoyed your company and *considered you easy to talk to*. It was the last part I found hard to believe."

"Oh." She eyed him askance. "Why? *You* never seem to have trouble talking to me. Or rather, lecturing me."

"It's either lecture you or stop up your mouth with kisses," he said dryly. "Talking to you isn't easy, because every time I'm near you I burn to carry you off to some secluded spot and do any number of wicked things with you."

She blinked, then gazed at him with such softness that it made his chest hurt. "Then why don't you?"

"Because you're a marquess's daughter and my employer's sister."

"What does that signify? You're an assistant magistrate and a famous Bow Street Runner—"

"And the bastard of nobody knows whom."

"Which merely makes you a fitting companion for a hellion with a reputation for recklessness."

The word *companion* resonated in his brain. What did she mean by it?

Then she pressed a kiss to his jaw, eroding his resistance and his reason, and he knew precisely what she meant.

He tried to set her off of him before he lost his mind entirely, but she looped her arms about his neck and wouldn't let go. "Show me."

"Show you what?"

"All the wicked things you want to do with me."

Desire bolted in a fever through his veins. "My God, Celia—"

"I won't believe a word you've said if you don't." Her gaze grew troubled. "I don't think you know what you want. Yesterday you gave me such lovely kisses and caresses and then at the ball you acted like you'd never met me."

"You were with your suitors," he said hoarsely.

"You could have danced with me. You didn't even ask me for one dance."

Having her on his lap was rousing him to a painful hardness. "Because I knew if I did, I would want . . . I would need . . ."

She kissed a path down his throat, turning his blood to fire. "Show me," she whispered. "Show me now what you want. What you need."

"I refuse to ruin you," he said, half as a caution to himself.

"You already have." With a coy glance, she untied his cravat and dragged it from around his neck. "When we return tomorrow everyone will know we spent the night together, and it won't matter if we did anything wicked or not. So why not indulge ourselves?"

The irrefutable logic of her argument didn't escape him. Nor did the fact that he was already flexing his hands convulsively on her waist to keep from sliding them up to cup the tender, delicate mounds of her pretty little breasts . . .

"I will not be another Ned, taking advantage of your innocence."

"You're nothing like him," she protested in a low voice. "You're honorable and strong and the only man I've ever wanted to show me how to be a woman." She caught his head in her hands. "And if you don't kiss me right this minute, Jackson Pinter, I swear I'll strip my clothing off one piece at a time until—"

He took her mouth savagely, his mind already filling with the image of her naked beneath him, just where he'd always wanted her. In his bed. In his life. How could he resist her? She was everything he'd ever desired, and his ability to fight it grew weaker with every caress of her soft hands, her soft lips.

"Jackson," she whispered against his mouth. "Show me how to be a woman. *Your* woman."

"My wife?" he murmured. "Because if we do this to-night . . ."

She drew back to stare at him. "Is that what you want? To have me as your wife?"

He gazed into the eyes that were haunted by insecurity and realized what she was asking. Did he want to secure as his wife the rich Lady Celia, whose lofty connections could further his ambitions?

Or did he want to make love to the brave woman who'd learned to shoot so she would never have to be afraid again, who'd kept her cousin's actions secret to protect her family from further scandal, and who now gazed up at him as if he were indeed the Lancelot to her Guinevere?

Tomorrow they would need a serious discussion about marriage and what it would mean, but for now, he didn't care about her grandmother's threats and his fears about their future. Not when he knew that Ned's cruel words still rang in her ears.

Tonight she needed to hear something else entirely.

"What I want," he said softly, "is you. Just *you*."

Chapter Eighteen

Tears stung Celia's eyes. He understood. He wanted *her*. Not her fortune or her connections, but her.

Then he made that clear by taking her mouth so ravenously she could hardly catch her breath. He cupped her breasts through her gown, and she exulted. He would be hers now. Her husband. *Forever*.

"In one respect, I understand why Ned behaved as he did," he murmured against her throat.

That took her by surprise. "What do you mean?"

"It must have driven him utterly mad to come close to having you, only to be denied." He thumbed her breasts, slowly, silkily, in a way so utterly unlike Ned's that it seemed a travesty to compare the two men. "Not that it excuses a damned thing he did—if I ever get the chance, I'll thrash him within an inch of his life. But if *I'd* ever come that near to Paradise . . ."

"Paradise?" With a heady laugh, she unbuttoned his waistcoat. "You're quite the poet for a Bow Street Runner."

"My uncle used to say that any man who can't appreciate poetry has no soul. I thought he was mad. Until now." Scouring her with his eyes, he reached around to the back of her to unfasten her gown, and his voice grew thick and husky. "'She walks in beauty, like the night / Of cloudless climes and starry skies'—it's the only lines of verse I remember. And they fit you perfectly."

A trill of excitement rang in her every vein. "Byron? You're quoting Lord *Byron?*" She shoved his waistcoat off. "That's not only poetry, but wicked poetry."

He urged her to stand, then stood, too, and turned her around so he could finish undoing her gown. "Not so high in the instep now, am I?"

No, indeed. "I wish I'd known you were thinking of me scandalously all this time." As her gown fell to the floor, she shivered, partly from the chill in the ramshackle cottage and partly from the thrill of knowing that Jackson was about to take her innocence. "I would have borne your lectures more easily."

With expert hands, he unfastened her corset. "And perhaps you would have been nicer to me."

"Perhaps." As her corset followed her gown to the floor, she faced him with a mischievous smile. "Or perhaps I would have tormented you differently."

"Oh?" he managed, though his eyes were devouring her in a way that made her every nerve sing. He left her with no doubt of his appreciation for her body.

His reaction differed so markedly from Ned's that she felt free to be coy, to tease. She untied her other petticoat and dropped it, backing away to step out of it. "For example, I might have worn smocks less often and low-cut gowns more."

His breathing grew labored as he stalked toward her, unbuttoning his shirt as he came. "That would have indeed been a torment."

"Because it would have made you want me?"

"I already wanted you, smocks and all. But it would have drawn other men to you like bees to nectar, and I would have had to restrain the urge to murder them for looking at you as I am now."

"Why, Mr. Pinter, were you jealous?" she teased, glad to have her suspicions confirmed.

His eyes met hers, suddenly solemn. "Why do you think I chose today to go to High Wycombe? Because I couldn't bear to watch you flirt with your suitors for one day more."

Oh, my. Who'd have guessed that Jackson could say such delicious things?

Then he dragged his shirt off. Merciful God in heaven, who'd have guessed that Jackson could *look* so delicious beneath his clothes? Though she'd had a hint of it when he'd worn evening attire, she hadn't expected *this*.

His nicely chiseled chest narrowed to a lean waist that showed no sign of running to fat. Dark hair swirled about his nipples, then trailed down to ring his navel before disappearing beneath his trousers. He had the body of a fencer rather than a wrestler, but his arms were muscled enough to explain how he'd managed to yank her onto the back of his horse so effortlessly this afternoon.

Then he unbuttoned his trousers and shucked them to reveal formfitting worsted drawers that showed every line of his well-wrought thighs and calves, not to mention the distinct bulge—

Oh, dear, she was staring. With a blush, she jerked her gaze away.

"Your turn, sweeting," he murmured. "Will you take off your shift? Or shall I?"

She reached for the ties, then felt a moment's hesitation as Ned's voice crept into her head: *Scrawny bitch with no tits—you don't have an ounce of anything female in you.*

As if Jackson knew exactly what halted her, he stepped forward to tip her chin up with his thumb, forcing her to meet his gaze. "I'd give anything to wipe Ned's words from your memory, but since I can't, I can at least add truths to counter the lies he spoke. Do you know what I see when I look at you, my lady?"

Sometimes when he called her "my lady," it felt like his way of putting distance between them. But right now the words held a reverence that stopped the breath in her throat.

"I see a woman of incredible elegance and strength." Keeping his gaze locked with hers, he dragged her chemise off her shoulders. "I see a fairy queen who could destroy a man with a word or enchant him with a smile."

He burrowed his fingers through her hair, tugging it free of its pins so that it tumbled down about her shoulders. With eyes that gleamed hotly in the firelight, he lifted one tress to kiss, then rub over his cheek.

"I see a lass with hair like rich chocolate, eyes that blend green and brown in a fathomless forest of color, and a face and form so lovely it humbles me to think of touching her, much less making love to her."

He tugged her chemise the rest of the way down her body, his gaze following it in a slow appraisal that blazed so hot and hungry that any lingering fear or embarrassment vanished in its wake.

His voice turned hoarse. "As for your breasts . . ." He bent his head to suck first one, then the other, his warm mouth playing over them so marvelously that she gasped. Then he drew back to murmur, "Ned was either blind or daft or both. Or more likely, a bald liar. Because no man in his right mind would ever think these anything but beautiful."

Tears welled in her eyes as he lifted her in his arms and carried her to the bed. How could she have thought him cold and passionless? He hid his feelings very well, but in times of great intensity, they shone bare upon his face. She was becoming more adept at reading them.

Right now she could easily read the desire in his eyes as he laid her on the bed and reached for the buttons of his drawers. Then he hesitated. "Are you sure about this?"

She rose up on her elbow to unbutton his drawers for him. "I'm very sure."

And clearly he was *quite* sure, for the minute she opened his drawers, his arousal burst out to surprise her with its thick, impressive rigidity.

Shortly after marrying, Minerva had explained exactly what happened in the bedchamber between a man and a woman, warning that a man's appendage could be rather daunting, and much different than those Celia had seen on horses and cows and hunting dogs.

Yes, it was different, but not really daunting. More like, oddly beautiful. Not to mention, fascinating in how it swayed a little as if buffeted by the wind.

"Ready for the rest?" he drawled, a hint of amusement in his voice.

"There's more?" When he shucked his drawers to reveal the ballocks hanging down, she said, "Oh. Of course. But I didn't expect them to be so hairy."

With a chuckle, he slid onto the bed beside her. "No more hairy than you are in the same place." And he put his hand right on her private part between her legs.

"Ohhhh," she said as she realized that their parts both mirrored and complemented each other's.

Then he began to rub her as she'd rubbed herself in bed, only much better, and everything went blank. "Jackson . . . heavens . . . *Jackson* . . . Is this one of those wicked things . . . you wanted to do with me?"

"Why?" His hand paused. "Does it bother you that I thought of touching you like this?"

"Certainly not. I thought of doing wicked things with *you*, too, you know. I imagined what it would be like to have you kissing me." Her voice lowered to a whisper. "Caressing me exactly like this, between the legs . . ."

Desire flamed in his face as he resumed his stroking. "Did you?" He rubbed her harder. "Like this?"

She arched up against his hand. "Oh, yes. Definitely . . . like that."

The devilish fellow smiled. "Where else did you imagine me touching you?"

"Oh, all over," she breathed.

"Perhaps here." He bent his head to suck her nipple, teasing it with his tongue until she gasped and threaded her fingers through his hair to hold him against her.

"Certainly there," she agreed as he lavished his attentions over first one breast, then the other.

Then he slid one finger inside her. "Or perhaps here," he murmured in his sinfully rough voice.

"My word!" she squeaked. "I never imagined *that*."

"*I* did," he said. "Plenty of times."

He dove deeply with his finger as his thumb moved in astonishing ways against a part of her that was aching and eager for his touch. Her breath shuddered out of her, her body rising up to meet his wicked, *wicked* hand.

"Lord help me, I had . . . *no* . . . idea." She squirmed, wanting more of that delicious feeling and feeling guilty that he was caressing her while she did nothing to please *him*. "When you thought of . . . wicked things . . . we could do, were there any . . . I could do to you?"

"Hell and blazes, yes." He shot her a heated glance, then took her hand and curled it around his aroused part. "Stroke me, sweeting." As she did so, his breath grew thick, heavy.

After only a few moments, he groaned, "Oh, God, stop . . . stop! Perhaps you'd better restrict your touching to . . . other parts of me."

"Didn't I do it right?" she whispered.

He uttered a harsh laugh. "Too well, I'm afraid. Some men need their pump primed, but mine has been primed for you so long . . ." He brushed a kiss over her breast. "Best not touch me there anymore, although you have free rein anywhere else."

After that, there were no words. He explored her; she explored him—his strong shoulders, his fine chest, the jaw she loved to kiss. She delighted in the feel of his flesh beneath her fingers, sinew and muscle dancing as he reacted to her touch. She adored that he couldn't hide how her caresses affected him. He was usually so controlled and hard to read. But she could read him here, in bed, and it made her heart soar.

So did the way he was caressing her, with firm, expert strokes, finding all the parts of her that yearned for him. She closed her eyes so she could relish every sensation, and soon she was breathing harder and harder, shimmying so wildly beneath his hand that she scarcely noticed he'd shifted to kneel between her legs until his hands drew her knees up and something bigger than a finger began easing up inside her.

Her eyes shot open. But just as she was feeling awkward and wondering if she looked as awkward as she felt, he murmured, "You're the most beautiful creature I ever beheld."

Instantly she relaxed. How did he always know the right thing to say? She ran her hands over his thick shoulders. "You're quite . . . attractive yourself, sir," she said, to take her mind off the thick flesh pressing up inside her.

"Don't mock me," he bit out.

"I'm not!" Was it possible *he* wasn't as sure of himself as he always seemed? "You must know you're handsome. I always thought so."

When gratification showed on his face, she was glad she'd said it.

He forged deeper, eyes alight with fierce hunger. "And I always thought you a goddess."

She eyed him skeptically. "Even when I tried your patience?"

"You tried my patience?" he quipped.

"You know I did."

Halting in his press inward, he turned solemn. "I'm afraid I'm about to try *your* patience, most sorely."

She gazed up at him, touched beyond words that he was being so gentle with her. Pulling his head down to her, she pressed a kiss to his lips, then whispered, "Make me yours. I can endure anything to be yours."

The words seemed to startle him, then make him grow even harder inside her, if that were possible. "We'll see," he murmured.

She had no time to register that odd response before he took her mouth. As he kissed her deeply, thoroughly, he thrust equally deeply inside her.

The swift pain made her gasp against his lips, but he just kept kissing her as he held still, letting her adjust to the tightness and the discomfort and the strange experience of being so closely joined to a man she still barely knew.

After a few moments he began moving, slowly at first, as if feeling his way along. He stared down at her with a searing gaze that made her stomach flip over. "Are you . . . all right?"

"Fine," she lied, though it still felt odd and uncomfortable to have him inside her. Fortunately, it was growing less so by the moment.

"I've imagined you like this . . . many times . . . naked, sharing my bed," he rasped, the fervent words warming her, making her relax. "You have no idea."

"I have *some* idea," she managed. "I imagined you, too."

He looked skeptical. "Like this?"

"Well, not exactly . . . I didn't know . . . what to expect." Or how shockingly intimate it would feel.

A lock of his dark hair fell over one eye, making him look more like a dangerous character and less like the formal Jackson she knew.

"And now that you do?" he asked.

"I like it." The motion had started to warm her below, to spark the same tingling she'd felt when he rubbed her. "It's like a very naughty waltz."

He choked out a laugh. "Yes. I lead. You follow."

You move between my legs.

Oh, so *that's* why people thought the waltz so scandalous! "I'll never be able to waltz again . . . without thinking of this," she breathed.

He bent to whisper, "Then I'll have to claim you for the next waltz."

She liked that word, *claim.*

"And the next . . . and the next . . ." He thrust more quickly into her and her tingling heightened, twisting into something hot and exciting and infinitely more thrilling than any waltz.

"Jackson . . . ohhh, *Jackson* . . ."

"Every waltz . . . from now . . . until eternity."

"Yes . . ." She felt as if she were spiraling upward, like sparks dancing up from the fire into the chimney and out, and now she was soaring, rising with him into the cloudless climes and starry skies where all the beauty walked. . . .

"Yes!" she cried as she reached that pinnacle. "Oh, yes, Jackson, yes . . . I'm yours . . . I'm yours . . . *yours* . . ."

And with a fierce groan, he drove in deep and spent himself inside her. "As am I . . ." he whispered against her ear while he shuddered and shook over her. "Yours. Always."

Chapter Nineteen

*H*etty and Oliver were having a brandy in his study before the guests began trooping down for dinner when Minerva entered, leading Celia's very anxious-looking maid.

"You have to hear what Gillie just told me," Minerva said, pushing the cowering maid forward. "I said she had to tell the two of you herself."

That roused Hetty's interest, since Celia had been conspicuously absent all day. "What is it, girl?"

When Gillie hesitated, Minerva said, "Celia does *not* have a headache. She has *not* been sleeping in her room all day with a dark cloth over her eyes."

Hetty burst into a laugh. "That is no surprise."

Gillie's gaze shot to Hetty's. "Beg your pardon, ma'am?"

"Come now, girl, I am no fool. I know your mistress cries 'headache' whenever she wants to shoot. I would have made her confess her subterfuge before now, but . . ." She let out a breath. "I grew tired of fighting her. I figured if I let her think she was fooling me, she might not be so stubborn about everything else."

"Well, *I* didn't know," Oliver said with a frown. "You could have told me."

"Would you have done anything about it?" Hetty asked.

"No, but—"

"She ain't come home, though," Gillie burst out.

Hetty's eyes narrowed. "What do you mean? She's usually back long before dark."

"Aye, that's what's got me worried, Mrs. Plumtree." Gillie wrung her hands. "She left right after dawn, and that ain't like her, either. She enjoys her sleep, she does. Then for her to be gone all day and into the evening . . ."

"Not to mention," Minerva put in, "that Mr. Pinter has been missing all day."

"Not missing," Oliver said. "He went off to follow some lead just after—"

"Dawn?" Minerva lifted an eyebrow. "Did he happen to say where he was going?"

A roiling began in Hetty's belly. "No. Just that it had something to do with Lewis's and Pru's murders."

"I suspect it had more to do with Celia," Minerva retorted.

Hetty began to suspect the same thing.

"Why?" Oliver asked.

"Last night," Minerva said, "Celia confessed that she and Mr. Pinter—or, as she calls him, Jackson—have been spending more time together alone than any of us realized. Apparently, they've kissed a number of times."

Hetty scowled. Matters had gone that far between them? And right under her nose?

"Good show, Pinter," Oliver murmured.

"Oliver!" Hetty chided him.

"What? It's plain as day that the two fancy each other. Thank God, they're finally doing something about it. Pinter probably took matters into his own hands and carried her off for a picnic or a drive, since they haven't had many chances to be alone together these past few days, with her other suitors around."

"Are you saying you have no problem with your sister spending an entire day alone with a man doing God knows what?" Hetty snapped.

"It's called courting." Oliver eyed her askance. "Don't tell me you disapprove. You've been trying to get her to marry for years. She finally has a suitor she really seems to like, and I for one applaud her."

"What if marriage is not what he has in mind?" Hetty spat, annoyed that her grandson could just gloss over the fact that Celia might be out there engaging in naughty activities with the Bow Street Runner.

"Don't be ridiculous. Pinter is an honorable man. He wouldn't ruin her."

"I don't think he's trying to, anyway," Minerva said slyly. "I think they've eloped."

"What!" Hetty said. "Why would you think that?"

Gillie jumped in to protest, "The miss would have said something to me if she were running off with a gentleman. I don't think—"

"Did she tell you that Mr. Pinter had been kissing her?" Minerva asked.

Gillie looked troubled. "Well, no, but—"

"I rest my case," Minerva said.

"I said 'no elopements,'" Hetty snapped.

"You were ready to waive that requirement for Gabe," Oliver pointed out. "I don't see why you can't do it for Celia."

She glared at him. "Are you blind, Oliver? Has it not occurred to you that Mr. Pinter might want to marry your sister for her fortune?"

"Oh, for God's sake, not Pinter."

His vehement defense of the man took her aback. She knew that Oliver liked the fellow, but she had not guessed how much.

Could Oliver be right about Mr. Pinter's character? Isaac seemed to agree with him. And she *had* warned the man that she would cut Celia off if he pursued her. So an elopement might mean he did not care about Celia's fortune.

On the other hand, it could mean he did not believe Hetty would actually hold to her threat. Or . . .

Another awful possibility leapt into Hetty's mind. "Oh, God. I am such a fool."

"Well, we all agree on that," Oliver said dryly.

She ignored her impudent grandson, caught up in a new concern. By threatening Mr. Pinter, she had thought to force him into revealing his true feelings. But what if the Bow Street Runner had simply decided to go around her? If he carried Celia off and did *not* marry her right away, it would force Hetty into having to consent to a marriage on *his* terms. Which meant she would have to give him Celia's inheritance if she wanted to save the girl's reputation.

Of course, there was always the possibility that he was really in love, and they were running off together because of Hetty's attempts to separate them.

She shook off that disturbing thought. Snatching the girl from her family in this secretive manner was not the behavior of a man in love. Not an honorable one, anyway. "Mr. Pinter might have a more devious reason for carrying Celia off than any of us have even considered. If you only knew—"

"If we only knew what?" Oliver asked, eyes narrowing.

Oh dear. She could not reveal to Oliver and Minerva what she had threatened Mr. Pinter with. One of them might tell Celia, and the girl would get all up in arms about it, without seeing how Hetty's scheme could elicit the truth.

"Mr. Pinter lied to my face about his involvement with Celia," she said stoutly. "He denied they had any interest in each other, all the while courting her behind my back. What is worse, he encouraged Celia to lie, too, for she reiterated his claim. That is not the action of an honorable man."

Minerva scowled. "You'll never convince me that the staid and upright Mr. Pinter would behave in such a scurrilous fashion."

"Nor me," Oliver said. "Besides, we are leaping to wild conclusions here. They may not be together at all. Celia may have forgotten the time and be even now trudging home in the darkness while Pinter is off on his expedition."

Hetty's pulse quieted a little. "Perhaps," she conceded. "In which case, all this speculation is for naught."

"Someone should head out to wherever it is Celia goes to shoot." Oliver glanced at Gillie. "Do you know where it might be?"

"I'm afraid not, sir. I never go with her when she shoots."

"Damn. Well, our first order of business is to find it. Then, if she's not there, we should search the estate. Gillie, check her room, make sure she didn't leave behind a note about where she was going to be or even about an elopement. Take Minerva with you."

As the two women headed for the door, Hetty called out, "Wait! Before we get our guests in an uproar over Celia's absence, perhaps we should handle this more discreetly."

Oliver crossed his arms over his chest. "What do you mean?"

"If she has *not* eloped with Mr. Pinter and there is no real cause for alarm, I do not want her potential suitors reconsidering their interest in her. Celia is the one who requested that they be invited to this affair. I assume she had a reason."

She's trying to gain a husband so precipitously only because you're forcing her to.

Ruthlessly, she pushed Mr. Pinter's words from her mind—she still had no idea what his motives were, and until she did, she could not trust what he said. "The duke is on the verge of offering for her, from what I understand," she continued, "and I would not want to ruin that for some idle speculation."

Though Minerva blinked at that, she conceded the point with a nod. "Perhaps Gran is right—we *should* proceed with caution. I'd hate to see Celia forced to marry Mr. Pinter out of some misapprehension, the way I was forced to marry Giles."

Oliver eyed her askance. "There was no 'misapprehension' involved in your wedding, my dear. You were caught lying half-naked in Masters's arms. You're lucky I didn't shoot the scoundrel right then and there. And you didn't seem too reluctant to marry him, either, as I recall."

Minerva sniffed. "That isn't the point. I just think we should be careful about alarming Celia's suitors until we're sure of what has happened. I suppose she might actually wish to wed one of them."

A sigh escaped Oliver. "You may be right." He thought a moment, then said, "Very well, here is what we'll do. Gran will tell everyone that my wife is in early labor. Since Maria has been resting all afternoon, no one has seen her, so that should be believable. Gran will say that I think it best that everyone go into town for an evening at the theater and a late supper. That will keep them out of our way. Isaac and Gran can be in charge of entertaining them in town."

"But I want to be here!" Gran protested.

"There's nothing you can do here but fret. In fact, Minerva should go with you." Overriding Minerva's protests, he went on firmly, "Keep our guests busy while we do our searching, and bring them home late. They'll sleep until noon, and if by then we haven't heard or found anything, we'll send everyone home."

"Why don't we just send them home now?" Minerva asked.

"Because it will take them time to pack up, and we won't be able to search during that time without their noticing."

Gran sighed. "True."

Oliver began to pace. He was always in his element during emergencies. "I wish we knew where Pinter had headed."

"John might know," Gran said. "He spoke to Mr. Pinter at length last night."

After ringing the bell for John, Oliver turned his attention to Gillie. "Go search Celia's room for notes. You can start that now—no one will see it." As Gillie headed for the door, he said, "But first, explain to Maria why she mustn't leave her room. Then send Jarret and Gabe down here, will you?"

He went to the window to look out and scowled. "Gabe and Jarret can search the estate, although it's going to take some time by lantern light with no moon. If we're lucky, Gabe might know where Celia goes to shoot. We'll involve the servants only if we have to. We don't want them talking to our guests' servants about what's going on."

John entered just then. "My lord, you wanted to see me?"

"Do you know where Mr. Pinter was headed today?"

"No, sir. He requested a list of former servants and their addresses a few days ago, and I got him confirmed information last night. He didn't say which servant he planned on visiting, though."

"But he did say he was visiting one today?" Gran prodded.

"Actually, no. He just took the list and thanked me." John brightened. "But perhaps one of the stable boys will know."

"Even if he told them, he could have lied," Gran pointed out. "Especially if he had designs on . . ." She cast a furtive glance at John. "Especially if he wanted to hide his true purpose."

With a roll of his eyes, Oliver dismissed John, then turned to Hetty. "You credit Pinter with more deviousness than I. Let's assume, for the moment, that he told the truth. If we can't learn from the servants where he headed, Giles and I will go to town and talk to Pinter's clerk and his aunt. One of them might know. He might even have returned home by now."

"Wouldn't he have come here first?" Gran pointed out.

"Not if he was hot on the heels of a lead in the case," Oliver drawled. "But now you've got me curious—what exactly do you have against Pinter that makes you so dead set against him for Celia?"

The sudden shift in subject took her off guard. "Nothing, I swear!" As Oliver continued to stare skeptically at her, she said, "I happen to know a bit about the man, that's all. And I've seen many of his kind through the years try to better themselves by—"

"Marrying above themselves?" Oliver said in a hard voice. "Like Mother?"

Hetty colored. "Your mother loved your father, no matter what else you might think about her. And though she was beneath him in rank, I made sure she was well-educated and had every advantage to make her a suitable wife to a marquess. While Mr. Pinter, until he was ten—"

"I know his history as well as you apparently do, Gran," Oliver broke in. "Did you think I hired the man without finding out everything about him first?"

She blinked. She had indeed thought that.

"No matter what his childhood," Oliver went on, "he has spent twenty-odd years making something of himself while we five sat on our arses mourning our parents. He had more to mourn than any of us, yet he worked hard to get where he is today." He stared her down. "I admire that. And I think that Celia could do a great deal worse than to marry Jackson Pinter."

Gran sniffed. "Well then, I only hope you are right about his character."

Oliver gave her a pitying smile. "And I hope one day you can see it as clearly as I." He came over to pat her on the shoulder. "Truthfully, I'm more worried about Pinter right now than I am about Celia. If they did decide to elope, it was probably at *her* instigation. Knowing my sister, they're already halfway to Gretna Green, and the poor man is beginning to regret he ever saw her."

Though his words were joking, Gran could hear the worry underlying his light tone.

Well, at least he was taking this seriously. And if anyone could find two runaway lovers and stop them before they did anything drastic, it was her grandson.

* * *

JACKSON LAY NEXT to Celia, perfectly content. With his body wrapped about hers, he scarcely noticed the chill in the room. He scarcely noticed anything but the fact that she was in his arms, naked, and that he'd finally made her his.

She was dozing now, but he didn't mind. In repose she lowered her guard and truly became the sprite he sometimes imagined her to be—with a half smile on her lips and her hair pouring over her shoulders like night rivers of gossamer silk.

With a soft sigh, she cuddled against him, and his heart flipped over in his chest.

The visceral response alarmed him. She might have agreed to become his wife, but matters were by no means settled. People did and said things in the heat of desire that they regretted on the morn, especially people whose lives were tied to great fortunes and age-old family connections.

She doesn't care about any of that.

Perhaps not. And perhaps if he and Celia could stay here forever, just the two of them in this cottage alone, making love and lying in each other's arms, they could make the rest of the world disappear. But they couldn't stay here. Aside from the murderers lurking about, there was her family to consider. They must be frantic, wondering what had happened to her, not realizing she was with him.

Once they did, would they be grateful that he meant to marry her? Or would they refuse to allow it? He had no idea what to expect. If he'd learned anything from his mother's tragic life, it was that the aristocracy had its own rules.

He wanted to think that the Sharpes were different, that they would support a marriage between him and Celia, but how could he be sure? He hadn't thought Mrs. Plumtree would oppose it, yet she had.

He sighed. Should he tell Celia that she might be cut off if she married him? That she might have to give up her comfortable life entirely?

No, how could he? It might prove an idle threat, and he would have caused a rift between her and her grandmother for nothing. If Mrs. Plumtree meant to cut Celia off, let her tell Celia herself. Then it wouldn't be on his head to explain to Celia why she was about to lose her fortune by marrying him.

Still, he needed to make sure she understood what marrying so far beneath her station might mean, fortune or no fortune. Her friends might abandon her. Her *family* might do so.

Celia might not want to endure that simply because he hadn't been able to keep his prick in his trousers for one night.

He gazed down at her. Ah, but he hoped she would. Marriage to Celia would be . . .

But he mustn't let himself hope for it too much. Not yet. He'd spent his childhood hoping for his father to return to save Mother and him and to claim him as a son, and all he'd gained was a childhood of private pain.

He was never putting himself through that again. Better to protect his heart. There would be plenty of time to lay it open for her when—*if*—he and Celia were married and joined for life.

But no matter what happened on the morrow, he would *never* regret having had this night with her.

She shivered in her sleep, and he realized that he, too, was growing colder. He left the bed to fetch her cloak and his surtout. When he returned, she was awake and watching him with a sleepy gaze.

"Did I doze off?" she asked as he climbed back in the bed.

"Yes." He spread the warm garments over them. "I imagine you got about as little sleep as I did last night."

"Less, probably. You left the ball early. I stayed up late talking to Minerva."

As she turned over to face him, the surtout slipped a little. He pulled it back into place, and the brandy flask in his pocket bumped his hand. After retrieving it, he offered her some.

She sipped the liquor, then smiled up at him and handed him the flask. "Do you know I've never had brandy before today?"

"I should hope not." He took a long swig. "Fine ladies do not drink brandy." Or share the beds of unrepentant bastards.

"That's a pity, if you ask me," she said cheerily as she snagged the flask and swallowed more. "I'm finding it most warming." She gulped more still. "Invigorating, even."

Her eyes were brighter now, and her cheeks flushed.

Uh oh. Bad enough that he'd ruined her. He was not going to get her drunk, too.

He took the flask from her. "That's enough brandy for you."

"Why?" She snuggled up close to him with a fetching pout. "No one will know."

"I will. And trust me, you'll regret it in the morning if you drink too much tonight."

She made a face at him. "I see that Proper Pinter has returned."

"Beg pardon?"

Mischief shone in her eyes. "That's how I thought of you whenever you lectured me. Proper Pinter, hoity-toity and high in the instep."

He lifted an eyebrow. "You can call me that after what we just did?"

"Why not?" She stretched and spread her arms in a wide arc above her head. "I feel quite delightful, and you're trying to spoil it."

With her breasts peeking out from beneath their improvised blanket, she looked like a goddess, inciting her subjects to riot in wild debauchery.

He shook his head ruefully. "I suppose I am."

Which is why he would save their serious discussion about marriage for the morrow. Besides, he didn't like being thought of as "Proper Pinter." He supported his head on one hand to gaze down into her lovely face. "Have you always called me 'Proper Pinter'? Or is this recent?"

"Ever since we met. Though not so much anymore."
She flashed him a coquettish smile. "After you kissed me,
I realized just how improper you could be."

"I can be downright scandalous when I want," he murmured, bending to give her a long, thorough kiss.

When he drew back, she looked pensive. "I don't suppose this was your first . . . well . . . intimate encounter."

"No. But neither have I had a hundred, like your
brothers."

"A hundred!" She looked horrified. "So many?"

He shouldn't have said that. "I'm probably exaggerating."

She thought a moment, then sighed. "Probably not.
They were awful rogues until they married." She gazed
up at him with an earnest expression. "Perhaps 'proper'
isn't so bad after all."

"I can think of worse nicknames," he said, remembering the wide variety of epithets flung at him in his youth.

"At least nobody ever called you Elf."

She looked so delightfully put out that he couldn't help
but chuckle. "How on earth did that come about, anyway?"

"I honestly don't know." She rested her head on her
hand. "Papa said it was because I had pointy ears, which
is nonsense, of course. And Nurse said it was because I
was small. But all children are small."

He gazed down at her pixie nose and the pensive expression on her heart-shaped face. "I have a theory."

"Oh?"

"Sometimes, when you're deep in thought, you have
an otherworldly look about you that makes one think of
creatures from another realm—sprites and dryads and

nymphs. I imagine it did make you look a bit like an elf when you were small."

She eyed him skeptically. "I don't look like an elf now, do I? Because I should warn you that no one in my family has been allowed to call me Elf in many years, upon pain of death. And I'm not rescinding that for you."

"Then I'll call you Fairy Queen. That's what you look like to me."

She cast him a dazzling smile. "You do give excellent compliments, Jackson. It quite redeems your other sins."

"And what sins are those?" he drawled.

"Being condescending. Hiding your true feelings." Eyes sparkling, she pulled his head down to hers. "Taking months and months in getting around to kissing me."

"I must have been mad," he murmured before kissing her again.

This time it led to more kisses, then caresses . . . the hot, sweet sort that set his blood aflame. Though he protested that she must be too sore to make love, she ignored him and did her best to rouse him to madness.

So he ensured she was rapt with enjoyment beneath him before he entered her again, plunging so deeply into her warmth that he thought he might perish of the pleasure.

It was only long afterward, as she lay asleep in his arms, that he realized he'd already stopped protecting his heart.

And that wouldn't do. Because if he weren't careful, he could easily find it trampled beneath the boots of the Sharpe family fortune.

Chapter Twenty

Celia was freezing. She pulled the oddly thick blanket over her bare shoulders just as she heard someone stoking up a fire nearby.

"Gillie," she muttered. "Put an extra log on, will you?"

"Not Gillie," said a man's voice, sounding vaguely irritated. "No servants here, I'm afraid. You'll have to settle for me."

She bolted upright, jerking the blanket to her chest as several things hit her at once. She wasn't in her own bed. She was naked. And Jackson stood a few feet away, wearing only a pair of drawers, an unbuttoned shirt, and a frown.

Everything from the night before came back to her—the race through the woods, the discovery of the cottage . . . the lovemaking.

Heat flooded her cheeks at that last memory.

He seemed to notice, for his expression softened before he picked up his pistol and began to clean it. The last time she'd seen it, it was loaded. When had he emptied it? And how long had he been up, anyway?

"Go back to sleep," he murmured. "There's still an hour before dawn. I'll wake you when it's closer to time to leave."

Was the man daft? Did he really think she could sleep while he walked about the cottage preparing for their escape from unknown assailants?

Apparently, he did. But since she couldn't oblige him, she shifted to her side to watch him work.

He was swift and efficient, rather like a soldier must be. In minutes, he had the pistol cleaned and shining before he loaded it with fresh, dry powder and a patch-wrapped ball. Then he packed up his gun kit and tucked it into one saddlebag before pulling out a stiff brush.

In the process, something fell from the bag, which he picked up, opening it to stare at it. From where she lay, it looked like a watch, but he was gazing at it too long for that.

Curiosity got the better of her. "What is it?"

He started, then carried the object over. She sat up, keeping his surtout tucked up around her breasts as he handed it to her. It was a rather large locket on a fob. When she opened it, she found three portrait miniatures, one of which was affixed to a metal leaf in the middle so that the first portrait sat alone and the second sat opposite the third.

"Uncle had them done by an artist friend of his after Mother and I went to live with him and Aunt Ada in London twenty-two years ago." Jackson pointed to the first image, of a pale and fragile young woman with dark hair and a wan smile. "That's Mother."

She stared at it, her heart in her throat. "She was beautiful."

"She was indeed." His voice grew choked. "Although less so in this portrait. She was already ill by the time this was done."

Hoping to lighten his mood, she looked at the other portrait, as blond as the first was dark, with merry eyes. "And this is your aunt, I take it?"

A faint smile touched his lips. "Yes. With my uncle opposite."

She stared at his uncle, a handsome man in his youth. "You look like him."

"That's impossible," he said dryly. "He's not my uncle by blood, remember? He married my mother's sister."

"Oh, right. I forgot." She gazed closely at the portrait. The man was slighter in build, but . . . "I still say you look like him."

Jackson's gaze narrowed on the portrait. Then he cast her a cold glance. "Don't be ridiculous. There's no resemblance at all."

"I grant you, his hair is arranged differently, but see there, where his nose is thin like yours, and his eyes are deeply set? And he has your jaw."

A strange look crossed his face, before he took the locket and snapped it shut. "He doesn't look like me. It's absurd—no one else has ever noticed any such thing."

As he headed back to the saddlebag with the locket, his back stiff, it dawned on her what he must have thought she was saying. Oh, dear. She hadn't been implying . . . She would never hint . . .

Oh, well. Best to leave that alone now. Any apology she could offer would only make it worse.

And clearly she didn't want to do that—he was now in quite a temper. Picking up the brush, he went to work on his muddy boots as if his life depended on making them shine.

"Would you like me to do that?" she asked.

"Have you ever cleaned boots before?"

"Well, no, but how hard can it be? I don't mind helping."

A shuttered look crossed his face, and his brushing grew positively manic. "Don't worry about it. I've done it every day of my life for the past twenty-five years, and I imagine I'll be doing it every day for the next thirty or more, God willing."

Oh, dear, Proud Pinter had shown up with a vengeance this morning. She was surprised he hadn't called her "my lady" yet.

"Don't you have servants at all?" she asked.

"Not to help me dress," he said in a hard tone as he brushed madly at his boots. "Men like me don't have valets. That probably won't change if . . . *when* we marry."

Had he really said "if"? Had it been a slip of the tongue borne of not being used to the thought? Or something else?

It set her on edge. And made her determined to banish Proud Pinter. "And why should you have a valet when you already know how to clean boots so well?" she quipped. "I do hope you're as good with lady's boots. I prefer mine brushed with horse hair, but if you insist on whatever you're using there, I suppose I can tolerate it."

He lifted a stern gaze to her, though he kept brushing. "You find this amusing, I take it."

"No, indeed," she said lightly. "What I find amusing is the idea of a Bow Street Runner taking a valet on his travels. Any decent valet would bemoan the damage to your hat every time someone took a shot at you. That could get annoying."

A smile tugged at his lips. "Perhaps a trifle, yes."

"And just imagine how he would despair over the effect that wind has on your cravat. Not to mention how gunpowder might stain your shirt cuffs."

He chuckled, then seemed to catch himself and turn pensive again. Setting his boots down, he fixed her with an earnest stare. "All joking aside, I should tell you that my daily life differs little from my traveling life."

"Oh?" she said, determined to keep the conversation light. "Cheapside must be quite poverty-stricken. You sleep on bug-ridden mattresses and eat poor meals every day, do you?"

He eyed her askance. "What I mean is, I have to fend for myself most of the time, not only when I travel, but at home. No one stokes up the fire before I rise or trims my quills or makes fanciful creatures out of sugar paste to decorate my birthday cakes. My few servants—"

"Ah, so you *do* have servants. I began to wonder how you had time to be a Bow Street Runner when you must always be washing your own clothes, cooking your own food, and possibly even constructing your own cabinets and weaving your own rugs."

He glowered at her. "This is all a joke to you."

"Oh, no," she said, turning as sober as he. "Not in the least. So tell me, *do* you have servants?"

"Yes," he bit out. "A maid-of-all-work, a cook, and a footboy."

"And a coachman?"

"I hire one for trips. Why?"

"I was remembering that you used your own equipage to transport Gabe and Minerva to Burton for Gran last spring."

A muscle worked in his jaw. "I do own a small traveling coach that I keep at a livery," he said almost defensively. "It was my uncle's. But in London, I travel by horse or hackney. Or I walk."

"I'm a grand walker myself," she said defiantly.

A snort escaped him. "Is that why you rode Lady Bell a mile to go shooting?" He strode over to finish packing up the saddlebags.

She frowned. "I had my lunch and my smock and gun kit and a pair of dueling pistols in my saddlebags, in addition to the rifle stuck in a saddle holster. So no, I didn't attempt to carry it all a mile."

"My point is . . ."

"I know what your point is. That you don't live as well as my family does. That being your wife will mean giving up some things." She stared him down. "I don't care." There. Let him weasel out of that one.

"You say that now, but you've never had to live without a hundred servants, meals prepared by a French cook and served on silver and china, and all of it in the confines of either a very spacious London town house or a three-hundred-and-sixty-five-room mansion."

"Well, I can hardly deny *that*," she said, her temper rising. "But it doesn't mean I'm incapable of doing without it all."

Taking her chemise from where he'd apparently hooked it by the fire the night before, he walked up to the bed and handed it to her. "You've never had to make do with only a couple of shifts and a small assortment of gowns. You're used to expensive jewelry, to silk and satin, with lace dripping from every delicate thing you own."

"Your aunt was wearing lace in that portrait," she pointed out. "And I would guess that her bonnet cost nearly as much as mine."

"Perhaps, but it's her Sunday best." He gestured to Celia's bonnet with a jerk of his hand. "*That* is what you wore to go *shooting*. You wouldn't even wear it to ride to town, I daresay."

The fact that he was right didn't mitigate her temper any. "What is the point of this lecture, Jackson? Have you changed your mind about marrying me?"

"No!" The vehemence in that one word soothed her hurt a little. He ran his fingers through his hair, then softened his tone. "Of course I want to marry you. I just want to make sure that you know what you're getting into."

Leaving the bed, she drew on her chemise, then began to dress. "You seem to forget that once we marry, I'll inherit a fortune. Granted, it won't buy a three-hundred-and-sixty-five-room mansion, but it ought to make us tolerably comfortable. And when you become Chief Magistrate—"

"That appointment is by no means certain." His eyes darkened as she wriggled into her drawers. "As for your fortune, I . . . um . . . there's . . ."

His voice trailed off as she sat down on the bed and pulled on one stocking, then tied her garter around it. She noticed how his gaze fixed on the bit of thigh she let show above the garter. In a burst of defiance, she donned her other stocking with excruciating slowness. Might as well remind him how they had come to this pass in the first place.

When his breath sharpened and he flexed his hands at his sides as if resisting the urge to grab her and kiss her senseless, she reveled in it.

"Yes? You were saying?" she taunted him. "Something about my fortune?"

His gaze snapped to her face, then turned stormy. "That is by no means certain either."

"Why not?"

He pulled on his own clothes with jerky movements that betrayed his agitation almost as much as did the bulge in his drawers. "Your grandmother might not approve of the marriage. She might decide not to give you your portion."

"Don't be ridiculous. Gran would never do such a thing." She stood to don her corset. "Her rule was that we had to marry, and she made it quite clear that she didn't care whom we married as long as we did so within the year."

Walking up behind her, he began to lace her up. "Let's say, for the sake of argument, that she changed her mind." His voice was harsh, labored. "Suppose she decides that she doesn't approve of me. Suppose she refuses to give you your fortune if you defy her. What then?"

A knot formed in her belly. Did the money matter so much to him? "Then we don't have her fortune. I told you. I don't care."

"That's what you said." His tone was flat, tense.

Feeling a growing chill in her belly, she drew on her gown so he could fasten that up, too. "You don't believe me."

He was silent for so long as he buttoned her up that it made her chest hurt. "I don't believe you know what living without all that would mean."

She whirled on him. She'd had enough of his condescension and his behaving as if he were now going to be stuck with some spoiled wife who couldn't survive in his world—a perfectly genteel world, from what she could tell. "If you want to get out of marrying me, Jackson—"

"That isn't what I'm saying."

"It certainly sounds that way." She shoved her feet into her half boots, then clapped her bonnet on her head, heedless of the fact that her hair was down and her hair pins were probably scattered to the four winds. "It's dawn. We'd better go."

He glanced toward the door, saw the gray light seeping in around the edges, then let out a low curse. "Yes, we'd better."

As she pulled on her gloves, he poured the remains of the pail of water over the fire, then took his coat from the window and his surtout from the bed and donned them both.

When he came toward her with her cloak and she tried to snatch it from him, he wouldn't let her. Instead, he laid it about her shoulders and began to tie it just as she had helped him with his surtout the night before.

Seething over his superior manner and his hints about her spoiled life, she refused to look at him.

With a muttered curse, he tipped up her chin and forced her to gaze into his eyes. "I'm merely trying to make sure that you take this seriously. That you know what you're about to get if you marry me."

There it was again. *If* you marry me. "Oh, believe me," she snapped, "I'm beginning to realize exactly what I'm about to get."

Proud and Proper Pinter all the time. Days of being made to feel guilty about coming from a family of privilege and fortune, punctuated with a few glorious nights of lovemaking.

Tears stung her eyes, and she pulled away from him, not wanting him to notice.

As she started for the door, he caught her by the shoulder. "Let me go first. There's probably a path to the road that was used by the poachers, but we can't be sure if anyone's lying in wait for us along it, so we need to move quickly and quietly. No talking. Stay as close behind me as you can, hold onto my coat, and be prepared to run if I say. Understood?"

"Yes." She wasn't so angry at him that she would ignore the danger they might find themselves in.

He opened the door, but before walking out, he turned and took her mouth in a long, heated kiss. When he drew back, his expression was a mix of need and frustration. "I will never let anyone hurt you. You know that, don't you?"

No one but yourself, you mean, she nearly said. Instead, she nodded.

"You trust me?"

"Of course." She trusted him to keep her safe, at least.

He nodded, then headed out the door with her at his heels. True to his competence as a Bow Street Runner, within moments he found a path she would never have noticed and started them down it.

As she followed him in utter silence, she replayed their conversation. Was she wrong to be so upset? He was a practical man, after all. She should add that to the list: Practical, Proper, and Proud Pinter. Everything that she was not.

Well, perhaps she had a *little* of his pride. She'd certainly found plenty when he was making her sound like some lofty lady who couldn't live without "fanciful creatures of sugar paste" to decorate her birthday cake.

She might not have minded that so much if he'd said he loved her, but love still hadn't entered the conversation.

You didn't say you loved him either.

No. Even though she did. Most awfully.

She groaned. When had that happened? When he'd saved her life? Or responded to her embarrassing revelations about Ned by threatening to shoot the man and then calling her a fairy queen? Or had it occurred when he was making love to her with such tenderness that she would never forget the glory of it?

Oh, it didn't matter when it had happened. She loved him. Despite his pride and his lectures and his determination to make her feel like a worthless aristocrat, she'd fallen in love with the wretched fellow.

But after everything he'd said, she'd be damned if she told him. If he wanted her love, he would have to make that clear. Right now, all he seemed to want was her body. And possibly her hand in marriage, though she wasn't even sure about *that* at the moment.

Still, last night he'd said he was hers always. If he'd meant it—and she had no reason to believe he didn't—then surely they could muddle through this together. That was close to a declaration of love, wasn't it?

It wasn't as if they'd have a choice anyway. Gran was going to make them marry.

That thought cheered her. Yes, they would have to marry. So he would just have to learn to deal with her fortune and her rank and her lack of ability to do without "silks and satins" and lace on her gowns.

And perhaps in the midst of all that, he could find a way to love her, too.

To Jackson's relief, they reached the road without incident. No doubt Celia's assailant had moved on once they had vanished. But that didn't mean they were out of danger—just that they were out of danger at the moment.

"Since we seem to be all right," Celia murmured as they began walking down the road, "do you think we could go back and check on Lady Bell?"

"That's unwise," Jackson said. "Whoever tried to kill you might anticipate just such an action and even now be lying in wait for you there."

"Oh. I hadn't thought of that. And what about *your* horse?"

He sighed. "If no one steals him between here and London, he'll make it to Cheapside well enough."

"I hope Lady Bell survived," she said wistfully.

"As soon as we reach the estate, we'll send someone back for her, I swear." He had his doubts about whether Lady Bell had made it but didn't voice them. Celia had enough to worry about at the moment.

Like his sobering pronouncements in the cottage. All right, so perhaps he'd done it up a bit too brown, but he wanted her going into marriage with open eyes. He wanted no recriminations when he couldn't live up to her expectations.

Yet her words stuck in his memory: *I know what your point is. That you don't live as well as my family does. That being your wife will mean giving up some things. I don't care.*

She said that now, but she might not feel the same later. *Have you changed your mind about marrying me?*

That made him wince. He didn't want to leave her with that fear. "Celia," he murmured, "about our earlier discussion . . ."

"You made yourself very clear. I'm not sure there's much more to say."

"Ah, but there is." He caught her gloved hand in his. "I do mean to marry you, you know. I would never abandon you now that . . . well . . ."

"I'm ruined?" she said dryly. "How kind of you."

"That's not what I meant, damn it."

"Of course it is. You're an honorable man, and honorable men behave honorably when they've ruined a woman. Whether or not they want to."

That fired his temper. "Now see here, I never said I didn't want to marry you. I certainly never—" He broke off at the sound of horses on the road, then hurried her into the woods.

"What the dev—"

"Shh," he muttered, placing his fingers over her mouth. "Someone's coming."

Her eyes went wide as she glanced to the road. They both held their breaths until a lumbering wagon came into view, drawn by two cart horses and driven by a skinny farmer with a pipe clenched between his teeth and a floppy beaver hat on his graying head.

Immediately, Jackson drew her back out onto the side of the road, then left her so he could step into the path of the oncoming wagon, waving his hands.

"Whoa!" cried the man as he pulled up on the reins. As soon as the horses halted, the farmer stood up on the wagon. "Are ye mad? I could've run ye down!"

Then he caught sight of Celia and blinked. "Beg pardon, madam." He tugged at his hat brim. "I didn't see you standing there."

Jackson forced a smile, hoping to look less alarming to

a stranger. "My wife and I were robbed by highwaymen last night, sir, and we could use your help."

The farmer eyed him suspiciously. "Highwaymen? On *this* road?"

Celia came to his side and curled her hand about his arm. "They shot my horse, and we ran into the woods to escape being shot ourselves. You didn't happen to see a dead horse as you came this way, did you?"

"No, but I heard tell of a horse found wounded in the shoulder when an early coach drove past. I believe they sent someone from town to look after it."

Celia sagged against Jackson. "Thank God."

"It's urgent that we go on to our destination," Jackson said. "If you'd be so kind as to let us ride with you as far as you're going . . ."

"I'm headed for the market in Ealing," the farmer said. "But I got a wagon full of apples, and there ain't no room back there for people, so—"

"There's ten pounds in it for you." Jackson drew out his purse and shook it until the coins clinked. "We ran off before the highwaymen could get it."

That changed the man's demeanor entirely. "Ten pounds will buy you a seat on the perch with me, it will," the man said cheerily. "Hell, ten pounds will buy you a seat and the apple cake me missus sent with me." He held up the pipe. "Not to mention a drag on this if you're so inclined."

Jackson fought a grimace. "Thank you, but seats on your perch will be quite enough."

It was only after they were settled next to the farmer that Jackson realized he couldn't carry on his discussion with Celia in front of the farmer who thought they were already married. That would have to wait until they were alone.

But they got no chance to be alone. When the farmer discovered that they were headed for Halstead Hall, he insisted upon bringing them through Ealing and right to the manor.

So that's how it happened that they rode up the drive to Halstead Hall midmorning with a wagon full of apples and a farmer who was eager to see, as he put it, "that place what's as big as a town."

Servants came running before they even reached the house. To Jackson's surprise, there was no sign of the Sharpe brothers, whom he'd expected to be out riding the estate looking for her.

Instead, Mrs. Plumtree herself and Mrs. Masters met them at the entrance to the manor.

"Are you married?" Mrs. Plumtree asked in a hard voice after Jackson had paid the wide-eyed farmer and sent him off happy.

"Not yet," Celia said, looking as confused as he felt.

"So you ran off to get married and then changed your mind, is that it?" Mrs. Masters asked.

"We didn't elope," Jackson said. "Someone tried to shoot Celia. We hid in the forest all night to elude them."

Mrs. Masters cried, "Good Lord!" while Mrs. Plumtree took control of the situation, hurrying them through the archway and ordering the servants to go fetch Lord Jarret and Lord Gabriel from the fields.

"Where are Oliver and Mr. Masters?" Celia asked her sister as they headed across the Crimson Courtyard.

"In London, attempting to discover what happened to Mr. Pinter," Mrs. Masters explained. "After you and I had our discussion night before last, I thought perhaps . . ." She cast Jackson a furtive glance. "We assumed that you had eloped."

That must have been quite the discussion. He would give anything to know what the two women had said.

Just then, Devonmont wandered out into the courtyard. "Ah, I was wondering where everyone was. Gone out shooting early, did you, Pinter?"

"Yes," Mrs. Plumtree said quickly, "Mr. Pinter was shooting, and Minerva and Celia went out to fetch him for breakfast."

"So your headache is better today, is it?" Devonmont asked Celia without a hint of suspicion.

What the bloody devil? Had none of her suitors noticed they were gone?

"Much better, thank you," Celia mumbled.

"If you're headed for breakfast, I'll join you," Devonmont said and offered Celia his arm.

"You go on," Mrs. Plumtree said quickly. "Mr. Pinter and the girls saw something suspicious on the grounds while they were out, so I need to talk to them about it a moment. They'll be in shortly."

That made Devonmont's eyes narrow, but apparently he knew better than to gainsay Mrs. Plumtree. With a shrug, he walked off toward the breakfast room.

They headed for Stoneville's study.

"What's going on, Gran?" Celia asked. "Why doesn't anyone seem to know we've been gone?"

"Don't you see, my lady?" Jackson said cynically as the truth dawned. "Your grandmother has managed to cover up our absence. She has apparently worked out a way to unruin you."

Celia glanced from him to her grandmother, incredulous. "You kept it entirely secret?"

Mrs. Plumtree shot him a dark look. "We'll discuss it once we reach a more private place, my dear."

Jackson snorted. And so began the undoing of his foolish hopes for a life with Celia. Mrs. Plumtree was determined to make sure they didn't marry. Which meant she would probably hold to her threats to cut Celia off.

Damn the woman to hell.

Now what? Should he reveal that he'd taken Celia's innocence?

Then he really *would* appear the devil in sheep's clothing, out to wrangle a marriage to Celia however he could. Besides, how could he embarrass her like that? She would never want her family to know what he and she had done; of that he was certain, given how she'd hidden Ned's near deflowering of her.

But neither did Jackson mean to abandon her. He was *not* going to behave like his father, refusing to be responsible for his actions.

If the tale he'd always believed about his father was even true. Jackson winced, remembering what Celia had said. . . .

No, she was wrong. He didn't resemble his uncle. No one else had ever said so. His father was some damned nobleman who'd ruined his mother. And Jackson wasn't going to follow in his footsteps by refusing to marry her.

But what if that's what Celia wants—freedom to marry whom she pleases?

His throat tightened. Now that she'd been saved the ignominy of being ruined, it might be exactly what she would want.

Even if she thought it wasn't, it might be best. The duke might marry her regardless—he only wanted a wife who wouldn't mind his family's madness. And though she said she didn't care about the money, how could she possibly understand the ramifications of losing her fortune? She had nothing to compare it to. Did he have the right to expect her to give it all up for him?

They entered his lordship's well-appointed study, with its Rembrandts and crystal brandy decanters and its mahogany and brass furnishings, and hopelessness swept over him. This was where she belonged, not in some cramped home in Cheapside, no matter how cheery and warm *he* found it.

"Now, Mr. Pinter," Mrs. Plumtree said, "please start at the beginning and tell us everything. Because if you did not set out to elope with my granddaughter, how the hell did the two of you end up in a position to be shot at?"

Chapter Twenty-one

*T*he entire time Jackson was explaining the events of the past two days, Celia marveled at his calm. She was a wreck of confused feelings while he spoke in his usual investigator's voice, as if they hadn't spent the night in a wildly passionate embrace, as if there were nothing between them.

How did he do it? Would she ever know the real him?

Coldly and unemotionally, he described Celia's dream and how she'd asked him to look into it, which had resulted in their traveling to High Wycombe together. But when he got to the part about Mama having an affair, both Minerva and Gran gasped.

"No," Minerva protested. "It can't be. I don't believe it."

"At first I didn't either," Celia admitted. "But I fear it might be true. It fits the circumstances in too many ways."

"Mrs. Plumtree," Jackson said, "have you any idea who might have been involved with your daughter?"

"I swear, this is the first I've heard anything of the sort." Gran looked visibly shaken. She paced to the fire, her cane coming down on the rug in choppy strokes, then returned to where Jackson stood. "But after Josiah died, I was struggling to keep the brewery going. I rarely spent time here. I wasn't aware that Lewis and Pru knew the Rawdons as well as all that. As for any other lover Pru might have had . . ." She trailed off with a sigh.

"You have no one to suspect," Jackson asked.

"No. I'm sorry."

"Perhaps Celia is mistaken," Minerva put in. "Perhaps it really was just a dream."

"Perhaps," Jackson said. "But given what your old nurse said, I doubt it."

"As soon as Oliver returns, we shall have to discuss this more," Gran said. "He may know more than he realizes. I will send for him—last I was told, he and Masters were at the town house hoping for word of your whereabouts." Her voice hardened. "But first, I want to hear about why you spent the night hiding out from killers in the forest."

Celia let out a shuddering breath. This would be sticky indeed.

With a terse nod, Jackson told a highly truncated version of what had happened. Celia expected nothing less—he *was* a gentleman, after all—yet it rankled that he could do it so easily. She was sure that if *she'd* told the tale, she'd be blushing to the tips of her ears.

His gaze locked with Gran's. "You understand, don't you, that we had no choice. We couldn't risk Lady Celia's safety by moving through the woods blindly at night, especially with no moon."

"Of course," Gran said. "You acted to protect her, and we are most grateful for that. Indeed, I am sure Oliver will compensate you most handsomely—"

"I don't want compensation for saving Celia's life," Jackson snapped, the only betrayal of his true feelings until now. Then he seemed to catch himself, and his tone turned more formal. "I behaved as any gentleman would."

"You certainly did," Minerva put in. "Gran didn't mean to insult you, I'm sure."

"In any case," Jackson said stiffly, "no matter what the circumstances, the only appropriate thing for me to do, having spent the night alone with her ladyship unchaperoned, is to offer marriage."

Appropriate? Marriage to her was the only *appropriate* thing to do?

Proper Pinter had arrived with a vengeance, and Celia was ready to strangle him. How could he propose a marriage to Gran as if it were merely some solution to a pesky problem? He wouldn't even look at her, for pity's sake!

"That is very good of you," Gran said. "Very gentlemanly, indeed. But I see no need for either of you to make such a precipitous decision right now." Her tone hardened. "Unless, of course, something more . . . scandalous occurred during your sojourn in the cottage?"

A short, tense silence fell on the room before Jackson said, "Certainly not." His voice softened a fraction. "Her ladyship is incapable of behaving scandalously."

How sweet of him to defend her honor to her family, but why wouldn't he look at her? And why had he offered such a cold proposal of marriage?

Last night, she'd thought she knew him. He'd seemed so gloriously infatuated with her, if not in love. But then this morning he'd turned into a different creature entirely, more proud and arrogant than any lord she'd ever known, and seemingly determined to convince her that a marriage between them would never work. Did he honestly think she could never fit into his world?

His lackluster proposal certainly made it seem so. And in that case, she wasn't sure she *wanted* to marry him. She certainly didn't want to spend the rest of her life being lectured about her spoiled nature and flawed character, no matter how glorious the man was in bed.

"And you, Mr. Pinter?" Gran asked him. "What is *your* capacity for behaving scandalously?"

"He has none," Celia choked out. "Mr. Pinter is always the most *proper* of gentlemen, trust me."

Though he stiffened, he gave no other sign that he felt the barb.

"In that case," Gran said, "I believe we can hush the entire incident up. You and Celia need not marry at all. Don't you agree, Mr. Pinter?"

Some strange message seemed to pass between Gran and him, for when he turned his gaze to Celia, it held a hopelessness that chilled her blood. "If that is what her ladyship wants."

What her ladyship wanted was some indication that all his sweet words and caresses from last night hadn't been impulses of a moment. What her ladyship wanted was for him to declare his desire to marry her with enthusiasm, instead of letting Gran bully him into withdrawing, or whatever it was that was occurring between them.

But clearly her ladyship wasn't going to get what she wanted. And that made her want to strike out. He wasn't the only one who could be "proper," blast him.

She forced a cool smile. "Her ladyship would like a hot bath and a nice long sleep and something in the way of food." She swallowed the hurt welling in her throat. "As you so carefully reminded me this morning, Mr. Pinter—we fine ladies don't endure severe deprivation well at all."

For a moment anger flared in his eyes, telling her that her aim had been true. But then that blasted veil came down over his face once more, and no emotion showed in his features whatsoever.

His words last night rose unbidden: *What I want is you. Just you.*

Foolishly, she'd believed him. She'd thought she was finally seeing the real Jackson Pinter, the one for whom passion and need swept away all other practical and societal considerations. But perhaps last night's Jackson was the aberration, and the real Jackson was the proud, proper, practical one.

"In that case, I should go," he clipped out. "While the trail is fresh, I must marshal officers to search the roads near High Wycombe and question any witnesses."

And just like that, he became the Bow Street Runner once more, entirely focused on matters far more important than a lady's silly hopes for a future with him.

He turned to Gran. "In the meantime, I don't think you should let Celia leave these walls until we've found whoever is determined to hurt her. And a guard should be placed on her door—"

"A guard!" Gran exclaimed. "Surely you do not think anyone inside Halstead Hall shot at you. They were all here yesterday afternoon while you two were gone."

"All?" he asked, one eyebrow raised. "All the suitors? The Plumtrees? The servants?"

"Yes," she snapped, "*all.* Minerva can attest to that."

"In truth, Mr. Pinter," Minerva said, "I can speak for all the guests. Indeed, we were hard-pressed to keep them entertained when they kept asking about how Celia was faring. As for the servants, surely you don't imagine that one of them would hurt her."

"Besides," Mrs. Plumtree said, "why would anyone here ride out to shoot at her in the woods when he could slip into her room and shoot her at his leisure?"

"All the same—" Jackson began.

"I'll be fine, Mr. Pinter," Celia put in. If he wasn't worried enough about her to stay and protect her himself, then she certainly wasn't going to put up with her family and half the servants hovering about trying to do so. Especially when all she wanted was to bury herself in her room alone and cry. "Please do not trouble yourself about my safety."

That got some reaction, but he masked it fairly quickly. "Very well. Since you all seem sure she will be safe here, I shall go search for Lady Celia's assailant elsewhere. If his lordship inquired about me in London, then my aunt has been informed I'm missing, so I'd be most grateful if one of you would send a message letting her know I'm well. Tell Stoneville that I'll return this evening, if I can, to report on what I've discovered." His voice grew rough. "And to make sure that Lady Celia is fine, of course."

Then he walked toward the door. Sudden tears burned Celia's eyes. Was he really going to act as if nothing had happened between them? How could he?

But just as he passed near her, he halted and turned to cast her a long, speaking glance. "Before then, my lady, if you should need anything, anything at all . . ."

And for a moment, she thought she saw the Jackson of last night.

Then he flashed her a self-deprecating smile. "Ah, but you have your family and a duke who's eager to marry you. Why should you need anything from me?"

Celia's heart broke as she watched him go. How could he throw the duke in her face when he *knew* she would never marry the man? Oh, that really took the cake! Jackson had inherited more of his noble sire's blood than he would admit.

My father was apparently quite the dashing young fellow, but he was a spoiled lord. . . .

Her throat grew raw. His father, her family, her—they were all of a piece to him. He wouldn't even give her a chance!

She wished she could curse the day that she'd ever met him, but she couldn't. She loved him. And there wasn't a thing she could do about it.

Her tears spilled down her cheeks, and Minerva saw them. "Oh, dearest," she said as she came to Celia's side. "Do you want me to fetch him back?"

"Don't you dare," Gran snapped. "Surely you do not want your sister to be forced into a marriage because of what is essentially an accident, do you?"

Celia shot her grandmother a wounded glance. "No, I would much prefer being forced into marriage because of some silly ultimatum."

Gran frowned. "I told you before, I only want—"

"For me to marry for love. For me to marry my choice." She jabbed her finger at the door. "Well, my choice just walked out because he thinks I can't manage in his world. Meanwhile, *you* seem to think I can't manage in mine, either. So where does that leave me?"

"What?" Gran said. "I never said you couldn't manage—"

"Didn't you? The only thing expected of a lady is to marry well. And since you obviously thought I couldn't succeed at that without some prodding—that none of us could—you concocted your stupid ultimatum."

As Gran stood there aghast, Celia added, "Well, I have a surprise for you. I'm not playing your game anymore. I'm not marrying *anyone*. And if you want to disinherit the lot of us, go ahead. I'd rather live in a ditch alone than marry a man I don't love just to meet your demands."

She rushed out the door. She'd had enough of Gran's machinations and Jackson's lack of faith in her. She'd had enough of her siblings' acquiescence with their grandmother's mad demand. It was time someone stood up to Gran.

And she was the only one left who could.

HETTY SCOWLED. SHE had done what she must, and she refused to feel guilty about it, no matter what Celia said.

"Congratulations, Gran," Minerva said coldly. "You just destroyed her chance for happiness. Well done."

"Do not be a fool. Mr. Pinter is not her chance for happiness. Did you hear his lackluster proposal?"

"Then you'd better hope that she doesn't end up *enceinte*. Because I don't believe a word either of them said about how they spent last night together."

Hetty paled. "You don't think Mr. Pinter would—"

"I think Mr. Pinter is as much in love with her as she is with him, and two people in love don't always restrain themselves. Even if they're both too foolish to admit it to you."

"No, you are wrong about that," Hetty said firmly. "If he had been in love with her, he would have insisted on a marriage. But he made only a halfhearted attempt because he thought that if he married her, I would—"

Too late, she caught herself.

"Would what?" Eyes narrowing, Minerva stalked toward her. "What did you threaten him with, Gran?"

Hetty drew herself up stiffly. "I did what I should have done with Pru. I acted to be sure that Mr. Pinter was not after her fortune. And I do not regret—"

"*What* did you tell him?" Minerva demanded.

Hetty could have ordered the girl not to be impudent and to stay out of it. But she did not want Minerva running off to Celia, making wild speculations. Better that Minerva knew the truth. Then she would understand.

"I told him I would cut Celia off if she married beneath her."

"Oh, Gran . . ." Minerva said in a disgusted voice.

"I was right to do it, too. Did you not see how he withdrew the moment I said that she need not marry him? Obviously, he thought there was no point in pursuing the marriage if he could not have her fortune!"

Minerva scowled at her. "I daresay he couldn't bear to see the woman he loved grow to hate him for being the *cause* of her losing her fortune!"

Isaac had said something similar, but Hetty had seen no sign that Mr. Pinter loved so deeply. "You are attributing very noble motives to our Mr. Pinter. How can you even be sure that he loves her? He was very cool today."

"According to Celia, he is very cool most of the time . . . except when he's kissing her with wild passion."

Oh, yes. She'd forgotten about all those kisses Minerva had mentioned yesterday. Nonetheless . . . "Perhaps he desires her, but—"

"While you were manipulating matters to your satisfaction, I was watching him. After you said they need not marry, he looked at Celia with such despair . . . Oh, Gran, you don't know what you've done. She loves him. And I truly believe he loves her. But each is convinced that the other doesn't care enough, and you're not helping. So now . . ."

"Now he needs to fight for her." Hetty considered their conversation in light of all that Minerva was telling her. "You heard what Celia said—'my choice just walked out that door because he thinks I can't manage in his world.'"

"He only thinks it because you told him she will lose everything if she marries him!"

"And that worries him?" Hetty crossed her arms over her chest. "Even when two people are from the same worlds, marriage is hard, my dear—you know that as well as anyone. But when they are from different worlds . . ."

Her voice grew stronger with her conviction. "If he has no faith in her ability to fit into his world *now*, only think what things will be like once they are married. He has to believe in her. And if he cannot . . ."

"Perhaps," Minerva conceded. "But Gran, it isn't your place to decide whether he can or not, whether she can rise to the challenge or not. They have to decide that themselves. You stepped in where you shouldn't, and I think you'll regret it down the road. Because if Celia continues to balk at your ultimatum—"

"She will not," Hetty said uneasily, remembering Isaac giving her the same warning. "She will come to her senses."

"And marry the man of *your* choice? Are you sure that's best? Because if she doesn't marry Mr. Pinter, that only leaves the duke, and she doesn't love him."

Hetty dragged in a heavy breath, remembering what Mr. Pinter had claimed, though Celia had never told her anything of the sort. "You do not know that for certain."

"I do. What's more, I think you know it, too. You seem to believe that in holding firm to your ultimatum, you're correcting the mistake you made in matching your daughter to a man like Papa. That if you can get us all happily married off, it will make up for what happened to them."

Minerva gazed at her with pity in her face. "But all you're doing is making the same mistake again. Because although Celia won't be marrying a fortune hunter if she marries the duke, she'll still be marrying a man who wants her for reasons that have nothing to do with how wonderful she is. So for your sake—and hers—I hope she sticks to her guns."

When Minerva headed for the door, Hetty called out, "Are you going to reveal to her what I told Mr. Pinter?"

Minerva paused. "I haven't decided. On the one hand, you might be right—he does need to fight for her. On the other hand, Celia is hurting . . ." She shot Hetty a weary glance. "Unlike you, Gran, I don't pretend to know what is best for everyone. I shall have to see what she needs from me."

After she left, Hetty stood frozen. What *did* Celia need? What did any of them need? She had thought they needed spouses, and it certainly seemed as if they were much happier now that they had married.

But what if she had been wrong about Celia? What if what Celia needed was something beyond Hetty's power to give?

That disturbing question haunted her for the rest of the morning.

Chapter Twenty-two

*D*espite several hours of searching, Jackson and his men found nothing to indicate who was trying to kill Celia. Not a bloody thing.

So, hours after leaving Halstead Hall, he rode toward Cheapside, seething with frustration. They'd combed the woods on either side of the road for a couple of miles. They'd found hoof marks in some soft mud, but that only told them that at least one assailant had lain in wait for them, which he'd already guessed. Whoever had attacked had been careful to leave few traces.

No one in the surrounding countryside had seen anything either. The assailants had well chosen their time to strike. His horse had turned up in a nearby field, but no sign remained of the villains. That meant Celia was still in danger, the target of God knows whom, for reasons he could only dimly be sure of.

And he'd given up the right to protect her himself.

He groaned. He could have told her grandmother to go to hell, that he was marrying Celia no matter what. But he hadn't. And though in his head he knew he'd been right to be cautious, it felt in his heart as if he'd been wrong.

He snorted. Hearts lied all the time. His heart had lied to him by telling him that rank and fortune didn't matter. He was better off not listening to it.

As you so carefully reminded me this morning, Mr. Pinter—we fine ladies don't endure severe deprivation well at all.

All right, so she'd said it with sarcasm and obvious anger, but it was true, even if she wouldn't admit it.

He'd reached the house. It was dark already, so he would stay just long enough to reassure his aunt that he was fine and perhaps eat something before he set off for Ealing again.

Handing his horse off to Jimmy, the footboy who'd been watching for him, he ordered the lad to fetch his carriage and a team from the livery, then headed up the stairs. Before he even reached the door, it swung open and his aunt burst out to grab him in her arms.

When she drew back, her reddened eyes and nose told him she'd been crying. "Thank heavens, you're all right!" she said in a voice thick with emotion. "Is it true you were shot at?"

Confound it all. "How did you hear that?"

Aunt Ada led him inside. "I sent Jimmy round to the Bow Street office this morning, where they told him that you were out searching for the villain who fired upon you and Lady Celia." She closed the door, then jerked him into her arms again. "After his lordship told me last night that you and Lady Celia were missing, I thought I'd have heart failure. He insisted that you must have run off to marry—but I knew you'd never do such a thing. It's not in your character."

She pulled back to gaze into his face. "Oh, my dear boy, I couldn't have borne it if I'd lost you, too. You're the only thing I have left of your—"

When she broke off, the blood draining from her countenance, he knew. Damn it all to hell, he knew for sure. He couldn't believe he hadn't guessed before now. Perhaps he hadn't wanted to know.

"Of my *what*, Aunt? And don't say 'mother.' You wouldn't have stopped if you'd meant her." He stared down at her, his throat tight, his breath lodged somewhere in his chest. "I'm the only thing you have left of *him*, right? My uncle. No, not my uncle." He uttered a mad laugh. "My *father*."

With a little moan, she turned to head down the hall.

The fact that she didn't deny it said it all. He followed her into the kitchen as an impotent rage seized him, directed at the man he'd always wanted to be his father. But not like this, not if it meant that the man had—

"It's true, isn't it?"

Her hands trembled as she pulled a plate of food out of the oven and laid it on the table.

Ignoring it, he turned her to face him. "Admit it, damn you!"

"How did you know?" she whispered. "When did you find out?"

"Lady Celia saw the miniatures and noticed a resemblance. I told her she was mad. Then I stared at it myself and saw it for the first time. I didn't want to believe it, but there *is* a resemblance."

"When you were a boy and your hair was lighter," she managed, "you looked less like him, but as you aged and your hair darkened, you started to look as he did when he was young. Fortunately, he changed as he aged, too, putting on weight and going bald. Still, he lived in terror that you might notice the resemblance in the miniature one day."

Jackson gave a cold laugh. "Clearly I'm blind about what matters most. I never saw it at all until Celia . . . Oh, God, how could you not have told me?"

"I wanted to, but your mother made us both swear not to. She didn't want you resenting him for her death or for not being there in your early years."

"Yes!" he said fiercely. "What of that? All those years I thought that I had some *arse* of a nobleman for a father . . ." His throat grew tight and raw. "Well, the *arse* part of that was right, wasn't it? He abandoned Mother and me."

"No, he did not," she said firmly. "He had no idea she was bearing his child when she left our house at twenty. Indeed, she had no idea herself until later. And *I* didn't even know they'd been together."

"But she left because he took advantage of her," he growled.

"It wasn't like that," Aunt Ada choked out as she went to fetch him some ale. "She revealed to me after you moved here that they were together only once. I was visiting a friend one night, and they drank too much wine and . . ." Her hands shook in pouring the ale. "He told me—*she* told me when I forced her to admit the truth—that they both regretted it deeply. That's why she left right after it occurred."

His aunt brought him the tankard, her eyes full of remorse as she pressed it into his hand. "She had some money she'd saved and a friend who was a seamstress. She thought she could manage on her own, but then once she was established as an unmarried lady, she found out she was with child and . . ."

"She stayed in Liverpool." He set the ale down. "And who could blame her for not wanting to come back where she would risk Uncle—my *father*—pawing her again?"

"Jackson . . ." she said in a pleading tone.

"So there was no elopement with a noble scoundrel, just my uncle— *Damn* it!" He dragged his fingers through his hair. "I don't even know how to think of him!"

"We tried to find her after she left, you know. But she didn't want to be found, didn't want me ever to learn of it. She didn't want to hurt me or ruin my marriage. I understand that." She seized his hand in hers. "I only wish it hadn't been so difficult for you two in Liverpool. I truly believe that if her seamstress friend had not lost her business . . ."

She sighed. "But by then, your mother had been away so long and had built up in her mind what awful things would happen if she returned. I don't think she realized how much you suffered at that charity school until that stupid boy almost killed you. That's when she swallowed her pride and came home. I was hurt for a long time after she told me the truth, but before she died, I forgave her. And him."

"Her, I understand, but how could you forgive *him*?" he ground out. "How could you not hate him for what he did?"

"I did hate him for a while. After she came back to us, I demanded that she tell me who your father was, and she kept refusing. Then your unc— Then *William* started saying I should leave her be, and I started noticing the guilt in his face whenever he looked at her."

She paced the kitchen, her hands tightly clenched together at her waist. "At first, I thought he blamed himself for not searching harder for her after she left. But soon I couldn't help noticing how tender he was with you, how immediately he'd taken you into his heart." Her voice grew choked. "And I guessed the truth."

Sweet God, what she must have suffered when she realized it. How had she borne it? "And then you had me underfoot," he said bitterly, "a living reminder that your sister and your husband had betrayed you. It must have been such a torment for you to look at me every day—"

"Don't you ever think such a thing!" she cried as she whirled on him. "You were my salvation, my darling boy. William and I couldn't have children. So when your mother brought you here . . ."

Tears rolled down her cheeks, and he pulled out his handkerchief to press into her hand.

She took a moment to compose herself, then went on in an aching voice, "You were worth any temporary difficulties that arose between me and William. I couldn't have asked for a better son. You're the light of my life." She smoothed back a lock of his hair. "Why else would I have worried so after hearing you were missing? If you only knew what a wretched night I had . . ."

As she began to cry, he drew her into his arms and held

her close, torn between guilt over her worry and a growing awe to see how much she loved him. How could that be, given the circumstances? Uncle William was his *father*. The devil had lain with Aunt Ada's own sister!

But there was no mistaking her sincerity about her feelings.

After a moment, she drew back and wiped her tears away with his handkerchief. "You know why Lady Celia noticed the resemblance between you and William, don't you?"

He stiffened. The last thing he wanted to discuss right now was Celia. "She has a good eye," he growled as he took a seat at the table.

"And she's memorized every line of your face. Because she loves you."

God, how he wished that were true.

"I'm not the only one to notice it either. His lordship said the same thing."

He stabbed the mutton chop. "And I'm sure he was ready to flay me alive at the very possibility."

"No, indeed." She thrust out her chin. "He was delighted when he thought that the two of you had eloped. He said it was about time."

"What?" Jackson gaped at her.

"I agreed with him. But I also assured him you would never behave so dishonorably. So then he and Mr. Masters got worried about you both. I promised to send a message to his grandmother's town house as soon as I heard anything. I went over there myself this morning to give them the news from Halstead Hall, and even though he'd already heard it himself he was most grateful to see me. *And* eager to see you again."

She had to be mistaking his lordship's reactions. "No doubt he wants his report," he muttered as he wolfed down some supper.

"No doubt he wants to know your intentions toward his sister. You did spend the night with her. That brings with it certain consequences."

"It's not what you think," he said defensively, though it was probably exactly what she thought. "We didn't have a choice."

"Of course not. No one spends the night in an abandoned ruin of a poacher's cottage by choice."

"Exactly." He blinked. "Wait, how did you know where we spent the night?"

"The message I got came from Lady Minerva, who has quite the writer's knack for describing situations." Her eyes narrowed on him. "It was clear that you are responsible for the young lady's ruin, despite the circumstances. So I do hope you offered marriage."

"Of course." He drank a healthy gulp of ale.

"And she turned you down?"

He turned the tankard in his hand. "Her grandmother had arranged matters so that no one but the family knew of it. Which means she didn't need to marry me."

"Did she say that?"

"She didn't have to." He swallowed more ale, then set the tankard firmly down. "Her grandmother made it painfully clear."

"So you took the opportunity to get out of a match you didn't want."

"No!" At her raised eyebrow, he scowled. "Now see here, I did my duty."

"I do hope you didn't put it like *that*: 'My lady, I know my duty. Would you please marry me?'"

"Certainly not. I said . . ."

What *had* he said?

The only appropriate thing for me to do, having spent the night alone with her ladyship unchaperoned, is to offer marriage.

Damn. Even *he* knew that was about as unromantic a proposal as a man ever offered a woman.

"It doesn't matter what I said," he grumbled. He toyed with the boiled potatoes, his appetite vanishing. "None of it matters. She could never fit in here, never be happy in such mean surroundings—"

"And you know this because . . ."

"Oh, for God's sake, you saw their town house," he snapped. "You saw how they live—it's grander than anything I could ever give her." Even if her grandmother allowed her to receive her fortune, which was doubtful.

"I see. So she's as missish as all that, is she?"

"She hasn't had the chance to be missish—she's never been anywhere but in the lap of luxury."

"Except for last night in that cottage. I suppose she ran you ragged, prodding you to make it more comfortable."

"Of course not. She would never—" He halted, remembering how she'd set about to feather their nest while he went in search of water. Seeing his aunt's raised eyebrow, he said, "She knew what she had to do."

"Did she? How odd for a pampered lady. Though I'm sure she complained constantly about the lack of heat and food and furnishings."

Hell and blazes, he could see where this was going. "She did not. But it was only one night, and we were hiding from killers."

"Trust me, Jackson, killers or no, if you'd hauled me about the woods and put me through such deprivation, I would have been complaining. Loudly. Repeatedly."

He pushed back from the table to eye her with abject skepticism. "No, you wouldn't. You'd make the best of things."

"And she didn't?"

With a hard glare, he crossed his arms over his chest. "One night in a cottage is hardly a good test of how well she'd endure a lifetime in Cheapside."

"So last night was a test, was it? And even so, she passed it. In response, you talked about duty and honor and such. Made her feel as if marrying her would be your concession to propriety. Have I judged the situation aright?"

It was getting harder to pretend that he'd behaved like anything but an arse this morning. "She has a bloody duke chomping at the bit to marry her, and you think she could be happy with *me*? Here?"

Aunt Ada planted her hands on her hips. "You know, I'm beginning to be insulted. I thought I'd made this quite a comfortable home, and now I find that you think it comparable to some hovel in the woods."

"That's not what I—"

"If you showed the same lack of feeling with her as you are with me right now, it's a wonder she didn't slap the tar out of you." She shook her head. "You decided her future without even considering her feelings. Don't you find that presumptuous?"

A frustrated breath escaped him. "It's not just the money; it's the difference in our stations. Even knowing who my father was, I'm no less a bastard and she's no less a lady. I still work for a living."

"And she's bothered by that? She's contemptuous of your station?"

It must have been difficult for you, starting so young in a place like Bow Street. You must have worked very hard to have risen so high in such a short time.

Celia had said those words with clear admiration. And she'd been willing to marry him even knowing he might never become Chief Magistrate. Indeed, she'd spent half the morning resisting all his attempts to tell her how difficult she might have it if they married.

Aunt Ada took his hesitation for a no. "That's the trouble with you, my boy. You're so ready to assume that others will turn their noses up at you that you ignore how they actually behave. You're well respected in the community. You've accomplished so much, yet you brace yourself for the cry of 'bastard' even when that cry isn't given."

He hated it when his aunt made sense, especially when it conflicted with what he was sure was right. Though he was getting less sure of it by the moment.

Her voice fell to a soft murmur. "Has it occurred to you that she made no complaint last night because she was with *you*? That being with you made the rest of it endurable? And that being without you might make all her fancy living intolerable?"

"No," he said acidly as he rose from the table and turned for the door, "that had not occurred to me."

She laid her hand on his arm to stay him. "Why not? Is it really so hard to believe that someone might truly love you for who you are?"

Anger welled up in him. "Yes, it is!" he spat. "When I would have given my soul to be called his son, my own father couldn't even bring himself to claim me! He didn't love me for who I am; how am I to believe that anyone else could?"

Profound sadness washed over her face, tinged with regret. "Oh, my dear boy, it was wrong of your mother to have told you that foolish tale she invented about your birth. And it was wrong of me—and William—to let it stand." She gripped his arm. "I know we made mistakes, the three of us. But surely you realize that you were always loved. By me, by your mother, and yes, by your father."

Tears trickled down her cheeks, but she swiped them away ruthlessly. "He was so proud of you, and rightfully so. If not for his fear of a scandal that could embarrass me and cost him his position, he would have shouted from the rooftops that you were his son. Never, ever think for one minute that he was ashamed of you. He loved you until the day he died."

The fervency of her words crawled inside the hard kernel that had always resented his supposed noble sire, eroding it.

For so many years, he'd lived with this pressure on his chest, this belief that his father hadn't wanted him badly enough to claim him. And her revelation that his uncle was his father had only eased the pain a little, for they'd kept that knowledge from him.

But if he were fair, he had to acknowledge that in their place he would have been cautious, too. He knew what it was like to suffer terrible slurs. His uncle would have never wanted that for Aunt Ada. And Uncle William had been able to do more for Jackson as a lauded magistrate than if he'd lost his position. Magistrates were expected to live exemplary lives; they weren't supposed to engage in what the law considered incest with their sisters-in-law.

Though it had been wrong of Uncle William to keep it from him, Jackson began to understand why he did. The man had been flawed. He'd made mistakes.

And so had *he*, in being so cautious with Celia. Certainly he hadn't given her a fair chance to accept *or* refuse his offer of marriage. At the very least, Celia deserved such a chance.

"I have to go, Aunt," he murmured. "I told his lordship I would return this evening to give him a full report, and it's getting late already."

"Yes, of course." Then she started. "Oh, I almost forgot in the midst of all that's been going on!" Reaching into her apron pocket, she pulled out a missive and handed it to him. "You received a letter from some people up north."

It was from the family of Mrs. Rawdon's former lady's maid, Elsie. They'd finally provided him with an address for her, in Chelsea. But if he went there now, he'd never make it to Halstead Hall before the family retired.

Confound it all, he ought to go interview Elsie tonight. What if she'd been involved with the shooting?

Somehow he doubted that. He just couldn't imagine some lady's maid lying in wait on the road to shoot them, then searching the woods. Besides, he had to see Celia. He couldn't bear to think of her lying in her bed hating him all night.

Shoving the letter in his pocket, he turned for the door.

"Before you leave," his aunt said, "answer one question for me. If Lady Celia weren't the daughter of a marquess—if she were some young woman you'd met at an assembly, the daughter of a baker or a tailor—would you hesitate to marry her?"

"No," he said, not even having to consider his answer. "If I could have her, I'd want for nothing else."

She seized his hand and squeezed it. "Then do whatever you must to secure her. Because if you don't make the attempt, you'll regret it the rest of your life."

Her words stayed with him throughout the hour and a half ride to Halstead Hall. They plagued him as his carriage approached the stable, and he noticed the other equipages there, which told him that the house party was still going on despite everything.

Her words were all he could think of as he was shown

into Stoneville's study. As Jackson waited for the marquess, whom he'd been told was still awake and would be with him presently, they wouldn't leave him.

Aunt Ada was right. If he didn't attempt to make Celia his, he would never withstand the loss of her.

Stoneville entered the study, a guarded expression on his face. "Well, well," he said as Jackson rose, "our missing investigator has shown up at last. Did you or your men find anything along the road to High Wycombe?"

"I'm afraid not, my lord."

As Stoneville took his seat behind the desk and bade Jackson sit as well, Jackson related everything he and Celia had discovered, though it was clear that his family had already acquainted him with the information about their mother's love affair.

After adding his own observations to that, Jackson then gave a thorough report of what had happened on the road, and what his suspicions were concerning why they'd been shot at. The marquess asked him several questions, which he answered as best he could.

"So you plan to speak to Elsie tomorrow?"

"First thing in the morning. I would have gone tonight, but I thought you needed to hear everything first."

"I appreciate that."

"Besides, I also wanted to know . . . that is . . ." Jackson braced himself for any reaction. "How is Lady Celia?"

Stoneville shot him a veiled glance. "She's well, considering all that has happened. She closeted herself in her room and told us she didn't want to see anyone." His gaze hardened. "Especially you. She said she wanted nothing to do with you from now on. She made me promise I would keep you away from her. Which makes me wonder exactly what happened last night."

Hell and blazes.

Time to state his intentions. Beating around the bush hadn't served him very well earlier. "It doesn't matter what happened. I am here to make things right. I want to marry your sister."

Stoneville eyed him closely. "Minerva seemed to think otherwise."

Jackson sighed. "I'm not surprised. I believe that I also left Lady Celia unsure of my intentions. I . . . um . . . made rather a hash of it when I proposed the first time."

The marquess chuckled. "I'll say."

Jackson cast him a startled glance.

"Yes, I heard all about your offer. Do forgive my amusement. If you'll recall, I made rather a hash of my own marriage proposal." He sobered. "I also understand that my grandmother had something to do with your reticence to offer marriage."

"I was not reticent," Jackson said fiercely. "I was never reticent about that. I've wanted to marry your sister almost from the moment I met her. And no matter what your grandmother thinks, it has nothing to do with her fortune or her position or—"

"I know." When Jackson blinked, the marquess smiled. "You forget—I've watched you work for nearly a year. I've listened to your opinions and heard of your fine reputation. I know a man of good character when I see one."

"Even if he's a bastard?" Jackson bit out.

"The Duke of Clarence has *ten* bastards and everyone turns a blind eye, so I don't see why we can't have at least one in the family. Or two, if you count Jarret's stepson." Stoneville smiled. "We Sharpes are hellions after all. We wouldn't want to become boring. What would the gossips have to talk about?"

His aunt's words leapt into his mind: *That's the trouble with you, my boy . . . You brace yourself for the cry of "bastard" even when that cry isn't given.*

"Your grandmother isn't so nonchalant about it," Jackson pointed out.

"True. And she may very well hold to her threat to cut Celia off."

"You know about that?"

"She let it slip to Minerva."

"Ah. So Lady Celia knows now, too," he said, not sure if that was a good or a bad thing.

"Actually, I don't think she does." He stared hard at Jackson. "Does it matter to you if Celia loses her fortune?"

"No, though I hate the thought of sentencing her to a life of sacrifice."

"Yet you still mean to offer marriage."

"I do, and this time I'll make sure she knows what your grandmother intends to do. But I hope it won't matter to her." He admitted what he'd realized after less than a day separated from her. "Because apparently I'm more selfish than I thought. I simply can't bear to be without her."

Stoneville's expression softened. "Now *that's* what you should say when next you see her."

"And when might that be?" Jackson asked.

"I don't know. I told you—she made me promise to keep you away. And the family has already retired for the evening." At Jackson's muttered oath, the marquess's voice softened. "Give her time. You have to talk to Elsie in the morning anyway, so come here after that and perhaps she will see you then."

Jackson was *not* going to wait until tomorrow, not when every moment away from her made her harden her heart against him.

He rose. "As you wish. But I left several personal items here while I was a guest at the house party, so if you don't mind, I'll fetch those before I leave." That would give him an excuse to find her room and make her listen.

"Very well." As Jackson headed for the door, Stoneville called out, "Your room is in the west wing, isn't it?"

Jackson halted to eye him warily. "Yes. Why?"

"You may not know that there's a shortcut through the south wing." The marquess stared steadily at him. The family resided in the south wing. "Indeed, I would love your opinion on a piece of art. I'm thinking of selling it, and you might know of a buyer. It's a fine military painting by Goya hanging right next to Celia's door, if you'd care to take a look on your way past."

He couldn't believe it—Stoneville was telling him how to find Celia's room.

"Just remember," Stoneville added, "if you should happen to run into anyone, explain that I wanted your opinion about some art."

"I appreciate your faith in my judgment, my lord," he said. "I will certainly take a look at that painting."

Stoneville's gaze hardened as he stood. "I trust that you'll behave like a gentleman while you're passing that way."

He bit back a hot retort—his lordship was one to talk. But the fact that the man was helping him with Celia was a small miracle, and he wasn't about to ignore that. "Yes. A perfect gentleman."

"Good. I'll hold you to that."

With a nod, Jackson hurried out into the hall. Even with Stoneville's sly urging in this endeavor, he hesitated to sneak about the house after the ladies had retired. But the sounds of drunken men from down one hallway told him that some of the gentlemen were still awake, so he hastened his steps. The last thing he wanted was to run into Celia's suitors right now. He wasn't sure he could trust himself around them.

Jackson had been in the south wing once before, when Stoneville had received him in dishabille, so he knew its layout. Fortunately, it took him only a few minutes to find Celia's room.

He knocked on Celia's door, but there was no answer. Should he pound on it to wake her?

Ah, but if she asked who was there and he told her, she might refuse to let him in. He glanced down at the ancient lock, and his eyes narrowed. Perhaps it would be better to have the element of surprise on his side.

Thank God he always traveled with his lock picks.

Chapter Twenty-three

Celia was awakened from a dead sleep by some sound. A knock? She wasn't sure. But whoever it was would knock again. Not that it would do them any good, because she wasn't letting anyone see her in her present state, eyes puffy from crying and her hair tangled from tossing and turning. It was a miracle she'd had any sleep after she'd spent hours fretting over Jackson.

She scowled. She *wasn't* going to think about *him* again.

Suddenly, a different sound came to her ears—a steady clicking at the door. By the light of the fire, she saw the handle shake.

Fear coursed through her. Good Lord, someone was trying to sneak into her room! And not someone with a key or they would have opened the door by now. Was it the same person who'd tried to kill her?

Then they were about to have a surprise. Soundlessly, she sat up and lifted the pistol she'd kept loaded on her bedside table ever since yesterday. Heart pounding, she waited until the door creaked open, then cocked the pistol and said, "I'd stop right there if I were you. I've got a gun trained on you, and I won't hesitate to use it."

There was a harsh intake of breath, followed by a low male voice saying, "It's me, Celia. Don't shoot."

"Jackson?" she said incredulously. "What the—"

"I had to see you." He opened the door and stepped inside.

Her heart still pounding, she carefully uncocked the gun and lowered it. "Go away."

"Not until we talk," he said steadily.

"I could have killed you, you know!"

"You could have," he agreed without a hint of his usual condescension on the subject of her and guns. "Next time I'll know better than to take you by surprise."

His eyes were dark, haunted. Then he stepped closer and seemed to notice that she wore only her chemise. When heat flared in his face, she lifted the gun again. "Oh, no, you are not going to waltz in here as if nothing has happened and expect to be taken into my bed without a word."

He held his hands up. "I wouldn't expect that."

The gun wavered in her hand as emotion clogged her throat. "You made it sound as if marrying me would be the w-worst sort of o-obligation . . ."

Pain slashed over his face. "I didn't mean to," he said, inching nearer. "I'm an idiot, I am."

"After last night, I th-thought you really cared about me, and th-then this morning—"

"I made you feel as if you were a pampered fool who could do nothing right," he said, now close enough to take the gun from her. He didn't. And even more amazingly, he seemed to understand her anger.

"I don't care what your house in Cheapside is like," she whispered, "and I don't care how many servants you have, and I don't care—"

"I know," he said hoarsely. "Either shoot me or put down the gun, sweeting, because I desperately want to hold you."

And she desperately wanted him to. Except that she couldn't bear to have him be tender with her, then turn cold in the morning again. "Not yet. I want to know why you became so formal once we got here, why you withdrew from me. Did you change your mind about wanting to marry me once you realized that Gran had made it unnecessary?"

"God, no." He thrust one hand through his hair. "There's something I have to tell you. And since it's going to make you want to shoot me—or someone, anyway— I'd feel much better saying it without a gun staring me in the face."

She hesitated, then nodded. "But you have to promise not to touch me until I say you can."

A faint smile touched his lips. "Very well."

"I mean it!"

Sobering, he backed up a few steps. "I'll stand over here. You put the gun on the bedside table where you can reach it if I misbehave, all right?"

"All right." She put down the gun, and then, feeling very exposed in her chemise, pulled a sheet up around her. "Before you start, you should know that I told Gran

I'm not going to marry anyone, ultimatum or not. So you see, I really don't care about my fortune. If I couldn't have you . . ."

"Ah, but you do have me, sweeting. I'm here because I couldn't bear to be without you."

Words that would have melted her yesterday only frustrated her now. "You always say such sweet things when we're alone, but tomorrow you'll act like Proper Pinter again, and it will all be forgot!"

He looked stricken. "Not this time, I swear."

"Why should this time be different than the last three times you kissed me and pretended it meant nothing?"

"For one thing, I just informed your brother I was going to marry you." When she gaped at him, he added, "How do you think I found out where your room was?"

She'd been on the verge of believing him until he said that. "Oliver would never allow you up here so late."

"Yet here I am."

"You're an investigator. You probably found out with your usual methods."

"I swear, I'm here because of your brother." He sighed. "Though he did make me promise to behave like a gentleman."

"That does sound like Oliver." And she wasn't sure whether to thank him for that. "So you're not here to seduce me."

"I'm here to convince you to marry me."

"Oh? The way you tried to convince me this morning?" she said acidly.

He flushed. "I realize now that I probably sounded a little . . . er . . ."

"Unenthusiastic?"

"Damn it, I was not unenthusiastic or reticent or any of that!"

She lifted an eyebrow.

"It threw me off guard when your grandmother said that everything could be hushed up. It occurred to me that you might prefer not to be forced into marriage just because I . . . because we . . ."

"Were intimate?"

He gave a terse nod.

"You thought I would prefer to forget that we'd shared a bed, so I could take some other man into my bed—a rich duke, for example?"

"No!" He shoved his hands into his pocket. "It wasn't like that. I didn't mean . . . I . . ."

He was flustered. She always liked him better then. It made him more approachable. If she weren't still so angry at him, she'd find it rather endearing.

A distinctly uncomfortable look crossed his face. "I didn't want to make things harder for you, all right?"

"No, you didn't want to make things harder for *you*. You didn't want to put up with a spoiled wife who might demand that you use her fortune for such things as lace and sugar creatures on cakes."

"What I didn't want was for my wife to lose her fortune just because she married me." A muscle worked in his jaw. "I wasn't hypothesizing when I said that your grandmother might cut you off. The truth is . . ." He hesitated, then squared his shoulders. "She told me that if you stooped to marry someone as low as I, she would cut you off completely. Your siblings would gain their inheritance, but you would get nothing."

That took Celia completely aback. "You're lying."

"I wish I were."

Celia thought back over the past few days, over his odd behavior and what he'd said, and suddenly several things made more sense. "When did she do that?"

"The night of the ball."

That was why he'd turned cold again, why he wouldn't dance with her. Why he'd avoided her, would have kept avoiding her if she hadn't insisted on going with him to High Wycombe.

It was also why he'd given her all those lectures about what life with him would be like in poor little Cheapside. Because he was sure Gran would cut her off after they married.

Yet he'd made love to her last night only after she'd agreed to become his wife. And he'd done it knowing she would be poor. That he would gain nothing from the marriage except a gently bred wife who might be a burden to him.

A lump caught in her throat. All his cautions this morning had been Practical Pinter realizing that he should prepare her for losing everything.

What I want is you. Just you.

Perhaps he'd really meant that. But if so, then it was time he acted like it. He must stop trying to do what he thought was right for her without consulting her.

"I know what you're thinking—" he began.

"Do you?" That was the trouble. He truly thought he did. "Enlighten me."

"You think I balked at marrying you because you would have no fortune."

"And is that the case?"

"No!" he said, clearly insulted.

"So you're saying you have too good a character to marry for financial reasons, but you think I have so bad a character as to assume that you would."

That seemed to catch him off guard. "I'm not saying that."

"Aren't you?" She hugged her knees to her chest. "When anyone implies that you're unprincipled because of the circumstances of your birth, you turn into Proud Pinter, as lofty as a lord. Yet you tar all the aristocracy with the same brush because of *their* birth. Does that seem fair?"

He gazed sullenly at her. "You forget that when you first asked me to investigate your suitors, you said you didn't want to marry someone lower in rank and wealth, who might prove to be a fortune hunter."

She winced. "I started out biased myself. The difference is, as I got to know how fine a man you are, I adjusted my opinions." Anger surged up in her as she remembered his parting words about the duke this morning. "Yet after all we'd meant to each other, you made it sound as if I'd go running off to marry the first rich duke who offered."

"Because you *deserve* a duke, damn it!" A troubled expression furrowed his brow. "You deserve a man who can give you the moon. I can't. I can give you a decent home in a decent part of town with decent people, but you . . ." His voice grew choked. "You're the most amazing woman I've ever known. It destroys me to think of what you'll have to give up to be with me."

"I told you before—I don't care!" she said hotly. "Why can't you believe me?"

He hesitated a long moment. "The truth?"

"Always."

"Because I can't imagine why you'd want me when you have men of rank and riches at your fingertips."

She gave a rueful laugh. "You grossly exaggerate my charms, but I can't complain. It's one of many things I adore about you—that you see a better version of me than I ever could." Remembering the wonderful words he'd said last night when she'd been so self-conscious, she left the bed to walk up to him. "Do you know what *I* see when I look at you?"

His wary gaze locked with hers. "Proper Pinter. *Proud* Pinter."

"Yes, but that's just who you show to the world to protect yourself." She reached up to stroke his cheek, reveling in the ragged breath that escaped him. "When you let down your guard, however, I see Jackson—who ferrets out the truth, no matter how hard. Who risks his own life to protect the weak. Who'd sacrifice anything to prevent me from having to sacrifice everything."

Catching her hand, he halted its path. "You see a saint," he said hoarsely. "I'm not a saint; I'm a man with needs and desires and a great many rough edges."

"I like your rough edges," she said with a soft smile. "If I'd really wanted a man of rank and riches, I probably would have married long ago. I always told myself I couldn't marry because no one wanted me, but the truth was, I didn't want any of them." She fingered a lock of his hair. "Apparently I was waiting for *you*, rough edges and all."

His eyes turned hot with wanting. Drawing her hand to his lips, he kissed the palm so tenderly that her heart leapt into her throat. When he lifted his head, he said, "Then marry me, rough edges and all."

She swallowed. "That's what you say now, when we're alone and you're caught up in—"

He covered her mouth with his, kissing her so fervently that she turned into a puddle of mush. Blast him—he always did that, too, when they were alone; it was when they were with others that he reconsidered their being together forever. And he still had said nothing of love.

"That's enough of that," she warned, drawing back from him. "Until you make a proper proposal, before my family, you're not sharing my bed."

"Sweeting—"

"Don't you 'sweeting' me, Jackson Pinter." She edged away from him. "I want Proper Pinter back now."

A mocking smile crossed his lips. "Sorry, love. I threw him out when I saw how he was mucking up my private life."

Love?

No, she wouldn't let that soften her. Not until she was sure he wouldn't turn cold later. "You told Oliver you'd behave like a gentleman."

"To hell with your brother." He stalked her with clear intent.

Even as she darted behind a chair to avoid him, excitement tore through her. "Aren't you still worried Gran will cut me off, and you'll be saddled with a spoiled wife and not enough money to please her?"

"To hell with your grandmother, too. For that matter, to hell with the money." He tossed the chair aside as if it were so much kindling; it clattered across the floor. "It's you I want."

"Jackson!" she cried as he approached her. "Someone might hear you!"

"Good." Catching her about the waist, he backed her toward the bed. "Then you'll be well and truly compromised, and there will be no more question of our marrying."

While she was still thrilling to the masterful way he'd decided to take charge, he tumbled her onto the bed, following her down to cover her body with his.

As she gaped at him, shocked to see her cautious love behave so delightfully incautious, he murmured, "Or better yet, they can find us here together in the morning and march us right to the church."

Then he took her mouth with his.

Chapter Twenty-four

Jackson wanted to crow when she opened her mouth to his kiss. He understood her anger—she had a right to it. And if he were a decent man, he'd do as she demanded and come back in the morning to make "a proper proposal" before her family.

But he wasn't taking the chance that *she* would change her mind by the light of day. This time he'd leave her craving him as badly as he craved her, even if he had to spend all night doing it.

He dragged his mouth along her jaw to her neck to plunder the tender flesh there. She turned her head to nip his earlobe, then whisper, "I should never have put down my gun, you devil."

"I told you," he rasped, "don't brandish a gun unless you mean to use it."

"I wish I'd shot you when I had the chance," she said in an aching voice, "just for being so cold to me this morning."

He'd hurt her badly, damn it. "I'll make it up to you." He fondled her breast, thumbing the nipple until she gasped. "After tonight, you'll never have cause to doubt me again."

"You made love to me before," she protested as he closed his mouth over her breast and sucked it through her nightshirt. "It meant nothing."

"It meant *everything*." He pushed himself up off her and glanced about until he saw what he was looking for. "But I tell you what." He reached over and grabbed the cord for the servant's bell, then pressed it into her hand. "I'll show you exactly how much you mean to me. And if at any moment, you question my sincerity, just ring that bell. Someone will come and make us marry, and that will be that."

She raised an eyebrow. "Our few servants aren't Johnny on the spot in this big house. That gives you plenty of time to run out or hide."

He slid off the bed and shucked his coat, then unbuttoned his waistcoat. "Not if we're naked and I'm in your bed, inside you." When she blinked at that blatant description, he lowered his voice. "Take off your nightshirt, sweeting."

With typical stubbornness, she just stared at him, so he swiftly removed the rest of his clothes, until he stood there in only his drawers. "I see you mean to torture me for my cruelty this morning."

"And what if I do?" she said, though her voice shook a little now, and her eyes drank him in.

That sent desire arrowing right to his cock, which was already thickening to unbearable proportions. He wriggled out of his drawers. He wasn't sure if he could restrain himself until he could pleasure her as thoroughly as he intended, but he was bloody well going to try.

"I admit you have the right to torment me." He knelt at her feet on the bed. "But I hope you'll give me the right to change your mind."

Before she knew what he planned, he slid her nightshirt up to bare her dusky triangle of hair, then bent and pressed a kiss right into the thick of it.

"Jackson!" she squeaked. "What are you doing?"

He spread her curls and smiled to see the pouting lips already wet for him. "Changing your mind," he said, then covered her there with his mouth.

"Oh . . . my . . . word," she whispered as he began to tongue her, enjoying every moan and gasp as she shimmied beneath him.

With a smile of triumph, he returned to pleasuring her in earnest, using teeth and tongue and lips to arouse her.

"Jackson . . . heavens . . . Jackson, you scoundrel, you!"

No one had ever called him a scoundrel, but under the circumstances it sounded like a compliment. The musky taste of her fired his blood, made his cock harden and his ballocks clench until he thought he'd die before he got to have her. And still he continued drinking her up, thrusting his tongue deep to keep from thinking how badly he wanted to thrust inside her.

Fortunately, it wasn't long before he had her writhing beneath him, rising to meet his mouth, and finally exploding in a violent release that made her cry out and clutch his head to her belly.

As she lay there quaking, he kissed her belly and thighs and the place where her loins ended and her buttocks began. If he weren't so overwhelmingly aroused himself, he would turn her over and kiss her from shoulders to soles, so he could mark every part of her as his.

His. For the first time, he began to believe it possible.

As he licked and caressed her navel, she gasped, "Your . . . wickedness . . . never ceases . . . to astound me, sir."

"I told you," he said, unable to keep the satisfaction from his voice, "every time I'm near you, I want to do wicked things with you."

He slid up her body, dragging her nightshirt as he went so he could see and touch the lovely breasts that regularly tormented his imagination. "Wicked, scandalous things." He tugged at her nipple with his teeth as he rubbed her below, keeping her aroused while he maneuvered himself between her legs.

Her eyes met his, now thoroughly glazed with desire.

"It's all I've been thinking about for weeks," he said hoarsely as he tugged her knees up and entered her with one fierce thrust. "All I dream about at night."

She closed her hands about his neck and arched up against him below.

"I never thought . . . the dream might come true." He buried himself over and over in her lush warmth. "Never thought . . . the lady could be mine."

"And now?"

Her cheeks were deliciously flushed, and her heart was gleaming in her eyes.

"Now I know I have no choice." He drove into her, claiming her. "I have to make the lady mine . . . no matter what the cost." He could feel his release stealing over him, ripping through him. Ruthlessly, he fought it, wanting them to reach their climax together. "Because without her . . . there *are* no dreams. Only nightmares."

Her eyes softened. Then she gasped and erupted, her sweet flesh convulsing on his cock and triggering his own climax. It swamped him with such a flood of feeling that he could no longer deny the truth.

He'd lost the battle to protect his heart.

"I love you," he murmured as he lost himself inside her. "I love you, my dearest Celia." When hope shone in her face, he said, "I'll always love you."

Then he collapsed atop her.

They lay there, joined together, for several moments. When he rolled off, she curled herself against him and stared into his face uncertainly. "Did you mean it?"

"Of course." He brushed a kiss over her lips. "I love you, sweeting."

Joy leapt in her face, but as he continued to stare at her, it shifted to something that looked remarkably like calculation. "I suppose you expect me to say something similar."

Though his breath caught in his throat, he arched an eyebrow. "Still torturing me for this morning?"

Pure mischief lit her pretty eyes. "Perhaps."

"Then I'll have to make you more sure of me," he drawled and reached for the bell cord.

"Don't you dare!" she cried, half frowning, half laughing, as he closed his hand around it.

"Do you love me?" he asked and dangled the cord over her head.

"I might," she teased. "A little. Do you still think me a spoiled lady?"

She grabbed for the cord, and he lifted it higher. "Probably no more spoiled than any other beautiful female used to getting her own way with men who adore her."

"At least you're mixing compliments with the insults now." She regarded him from beneath lowered lashes. "So you adore me, do you?"

"Madly. Passionately." He released the cord. "And no, I don't think you're spoiled. If I'd ever had any doubt, my aunt banished it completely."

"Your aunt?"

"I told her everything . . . well, not *everything*, but the important parts. And after she pointed out that I'm probably the worst suitor ever when it comes to proposing, she defended your behavior this morning with great enthusiasm."

A devilish smile crossed her lips. "I think I'm going to like your aunt."

"I'm sure you will. The two of you are peas in a pod." He debated whether to tell her the rest, but decided she should know. "As it turns out, you were right about the resemblance between me and my uncle. I . . . um . . . had a long talk with Aunt Ada, and it seems Uncle William was . . . not who I always thought."

The fact that she took his meaning at once told him she'd figured that out for herself already. "I'm sorry, Jackson."

"Don't be. If I could choose any man as my father, it would be him." He told her the entire tale, then added, "So you see, I don't even have any secret noble blood to commend me."

"In that case," she teased, "the wedding is off."

He covered her breast with his hand. "I suppose I'll have to do more persuading."

"Do your worst," she said lightly, "but I warn you, a lady never surrenders."

"We'll see about that," he murmured before seizing her mouth in a hot kiss.

Sometime later, as they lay entwined again, completely spent, she nuzzled his shoulder and said, "I do love you, you know."

"I thought you might."

She cast him a look of mock outrage. "Cocky devil! You can be as arrogant as my brothers at times."

"More so. Because I'm going to demand that we marry as soon as possible." He swept his hand over her belly. "After all our activity, you might even now be carrying my son. And no son of mine will be born a bastard."

Her eyes gleamed up at him. "It could be a daughter."

"No *daughter* of mine will be born a bastard either," he said.

"And will you let me teach her to shoot?"

"No need. If we have a daughter, no man will be allowed within a mile of her until she's thirty."

She laughed gaily. "Then I pray, for our child's sake, that we don't have a daughter." She cuddled close. "But if we do, I still want to teach her to shoot. It never hurts a woman to be prepared."

A lump stuck in his throat at the thought of all the things that had made her so wary—her parents' deaths, Ned's idiocy . . . being shot at. "That reminds me, I have to go."

"You do indeed," she agreed. "Much as you joke about it, it wouldn't do for anyone to find you here. My brothers are unpredictable, and Gran might just chase you around the manor with her cane."

"I can handle your brothers and grandmother. Unfortunately, there's still a killer after you, and I must find out who."

"Did you learn anything today?"

As he got dressed, he told her everything he'd discovered. When he came to the part about the letter concerning Elsie, however, she sat up. "You'll see her first thing, won't you?"

"I'd planned to come here first, so I could propose to you in a manner befitting your station."

"Never mind about that," she said with a dismissive wave of her hand. "If you do that first, we'll spend the entire day in discussions and recriminations and eventually, hopefully, in celebration. Before that, I want to hear what Elsie has to say. She might know the truth about Mama!"

"She might. But don't get your hopes up."

"If you visit her early enough," she pointed out, "you can be here before anyone even rises." She smiled at him.

"And bring your aunt, too. I very much want to meet her."

"I can already see that you and she will be thick as thieves."

"I do hope so."

The dreamy look on her face made his heart catch in his throat. Oh God, what he wouldn't give to keep that look there forever. But what if he couldn't? What if—

"Oh no, you don't," Celia said. "I can already see Proud Pinter creeping in."

He laughed. She knew him so well.

"Hand me your cravat," she said, snapping her fingers.

"What?"

"I shall hold on to it, and if you try to deny me again, I'll leave it in my bedclothes and make sure Minerva finds it."

He chuckled. "No need for that." Coming over to the bed, he bent to kiss her pouting mouth. "I swear I'll be here as early as I can tomorrow, ready to do battle for you, my love."

"You'd better," she muttered. As he headed for the door, he heard her add, "I could still ring the bell, you know."

He grinned at her. "Go ahead, my lady. I'll stand right here while you throw the house into an uproar."

That seemed to reassure her, for she made a face, then said, "Oh, go on with you."

He left the room smiling. But he didn't stay smiling for long. He'd been so caught up in her that he wasn't careful leaving and had only gone a few paces down the hall when he realized someone stood at the other end staring at him.

Ned, of all people. The bastard swaggered toward him with a sneer. He'd obviously witnessed Jackson leaving Celia's room.

"What are you doing up here?" Jackson demanded.

"Not that it's your business, but I've been playing cards with my cousins, who suggested I stay the night." He cast Jackson a sly look. "It appears that the upstanding Mr. Pinter isn't so upstanding after all. Not that I'm surprised you would take advantage of my pretty cousin's disregard for decency, but—"

The words were barely out of the man's mouth before Jackson had him by the throat and shoved up against the wall. As Ned clawed at Jackson's fingers, his eyes wide with alarm, Jackson hissed, "Speak of my future wife in anything but the most reverent of tones again, and it will be pistols at dawn."

He bent to press his mouth to Ned's ear. "I know what you did to her when she was fourteen. You got away with it then because she was scared and naïve and thought everyone would blame her. But we both know that if her brothers learned of it, they would cut off your ballocks and stuff them down your throat. If I didn't fear it would shame her further, I'd do it myself."

Drawing back to stare into the arse's face, he made sure Ned thoroughly understood his threat before releasing the bastard. "But if I ever catch you so much as whispering a sly word in her ear, you'll wake up deep in the bowels of some gaol where no one will ever find you. Do I make myself perfectly clear?"

Ned blinked. "Perfectly, sir."

"Good."

He watched until Ned had passed Celia's door, gone down to his own room, and entered it. Then Jackson turned for the stairs.

The first thing he was going to do after he and Celia married was make sure her cousin was banned from Halstead Hall forever.

Chapter Twenty-five

Celia woke feeling rested, happy, and in love. Jackson loved her! And today he would come and propose marriage and all would be well.

She only wished that it didn't mean Gran would win, but wasn't foolish enough to cut off her nose to spite her face. And she did hate to think of her siblings losing their inheritances because of her.

Leaving the bed, she rang for Gillie. As the maid came in, she said, "Isn't it a *lovely* day, Gillie?"

Since Gillie had left her crying her eyes out the previous day, she looked a bit perplexed. "Indeed it is, milady."

As Gillie helped her dress, Celia wondered if she could take the girl with her to live in Cheapside. Could Jackson afford a lady's maid for her if Gran really did cut them off?

But Gran wouldn't do that. Oliver would never let her, would he? Not that it mattered. As long as she had Jackson, she didn't care what she faced in Cheapside.

"What time is it?" she asked Gillie as the girl arranged her hair.

"It's nearly eleven."

"I don't suppose Mr. Pinter has arrived yet this morning." Celia fought a smile when the girl shot her an astonished look.

"No, milady. Not that I know of."

If he went to talk with Elsie, it was probably too early for him to be here, she thought with a sigh.

As Gillie hunted for her mistress's favorite mob cap, Celia wandered to the window. It was a lovely day to become betrothed to Jackson. The sun was shining, banishing the usual winter gloom. It was so clear that she could see the road and a carriage coming—

Jackson! He was here after all! And he'd come in his carriage, too, like a fine gentleman. No doubt it was because he had his aunt with him, but still, it showed he was serious about this marriage proposal.

She should probably wait up here like a proper lady until someone came to fetch her, but she didn't feel like a proper lady today. Grabbing her mob cap from Gillie, she clapped it on her head, raced down the hall, and then down the stairs. Only minutes later she'd reached the drive, where she forced herself not to run but instead walk semi-sedately toward the equipage she could now see at the other end.

But as it came closer, she realized it wasn't Jackson's coach. Blast, blast, and more blast. It was the cursed Visconde de Basto. She'd completely forgotten about the house party, which didn't end until tomorrow. This was around the time he always came.

The last person she wanted to see at the moment was one of her suitors. Unfortunately, she couldn't get out of it now. The carriage was slowing already. He'd seen her.

It stopped opposite her, and he leapt out. "My lady! How delightful to come across you this way. I had heard you were ill."

She forced a smile. "I'm feeling much better now." And she would be feeling better still once she could be freed of her suitors.

He offered her his arm, and she took it. Motioning to his coachman to drive beside them, he led her back toward the manor.

"You're looking very lovely today."

"Thank you." Her second smile was more genuine. He couldn't help it that she had no romantic interest in him; no need to be rude to the man.

"You have a mystical glow about you. Like a nymph of the forest. Or a fairy."

Really, why were men always thinking she looked like something otherworldly? And where had they all been when she'd been interested in finding a man?

Although what she'd told Jackson last night was true—she'd never really been interested in the men she met in society. Men like the viscount merely left her impatient to be away. Perhaps she'd always preferred men with rough edges, and she just hadn't realized it until now.

"It's no wonder your family calls you Elf," he said genially. "In some respects, it suits you."

"I *hate* that nickname, I must confess," she said. "Which is why no one has called me that since I was a chi—"

She caught herself. How could he have heard her called that? She'd threatened her family with shooting if they ever did, and they'd taken her at her word.

As a chill passed through her, she asked in as pleasant a tone as she could muster, "When did you hear someone call me Elf? I must have missed it. I would have given them what for."

She risked a glance at his face. It seemed frozen in a smile that looked utterly false.

"Oh, some time or other," he said evasively. "Perhaps you were not around."

"That must be it."

Except none of her family would have dared.

She started considering some odd things. Given the age Jackson had postulated for him, he was only a little younger than Papa would be now. Her conversation with the viscount the other day went through her mind—the discussion of her parents and their deaths, his curiosity about her mother's attraction to Papa . . .

Odd questions or perfectly normal?

Oh, she was being absurd. If he'd been Mama's lover, why would he return here and risk being caught? Besides, Mama's lover had *not* been Portuguese. She would have remembered that.

Unless . . .

"It's funny about nicknames," she said gamely. "You called me something the other day in Portuguese that I thought was very musical. I think you said that it meant 'bright beauty.' Something *brilhante?*"

"Bright soul is what I called you—*alma brilhante*," he said, his eyes suddenly hard on her. "Bright beauty would be *beleza brilhante.*"

Her breath stuck in her throat, and she had to pull her gaze from his to hide her consternation. *Mia dolce bellezza.*

What if it hadn't been Italian she'd heard, but Portuguese? A four-year-old would have heard what she knew already—the Italian phrase—and the words might sound much the same. *Dolce* meant "sweet" in Italian. If *beleza* and *bellezza* both meant beauty, then perhaps *dolce* had its Portuguese correspondent, too.

"Or perhaps you are thinking of *'minha doce beleza,'*" he murmured, as if he'd read her mind. "It means, 'my sweet beauty.'"

Her gaze shot to him, and her heart sank. He was staring at her with complete understanding.

"You remember that day in the nursery, do you not?" he asked in a choked voice. "I cannot believe it. I had hoped you were sleeping or would not remember after all these years, but—"

"I-I don't know what you're talking about."

His hand gripped her hard, and he barked something to his driver in Portuguese.

"Let go of me!" She tried to pull free.

Before she could knee him as Jackson had told her to do, he drew a pistol out of his coat pocket and said in a low voice, "I regret to say, my lady, that you will have to come with me."

The coach stopped. His two grooms jumped down and grabbed her, throwing her through the door that the viscount opened for them. Then the viscount leapt in after her, along with one of the grooms.

As the carriage turned around and headed down the drive, she thrust her head out the window and screamed, but the viscount forced his hand over her mouth. "Shh, I will not hurt you, I swear."

She bit his hand, and he cursed foully. If he was going to shoot her, she would make him do it here in front of her family, blast it! She wasn't going to end up dead in some hunting lodge, with no one ever knowing what had happened and why.

"If you do not be still," he growled. "I will shoot that groom running up the road from the house right now."

Following after the coach was one of Halstead Hall's grooms. She didn't want him to die for her sake. She wasn't sure if he'd seen what happened, but if he had, he would know the coach. He would know who had taken her.

He would tell Jackson, and Jackson would come after her. Ah yes, Jackson should be heading down this road any moment! They might even pass him—she would watch for him out the window. In the meantime, she had to survive until he could get to her.

Disgusted at how she'd put herself right into the viscount's clutches, she threw herself back against the seat. How could she have been so rash as to ask him about "beauty"? She'd thought she was being subtle, and she'd wanted . . . needed to know the truth about Mama, but it had been foolish under the circumstances.

"Where is your pistol?" he demanded now that she'd stopped fighting him. "Give it to me, or I shall have my man search you for it."

She thought about lying to him, but she didn't want that grubby servant touching her. "I don't have it. I left it in my room, I swear."

He ran his gaze over her, but her claim seemed to satisfy him. And why wouldn't it? She had no reticule, no apron, no pockets. She hadn't even thrown on her cloak.

Oh, what had she been thinking to run out of the house without anything, and especially without her pistol? That's what she got for being rash. Jackson was right—sometimes she did go off half-cocked, and this time it would be her undoing.

"My family knows who you are," she lied. "They know what you did with Mama."

He snorted. "If that were true, you would not have walked with me. You would have run back to the house the moment you saw me." He eyed her closely. "It was the Elf that gave me away, was it not? A foolish mistake on my part. I did not realize your family no longer called you that."

"That groom saw your carriage, you know. He may have even seen you carry me off. He'll tell my family, and they'll come after you."

"Which is why we are racing so fast along the road.

And why I told the driver to turn onto another route as soon as he has the chance."

That meant Jackson wouldn't come across her on his way to the manor. Despair swept her. "It doesn't matter," she pointed out. "They know where you live."

"We are not going where I live," he said in a hard voice. "I am never returning there again."

No, no, no . . . if he went somewhere Jackson didn't expect, then he wouldn't know where to find her! Not that it mattered—she would probably be dead before they traveled very far.

Blast it, she was *not* going to die and let this scoundrel get away with it!

"If you stop here and let me out, you'll have plenty of time to get away. I promise not to tell a soul who you are."

"You must think me a very great fool," he said dryly.

"Please," she said, not averse to begging for her life. "If you ever had any love for Mama at all, you will not kill her daughter."

He stared at her aghast. "I have no desire to kill you, my sweet. These two days without you have been agony."

She snorted. "Is that why you had a loaded pistol in your pocket?"

"I only carried it because of what I heard in Ealing yesterday, about a couple shot at by highwaymen on the roads hereabouts."

"Now who's the fool? We both know that wasn't highwaymen. You were the one who shot at us."

"I haven't shot at anyone! And us? Who is *us*?" He looked genuinely surprised. "How could you think I would shoot at you? I find you intoxicating . . . wonderful. I have been seriously courting you!"

"And you think I would marry my mother's lover? Are you mad?"

"It is not so strange an idea," he said, though he looked as if it had just occurred to him. "Until you knew I was her lover, you accepted my attentions eagerly."

Blast. Her foolish plan to use her suitors to force Gran's hand was coming back to haunt her. "But I know now," she said hotly. "And that changes everything."

"Ah, such fire, such passion. You are everything I wish for in a wife." His eyes held an almost feverish light. "You are so much like her, beautiful and haunted."

"I'm nothing like Mama," she bit out, shocked that he was insisting he meant to marry her. "Everyone says so. I'm taller and thinner, and my hair is darker—"

"It's not in your looks, but in the turn of your countenance, the way you smile. The softness of your eyes. She had soft eyes, your mother." His voice grew bitter. "And your bastard of a father never appreciated them."

"So you killed him," she whispered.

"What? No!" He scowled at her. "I see what you're thinking, but it's not true. I did *not* kill your parents."

Chapter Twenty-six

*I*mpatiently, Jackson paced the tiny drawing room in the lodging house where Elsie lived. Her landlady had told Jackson that Elsie had been searching for a situation ever since her arrival in London and was due to arrive back from an interview any moment.

"Sit down, Jackson," his aunt said. She had come here with him because he intended to go to Ealing afterward. "The woman will get here when she gets here. And Lady Celia will understand. You said she knew where you were going."

"Yes, but it makes me nervous to leave her alone with a killer roaming about."

"You determined that it wasn't the Plumtrees who shot at you two, so it's doubtful anyone else inside the house would try to hurt her, isn't it?"

He halted in front of her. "I still don't trust Desmond and Ned. That man—"

The door opened, and a woman walked in, smiling. "Good day to you, sir. My landlady says you wished to see me. Is it about a position?"

She couldn't have been more than forty, with fine features and a trim figure. He wouldn't have been surprised to hear that Lewis Sharpe had taken a fancy to her, although he didn't now believe that was the case.

"You're Elsie Watkins?" he asked.

She nodded.

"You once served as lady's maid to Mrs. Augustus Rawdon?"

Fear replaced the amiability in her face. "I beg your pardon, sir, I believe you have me confused with someone else."

She turned toward the door.

He took a stab at guessing the source of her fear and said, "I'm not connected with the Rawdons. I'm here on behalf of the Sharpe family. And they have a right to know the truth about what happened to their parents."

When she halted, her back stiff, he came up behind her. "I'm Jackson Pinter, Lady Celia's fiancé. You may remember her—she was the youngest of the Sharpe children. I'm investigating her parents' deaths, and I hope you can clarify a few matters about your former employers that would help my investigation."

Slowly she faced him. "You're the man who talked to Benny, aren't you?"

"You talked to him, too."

She swallowed. "He knows the same things as I, so if you already knew that he came to see me, then you must have spoken with him again, and there's nothing more I can tell—"

"Benny's dead. Someone killed him on the road from Manchester."

If he'd ever suspected Elsie of being involved in it, that suspicion vanished when she went white and looked as if she would crumple. Taking hold of her arm, he led her to the settee.

His aunt drew a vial of smelling salts from her reticule and hastened to her side. "Here you are, my dear. This will help."

Elsie allowed Aunt Ada to minister to her a moment, then gazed up at Jackson. "I had no idea about Benny. I left the Rawdons' employ the very day he came to see me."

"The *Rawdons'* employ?" Jackson said. "They're in Manchester? But I thought Captain Rawdon was posted to Gibraltar."

"He was, until six months ago. Mrs. Rawdon grew homesick, so he resigned his post and returned to England. At least that's what they told me. They asked me to keep it to myself. They wanted to live quietly here, away from all their former friends. Mrs. Rawdon had inherited a property in Manchester, so that's where they went."

She sniffed more of the salts. "I didn't question that—they were always a peculiar couple. And she said she remembered my service fondly, so that was why she hired me." Her voice hardened. "I believed her, too, until Benny led me to think otherwise."

Jackson sat next to her. "What did Benny tell you?"

"You have to understand, the Rawdons visited the Sharpes often in those years, so Benny and I became . . . sweethearts. We talked about things. After you visited him to ask where his ladyship was going the day they died, he got nervous."

"Because he knew about the affair between Lady Stoneville and Captain Rawdon," Jackson guessed.

She colored. "He suspected. And he suspected that I knew even more."

"Did you?"

"Nothing for certain. My mistress always claimed they were having an affair, but she was the jealous sort. She always saw women after her husband where there were none."

Her eyes filled with worry. "But Benny and I had always truly believed that Lady Stoneville killed her husband. The constable said it, so we assumed there must be clear evidence of it. That the affair might have taken place seemed inconsequential. We didn't want to reveal such an awful thing about her ladyship. Let the dead rest in peace and all that."

"Then I came along and said there were questions in the matter of the deaths."

She nodded. "It upset Benny that there might be more to it than we'd thought. He decided to look for me, so we could consult on how much to reveal to you. But when he found me at my current post, he was alarmed to learn I was working for the Rawdons again. He worried that they were involved in the deaths. He considered it suspicious that the Rawdons wanted to keep their presence in England secret, yet they'd sought me out to hire me."

"He probably suspected, as do I, that they wanted to keep you—and whatever you knew—under their thumb."

"Benny begged me to leave with him that very day." She cast Jackson's aunt a furtive glance. "I told him I wasn't the sort to run off with a man alone, sweetheart or no. Besides, I wasn't giving up a well-paying post on such flimsy evidence. So he went without me."

An anxious expression crossed her face. "But my master saw him leave, and afterward he asked me all sorts of questions—why Benny had come, what it was about. It spooked me. I got through it as best I could, pretending it was merely a social visit, but after everything Benny told me, it made me quite nervous. That night after everyone was asleep, I packed up and left."

"And you never saw Benny again."

"No. I thought I might catch up to him on the road, but I never did." She stared into his face, her eyes troubled. "You don't think the captain killed him, do you?"

"Someone did, and it's looking more and more as if it were one of the Rawdons. Just consider yourself lucky that you escaped."

"I told my parents not to give anyone my direction, so you can understand my shock when you turned up here."

"I explained to them that you might be witness to a murder, so they thought it best to cooperate. Especially since I said you might be in danger. I asked them not to tell you of it, however." He flashed her a wan smile. "I'm sorry, but I couldn't take the chance that you were involved."

"I understand."

"So you still don't know for certain whether the captain and Lady Stoneville were engaged in an affair."

"No, but Benny told me that he'd seen the captain return very agitated late in the afternoon the day of the picnic, around dusk."

"I don't suppose he mentioned what horse he rode."

That seemed to perplex her. "I'm sorry, but no."

It didn't matter. Jackson was nearly convinced that the mysterious man on the horse had been Captain Rawdon. But if that were the case and Rawdon had killed them, why had Desmond seen the man riding toward the lodge?

Unless Mrs. Rawdon had fired the shots.

He sat back and mused aloud. "What I don't understand is why the Rawdons returned to England in the first place. If they were afraid of being suspected of murder, why come back at all?"

"I heard them argue once about their being here. I gather that he didn't really want to stay. He wanted to go back to Portugal to live, but she was tired of foreign climes, and—"

"Back to Portugal?" he asked, a chill running down his spine. "They lived in Portugal at one time?"

"Oh, yes. The captain's grandmother was Portuguese. He has family there. During the war in Portugal and Spain, I'm told he helped to train a great many Portuguese troops, since he spoke such fluent Portuguese. I believe there's even some obscure title in his family—"

"Sweet God," Jackson said hoarsely. "The Portuguese viscount. Captain Rawdon is the Visconde de Basto."

* * *

CELIA STARED AT the viscount, shocked by his assertion. "I heard Mama agree to meet you at the hunting lodge. If it wasn't you who killed her and Papa, then who could it have been?"

A shuttered look crossed his face. "I do not know. I arrived there after it happened, to find them dead."

Should she believe him? His arriving afterward did fit with the information Desmond had given them, but it also meant they'd been entirely wrong about Captain Rawdon being Mama's lover. The viscount had been the one to meet Mama at the hunting lodge.

Yet something wasn't right. If Mama had been so closely involved with a Portuguese viscount as to have allowed him into the nursery, how could *no one* have known about it? He must have been a guest at the house party, and surely someone would remember him. Gran might not, because she had arrived late, but Oliver and Jarret would have seen him. Wouldn't they have found it odd that two Portuguese gentlemen had moved in the family's sphere?

Besides, she could swear that Mama's lover hadn't had a foreign accent. Then again, there was that blasted phrase. "One thing puzzles me about that day in the nursery," she ventured. As long as she was trapped with him, she should find out all she could. "Why would you call Mama the same thing in Portuguese that Papa always called her in Italian?"

He stiffened. "It was a joke between us. I used to say that he was my wicked twin, that he loved her for her money and I loved her for herself."

"It couldn't have been much of a joke: she didn't seem to like it when you called her that."

A frown knit his brow. "Your mother hated to be reminded that her husband did not love and respect her as he ought. I should not have said it. I never meant to hurt her."

Celia remembered what Jackson had said: *She was feeling guilty over what she'd been doing, so she lashed out at Oliver to cover her own guilt.* Oliver might not have been the only person she lashed out at.

But that brought to mind other things: what Mrs. Rawdon had done that day, what she'd said to Mama, Mama's reaction. Why would Mama have been envious of Mrs. Rawdon if the woman's husband hadn't been her lover?

Unless . . .

Celia stifled a groan. What if Oliver and Jarret hadn't recognized the Portuguese lover because *that* had been the disguise? The heavy beard, the accent . . . the dyed hair to change his age.

A chill crept over her. What if the viscount was Captain Rawdon?

But then why persist in the disguise now that she had remembered him from the nursery? Why continue this strange masquerade?

Because he really does want to marry you. And he doesn't know *that we suspect the Rawdons.*

The ramifications of that hit her. He couldn't possibly know. They'd never spoken of any details around him. He might not know about Mrs. Rawdon seducing Oliver to strike back at Mama either. Surely the woman wouldn't have told her husband. And if the captain believed that the family knew nothing to connect the Rawdons intimately with Mama and Papa, then he would think himself able to keep up the masquerade indefinitely.

But then what about his wife? Where was she? Could she be dead now?

Then it hit her. The invalid sister, of course, whom he'd never introduced to them. Perhaps his wife really was an invalid. Or perhaps he just feared she wouldn't be as good at masquerading as he was.

That's why he spent his evenings in town, too. His wife might have agreed to let him "court" Celia to find out what she knew, but the woman would never have let him too far out of her sight. Not if she knew he'd strayed before.

So if he truly intended to marry Celia as the viscount, even though he had a wife, it made sense that he was maintaining the masquerade. And it probably wouldn't be a good idea for Celia to let him know that she'd realized who he really was. As long as he thought there was a chance of his marrying her, he had no reason to kill her.

That left her with no choice—she had to let him keep up the façade until she could catch him with his guard down and get the pistol. Or until Jackson found her. Because she had to have faith that Jackson would find her somehow.

She just hoped he found her in time.

Chapter Twenty-seven

Jackson had left his aunt in charge of arranging for Bow Street officers to be sent to Bedford Square, where the supposed viscount's town house lay.

Elsie had also mentioned that the Rawdons had a family town house in Paddington, but it had been closed up for years. Jackson would have preferred to send men there, too, but Paddington was out of Bow Street's jurisdiction. Besides, Rawdon surely wouldn't go there if he was trying to keep his identity secret.

With any luck, the Bow Street officers would find Rawdon at home in Bedford Square with his wife. If not, Jackson hoped to catch up to him at the manor, perhaps even before Celia saw him. It was early still—during the house party, the guests had all risen late.

The "viscount" sometimes came early, but if no one was up, he'd be forced to cool his heels. And the man had apparently been there all day yesterday without once approaching her. As long as he didn't realize anyone had guessed his true identity, she might remain safe.

Or so Jackson kept telling himself. Because th

alternative—that the bastard would get his hands on her somehow—was too chilling to contemplate.

The first sign Jackson had that something was wrong came as his carriage raced up the drive at Halstead Hall. Far too many people rushed out to meet the coach, and far too many of them were the family—Mrs. Masters and the wives of the Sharpe brothers along with Mrs. Plumtree and General Waverly, her suitor. Since none of them was Celia, his pulse began to thunder in his ears.

As soon as the carriage slowed, he leapt out. He barked an order to the grooms to change out his horses, then turned to Mrs. Masters. "Where's Celia?" he demanded. "Why have you all come to greet me?"

Wearing a concerned expression that struck him to the heart, she said, "One of the grooms thinks he saw her being forced into the Visconde de Basto's carriage an hour ago."

His heart plummeted into his stomach. He couldn't believe it. "I'm too late." He stared at them in a daze as his world crashed before him. "Oh my God, I'm too late."

"Don't worry, Pinter," General Waverly said. "As soon as the groom told us of it, we sent the guests and the Plumtrees home so the Sharpe brothers and Mr. Masters could ride out after Basto and Celia. Mr. Masters went the nearest route to Gretna Green, and the brothers headed for his address in London, in case he went there."

"He didn't go there," Jackson said hoarsely. "The man's not stupid. He'd know that we'd go first to his house in town. Or what we believe is his house in town, anyway."

That made Mrs. Plumtree blink. "What do you mean?"

Jackson glared at her. This was her damned fault, for forcing Celia into seeking out suitors. "I have reason to think that Basto is actually Captain Rawdon," he said, refusing to mince words with her. "And since one of the Rawdons may very well have killed your daughter and son-in-law . . ."

The color drained from her face, and she staggered back with a little moan. Waverly caught her, supporting her with an arm about her waist. "Are you certain that Basto is Rawdon?" he asked.

"Certain enough," Jackson bit out. God, how he wished he weren't. "I just spent an hour interviewing his wife's former lady's maid, whose tale convinced me that he's been courting Celia all this time to determine if she remembers seeing him with her mother. So this abduction isn't about a marriage; it's about eliminating the last living witness to acts that either he or his wife almost undoubtedly committed."

Mrs. Plumtree gasped, but he had no time, and even less inclination, to comfort her. Casting her a withering glance, he said, "I have to go."

She cried, "Wait, where are you going?"

The grooms weren't yet done changing the horses, so he spared a moment for her. "Elsie mentioned that Mrs. Rawdon's family has a town house in Paddington. On the slim chance that he might go there, I'm headed there."

"Let me go with you." Mrs. Plumtree pushed away from Waverly. "Please, Mr. Pinter, if I stay here with no news, I will go mad."

"Good!" Bitter words rose in his throat, threatening to choke him if they remained unsaid. "You deserve it. She probably didn't survive ten minutes in his presence. Why should he let her live after he's killed her parents and Benny? After he shot at us on the road?" The thought of Celia dead drove a dagger through his heart, sparking more angry words. "And it is all your doing. You forced her into seeking suitors she didn't want and thus threw her into his clutches. She would have been safe, living her life, if not for you."

"Pinter, that's a little strong, don't you think?" Waverly said gruffly.

"It's not strong enough." Jackson strode up to Hetty, unable to restrain his fury one moment longer. "Do you know why she's been encouraging the viscount and the earl and the bloody duke? Because she was sure you believed she *couldn't* marry."

He thought of how insecure she'd been, how badly she'd wanted to show her family that she was a woman they could be proud of. It made him want to strike out all the more at the obstinate matron before him.

"She hoped to garner such impressive offers of marriage that you would finally accept she was marriageable and would let her out of your ultimatum. That was her plan. Until she fell in love with me. Apparently she made a bad choice there, too, since I have failed her. And now the only woman I have ever loved—"

He broke off with a choked moan. "I have to go. I have to try to get her back, even if there is small hope of it."

If he hadn't been such a fool yesterday, if he'd made his

"proper proposal" then, they could have sent the damned viscount away, and he wouldn't be in agony now. But he'd had to cling to his stupid pride instead. He would never forgive himself for that, never forgive himself for putting her in danger.

How would he live if she died?

As he turned for the carriage, Lady Gabriel called out, "She carries a pistol, so there is *some* hope."

He nodded as he jumped into the coach, but her words offered little reassurance. Rawdon knew that she carried a pistol, so he'd probably relieved her of it the moment he'd gotten her into that carriage.

Still, perhaps she had it and would get to use it. Jackson had no choice but to pray that she would. If he didn't hope for something of the sort, he would go stark raving mad. Because life without Celia wouldn't be worth living.

The irony of that struck him as the coach pulled away. How foolish he'd been to worry about his ability to provide her with suitable gowns and servants and all that rot. How could he have contemplated for even one moment throwing her away for such trivial reasons?

Right now, only one thing mattered—that Celia stayed alive. Because if he ever got the chance to hold her in his arms again, he wouldn't give a bloody damn about the rest of it.

CELIA *HAD TO* get the pistol away from Captain Rawdon somehow. It was her only chance for survival. If she could get him to stop the carriage, preferably where there were people around, she might manage it, but though she'd asked him a couple of times to stop on the pretext of needing to relieve herself, so far he'd refused.

Blasted scoundrel. How far did he mean to travel? It seemed as though they were avoiding the city, for they'd taken a different road than the one leading into town that the Sharpes always used. Was he carrying her straight to Gretna Green?

That was the only place they could go to marry—she might be of age, but marrying in England, even with a special license, would require her consent, and he had to know she wouldn't give it. It would be much easier to find someone who would marry them without that in Scotland.

"Almost there now, my love," he murmured. He seemed distracted, absorbed in some private world to which she wasn't privy.

"Where?"

He didn't answer. Oh, Lord, did he mean to shoot her somewhere outside of town and bury her?

The second she was out of this carriage, she would fight. If he meant to kill her, he'd have to shoot a moving target. Of course, his manservant was probably armed as well, and he had other men. . . .

Despair gripped her. How was she to get out of this?

They halted abruptly. His servant stepped out, looked around, then motioned the viscount out. Two of the manservants grabbed her between them and carried her kicking and screaming in the back entrance of what looked like a perfectly respectable house on the outskirts of London.

There were no other houses directly nearby. Blast it all, where had he brought her? And why? Wherever it was, no one had been here in some time. The inside of the house looked deserted. All the furniture was shrouded in canvas covers, and there seemed to be no servants about.

His men released her inside what looked like a large study with only one door. After barking some orders to her captors in Portuguese, Rawdon shut the door and stepped in front of it to block it.

She flew to the one window, but it was locked, and all she could see outside was a garden. Screaming would do her no good. No one was close enough to hear her.

Whirling on him, she cried, "What are we doing here? Where *are* we, blast it?"

He shot her an irritated glance as he paced before the door. "Leave me alone. I have to think."

"About what?" She planted her hands on her hips. "Do you mean to keep me here? And for how long?"

"Quiet!" he roared. "Let me think!"

She shrank back. Best be careful of provoking him. And what did he have to think about?

As he continued to pace, obviously agitated and muttering to himself, it dawned on her. He must not have planned this abduction. When he'd suggested that he marry her, he'd seemed as surprised by the idea as she.

If he had planned it, surely they would already be on the road to Gretna Green. He would have brought supplies and made provision for stops along the road.

Dear Lord. He had come to court her—or to find out how much she knew about her parents' deaths, more likely—but when she'd recognized him, he'd made a spur-of-the-moment decision to abduct her. Which meant he had no idea how to proceed.

That could work in her favor. She could guide him in a direction that better suited her. Or at least that better slowed him down until she could find a way to escape or grab his pistol, whichever came first.

Deliberately she softened her tone. "My dear Lord Basto, I realize that you have much on your mind at the moment, but I have certain needs. If there is a retiring room . . ."

His gaze shot to her, worried, distracted. "I'm sorry, but as you say, I have much on my mind. It won't be long now. If you can just wait a bit more, I shall be in a position to give you every comfort, my love."

She gritted her teeth. She'd hoped that a few moments away from him would allow her a chance to escape. Still, it was a good thing she didn't really need a retiring room just yet, because if she had access to one, she might be tempted to throw a chamber pot at him just for calling her "my love."

"Something to drink would be nice, as well," she said. "I'm thirsty."

"All in good time, my dear, all in good time." He waved vaguely in the direction of what looked like a chair behind the desk, covered by canvas. "Why don't you take a seat until we leave?"

"When will that be?"

He began to pace again. "Soon, I hope. I have to arrange . . . certain matters concerning our journey."

"Up north?" she prodded.

"Not exactly. I think it best if we—" He broke off, as if realizing he'd said more than he should.

Oh, dear, not up north? She should keep him talking, keep him thinking about the difficulties of his improvised plan. Perhaps if she could get him to realize that none of this would work, he would let her go.

"Are there no provisions here?" she asked.

"This house hasn't been used in some time. It belongs to a . . . friend of mine."

A friend? Or him and his wife?

She dearly hoped it was the latter. Jackson didn't yet know that the viscount was Captain Rawdon, but there was more chance of his finding that out on his own than of his figuring out who some friend of the viscount's was.

She asked him more questions, but he grew agitated and ordered her to keep quiet. Agitated was bad. People started shooting when they were agitated. So she stopped talking and turned her attention to figuring out how she could escape.

A long time passed as she considered and discarded several possibilities. Getting the gun from him seemed unlikely—he held it always at the ready and any time she even stepped near him, he brandished it at her. Could she pretend to be sick? He would rush to her side, and she could grab the gun?

But if he called in one of his men instead, she would lose that advantage. She might need it in a pinch. So far, it didn't look as if he meant to kill her. She could take comfort in that.

Perhaps if she threw something at him, he would fire, then she could get away while he was fumbling to reload. She discarded that idea within moments, as his men came in and out, responding to various orders. Even if she got past him, she'd have to get past *them*, and there were at least three.

What she wouldn't give at present to know Portuguese. Especially when he seemed to grow even more upset after one of them gave him some report.

As soon as the fellow left, he turned to her. "My man tells me there are officers of the law at my doorstep in Bedford Square."

Jackson! If they could unravel the truth . . .

"What did you mean when you said that someone shot at you yesterday?" the "viscount" asked.

She blinked. "Just what I said. I went with . . . a friend to talk to our old nurse who lives in High Wycombe about what happened the day my parents were murdered, and on our way home, someone shot at us. We were forced to hide out until it was safe."

"Damn her to hell," he muttered under his breath.

Her? His wife? And he'd just dropped his accent, too. Should she mention that? Or pretend she hadn't noticed?

"Her who?" she asked.

He dragged his fingers through his hair. "My . . . er . . . sister. She doesn't approve of my courtship of you."

Celia practically bit her tongue off trying to keep silent on *that* score. "So you believe she shot at me?"

"I don't know. But it's something she would do."

"Yet you still expect me to marry you, even though I'm likely to lose my life over it?"

Though his color turned gray, he came toward her with concern in his expression. "That will not happen. I won't allow it. You and I will go aboard a ship to Portugal and leave her and this damned country behind."

Oh, dear, he meant to carry her aboard a *ship*? No wonder he thought he could marry her with impunity.

"My sister may fend for herself, for all I care," he went on. His eyes softened on her. "As long as I have you—"

"You bastard!" came a voice from behind him. "I should have known you were planning to desert me. When have you ever cared about your wife?"

As he whirled toward the door, an older woman wearing an expensive cloak walked in.

Uh oh. Mrs. Rawdon had finally made her appearance.

Blond and blue-eyed, she must once have been very pretty, but bitterness and tropical travel seemed to have eroded her looks. Perhaps the sour temperament that evidenced itself in her fierce frown had something to do with it, too.

"Damn you!" Rawdon cried. "How did you know we were here?"

"Don't insult my intelligence," she said contemptuously. "Did you think I was going to let you go a-courting every day to Halstead Hall without having a servant of yours in my pay? The minute you landed here, he came running to tell me. I got out a side door while officers demanded to see me.

"And here I find you were planning to elope—*elope,* mind you—with this . . . this . . . chit." She sneered at Celia. "Not that I'm surprised—after all these years, I'm well used to your tricks."

"My *tricks?*" he hissed. "I only ever betrayed you with one woman, but you have never let me forget it."

"And why should I?" she growled. "Long before that, I bought you body and soul. For all your talk about your lofty relations in Portugal—who don't give a damn about you—everything you own comes from *my* family's money. Yet you were ready to throw it all away because some stupid marquess's wife was unhappy in her marriage."

Celia kept an eye on Rawdon's pistol, but he had the weapon firmly in his control. What's more, his wife was facing Celia, so the woman would notice any move she made in his direction and would alert him.

"I wouldn't let you do it then," Mrs. Rawdon went on, "and I'm not going to let you do it now. Certainly not for some timid chit half my age."

Timid? He must not have told his wife much about her, had he?

But that could work to her advantage. "Please, Mrs. Rawdon," she said in her best little-girl voice, even as she edged closer to the door, "I don't want to run away with your husband, so if you'll just let me go—"

"Do you think I'm stupid, missy?" Mrs. Rawdon snorted. "My servant told me all about my husband's fawning over you, and your ready responses. Of course, *Augustus* said it was all to convince you to confide in him, so he could learn how much you knew about your parents' deaths, but it didn't take me long to figure out he was lying. I could see all the signs of infatuation. I saw the same ones when he began falling for your damned mother."

Mrs. Rawdon pulled a pair of dueling pistols out from beneath her cloak. "Well, girl, my servant and I may have missed you on the road to High Wycombe, but this time my aim will be true."

Celia's heart stopped in her throat just as Captain Rawdon stepped between them and aimed his own pistol at his wife. "You're not doing this again, Lilith. I wasn't there to stop you last time, but this time, I will die before I let you shoot another innocent woman. I've spent half my life covering up for you, and I'm not doing it anymore. I'll kill you first."

She laughed. "You don't have the stones."

Celia feared his wife might be right, for the captain's pistol wavered.

Oh God, this was what had happened to Mama and Papa. Mrs. Rawdon must have aimed for Mama, Papa had stepped in to protect her, she'd shot him, and then she'd shot Mama.

"I swear I will do it," he growled as he steadied the pistol on her.

Mrs. Rawdon fired, and Captain Rawdon fell, hitting his head against the corner of the desk as he went down. Knowing she would be next, Celia threw herself on him, pretending to weep, and extricated the pistol from his limp hands.

But as she came up aiming, Jackson stepped into the room behind Mrs. Rawdon. "Put the gun down, madam. Now."

Mrs. Rawdon's eyes narrowed, and she began to turn toward Jackson. Celia fired, hitting the gun in her right hand and sending it flying. But apparently that was the spent one, for Mrs. Rawdon was already steadying the other to shoot Jackson when he fired at her.

Mrs. Rawdon crumpled. Her pistol went off, but the bullet embedded itself in the doorframe just to the right of Jackson. Then she collapsed on the floor, still clutching her gun.

Jackson had shot her right through the heart.

Chapter Twenty-eight

*J*ackson knelt and made sure that Mrs. Rawdon was as dead as she appeared, then rose to look at Celia.

Her gaze was fixed on Mrs. Rawdon. As the pistol fell from her numb fingers, she took the few steps to where he stood and stared down at Mrs. Rawdon and the hole in her chest.

He dragged Celia into his arms and forced her head against his shoulder. "Don't look, my love. Try not to look."

She was trembling now, belatedly reacting. "So much blood," she whispered. "I can't believe it." She lifted her face to him. "All these years of shooting, and I've never seen a person shot."

"Better her than you," he said hoarsely. "After everything she did—" His voice turned fierce. "It was right that she was the one to die. I couldn't have borne it if it had been you."

Tears started in her eyes as she hugged him tightly. "I'm so sorry, my darling. I would never have gone near him if I'd guessed that the viscount was Captain Rawdon."

"I know. I only made the connection after speaking to Elsie."

"Is he—"

Jackson glanced past her to the captain, who lay so still that Jackson suspected he too was dead. "I don't think he made it." His eyes narrowed on the gun lying near the man, the one Celia had used. "That's not your pistol."

"I didn't have mine." She cast him a teary glance. "I thought it was you coming up the drive this morning, and I ran out to meet you without thinking. Oh, what good is it for me to carry a pistol if I don't have it when I need it?" She cast a fleeting glance at the captain and the slow spread of blood over his left side. "I'm not sure I ever want to shoot again, anyway."

He cupped her head in his hands so she couldn't see the blood. "I pray that it's never a necessity. But if you find in time that you want to return to shooting, I don't mind. As long as you let me be the one to keep you safe."

As the fear plaguing him the past few hours caught up to him, he kissed her hard, wanting to reassure himself that all was well, that *they* were well. When he drew back, she looked calmer.

Then a sudden alarm hit her. "The captain's men. Where—"

"I took care of the fellow near the door, but I didn't see any others. No doubt they went running the second Mrs. Rawdon showed up packing her pistols. They probably knew what she was capable of. In any case, my men should be here any moment. After I arrived and noticed 'Basto's' carriage in back, I sent my coachman on to Bedford Square to fetch the officers my aunt sent there after we talked to Elsie this morning."

She cast him a tremulous smile. "I knew you would guess the truth eventually. I just kept telling myself that if I could stall him long enough, you would come for me."

Her faith in him brought a lump to his throat. He kissed her hair, her cold brow, her dampening cheeks. "You did very well without me, my love. But I'm sorry you had to see her die."

"After all she did, I should hate her. She killed Mama and Papa. She's the one who fired on us. And I suspect she killed Benny, too." She slanted a quick glance at the body. "But now she doesn't look dangerous at all. She just looks like a poor sad woman, thwarted in love."

A moan sounded from nearby. They turned in shock to see the captain move.

"He's alive," Celia said. "I don't believe it!"

They hurried over to him, and Jackson knelt to examine his wound. "The bullet seems to have missed his heart," he told her. "He hit his head hard enough on the desk to knock him senseless, but if we can get him to a doctor he may still survive."

The captain's eyes fluttered open. "Is my wife—"

"She's dead," Celia said softly. "I'm sorry."

Before Rawdon could do more than moan, a swarm of officers entered the room.

"Fetch a doctor right away," Jackson ordered one of them, who immediately left to do so.

"She killed . . . the Sharpes, you know," Rawdon said as Jackson shrugged out of his surtout and folded it to put under his head and shoulders in an attempt to make him more comfortable. "Before I could—"

"Lie still now," Jackson murmured. "The doctor will be here soon."

"No," Rawdon said. "I must speak while I can, in case . . ." He shot Celia a long glance. "Forgive me, my dear. I should never . . . have risked your life." He gave a choked laugh. "I should have known she'd find out. She always finds out."

"How did she learn about your assignation that day?" Celia asked.

"She . . . overheard me and Pru in the nursery. Lilith had followed me there. I didn't find out until later, after she'd shot—" He swallowed hard. "I was the one to discover your parents' bodies in the hunting lodge. She was . . . hiding in some closet—I don't know why."

"To avoid Desmond, most likely," Jackson murmured to Celia.

"When she heard me, she came out," Rawdon went on. "She knew I'd . . . recognize the pistols as hers. I taught her to shoot when it looked as if she might . . . be traveling abroad with me. I never dreamed she would . . ."

He dragged in a shuddering breath. "Anyway, she was . . . hysterical. It took some time to get the story from her. She said . . . she'd earlier threatened Pru to stay away from me."

Threatened her? Oh, yes, Jackson recalled—when Mrs. Rawdon seduced the young Stoneville. That had been the threat. If he remembered right, Stoneville had left the room while the women were still in there together.

Perhaps Mrs. Rawdon had made an even more tangible threat then.

The captain went on. "But Pru went to the hunting lodge anyway, not knowing that Lilith knew of our . . . assignation. Lilith lay in wait for Pru. She said . . . the pistols had only been meant to frighten her. But while they quarreled, your father came in . . . and got between them. The gun went off, killing him. So she shot your mother . . . in a panic."

Rawdon's eyes went cold. "I knew that was a lie. Since shooting Lewis . . . had been an accident, she wouldn't . . . have been prosecuted. But with the marquess dead . . . your mother would be free to be with me. Lilith couldn't stand . . . the thought that I might leave her. So she killed Pru."

The captain cast Celia a remorseful glance. "I wanted to turn her in . . . but she threatened to accuse me . . . of Lewis's murder. Who would gainsay her? Her word against mine."

Desmond could have revealed the truth, but the captain wouldn't have known that.

"Besides," he added in a voice of self-loathing, "Lilith had all the money. And I couldn't live . . . without the money."

"So you covered for her." Celia swallowed. "She killed Benny, too, didn't she?"

"Benny?" He frowned. "That groom who came to see Elsie?"

"He was found dead on the road from Manchester," Jackson put in.

The captain closed his eyes with a groan. "I told her about him. She said . . . she'd make sure he never talked. I figured she'd . . . offer him money. She was always offering people money . . . to keep silent." His eyes opened again. "Poor fellow barely knew anything . . . worth worrying about. I told her that."

His gaze grew distant. "We should never have returned to England, but she said . . . what good was money if she couldn't be part of society . . . couldn't go to the London theater, couldn't . . ."

He shook his head. "I wouldn't have come back if I'd thought anyone suspected . . . After nineteen years of nothing in the papers . . . Even so, I insisted on going to Manchester first . . . being circumspect while I . . . tried to learn if anyone suspected anything. After Benny came . . . she insisted we go see what we could learn in London."

"How did she know about me and Celia going to visit Mrs. Duffett?" Jackson asked.

When Rawdon looked blank, Celia explained to Jackson, "She had one of his servants spying for her. I thought I felt someone watching us all at the ball. The servant must have told her that night that you were pursuing leads the next day, so he and she came out to follow you that morning, but when she saw I was with you she took her chance to kill me. It was them pursuing us in the woods. She admitted it. I gather that she'd realized her husband was growing enamored of me."

Anger surged up in him again at that.

"She was always jealous," the captain said. "Always . . . so . . . damned . . . jealous . . ." His voice fell to a whisper, and Celia bent close to listen while Jackson called out to his men, "Where's that doctor, damn it?"

Jackson felt for a pulse. It was there, but the man needed help. Fortunately, the doctor arrived moments later, and Jackson turned Rawdon over to his care.

Then Stoneville and his brothers rushed in, along with Aunt Ada.

"You're all right!" she exclaimed as she raced over to grab Jackson. "Thank the good Lord!"

Meanwhile, Celia's brothers were taking turns squeezing the life out of her.

When the Sharpes were done satisfying themselves that Celia was fine, Stoneville turned to Jackson. "Look here, Pinter, if you don't mind, we'll take Celia back to Halstead Hall so we can set Gran's mind at ease while you're busy here."

Celia grabbed Jackson's elbow. "I'm not going without Jackson."

He covered her hand, holding it there. "We'll be along shortly. You three go on and let Mrs. Plumtree know we're well. After I arrange some matters here, Celia and my aunt and I will be right behind you. I can tell you everything then."

The brothers exchanged speculative glances, but didn't question his right to take care of her.

Thank God. Because now that he had her back, he wasn't letting her out of his sight for a very long time.

* * *

AS THEY APPROACHED Halstead Hall two hours later, Celia got choked up. She'd thought she might never see it again.

Jackson took her hand. "Are you all right?"

"I'm just so glad to be here." She gazed up at him. "With you."

His aunt pretended to be staring out the window, but Celia could still see her smile to herself.

Celia liked Ada Norris. She was the only person Celia had ever seen, besides herself, who could get away with teasing Jackson.

Certainly his men would never attempt it. Celia had watched with growing admiration earlier as Jackson had expertly taken charge of the scene after her brothers left. The other Runners followed his orders without question. They rounded up Rawdon's Portuguese servants and Mrs. Rawdon's henchman. They gathered evidence to use against the captain, assuming he lived to be tried for Celia's kidnapping and his part in covering up the deaths of her parents.

And when they took Jackson's report about the shootings, they handled it carefully, allowing him to keep her out of it as much as possible, undoubtedly because of her status. Even after the Chief Magistrate arrived, Jackson's word that he would bring her to the Bow Street offices in a few days so she could answer questions was all that was required to have them finally allowed to leave the place with Celia and his aunt.

Now his carriage pulled up in front of Halstead Hall. Every member of her family was out in front to greet them, and as soon as Celia stepped down, chaos ensued. They were all laughing and crying and talking and hugging at once. Jackson stood back with his aunt, as if he understood that her family needed their own reassurances that she was fine.

Then Gran hushed them all. "I have something to tell you, Celia," she said, her voice hoarse with emotion. "From now on, your life is your own. If you want to marry, fine. If you do not want to marry, that is fine, too. Either way, you and your brothers and sister will all inherit." She cast an apologetic glance in Jackson's direction. "Mr. Pinter made it quite plain this morning that today's disaster would never have happened if not for my arrogant ultimatum."

Jackson winced. "About that, Mrs. Plumtree—"

"You were right, Mr. Pinter." She glanced around at her family as General Waverly came to stand beside her. "And you were not the only one who pointed out how wrongheaded I was. Isaac and Minerva tried to show me the error of my ways, too, as did all of you at one time. But until this morning, I was too stubborn to listen."

With a wan smile, she took the general's arm. "I told myself that I knew no other way to push you children past this hard part of your lives. But I see now that it was not my place to push you at all."

"Perhaps not, but we're glad you did," Oliver put in. "If you hadn't, we wouldn't have found out the truth about Mother's and Father's deaths." He looped his arm around

Maria's shoulder. "We wouldn't have found our wonderful spouses."

"All the same," she said, "though it is too late to rescind my ultimatum for the rest of you, I can make amends by doing it for Celia." She stepped forward to kiss Celia's cheek and gaze tenderly into her face. "And one more thing, my dear. I never for one moment thought you incapable of finding a husband. Because any man would be a fool not to want to marry you."

The words healed the last of the hurt Celia had felt ever since Gran had laid down her demand. "Thank you, Gran," she whispered as she hugged her.

Then Jackson moved forward to stand before Celia. "Your grandmother is right." He dropped to one knee and took her hand. "My dear wonderful love," he said as he stared up into her face, "I realize I'm not allowing you time to enjoy your newfound freedom, but I can't help it. I'm a selfish man, and I can't take the chance of losing you again."

She beamed down at him, her heart in her throat.

He kissed her hand. "I don't care about your shooting, and I don't care about your fortune, and I don't care if we live in a hovel for the rest of our lives. As long as we're together, I'll be content. Because I love you, and I can't live without you. And I'd be honored beyond words if you'd consent to be my wife."

After everything she'd been through the past few days, she burst into tears. When alarm showed on his face, she squeezed his hands and fought to regain control enough to choke out, "Yes, Jackson, yes. With all my heart, yes!"

Love shining in his face, he rose and kissed her amid a mix of wild cheers and laughter.

When he drew back, Gabe cried, "That's a much better kiss than the one you gave her when you won the shooting match!"

"And a much better proposal of marriage than the one you gave her yesterday morning!" Minerva chimed in.

"Leave him be!" Celia chided as Jackson went red about the ears. "He saved my life twice, figured out who killed Mama and Papa, and taught Gran some humility. We can't all be good at *everything*, you know."

Amid the laughter, he kissed her again, but her family didn't let *that* go on for long. It was cold outside, after all. Gran herded them inside to the great hall, where the servants had brought out refreshments. There, everyone had to take turns congratulating them and clamoring for all the usual details of how it had started and when it had become true love.

Once their curiosity was satisfied and they'd met Jackson's aunt, he and Celia took turns telling them what had really happened to Mama and Papa.

When they finished, Oliver said into the stillness, "So Father tried to save Mother?"

Celia nodded. "He stepped between Mrs. Rawdon and Mama. He gave his life for her."

"Then perhaps they did love each other a little, even at the end," Minerva ventured.

"I like to think it was more than just a little," Celia said. "That morning when I overheard them in the nursery, she seemed very uneasy with the captain. So I prefer to think that she persisted in going to the hunting lodge because she wanted to break things off with the captain in person. And I prefer to think that Papa went there to try to win her back."

She gazed at the family she loved so very dearly. "We can never know the truth of what was in their hearts. So what does it hurt to trust in a dream that could be just as true as the nightmare we've believed all these years?"

There was a long silence. Then Jarret said, "Hear, hear, sis. I'll drink to that." Slipping his arm around Annabel's waist, he raised a glass. "To Mother and Father and the love that might have been."

Everyone joined in the toast.

Much later, when the family had settled down into smaller groups and Jackson's aunt was having a long, involved chat with Gran, he drew Celia aside.

"There's one thing I'm curious about," he said. "Right before the doctor arrived this afternoon, Rawdon whispered something to you. What was it?"

Celia slid her hand into the crook of his elbow. "He said that when Mrs. Rawdon fired, she missed his heart because she loved him too deeply to go through with killing him."

"Do you believe that?" he asked, looking skeptical.

"No. I believe she might have missed him on purpose, but what she felt was obsession and jealousy, not love."

She nodded toward his aunt. "Love is when you endure pain for the sake of a beloved sister and husband, if that's what it takes to nurture the child of their illicit union."

Then she glanced at Gran. "Love is sometimes do-ing the wrong things because you're at your wit's end in knowing how to help your family."

He drew her into his arms. "Love is taking chances when every rational part of you screams, 'Don't risk it.' Because it's only when your heart has been ripped open that you get a chance to find the one person capable of making it whole."

With her own heart beating wildly, she smiled at him. "And you say you aren't poetic."

"Well," he said, with a glint in his eye, "perhaps a few of us *can* be good at everything."

And as he pulled her into a dark corner and kissed her with great sweetness, she acknowledged that at some things, he was very good indeed.

Epilogue

On a cold but bright St. Valentine's Day, Jackson and his wife and aunt attended the wedding of Mrs. Plumtree to General Waverly in Halstead Hall chapel. Jackson was truly happy for the couple. She'd admitted shortly after his betrothal to Celia that she'd only threatened to disinherit her granddaughter to test his love. Since she unabashedly acknowledged her fault in the matter, he'd forgiven her. Indeed, they'd mended fences to such an extent that she insisted he call her Gran as the other spouses did.

Now, as they headed for the great hall, his wife and aunt began discussing gowns and flowers and things beyond his ken, but he didn't mind. The two ladies were always so lively. He'd never imagined he would enjoy having two magpies in his house, but he did, especially since they fussed over him a great deal.

In the end, all his fears about how well Celia would manage in Cheapside had come to naught. They *had* added a couple of servants and were making renovations to the house, but those were things he might have done on his own.

Best of all, having come from a large family, Celia seemed to like having his aunt around. And Aunt Ada was careful to give them some privacy often, going to visit various friends for days on end.

"Didn't Gran make a beautiful bride, Jackson?" Celia asked.

"Hmm? Yes. Beautiful." He covered her gloved hand with his. "Though not nearly as beautiful a bride as you were."

She smiled. "Flatterer."

"Not a bit. It's the absolute truth."

"You *were* a gorgeous bride," Aunt Ada agreed. "That veil with the rosettes . . ."

And they were off again, discussing gauze and ribbons and something called a furbelow. That last one sounded dirty, but he figured it probably wasn't, if they were discussing it with such enthusiasm.

The three of them entered the great hall, where the wedding breakfast was to be held. He gazed down into his wife's animated features and felt the usual clutch to his heart. Would he ever stop feeling it, this pleasure of knowing she was his? That she would always be his?

He'd been told that the feeling would mute over time, but he doubted that. Two months after his wedding, there were still days when he looked at her and felt as if he'd stumbled into a dream from which he'd awaken any moment to find himself bereft again.

"Mr. Pinter!" called a voice, and he glanced over to see Freddy Dunse, Lady Stoneville's American cousin, heading for him. He and Freddy had played a small part in bringing Stoneville and his wife together a year ago, almost to the day.

As Freddy reached them, Celia looped her arm through Jackson's and said proudly, "You have to call him Sir Jackson now, Freddy. He was knighted for solving Mama's and Papa's murders. *And* for saving me from the villains responsible."

"Which is also why they made him Chief Magistrate," Aunt Ada pointed out, still preening with pride over both preferments. "About time, I say."

Jackson sighed. His two magpies had been boasting of his success to everyone they saw. "Ignore them, Freddy. You can call me whatever you please." Having spent most of his life despising people of rank, he still wasn't sure how he felt about being one of them.

"Oh, but that's why I want to talk to you, old chap!" Freddy said. "I want to hear firsthand the tale of how you rescued Lady Celia . . . Lady Pinter . . . oh, whatever you English call the knighted ladies."

"Lady Pinter," Celia said firmly.

She'd had a choice between keeping her loftier title or taking Jackson's name upon her marriage. It still pleased him that she'd chosen the latter.

"And ladies can't be knighted," Celia added gently, "only men."

"Though in this case the lady deserved to be knighted, since she played a part in catching the villain," Jackson said.

"She *did*?" Freddy gazed at Celia with new admiration. "Tell me *everything*. I want to hear whatever they left out of the papers. Were there swords? I know someone was shot. Was there lots and lots of blood?"

"Freddy!" Celia exclaimed as Aunt Ada gaped at Freddy, aghast. "We're not going to talk about that at Gran's wedding!"

"I don't know why not. She married a general. He knows something about guns and blood, I daresay."

"Then go talk to *him*," Celia said. "I swear, you're as bad as your cousin."

That was true. Lady Stoneville had quite the fondness for vivid accounts of murder and mayhem.

But Freddy had another, more compelling fondness. Jackson leaned over to murmur, "There's pie, my good fellow. Right over there. Three kinds."

"Steak and kidney?" Freddy asked, eyes lighting up.

"You'll have to go see. I haven't had any yet."

That was all it took to have Freddy bounding over to his wife Jane and dragging her to the table to help him figure out what kind of pie it was.

"Good heavens," Aunt Ada exclaimed. "What is the matter with that young man?"

"He's a good sort. He's just a little . . . different. And speaking of different . . ." Jackson murmured as he saw Ned ambling toward them.

Celia followed Jackson's gaze and tensed.

Then Ned spotted them, and the blood drained from his face. He very markedly turned and walked in another direction.

"What was that all about?" Celia asked.

"Who knows?" Jackson said, though he allowed himself a private little smile.

"Oh, look," Aunt Ada said, "the newlyweds have entered. I must go pay my respects. Are you coming, Jackson?"

"Go on," he said. "We'll be there in a minute."

Someone else was approaching, and Jackson was none too happy about it. He hadn't seen Devonmont since the house party and wouldn't mind never seeing the man again, but since Devonmont was his new sister-in-law's cousin, that was unlikely.

As the man neared them, Celia cast Jackson an assessing glance. "You do know he never meant a thing to me."

"That makes me only slightly less inclined to smash his face in."

"Jackson!" she said laughingly. "You would never do any such thing."

"Try me." He glanced at her. "Don't let this sober façade fool you, sweeting. When it comes to you, I can be as jealous as the next man."

"Well, you have no reason." She leaned up to kiss his cheek and whisper, "You're the only man I'll ever love."

He was still reveling in that remark when Devonmont reached them. "I take it this would not be a good time for me to kiss the bride?" he drawled.

Jackson glared at him.

"That's what I thought," Devonmont said, laughing. "But seriously, Pinter, you're a very lucky man."

"How well I know it," Jackson said.

"And I say most sincerely that your wife is a very lucky woman as well."

Jackson was taken aback. "Thank you, sir," he managed.

After Devonmont nodded and walked away, Celia said, "Surely that softens you toward him a little."

"Perhaps," Jackson conceded. "Though it's a good thing Lyons isn't here. I don't think I could be civil to both in one day."

She was still laughing when her grandmother rang a bell to gain their attention.

"Thank you all for joining me in celebrating my wedding." Gran tucked her hand into the crook of her new husband's elbow. "I may be an old fool sometimes, but I am a happy old fool."

She gazed around at the guests, who consisted of only her family and close relations like Devonmont. "As you know, little more than a year ago, I was ashamed of how my grandchildren were living their lives and mortified that they were called 'hellions' by everyone in society. So I took measures that I came to see were a bit harsh.

"Yet my grandchildren not only rose to the challenge I set for them, but exceeded it. What is more, I have come to understand that their being hellions is not all bad—if not for their strong wills, I doubt they would have found such wonderful spouses or succeeded so admirably in their various endeavors. So today I wish to tell them two things. One, I am tremendously proud of my hellions."

That brought a round of applause, which made her color.

When she went on, her voice was choked. "And two, thank you for giving me such beautiful great-grand-children—at last." As laughter filled the room, a sparkle entered her eye. "I promise to dote on them and indulge them—"

"And not meddle in their lives?" Jarret called out.

"That, I do not promise," she said archly, which brought another round of laughter. "Although I shall *try* to restrain my meddling to matters within my purview."

"I daresay your brothers find that less than reassuring," Jackson told Celia.

She got a funny look on her face, as did his aunt. He didn't have a chance to wonder about it, however, before toasts were being proposed and the hall became a veritable sea of congratulations and speechmaking.

After that was done and people began to mingle, helping themselves to the food laid out on the large tables, Mrs. Masters hurried up to her sister to say, "I'm going up to see the babies. Do you and Mrs. Norris wish to come?"

"Let's all go," Celia said, taking firm hold of Jackson's arm.

"All right," he said, a bit bewildered by her determination to drag him along. He'd seen the babies just last month. Still, Aunt Ada hadn't yet, and he supposed he could endure seeing them again.

When they entered the nursery, the new nurse instantly cautioned them to be quiet, since both infants were sleeping.

Last time he and Celia had entered the nursery, he'd briefly worried about her reaction to being in it so soon after they'd learned the truth about her parents' deaths, but her infatuation with the new babies had seemed to banish any bad memories.

Today, however, he wondered if those memories had returned. She was oddly pensive. She said nothing as they gazed at Lady Prudence Sharpe, Stoneville's plump golden-haired daughter, who looked like a cherub out of a painting. Even Jackson couldn't help agreeing with his aunt that the babe was "adorable."

Celia remained silent when they went to stare at Master Hugh Sharpe, Jarret's son and heir, a black-headed, restless child who sucked his thumb in his sleep.

"That one is a little hellion in the making," his aunt predicted. Mrs. Masters agreed.

Then Aunt Ada glanced at Mrs. Masters. "Perhaps we should return to the breakfast."

"Absolutely," Mrs. Masters said with a veiled look at Celia.

"We'll be along soon," Celia said, to his surprise.

His surprise grew more acute when the other two insisted on taking the nurse with them. "Alone at last," he murmured, thinking Celia might want a private moment with him. Though the nursery was a strange place for it.

"Yes. I have something to tell you, Jackson." Taking his hand, she laid it on her belly. "I'm fairly certain that you and I are going to have a child of our own soon."

He stared at her, stunned speechless.

At his continued silence, an anxious look crossed her face. "I know it's perhaps a bit sooner than we expected, but—"

"It's wonderful," he choked out. "Absolutely wonderful." He smoothed his hand over her belly. "I can't imagine anything better than having a child with you, my love. But are you sure?"

She relaxed. "As sure as anyone can be at this point. Your aunt and I think I may be nearly three months along, so . . ."

When she trailed off with a blush, he added up numbers in his head, then let out a laugh. "It probably happened that night in the cottage."

"Or the night in my bedchamber."

"Then it's a good thing I came to my senses and gave you that 'proper proposal' you demanded. Or I'd be staring down the barrel of your percussion rifle just about now."

"I doubt that. I would just have married the duke," she teased.

He scowled. "Over my dead body."

She laughed. "You know perfectly well you would have proposed long before I knew I was with child."

"Ah, but would you have said yes? I thought you once told me that a lady never surrenders."

"She doesn't." Eyes sparkling, she buried her fingers in his hair and drew his head down to hers. "Except where love is concerned. I've come to realize that in matters of love, a clever lady *always* surrenders."

Love Sabrina Jeffries?
Turn the page for a sneak peek at
her exciting Christmas hardcover,
featuring Pierce Waverly from
To Wed a Wild Lord!

amilla Stuart's cheeks heated as she gaped at Pierce Waverly, the Earl of Devonmont. How dare he refuse to remain here, visiting his own mother for Christmas, unless Camilla agree to spend her nights with him! What a despicable, wicked—

Then her brain caught up with her moral outrage. The earl wore a very calculating expression, as if he knew exactly what her reaction would be.

Oh, of course! He was making this up as he went along, the devilish creature. He wanted her to be so insulted by his proposition that she left him alone and stopped plaguing him about his estrangement from his mother.

That made far more sense than believing he actually meant it. She wasn't the sort of woman whom fashionable rakehells tried to seduce. The very idea was preposterous.

She forced herself to look bewildered. "I'm afraid I don't understand, my lord. How could I possibly entertain a worldly man like you?"

His sudden black frown strengthened her conviction that his supposed bargain was a bluff. "I am quite certain that you take my meaning. After dinner is over every night and my mother has retired, you and I will have our own little party. Here. In my bedchamber, where you can slip in and out without being noticed. If I must spend my dinners with her, then you must spend your nights with *me*."

"Entertaining you," she said primly, buying time to figure out what answer would best gain her what she wanted. "Yes, I understand that part. I'm just not sure what kind of entertainment you want."

He gritted his teeth. "Oh, for the love of God, you know precisely what kind of entertainment a 'worldly man' like me enjoys."

Now that she had caught on to his game, it was all she could do not to laugh at him. He was so transparent. What was wrong with all those women in London that they didn't see right through him?

"On the contrary, my lord," she said blithely. "I *don't* know you well enough to know what you enjoy. Perhaps you would prefer that I sing for you, or dance, or read you a good play. I understand there is quite an extensive library at Montcliff. Your mother says you bought most of the books for it yourself. I'm sure there is some volume of—"

"I am not talking about you reading to me!" he practically shouted.

When she merely gazed at him with a feigned expression of innocence, he changed his demeanor. His brown eyes turned sultry, and a sensual smile crossed his lips. "I am speaking of the kind of entertainment most widows prefer."

My, my, no wonder London ladies were rumored to regularly jump into his bed. When he looked that way at a woman and spoke in that decidedly seductive voice, the average female probably melted into a puddle at his feet.

So it was a good thing that she was *not* an average female. Before she had become paid companion to his mother, she'd had the occasional lascivious offer from scoundrels who liked to prey on unprotected females. Fortunately, she'd always known how to handle them.

This was a trickier situation, however. If she wasn't an average female, he was definitely not an average scoundrel, either.

She pretended to muse for a moment. "Entertainment that widows prefer . . . Works of charity? Taking care of their families? No, those aren't actually entertaining, though they do pass the time." She cocked her head. "I confess, my lord, that you have me at a complete loss."

Uh oh, that was probably doing it up too brown, for understanding suddenly shone in his face. "You're deliberately provoking me. Well then, I'll spell out what you're pretending not to understand. You would spend those evenings in my bed. Is that clear enough?"

He said it in such a peeved manner that she couldn't help but laugh. "Clear indeed, though preposterous."

His gaze narrowed on her. "Preposterous, how?"

Time to let him know that she had caught on to his game. "I'm aware of your reputation, sir. I'm not the sort of woman you like to take to bed."

Something glinted in his eyes that looked remarkably like admiration. "I thought you said you didn't know me all that well," he drawled.

"I know what kind of women you are most often seen with. And by all accounts, they are tall, blowsy blondes with porcelain skin and clever hands."

He looked startled. "You *do* know my reputation."

She shrugged. "I read the papers. And your mother likes to hear all the stories of you, even the salacious ones."

Mention of his mother made his gaze harden. "Then you should know that men like me aren't usually discriminating in their choice of female entertainment."

"Oh, but no matter how bored you might be in the country, I'm sure you're discriminating enough not to wish to bed a short, mousy, freckled servant, when you can have any beautiful blond actress or opera singer instead," she said coolly.

Crossing his arms over his chest, he dragged his gaze down her, then circled her in a slow, careful assessment that made her nervous. A pity that he wasn't a mere perfumed dandy; she could have handled one of those easily enough. But this sharp-witted rakehell with hidden secrets was unpredictable.

Camilla had never liked the unpredictable.

"And what if I were to say that I really *am* that indiscriminate? Would you then share my bed in exchange for my spending Christmas here with my mother?"

She swallowed. Why did he persist in bluffing when he knew she had caught on to him?

Oh, what did it matter? He would never truly want her in his bed, and they both knew it. Might as well call his bluff. "Why not? You *are* rumored to be quite good at that sort of thing." She couldn't keep the edge from her voice. "Besides, the likelihood of my ever again having the chance to be seduced by such a notorious fellow as yourself is slim."

He blinked at her frank statement, then flashed her a rueful smile. "Good God, Mrs. Stuart, remind me never to play cards with you. I daresay you're quite a terror at the gaming tables."

She bit back a smile of her own. "I confess I've won a hand or two at whist in my life."

"More than a hand or two, I'd wager." He let out a long breath. "All right then, let me propose a bargain that we both could actually adhere to." He searched her face. "I'll do as you wish—I'll go to dinner with you and Mother every evening until Christmas. Afterward, you will come here to join me in one of your more innocuous entertainments for the evening." He raised an eyebrow. "It's the least you can do, if you mean to force me into moldering in the country for two weeks."

She let out a breath. She'd won! "I am happy to attempt to entertain you, my lord, if you will just give your mother some time with you. That's all I ask."

"I'm not finished." He gazed steadily at her. "In exchange for my allowing this farce to continue until Christmas, you must agree never again to try to force my hand in the matter of my mother."

When she drew a breath as if to speak, he added, more firmly, "Two weeks of watching me and Mother together should demonstrate to you why you have no business involving yourself in our relationship. But even if it doesn't, Christmas Day must mark the end of your meddling—or I will dismiss you without a qualm. Am I understood?"

"Yes, my lord," she said, suitably chastened. She *had* overstepped her bounds in sending that misleading letter to him.

He frowned. "In this room, do not call me 'my lord.' It reminds me too much of . . ." He paused. "Just call me Devonmont. That will do."

"Very well, my . . . Devonmont."

A heavy sigh escaped him. "I must be out of my mind to be letting you off so easily, after what you did."

"Easily?" she couldn't resist quipping. "Have you forgotten that I will have to entertain you every evening?"

His lips quirked as if he fought a smile. "Ah, yes, that will be such a trial for you. And I expect very rousing entertainment. At the very least, you must show me your . . . reputed ability at whist, so I can trounce you." He sobered. "If I have to endure this house every night, then you, my dear, will join me in my suffering."

The bitter remark gave her pause. Hadn't Lady Devonmont said that this was the original manor house on the estate? The one where he'd grown up?

As if realizing he'd revealed more than he'd meant to, he broke into a grin. "It won't be so very difficult, I promise. I can be charming when I want to be, you know."

"No doubt," she said dryly.

He stared at her a long moment, his grin fading. "Well then, we're agreed. I'll see you here this evening after Mother has retired."

And after she had put her young son, Jasper, to bed, though she couldn't say that.

Still, she hesitated, wanting to confirm one thing. Perhaps she shouldn't press the matter, but in for a penny, in for a pound. "And you will come down to dinner, sir? This very evening?"

His face turned rigid. "That's the agreement, isn't it?"

She let out a breath. "I was just making sure."

"Whatever else you may think of me," he said sharply, "I do honor my promises."

"Of course, my lo— Devonmont."

She turned for the door, relief swamping her. She had braved the lion's den and survived. She'd even won. Spending evenings with his lordship would be no sacrifice at all compared to that.

"One more thing, Mrs. Stuart," he said as she reached the door.

She paused to look back at him.

"You were right when you said that I am discriminating in my choice of bed partners. But you are not remotely mousy." His gaze scoured her, this time with decided heat that she could tell wasn't the least bit feigned.

It left her torn between pleasure and alarmed by the possibility that he might consider her worthy of seducing. The last thing she needed in her life right now was a lover; not with Jasper to take care of.

Only when he had her thoroughly agitated, and not just from concern over her virtue, did he lower his voice to a husky drawl. "Fortunately for you, I'm not in the habit of abusing the trust of those in my employ. So as long as you want me to play the respectable gentleman, I will do so."

He fixed her with a smoldering look. "But let me warn you. Give me an inch, and I will take two miles. If you offer more, I will be only too happy to take you into my bed."

"Then I shall have to be careful not to offer more, shan't I?" And with that, she slipped from the room.

But as she made her way down the hall, with her knees shaking and her hands clammy, she knew that this bargain might not be quite so easy to keep. Because she wasn't as averse to the idea of being in the earl's bed as she should be.